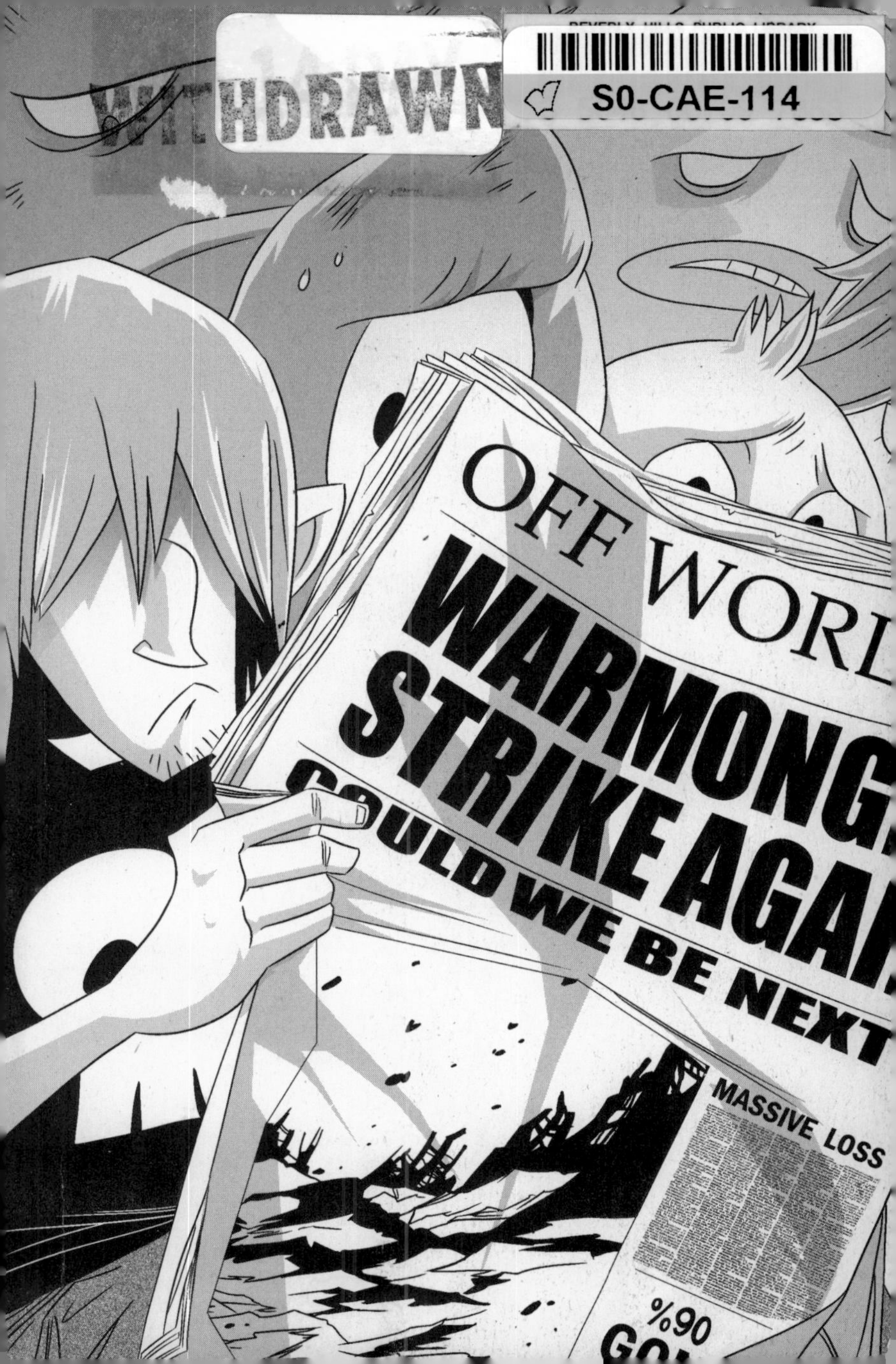
OFF WORL
WARMONG
STRIKE AGA
OULD WE BE NEXT
MASSIVE LOSS
%90

Snow Vol.1
Created By Morgan Luthi

Lettering - Lucas Rivera
Cover Layout - James Lee

Editor - Paul Morrissey
Digital Imaging Manager - Chris Buford
Pre-Production Supervisor - Erika Terriquez
Art Director - Anne Marie Horne
Managing Editor - Vy Nguyen
Production Manager - Liz Brizzi
VP of Production - Ron Klamert
Editor-in-Chief - Rob Tokar
Publisher - Mike Kiley
President and C.O.O. - John Parker
C.E.O. and Chief Creative Officer - Stuart Levy

A  Manga

TOKYOPOP Inc.
5900 Wilshire Blvd. Suite 2000
Los Angeles, CA 90036

E-mail: info@TOKYOPOP.com
Come visit us online at www.TOKYOPOP.com

ISBN: 1-59816-743-X

First TOKYOPOP printing: October 2006
10 9 8 7 6 5 4 3 2 1
Printed in the USA

SNOW

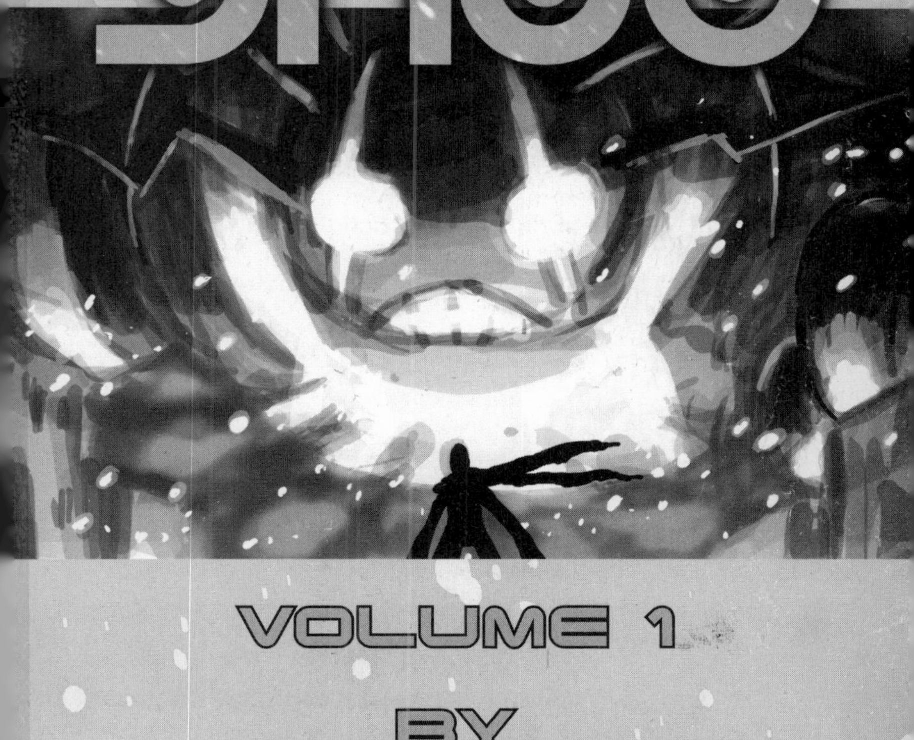

VOLUME 1

BY MORGAN LUTHI

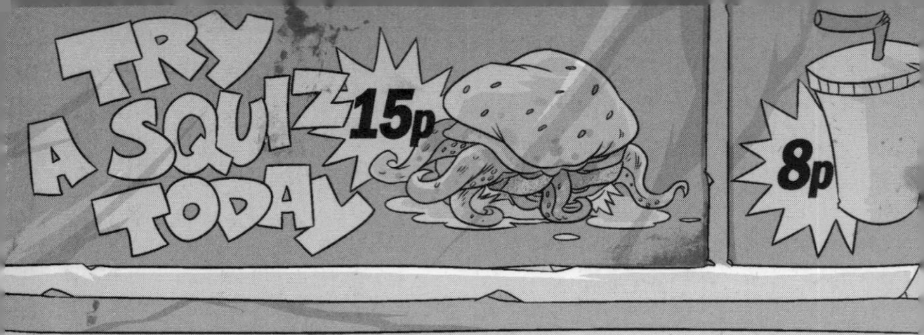
TRY A SQUIZ TODAY
15p
8p

TABLE OF CONTENTS

Ask for Extra Cheese!

OPEN 10:30 a.m. to 1:00 a.m.
........................Fri. and Sat. until 1:30 a.m.

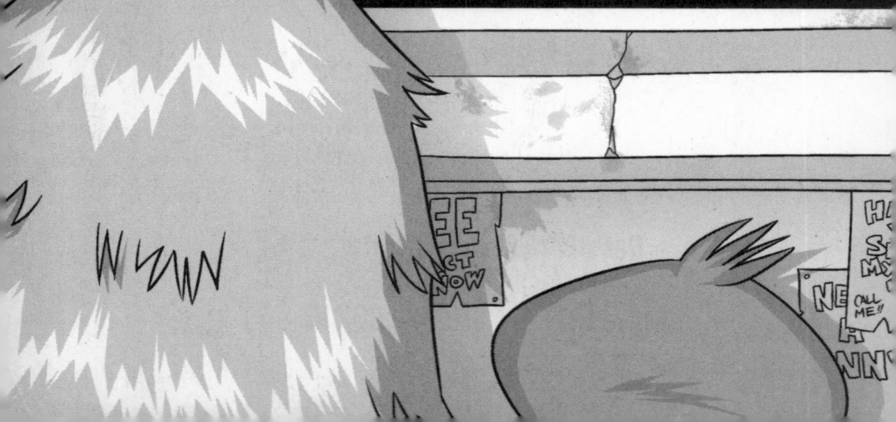
CALL ME!!

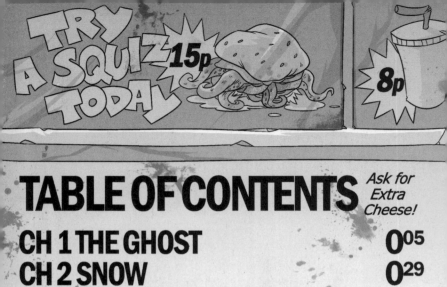

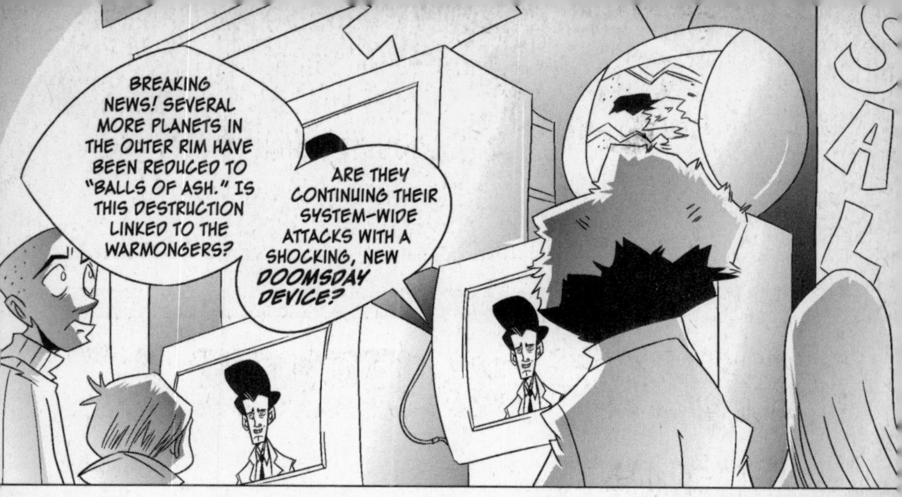
BREAKING NEWS! SEVERAL MORE PLANETS IN THE OUTER RIM HAVE BEEN REDUCED TO "BALLS OF ASH." IS THIS DESTRUCTION LINKED TO THE WARMONGERS?
ARE THEY CONTINUING THEIR SYSTEM-WIDE ATTACKS WITH A SHOCKING, NEW *DOOMSDAY DEVICE?*

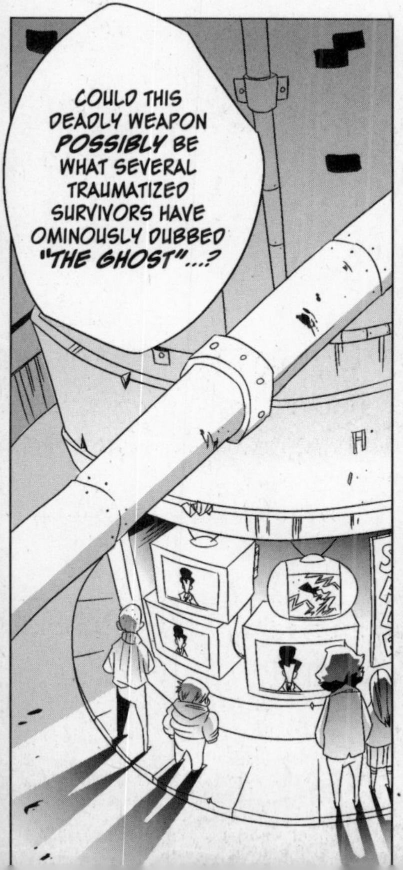
COULD THIS DEADLY WEAPON *POSSIBLY* BE WHAT SEVERAL TRAUMATIZED SURVIVORS HAVE OMINOUSLY DUBBED *"THE GHOST"...?*

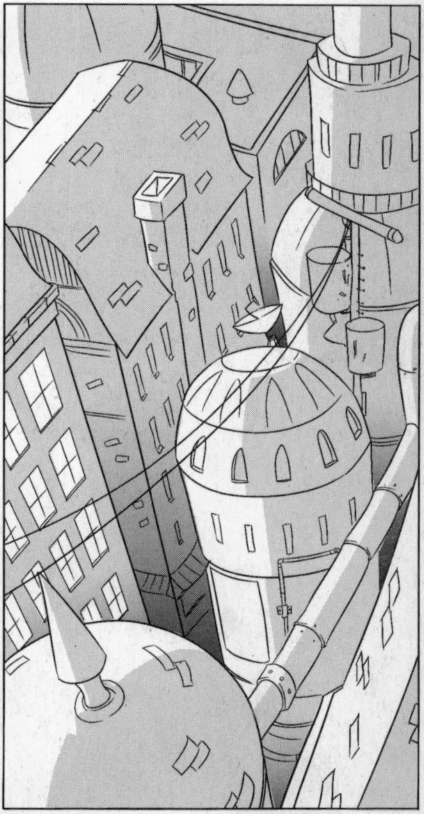

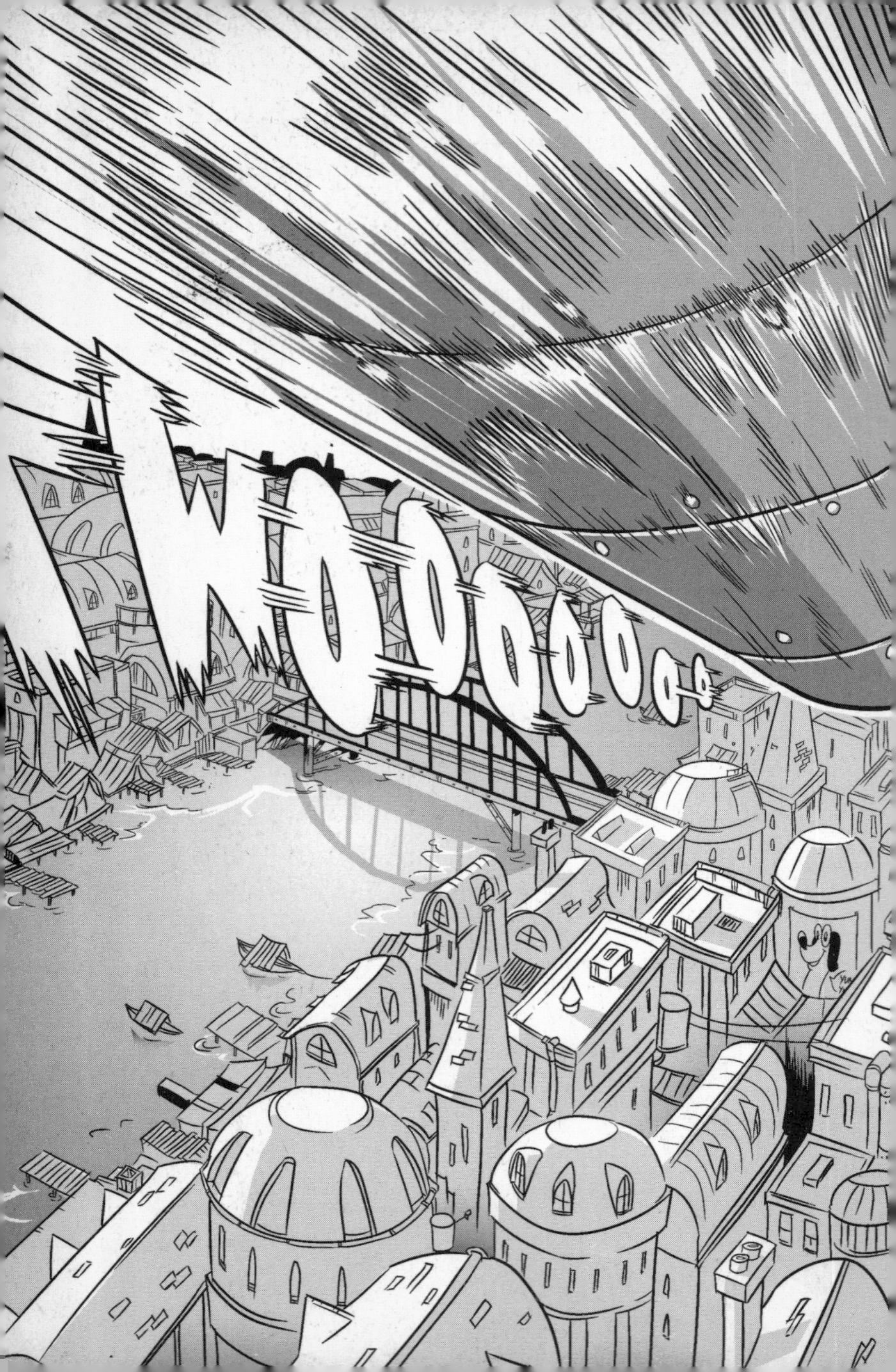
WOOOOOOO

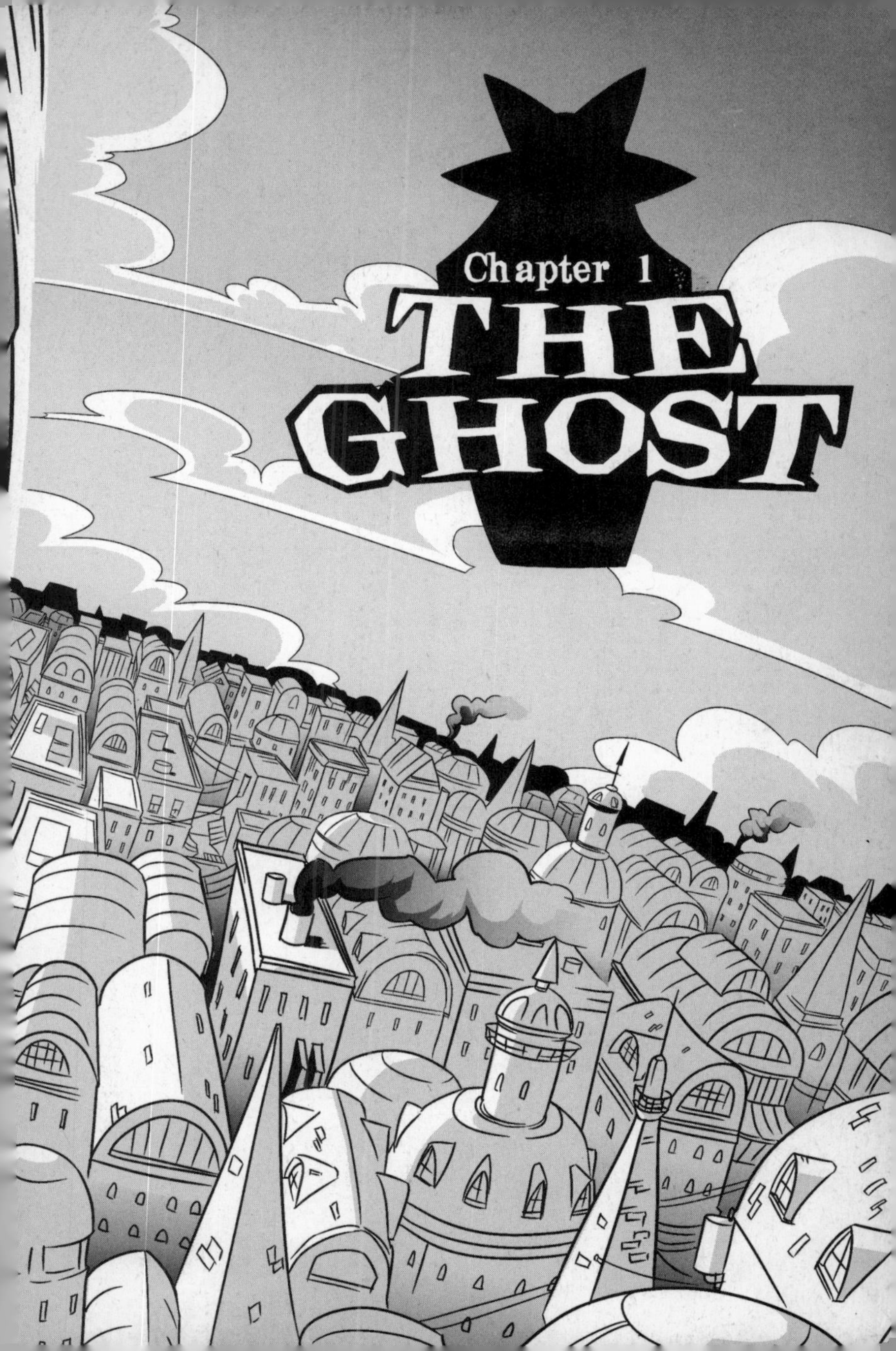
Chapter 1
THE GHOST

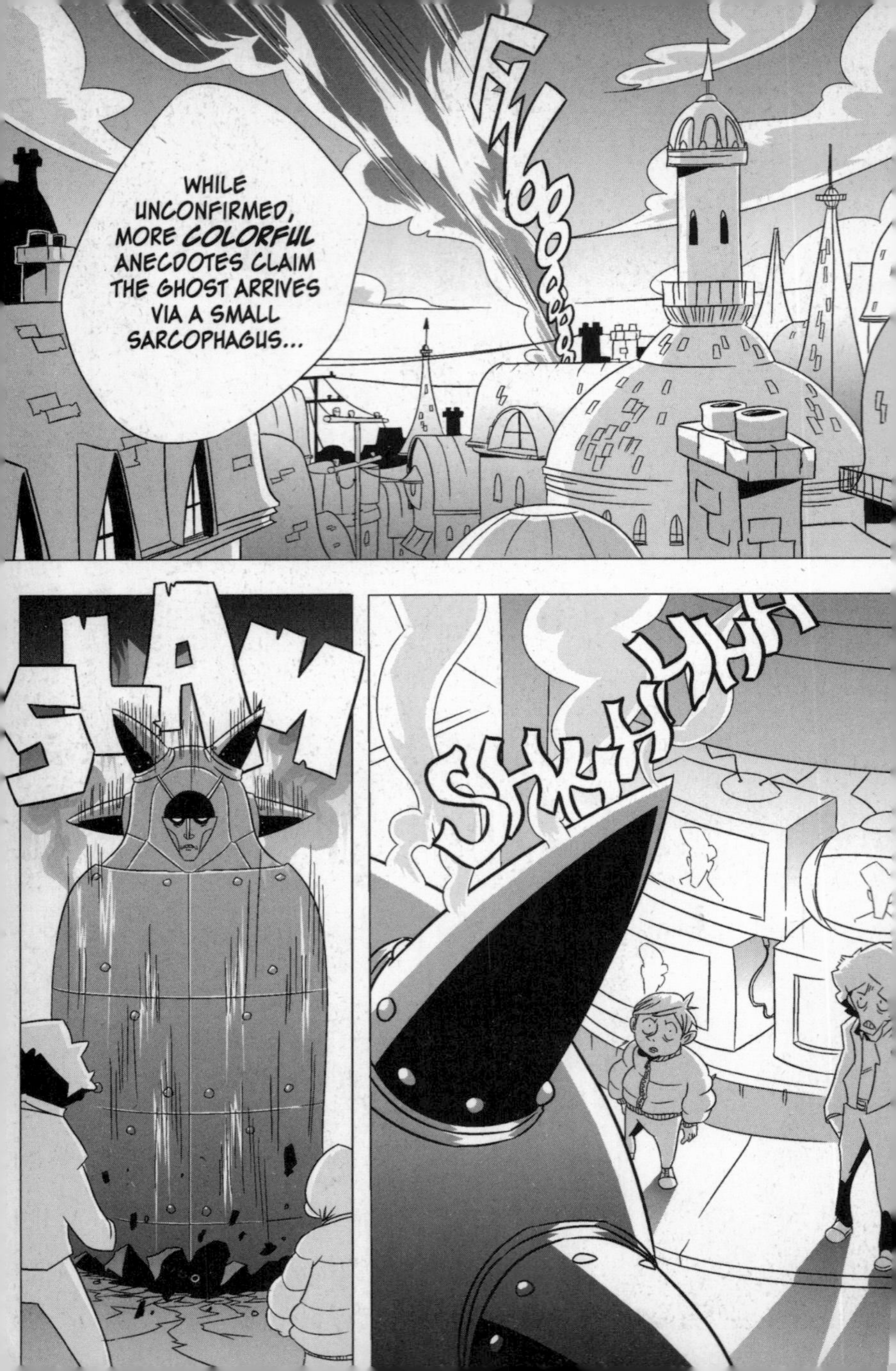
WHILE UNCONFIRMED, MORE **COLORFUL** ANECDOTES CLAIM THE GHOST ARRIVES VIA A SMALL SARCOPHAGUS...
SLAM

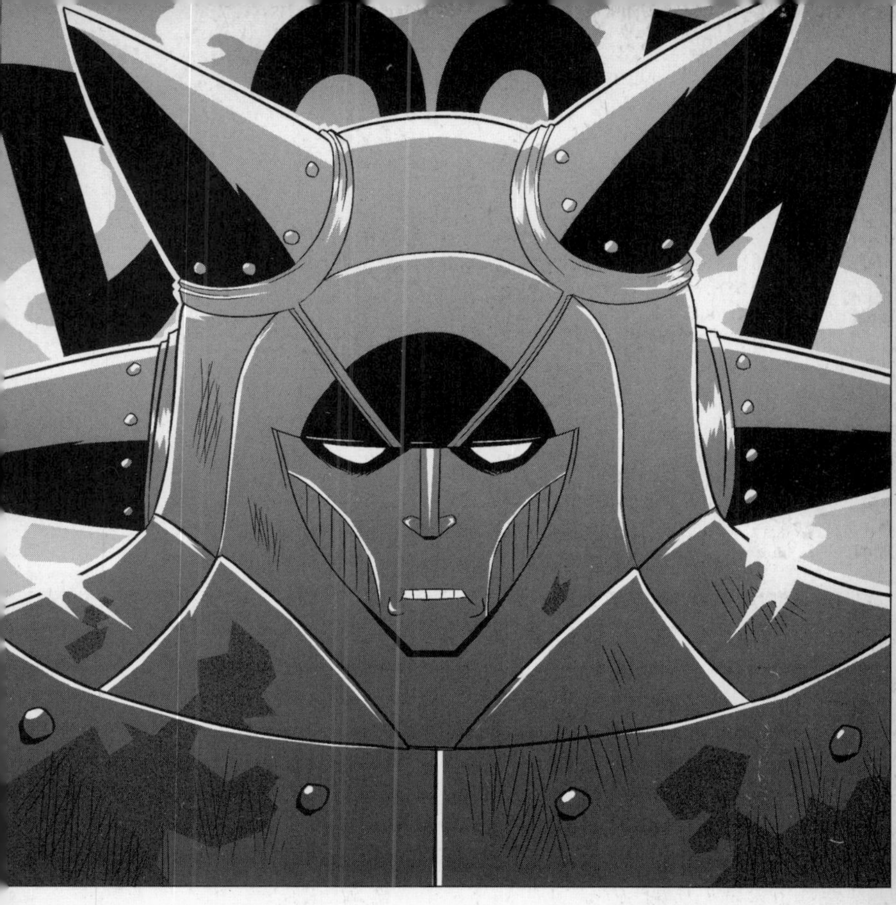
DOOM

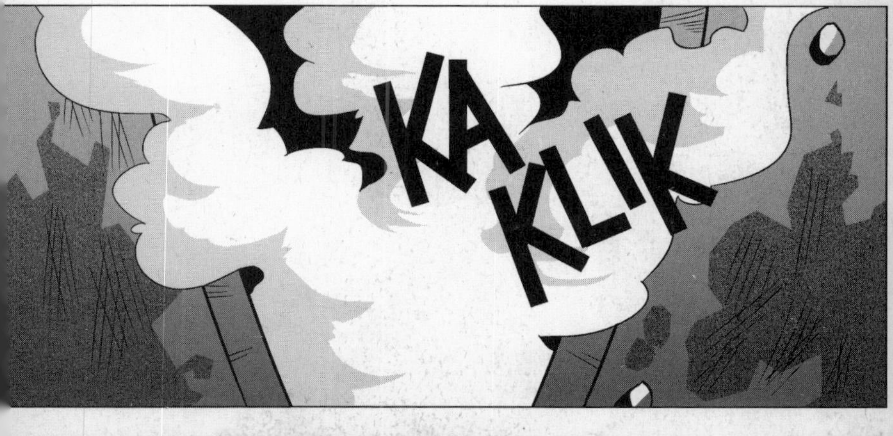
KA
KLIK

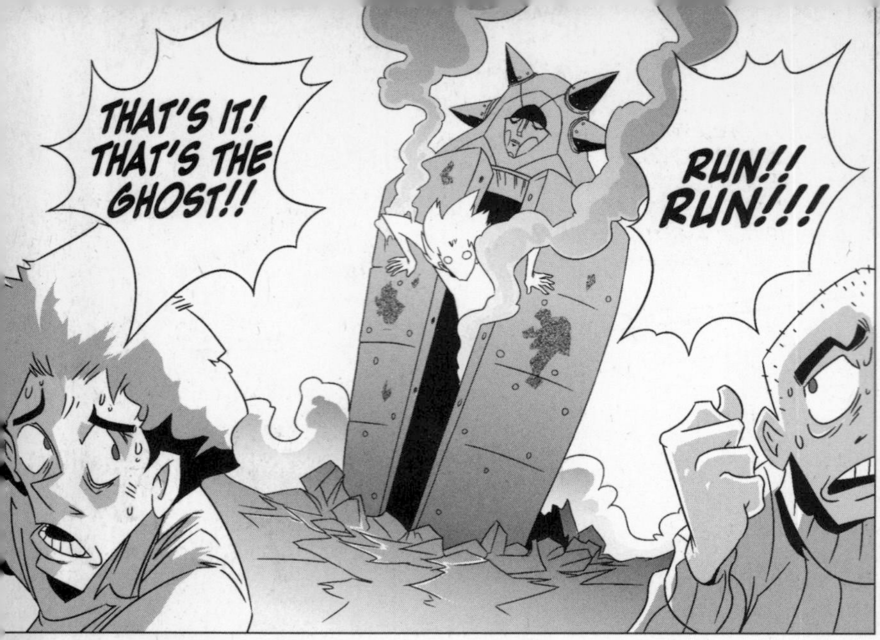
THAT'S IT! THAT'S THE GHOST!!
RUN!! RUN!!!

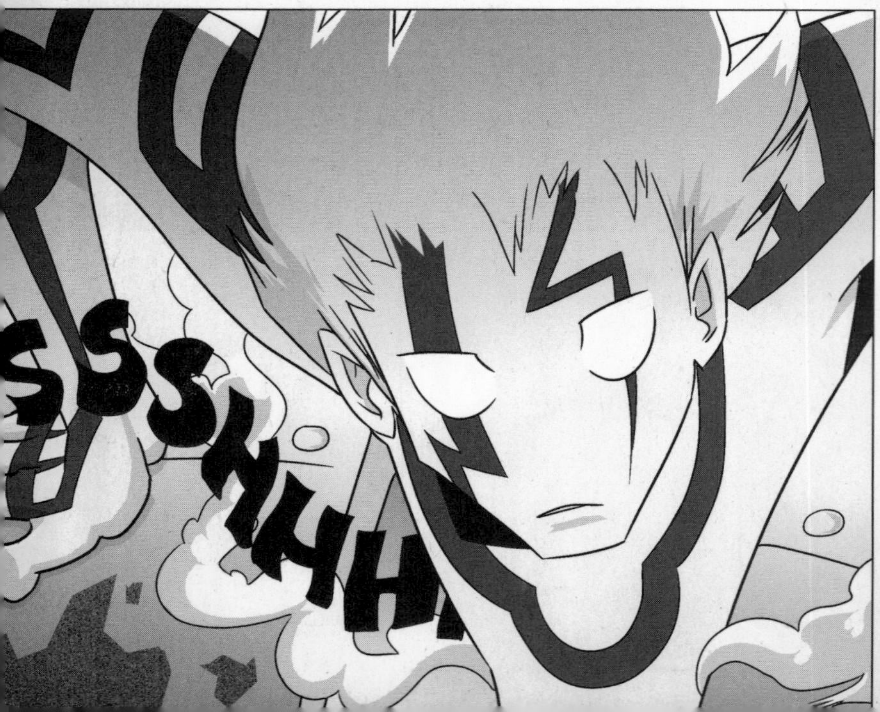
SSSHHHH

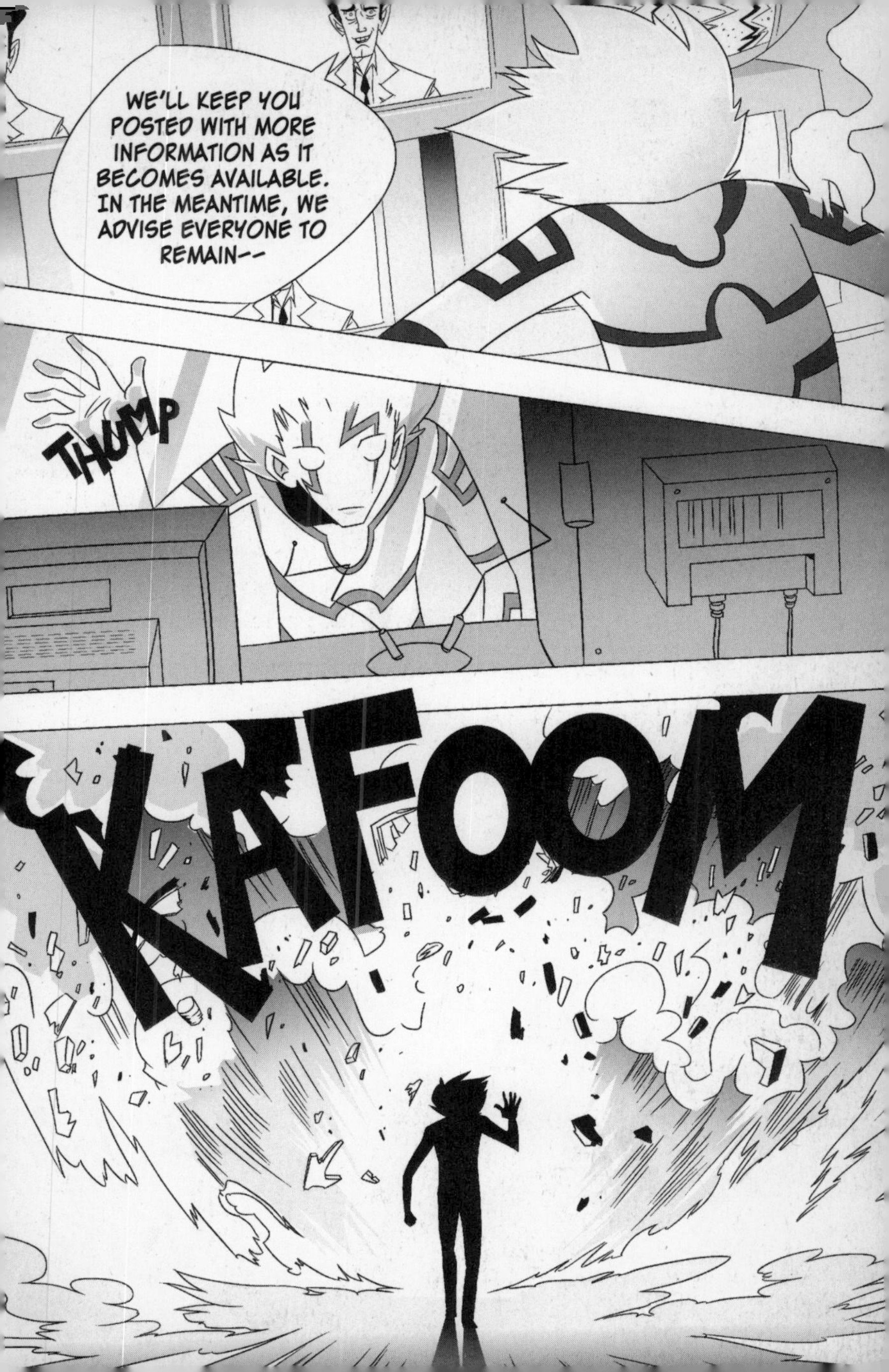
WE'LL KEEP YOU POSTED WITH MORE INFORMATION AS IT BECOMES AVAILABLE. IN THE MEANTIME, WE ADVISE EVERYONE TO REMAIN--
THUMP
KAFOOM

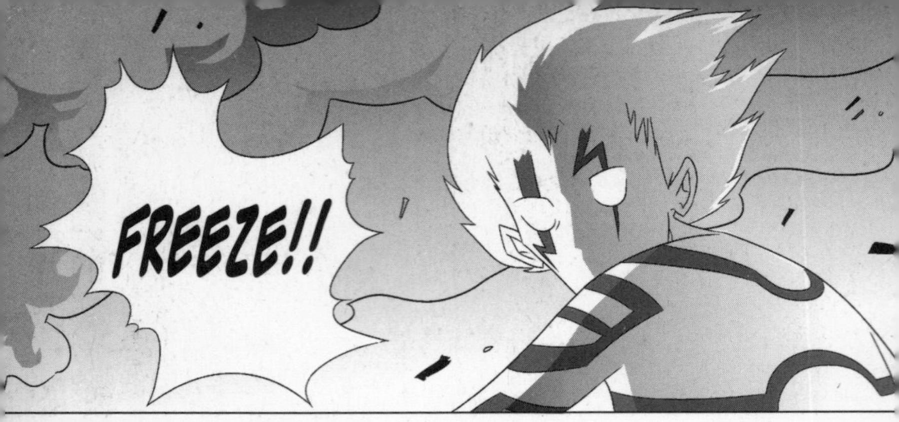
FREEZE!!
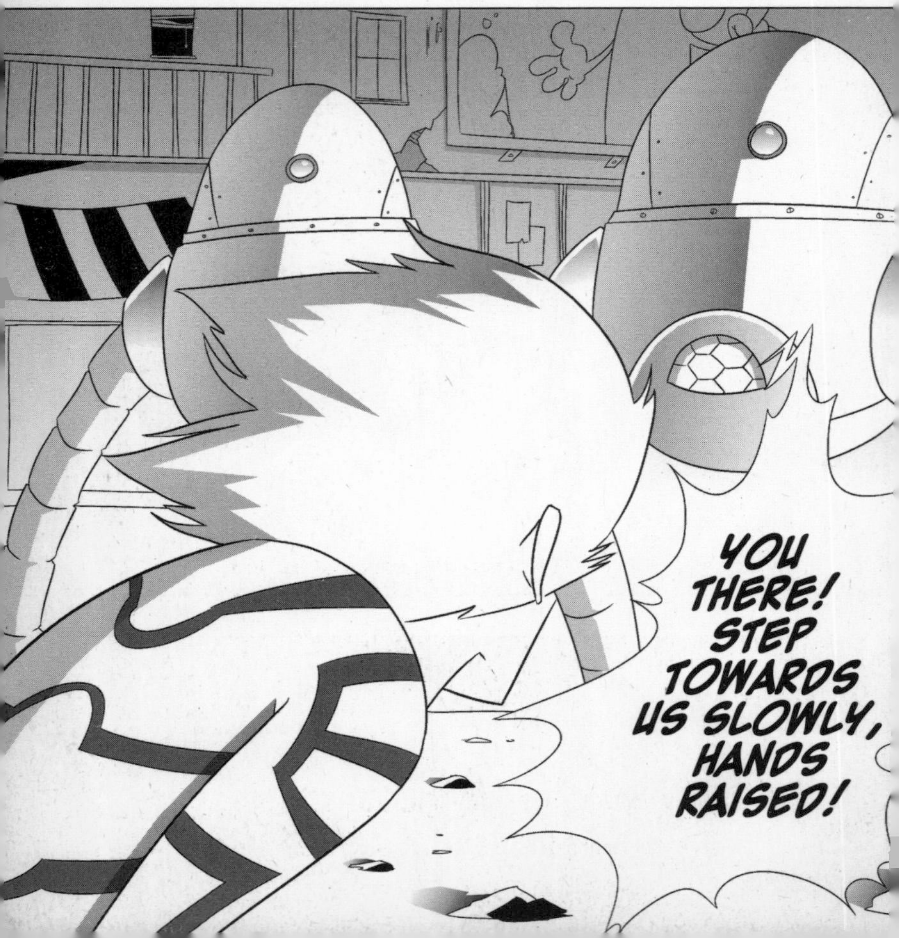
YOU THERE! STEP TOWARDS US SLOWLY, HANDS RAISED!

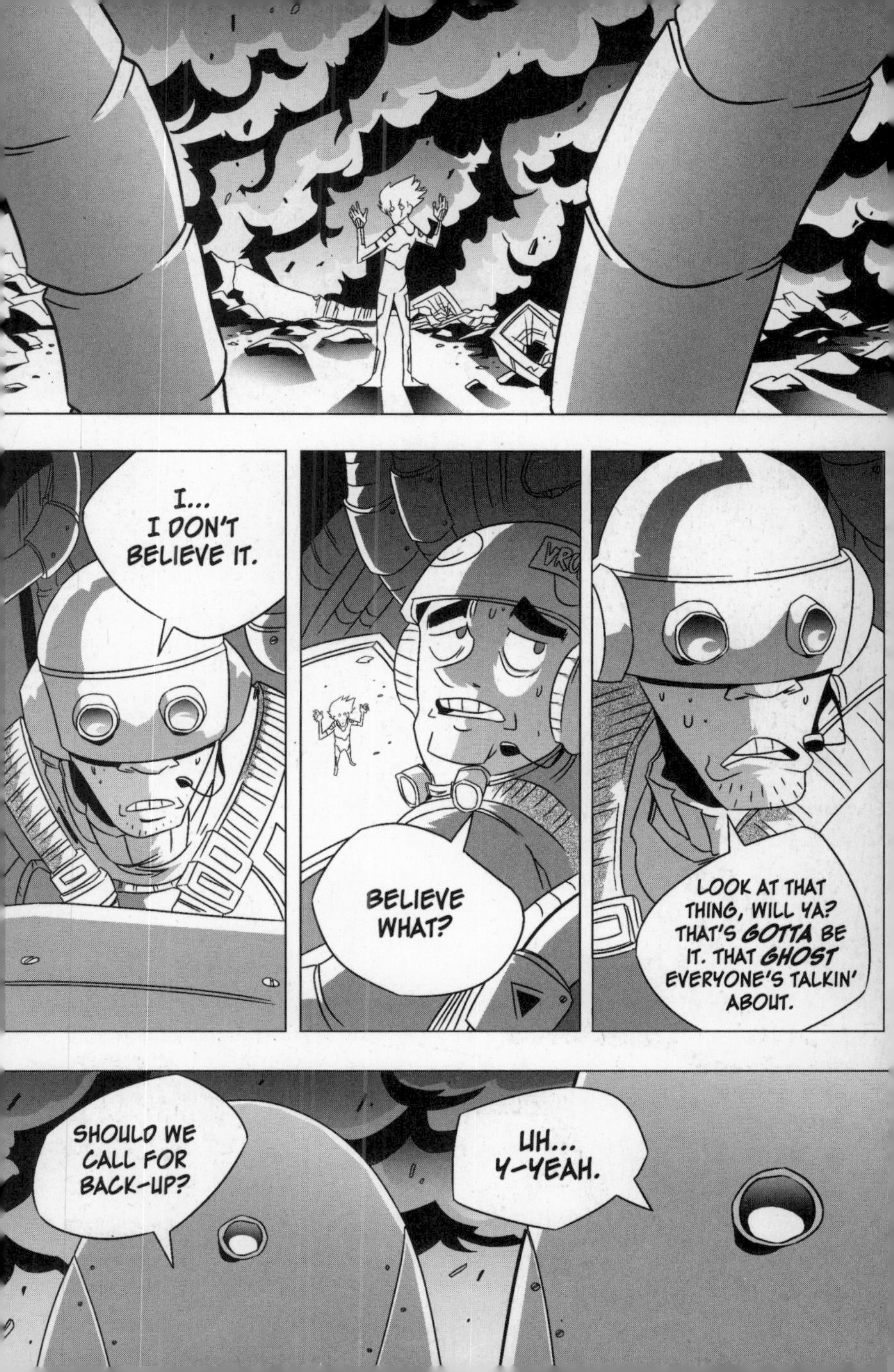
I... I DON'T BELIEVE IT.
BELIEVE WHAT?
LOOK AT THAT THING, WILL YA? THAT'S GOTTA BE IT. THAT GHOST EVERYONE'S TALKIN' ABOUT.
SHOULD WE CALL FOR BACK-UP?
UH... Y-YEAH.

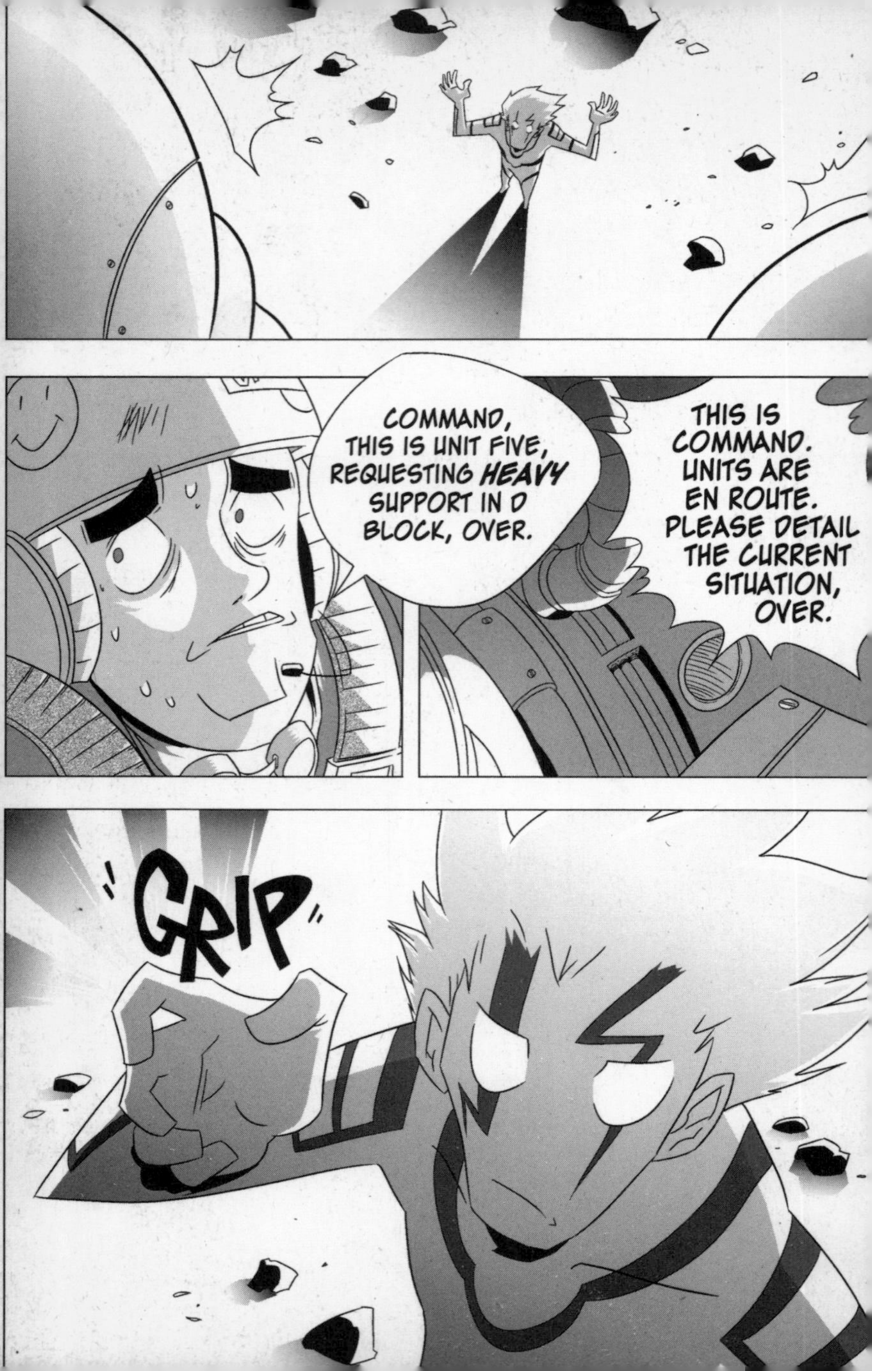
COMMAND, THIS IS UNIT FIVE, REQUESTING HEAVY SUPPORT IN D BLOCK, OVER.
THIS IS COMMAND. UNITS ARE EN ROUTE. PLEASE DETAIL THE CURRENT SITUATION, OVER.
GRIP

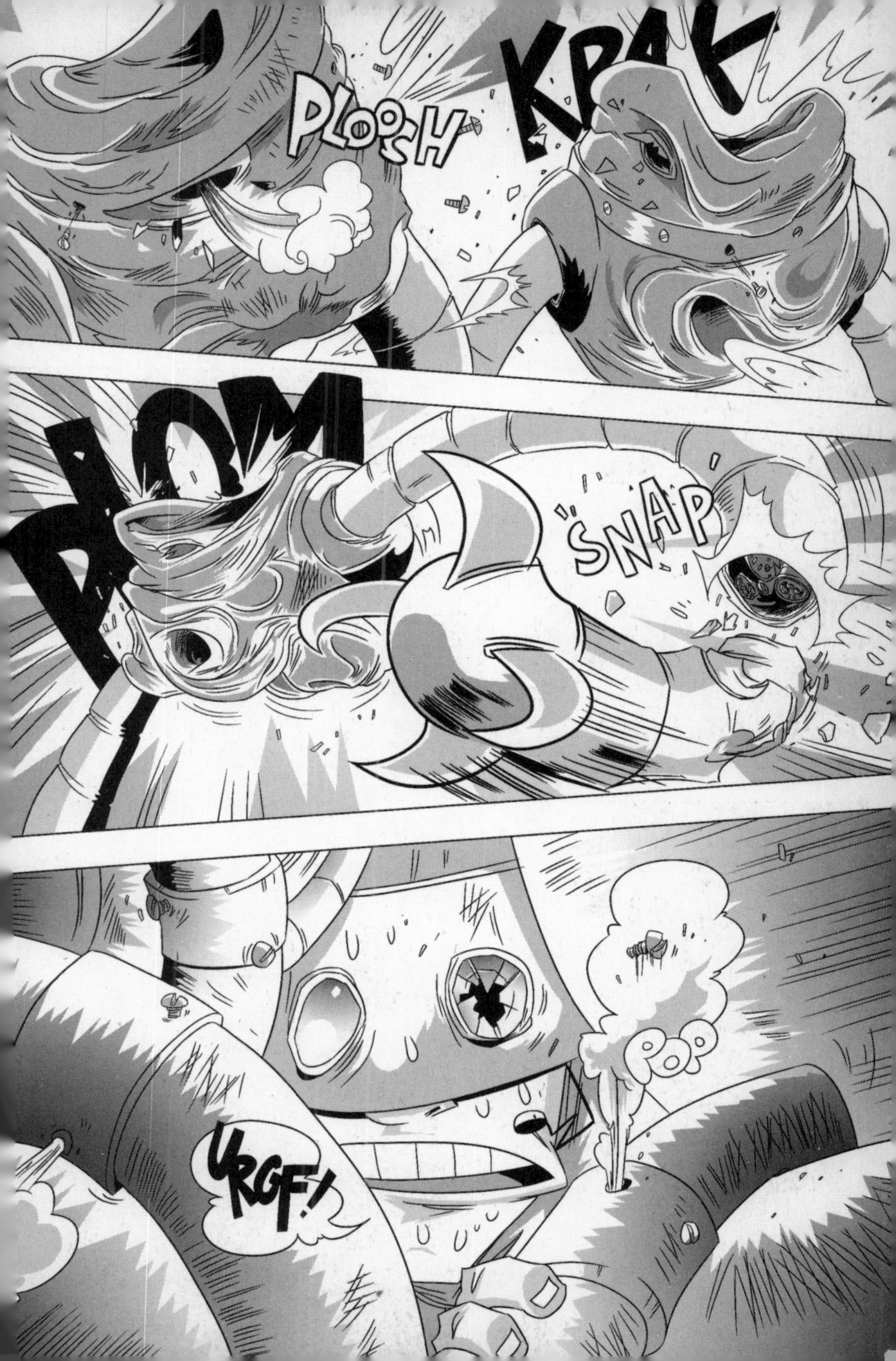
KRAK
PLOOSH
SNAP
BOOM
POP
URGF!

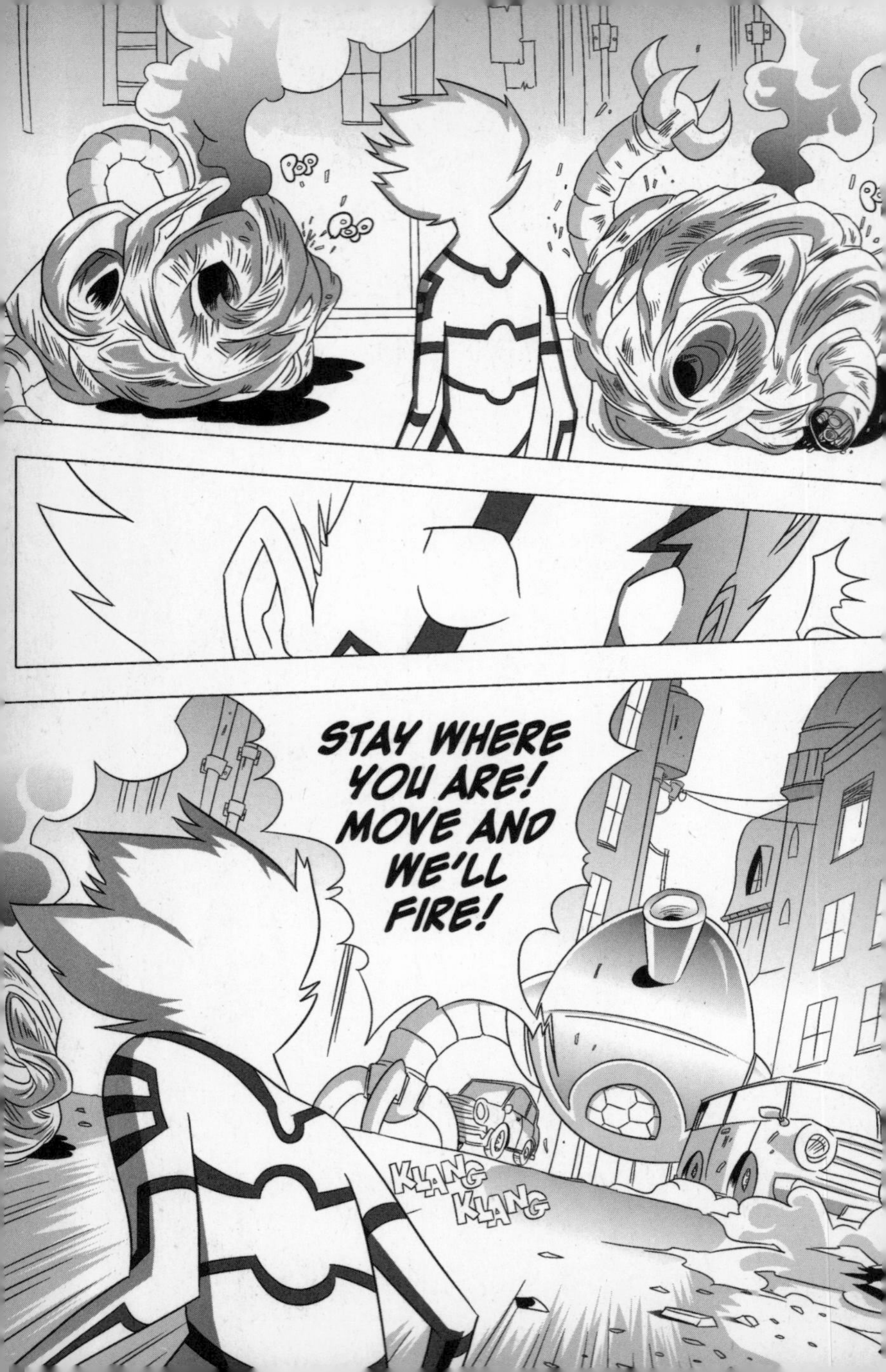

POP
POP
POP
STAY WHERE YOU ARE! MOVE AND WE'LL FIRE!
KLANG KLANG

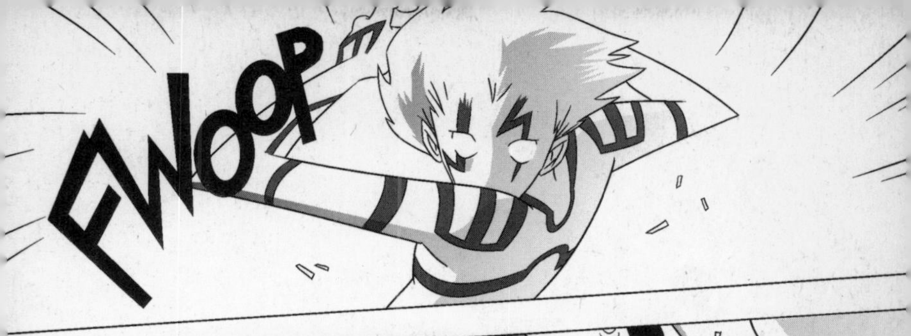
FWOOP

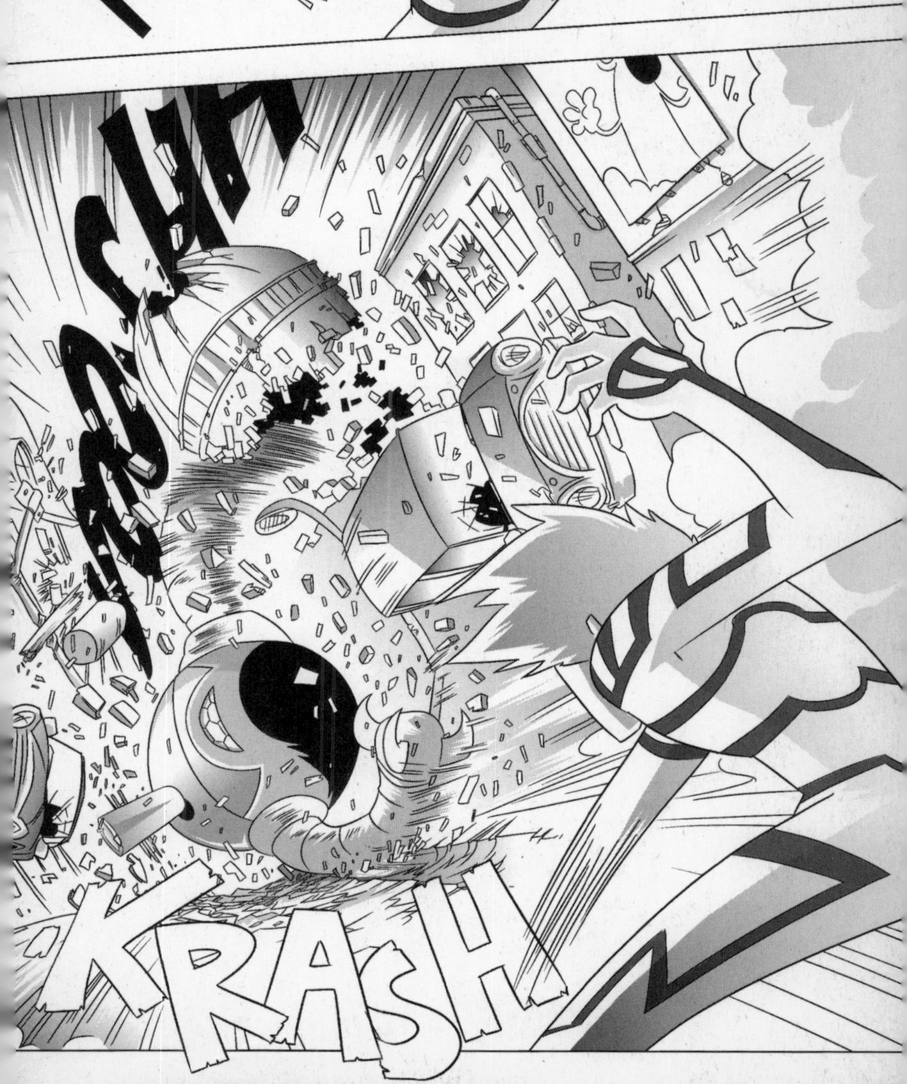
KRASH

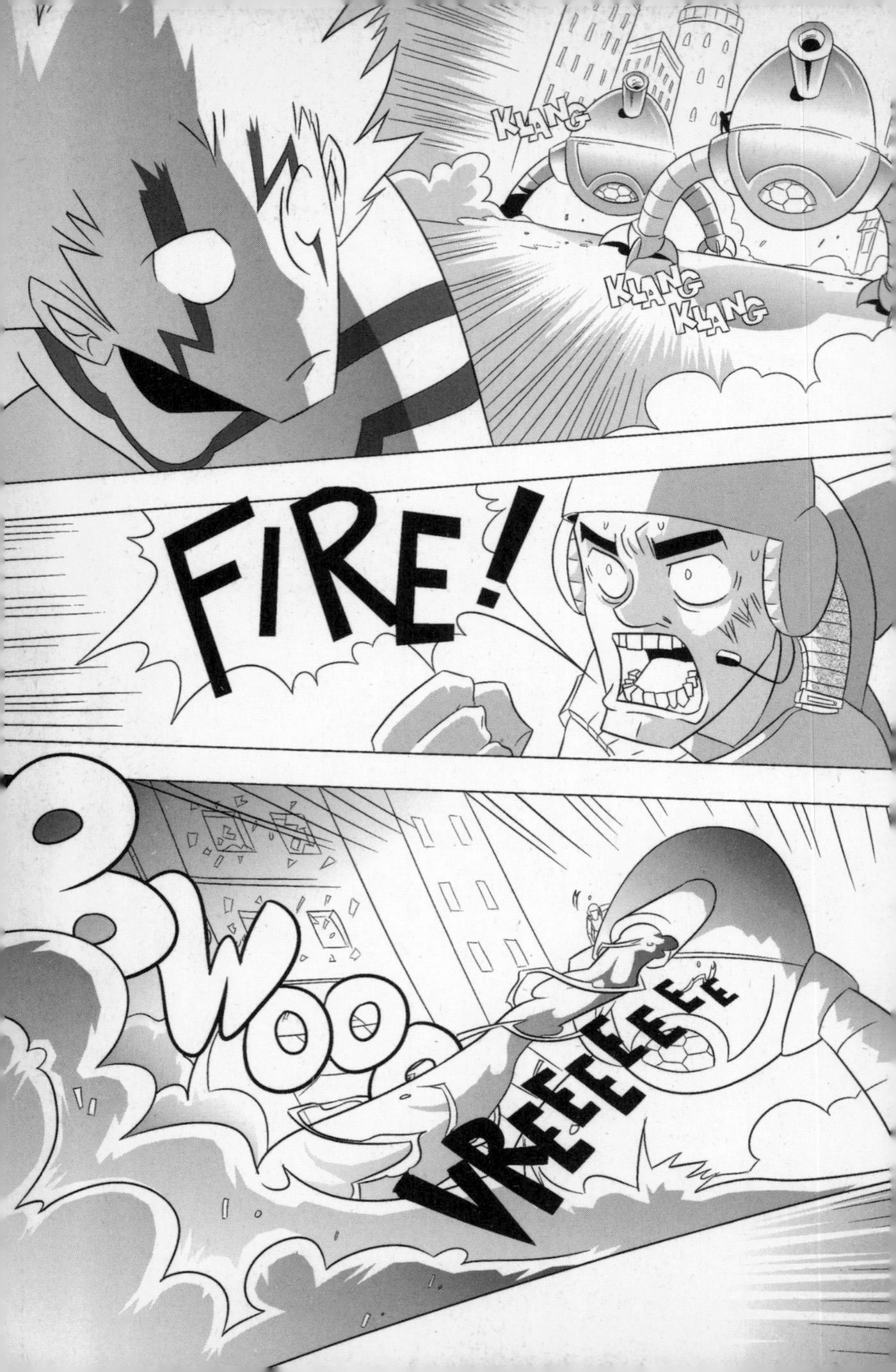
KLANG
KLANG
KLANG
FIRE!
VREEEEEEE
BWOOO

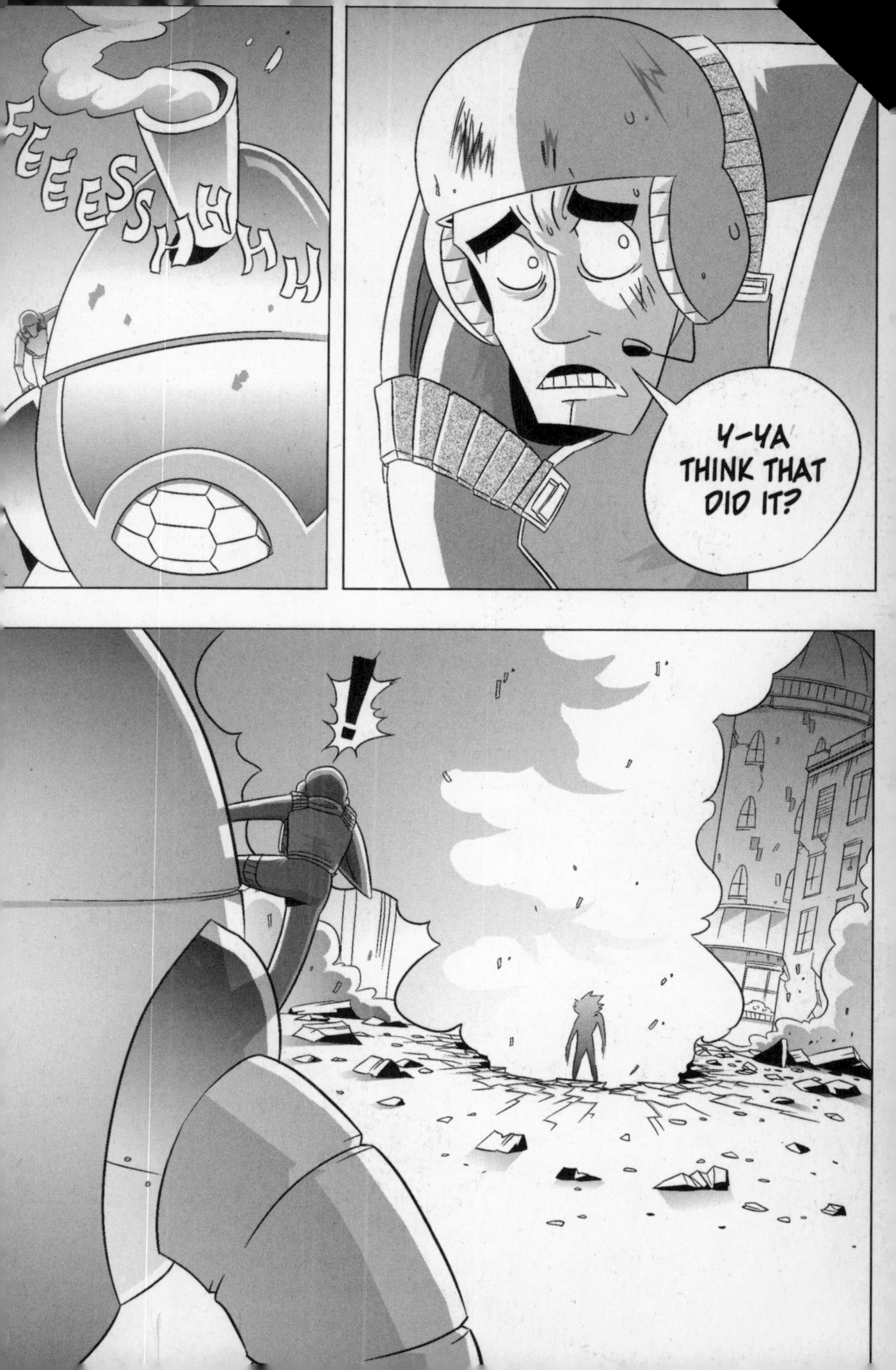
FEEESSHHHHH
Y-YA THINK THAT DID IT?
!

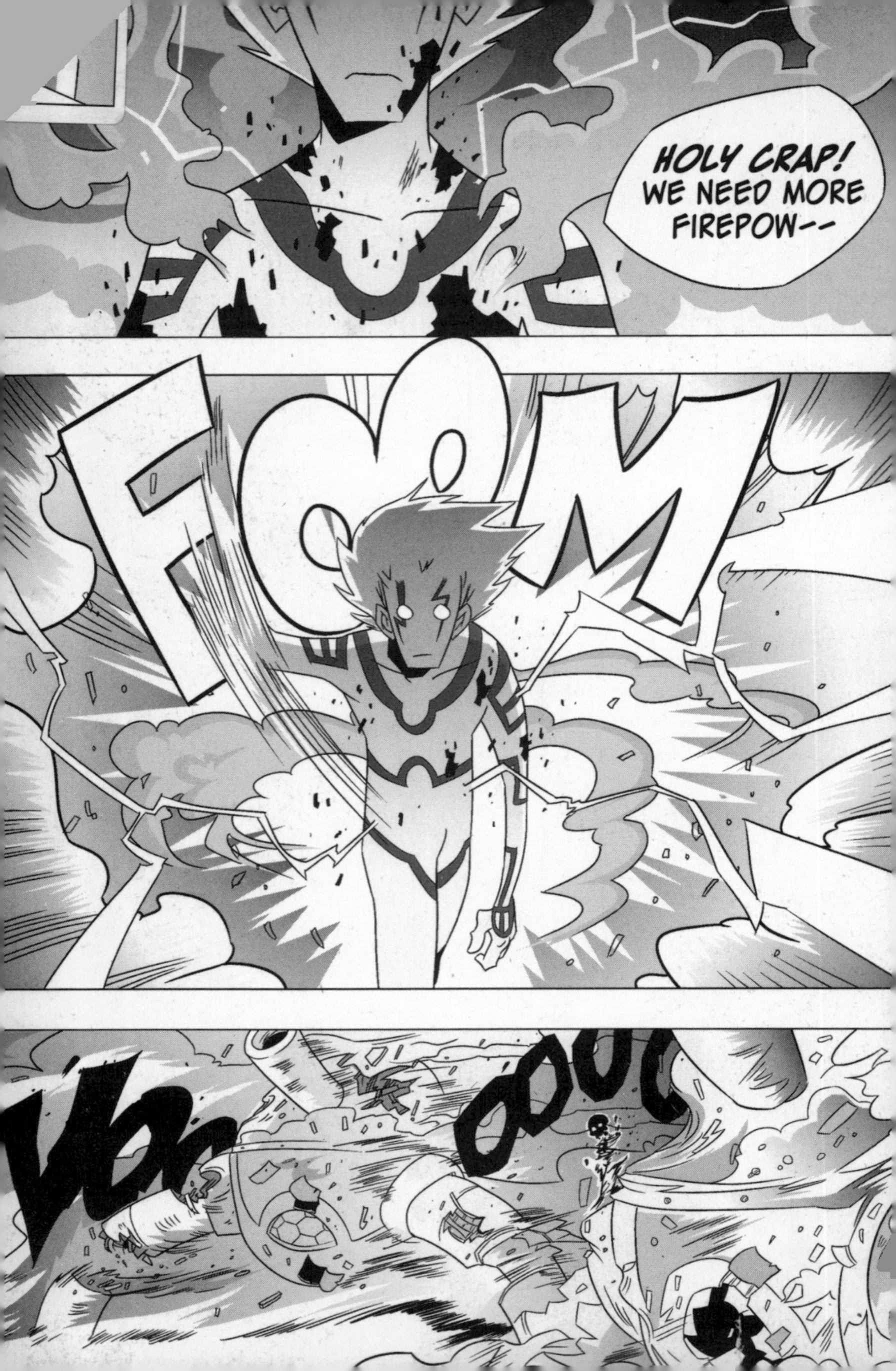
HOLY CRAP! WE NEED MORE FIREPOW--
FOOM

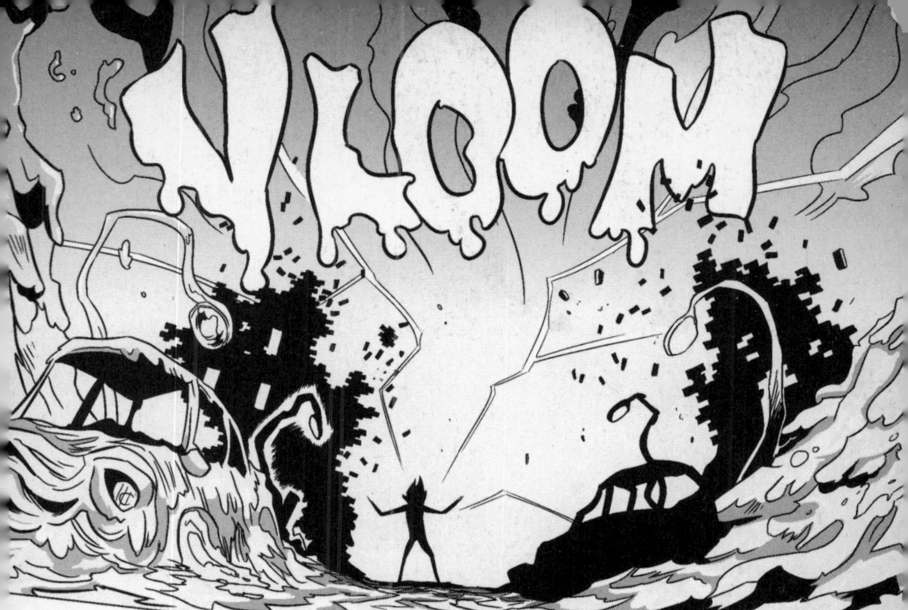

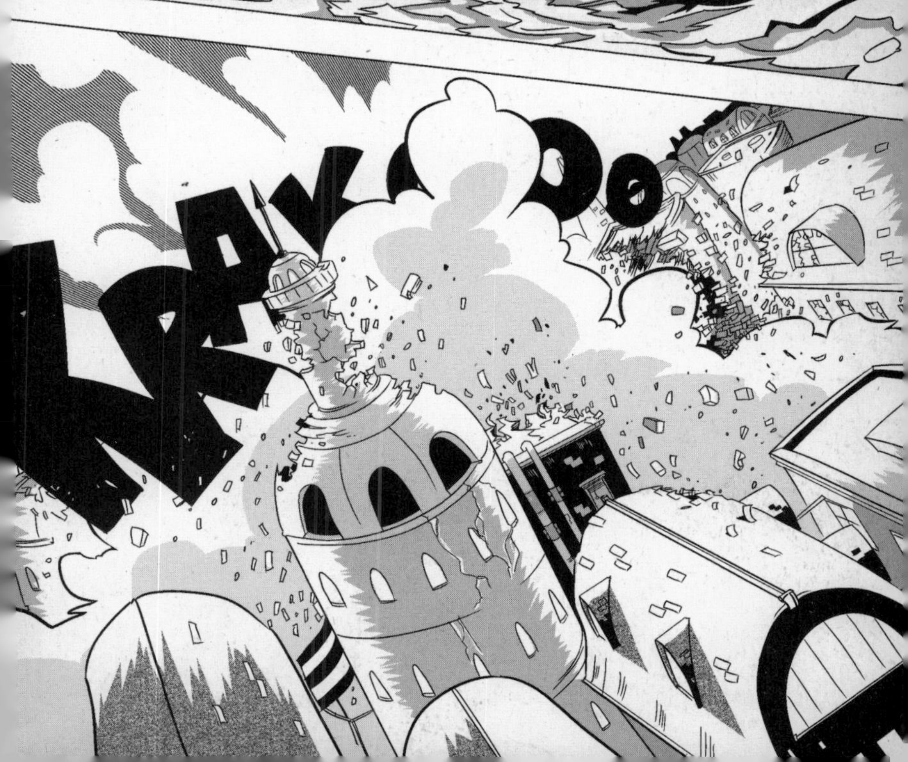

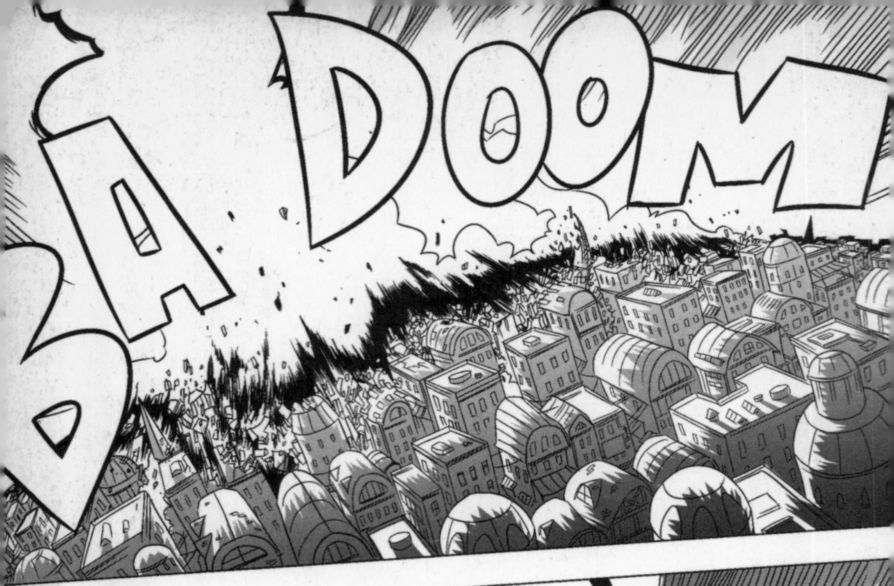
ADOOM
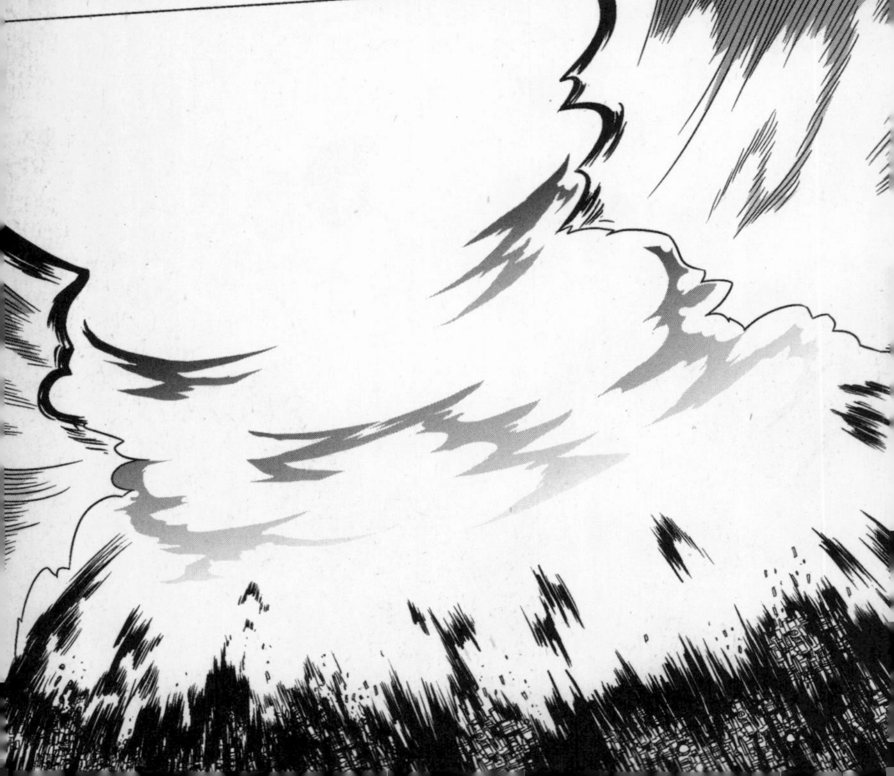

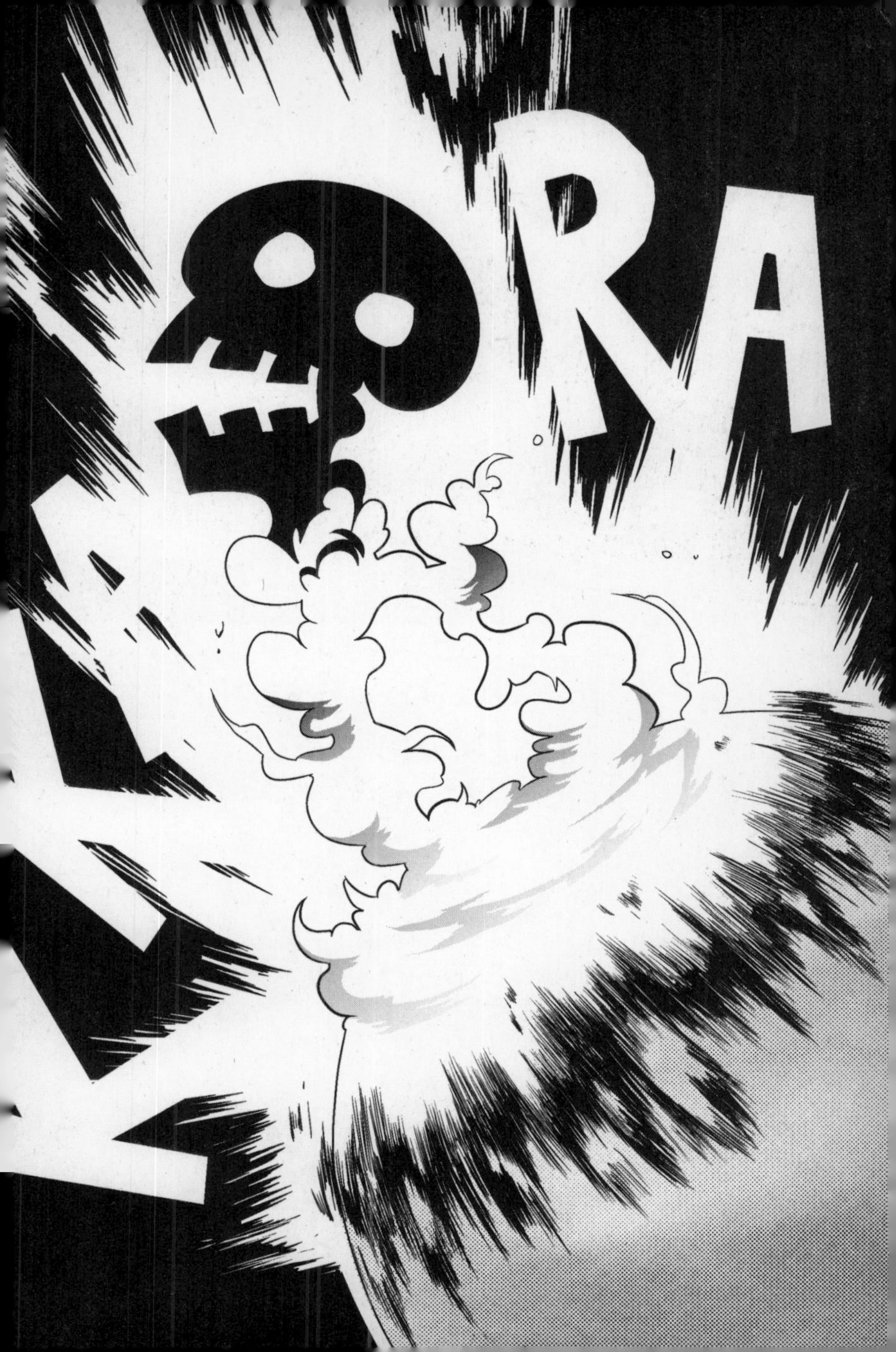

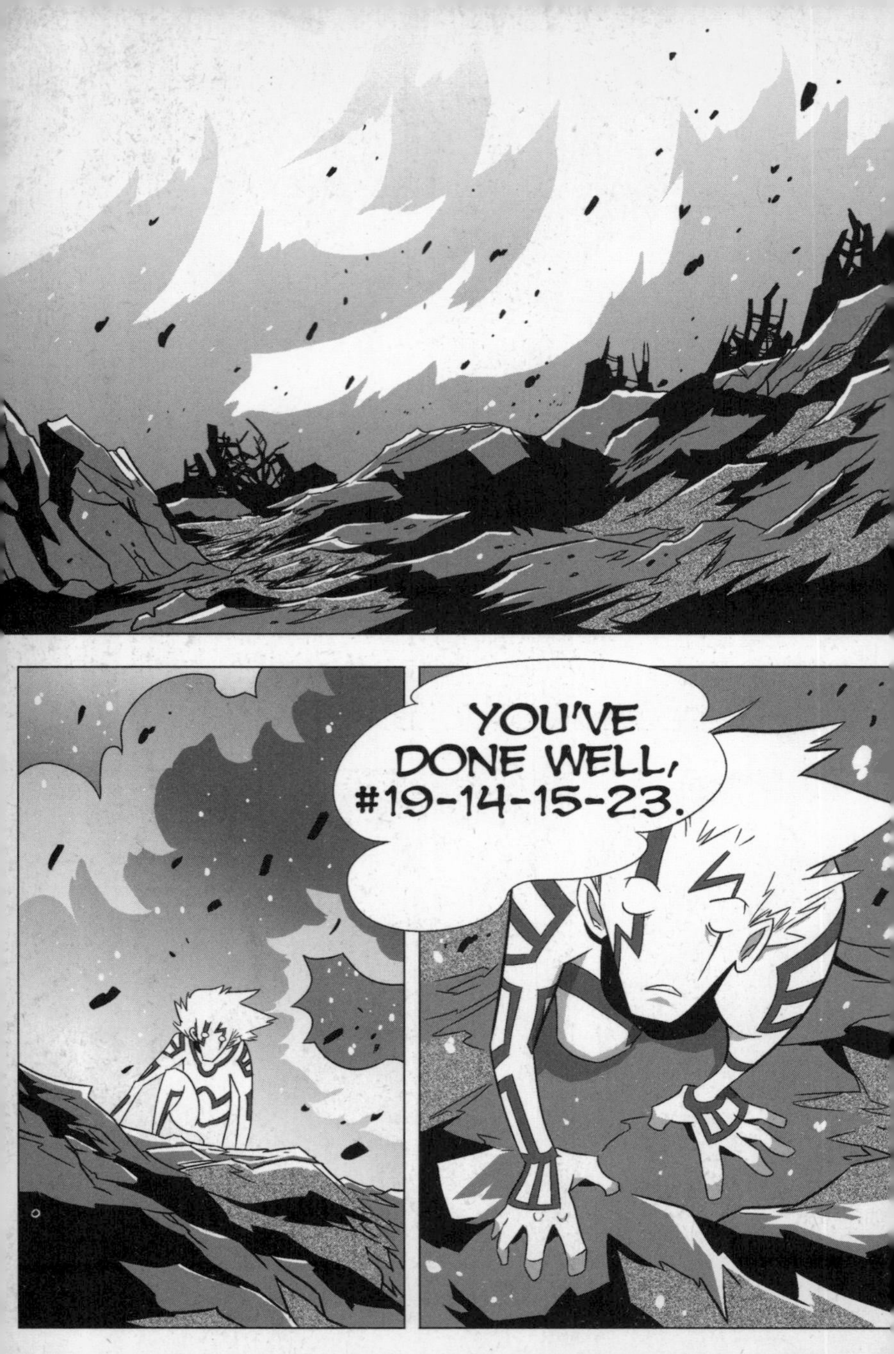
YOU'VE DONE WELL, #19-14-15-23.

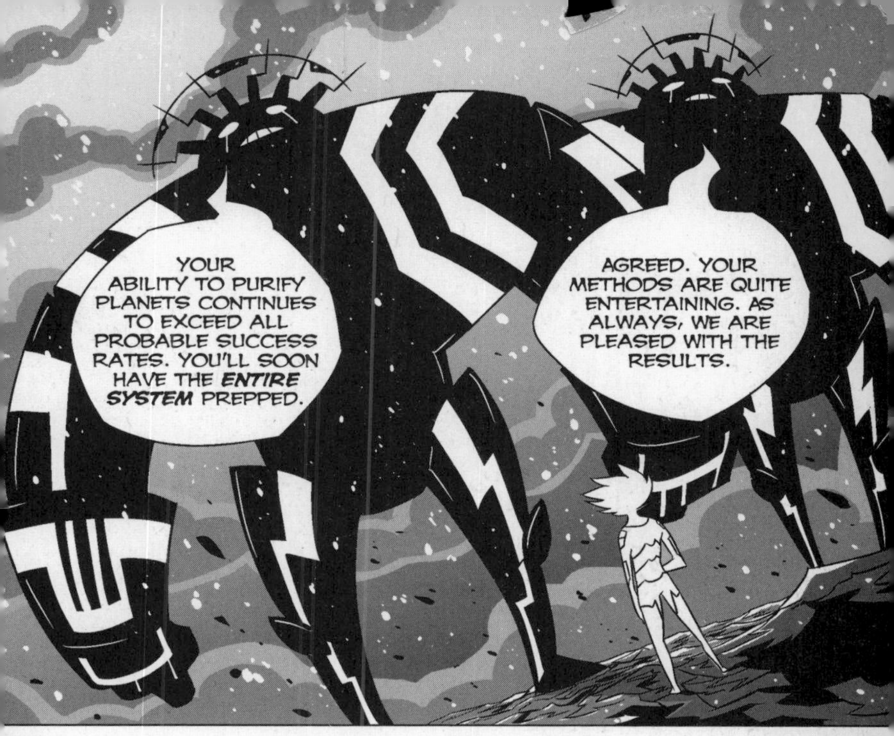
YOUR ABILITY TO PURIFY PLANETS CONTINUES TO EXCEED ALL PROBABLE SUCCESS RATES. YOU'LL SOON HAVE THE *ENTIRE SYSTEM* PREPPED.
AGREED. YOUR METHODS ARE QUITE ENTERTAINING. AS ALWAYS, WE ARE PLEASED WITH THE RESULTS.
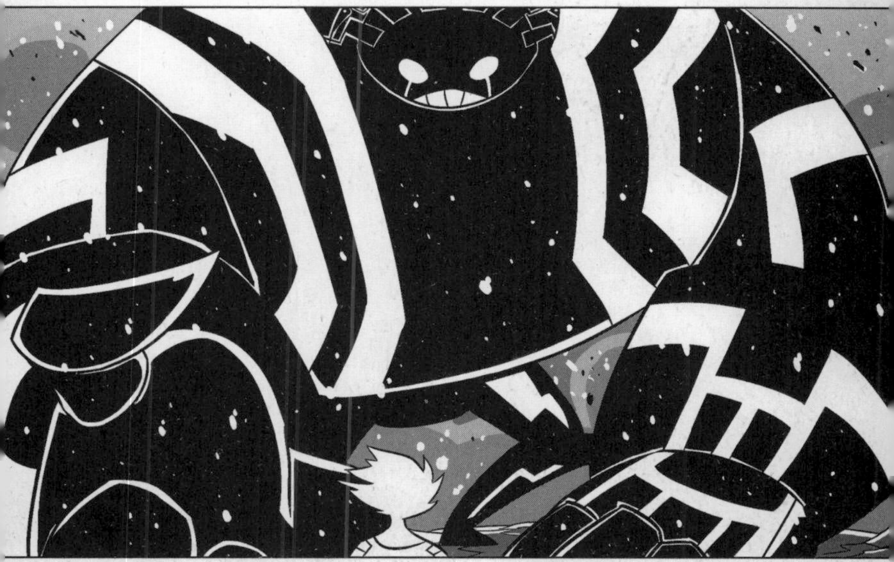

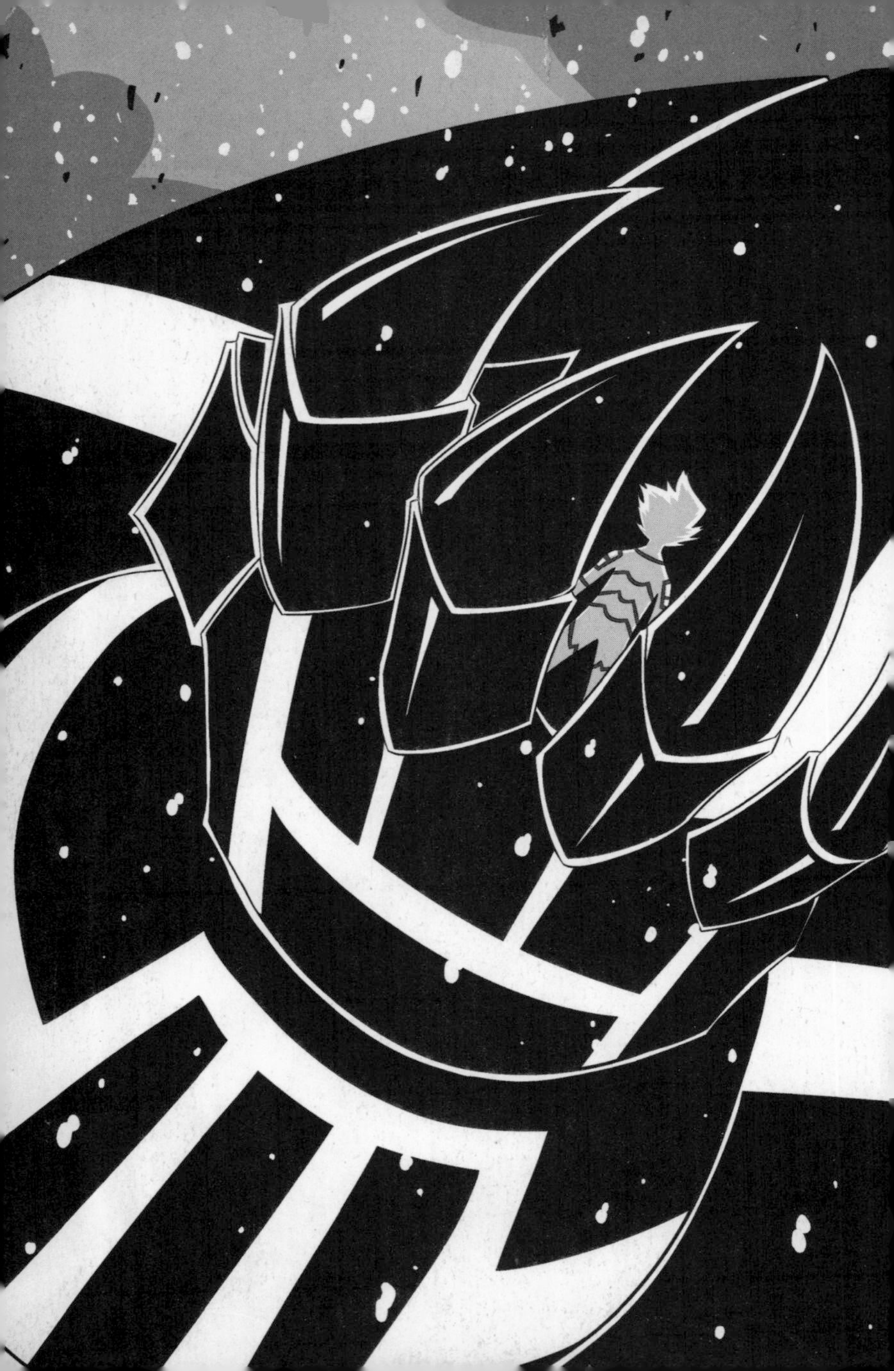

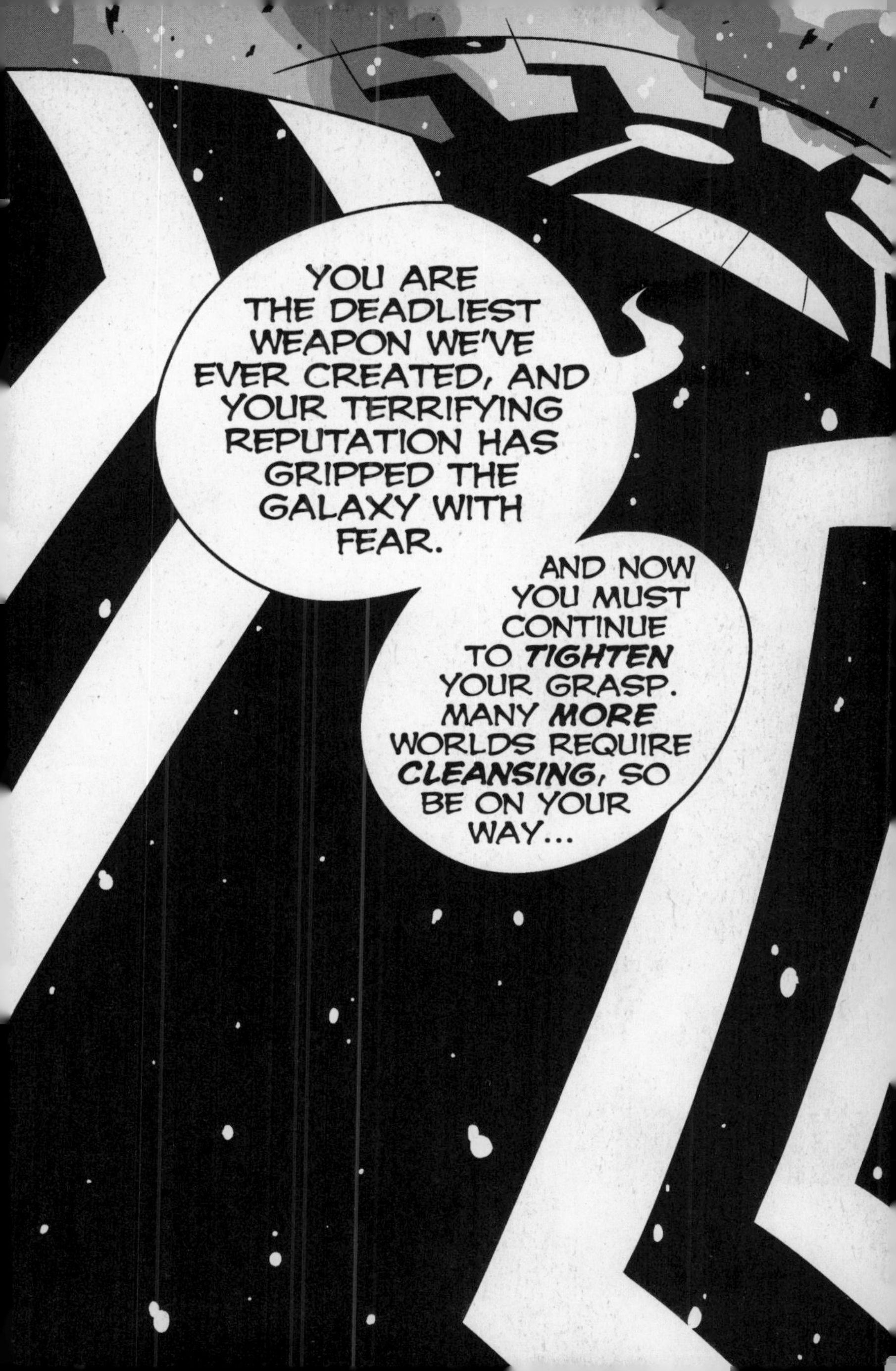
YOU ARE THE DEADLIEST WEAPON WE'VE EVER CREATED, AND YOUR TERRIFYING REPUTATION HAS GRIPPED THE GALAXY WITH FEAR.
AND NOW YOU MUST CONTINUE TO TIGHTEN YOUR GRASP. MANY MORE WORLDS REQUIRE CLEANSING, SO BE ON YOUR WAY...

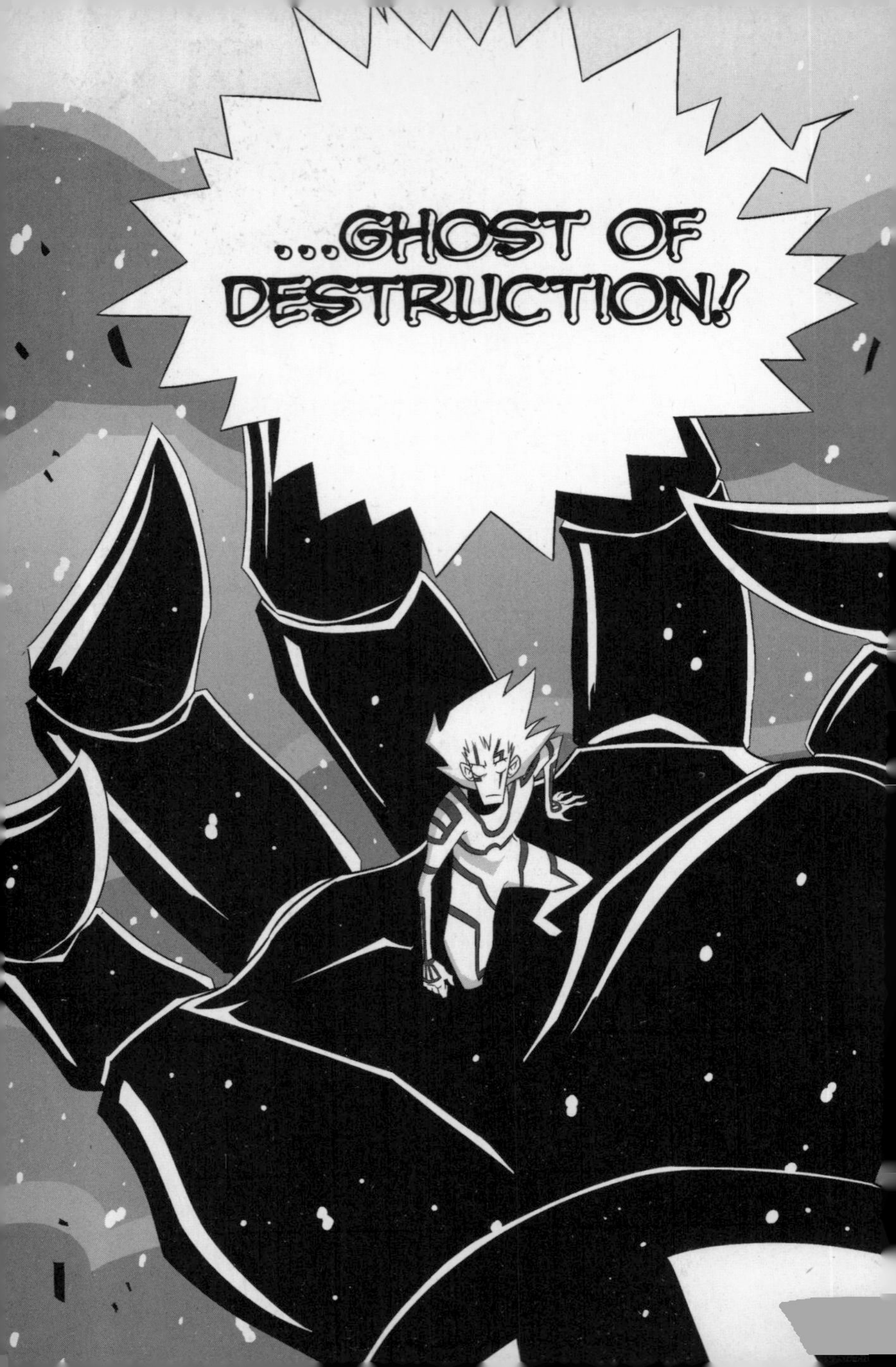
...GHOST OF DESTRUCTION!

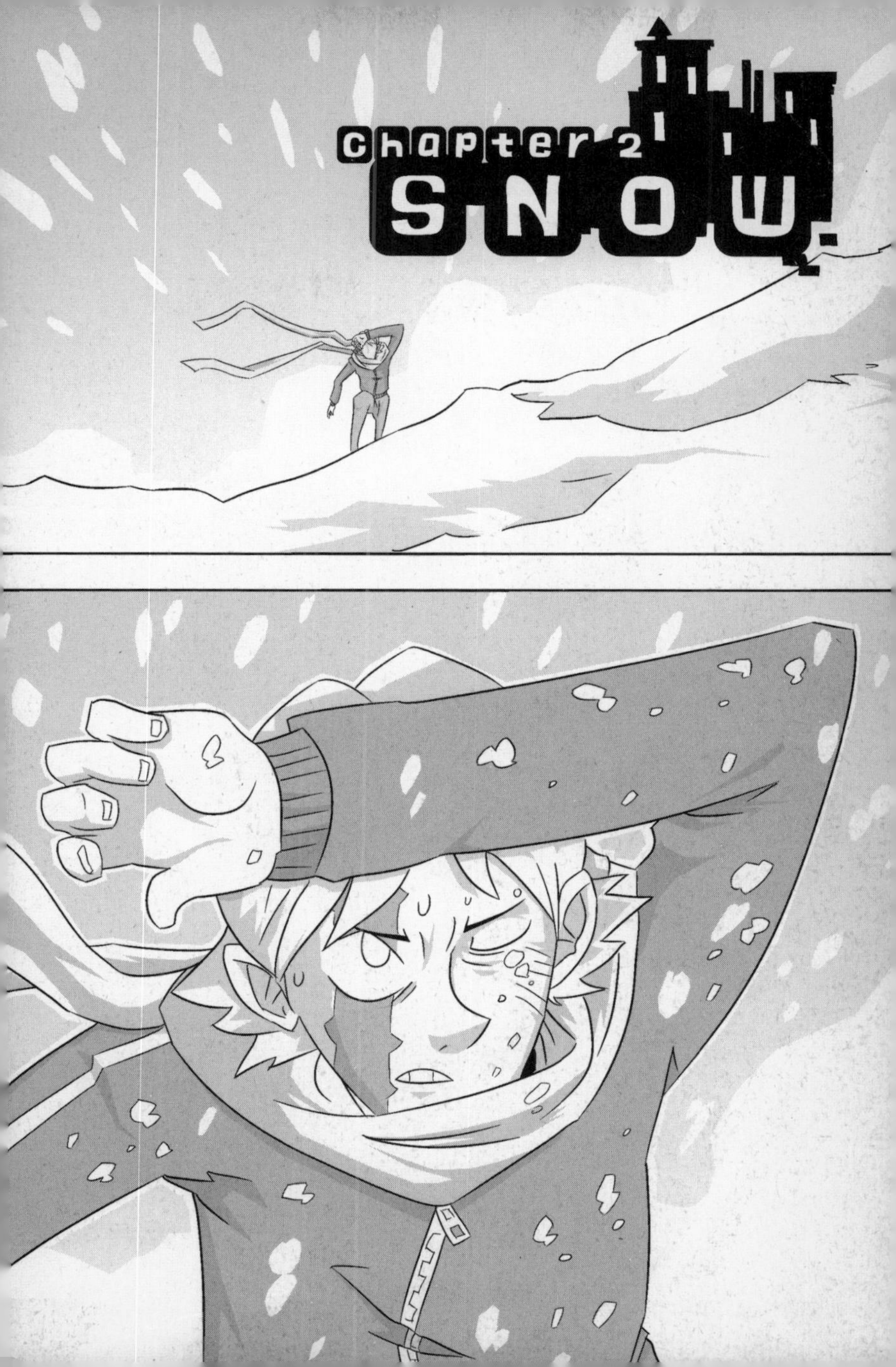
Chapter 2
SNOW

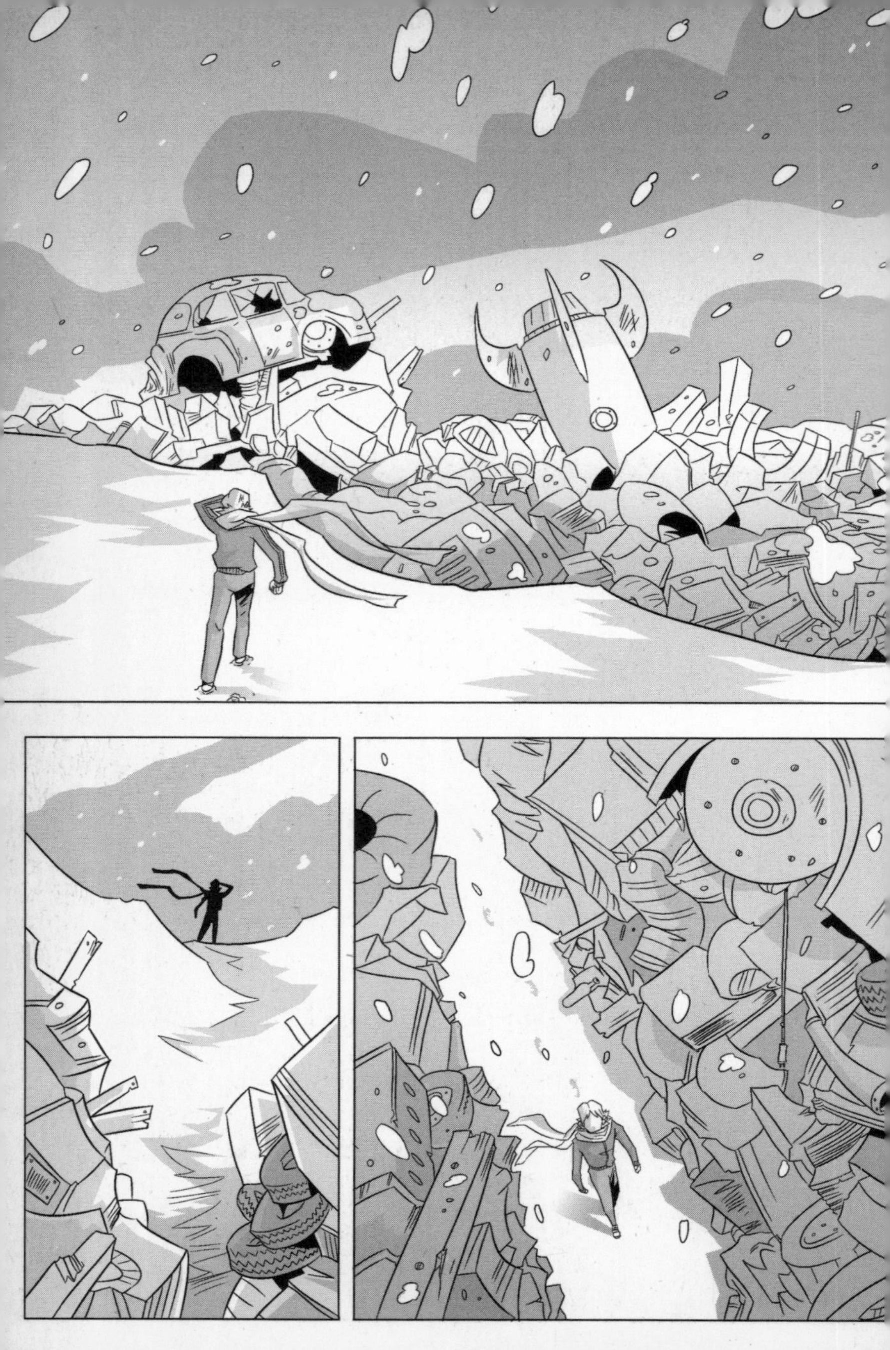

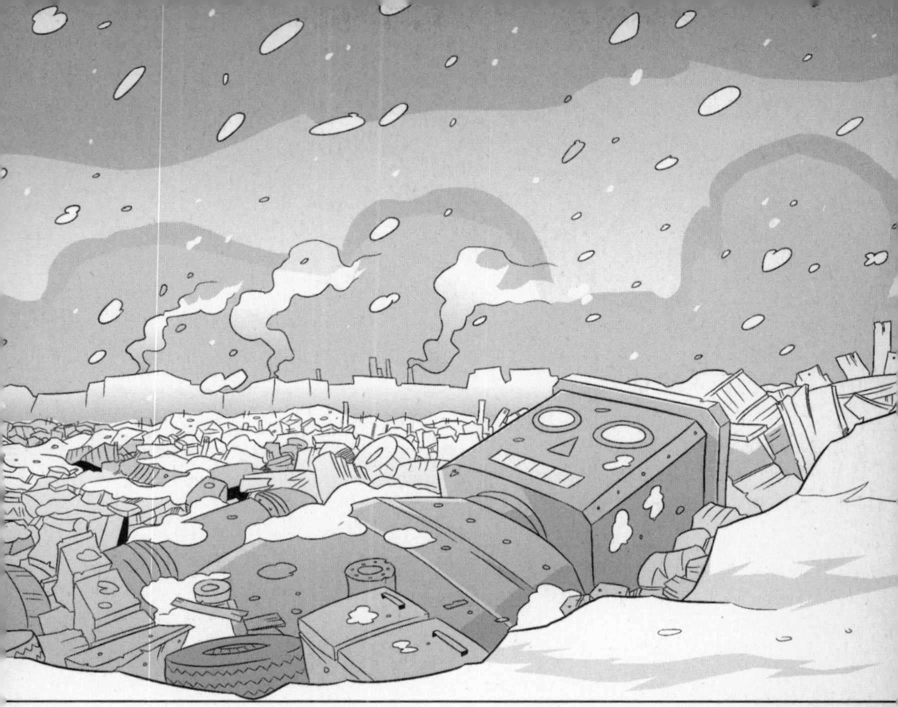

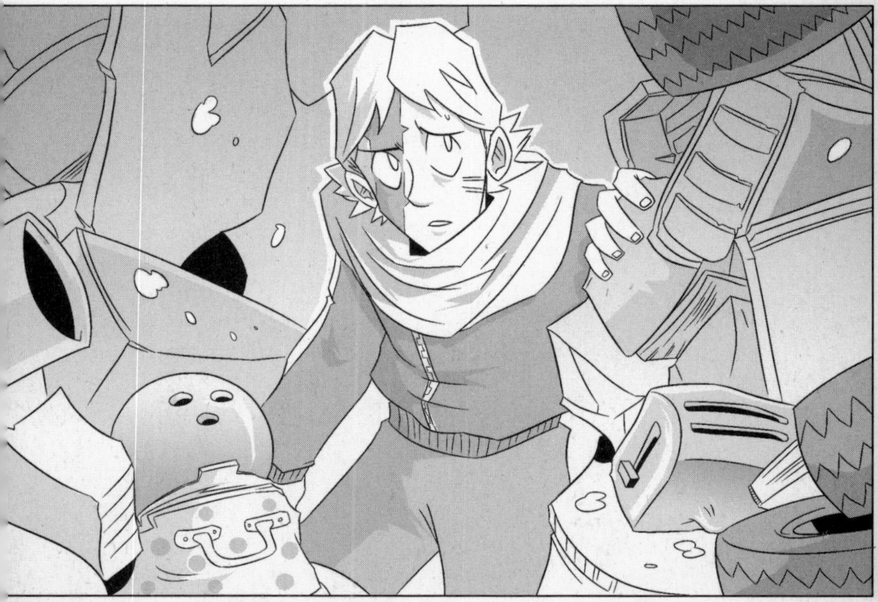

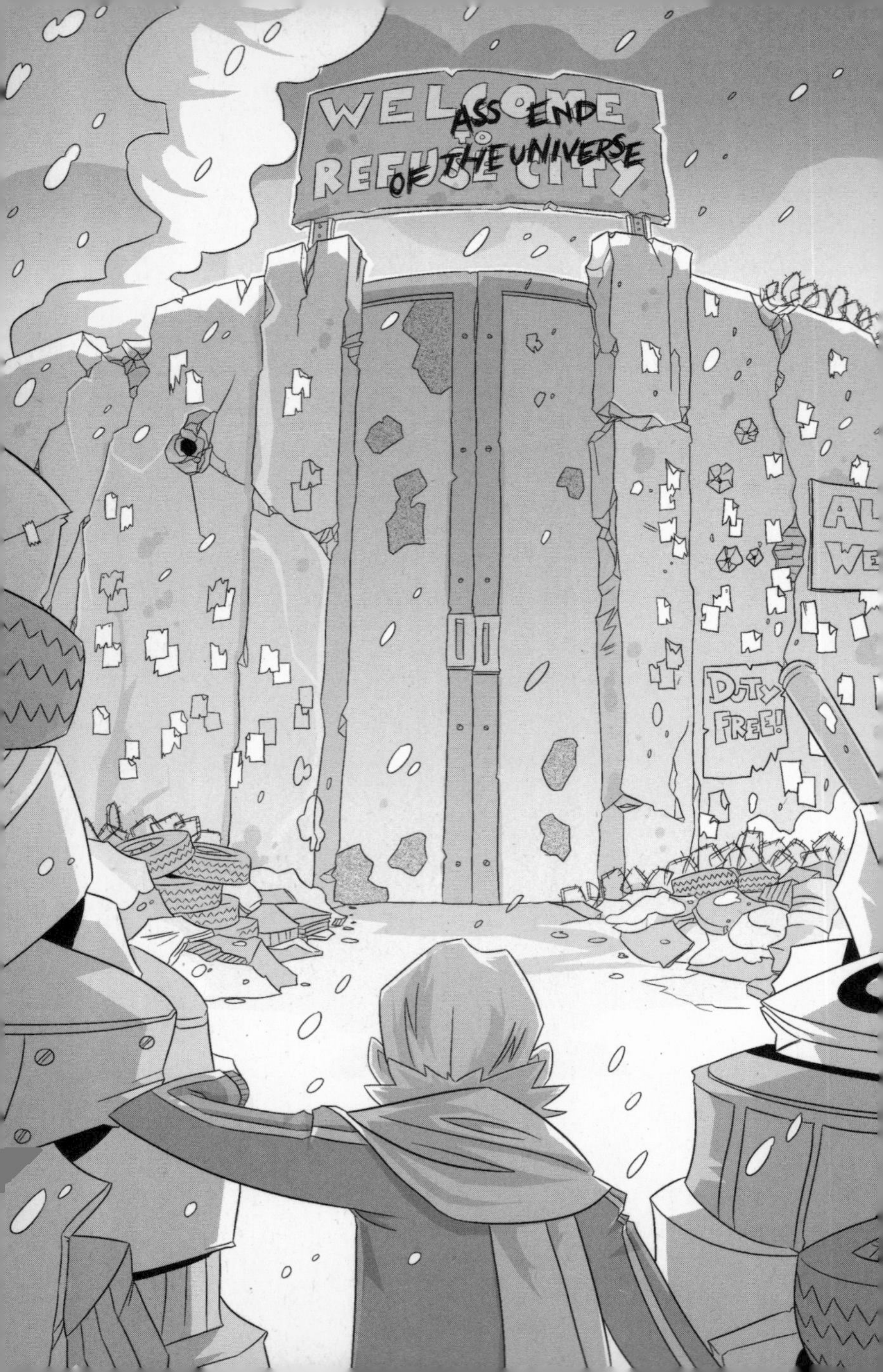
WELCOME TO REFUSE CITY
ASS END OF THE UNIVERSE
DUTY FREE!

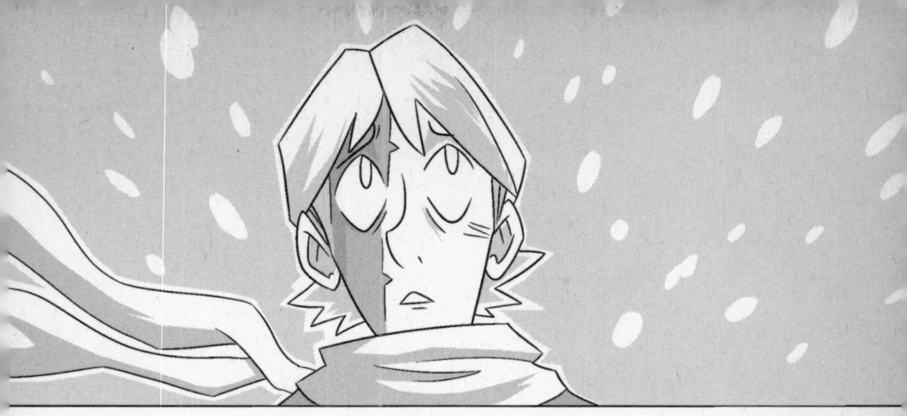
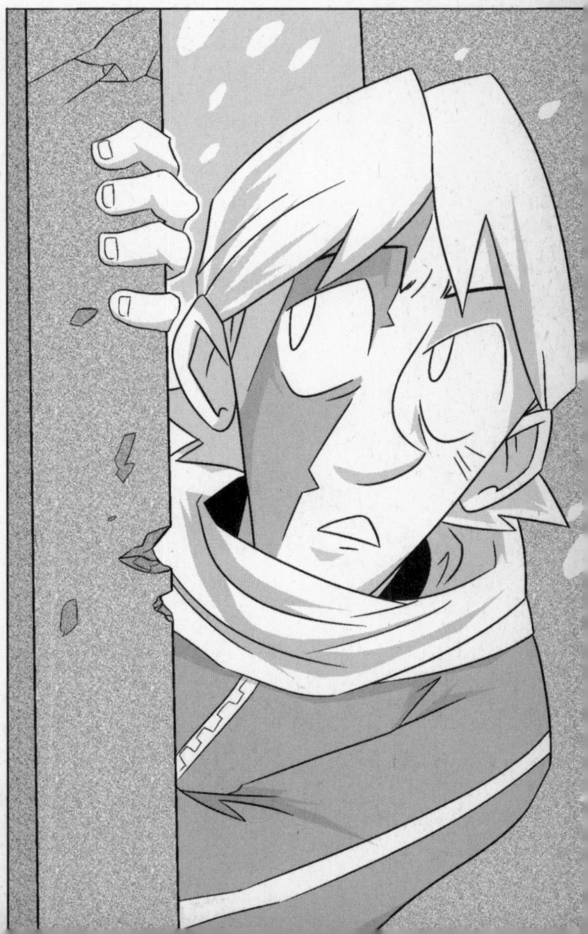
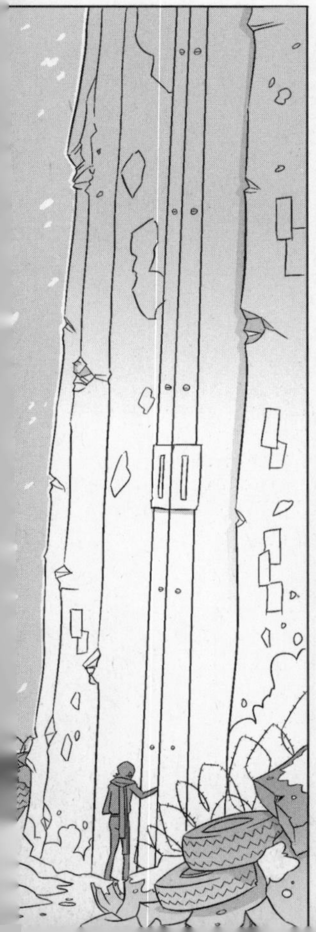

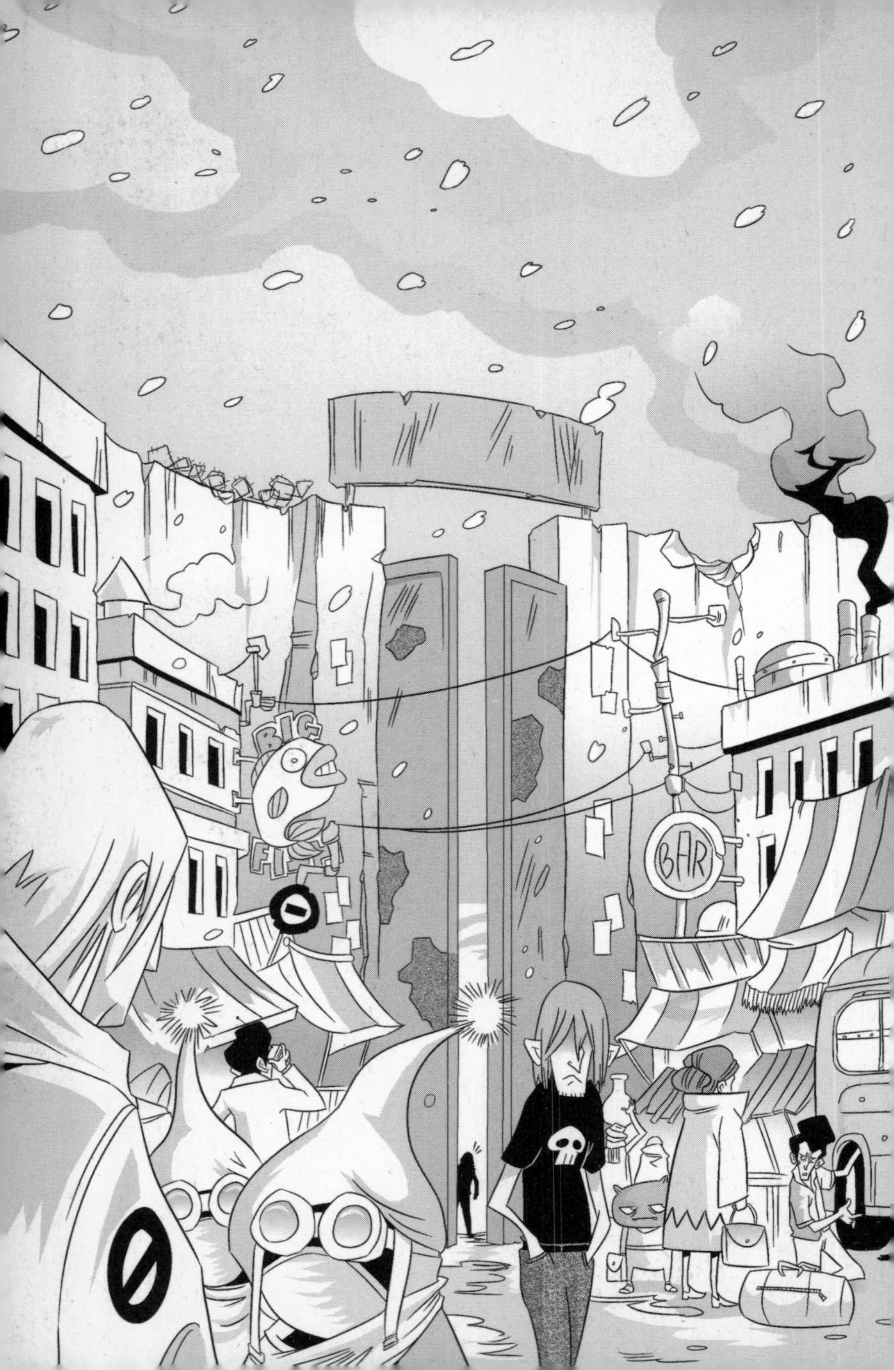
BIG
BAR

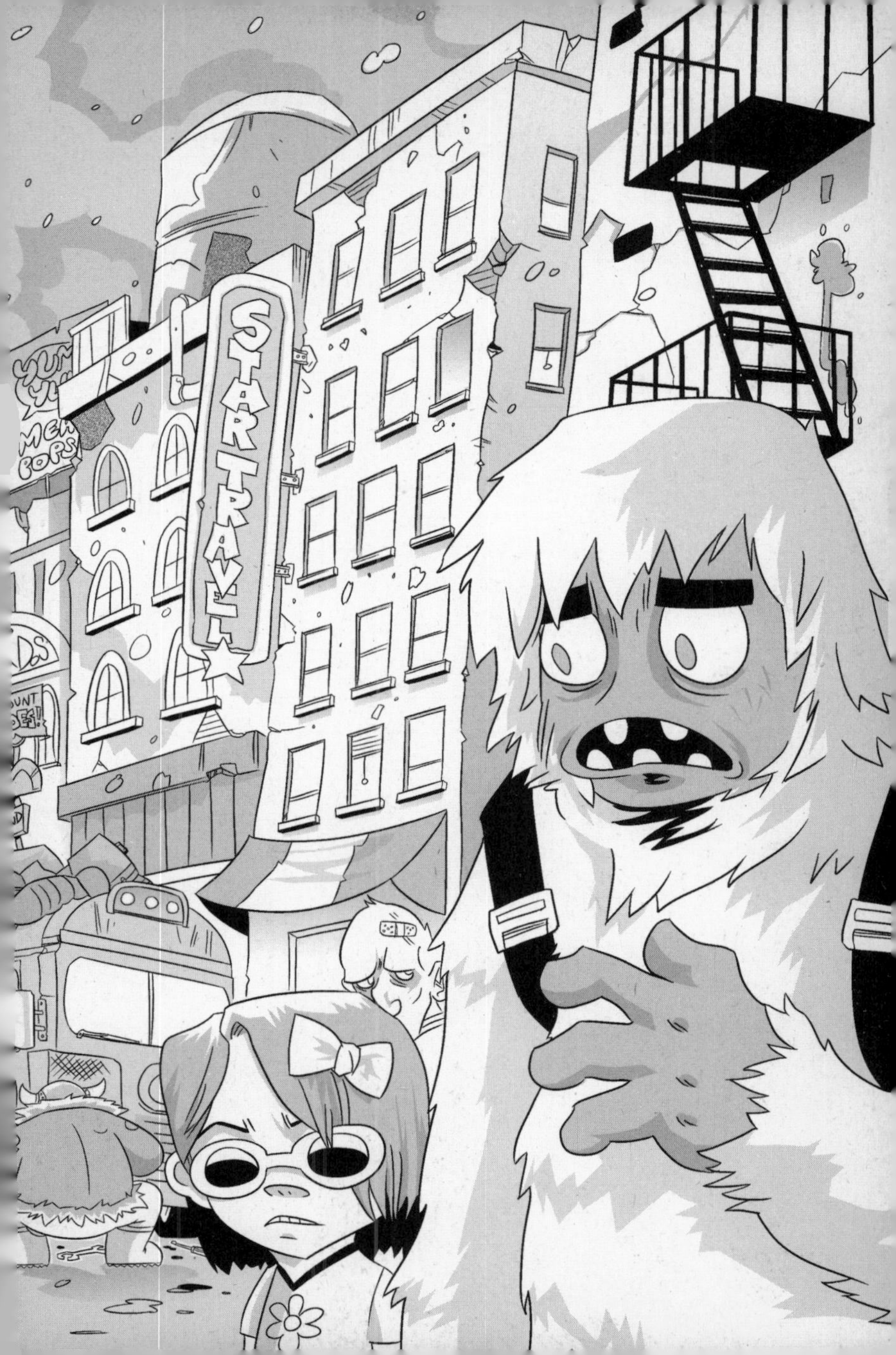
STAR TRAVEL
POPS

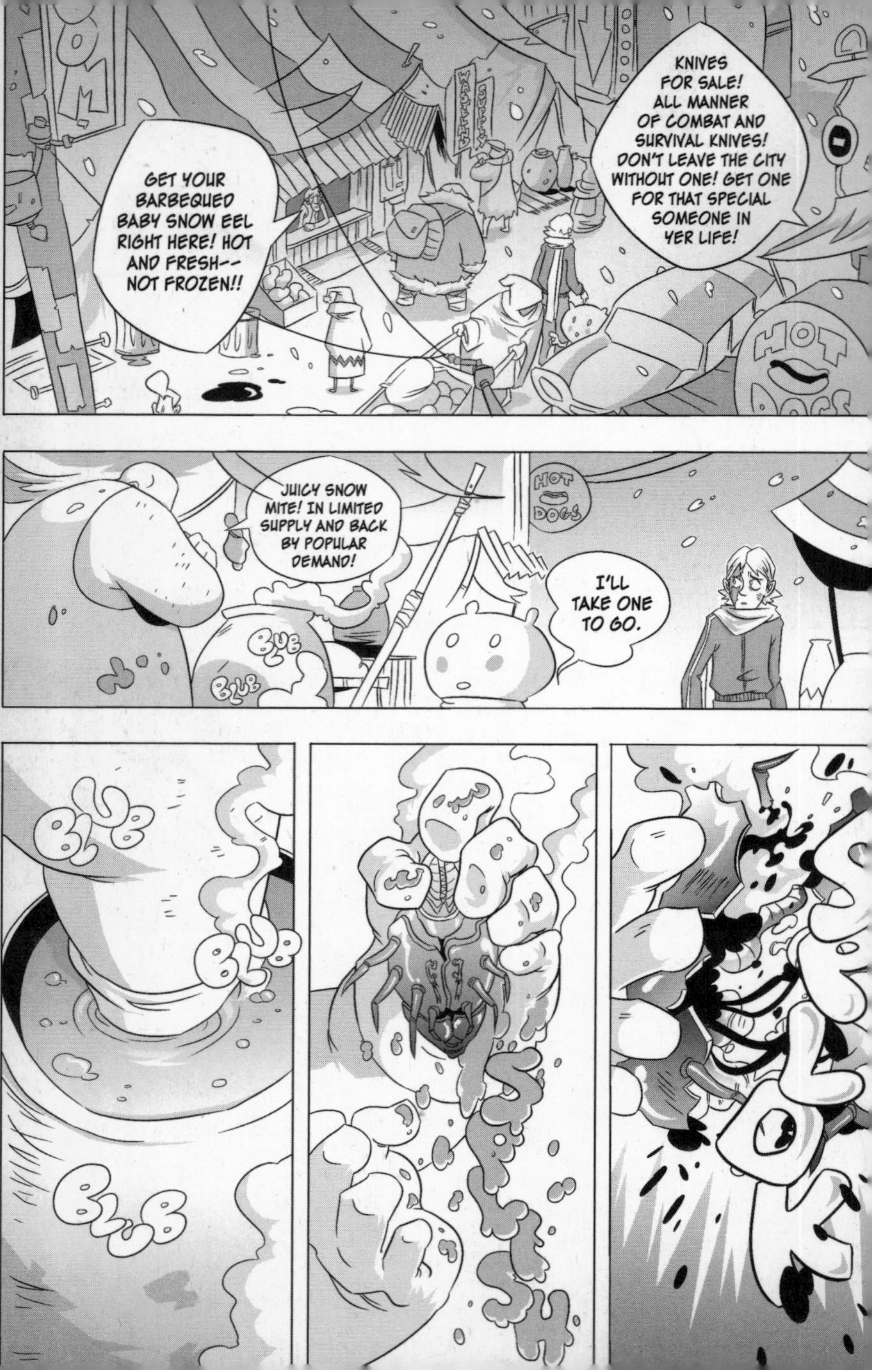
GET YOUR BARBEQUED BABY SNOW EEL RIGHT HERE! HOT AND FRESH-- NOT FROZEN!!
KNIVES FOR SALE! ALL MANNER OF COMBAT AND SURVIVAL KNIVES! DON'T LEAVE THE CITY WITHOUT ONE! GET ONE FOR THAT SPECIAL SOMEONE IN YER LIFE!
HOT DOGS
JUICY SNOW MITE! IN LIMITED SUPPLY AND BACK BY POPULAR DEMAND!
HOT DOGS
I'LL TAKE ONE TO GO.
BLUB
BLUB
BLUB
BLUB
BLUB

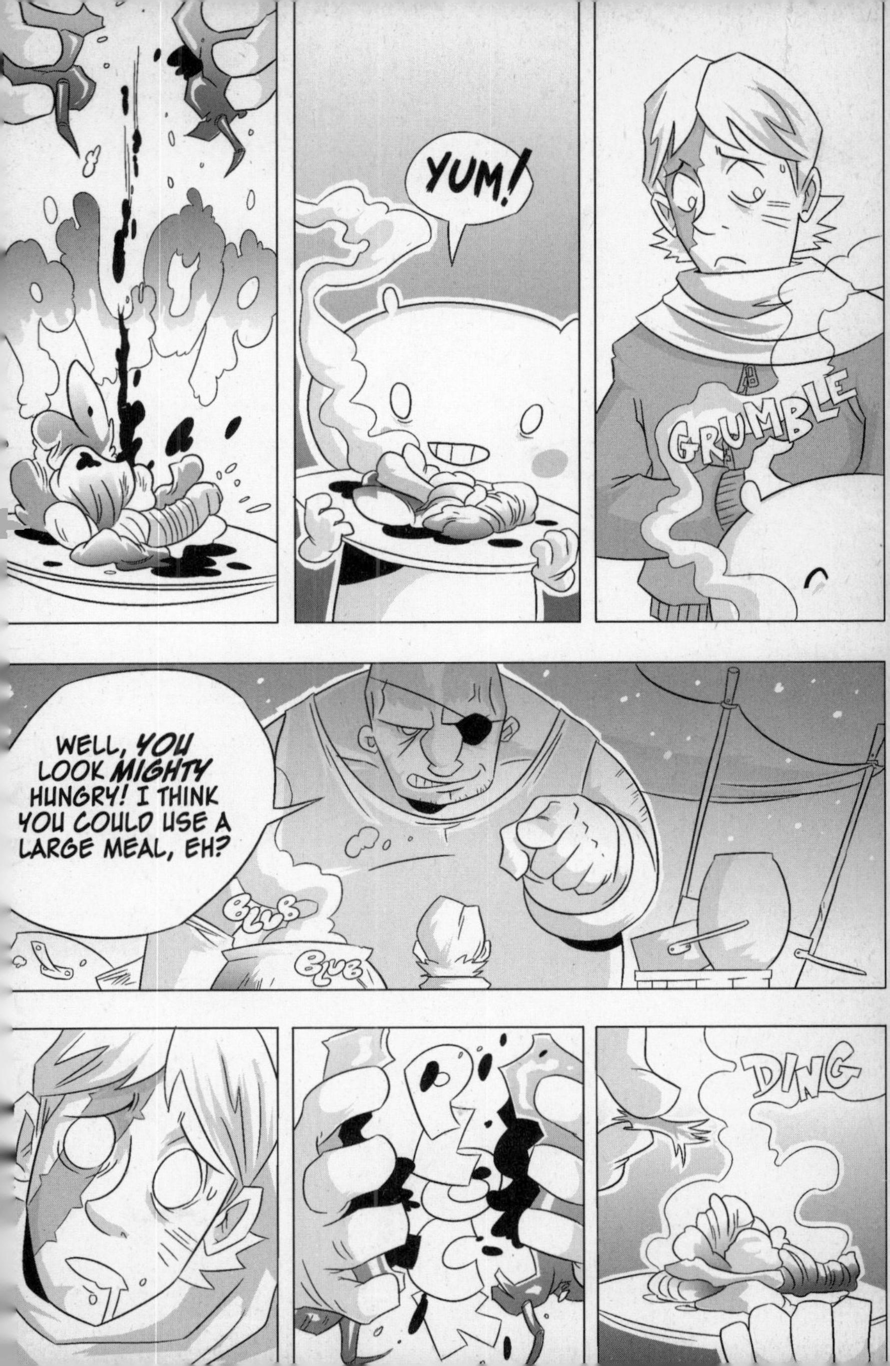
YUM!
GRUMBLE
WELL, YOU LOOK MIGHTY HUNGRY! I THINK YOU COULD USE A LARGE MEAL, EH?
BLUB
BLUB
DING

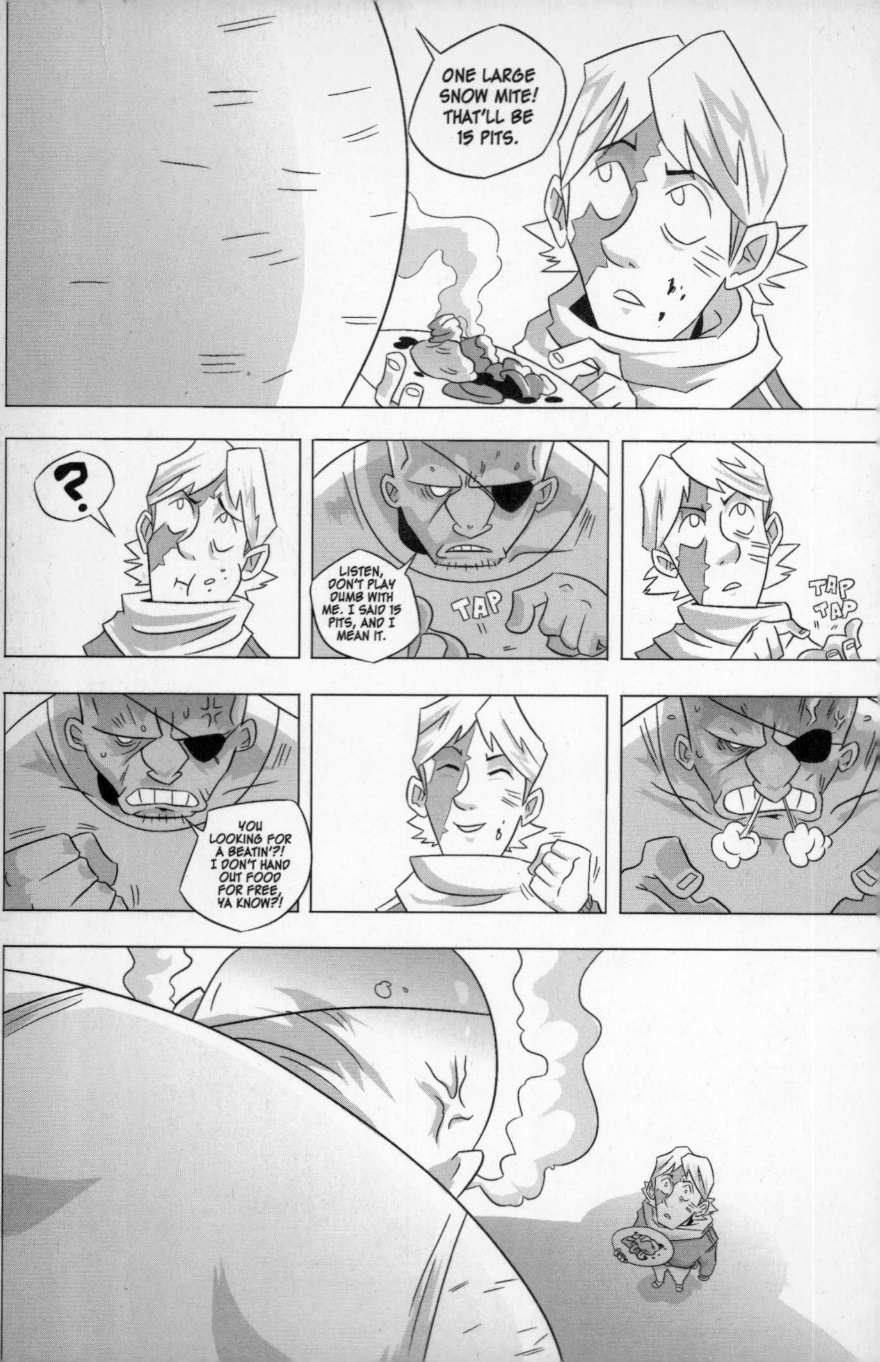
ONE LARGE SNOW MITE! THAT'LL BE 15 PITS.
?
LISTEN, DON'T PLAY DUMB WITH ME. I SAID 15 PITS, AND I MEAN IT.
TAP
TAP TAP
YOU LOOKING FOR A BEATIN'?! I DON'T HAND OUT FOOD FOR FREE, YA KNOW?!

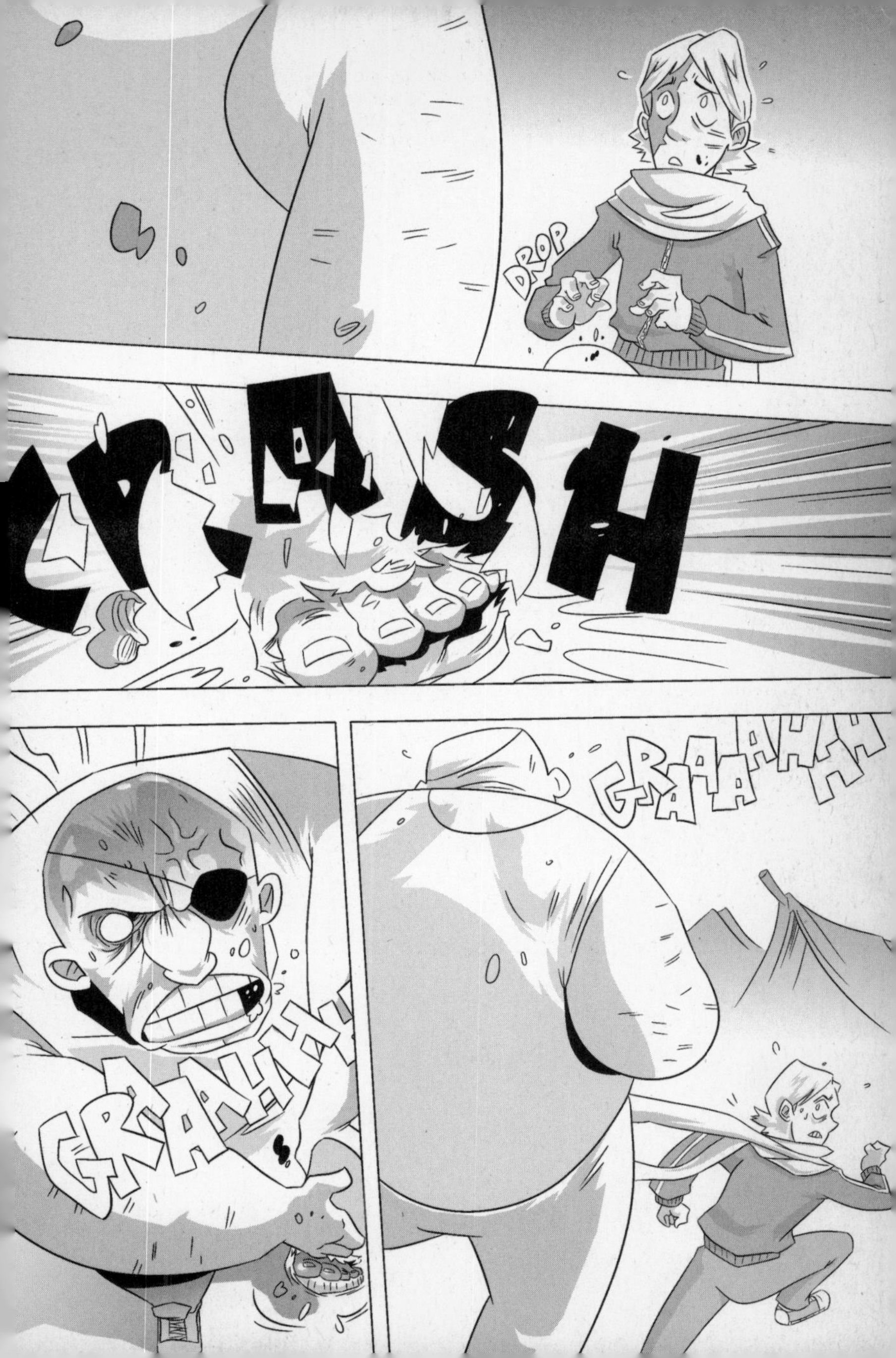
DROP
CRASH
GRAAAHHH
GRAAHHH

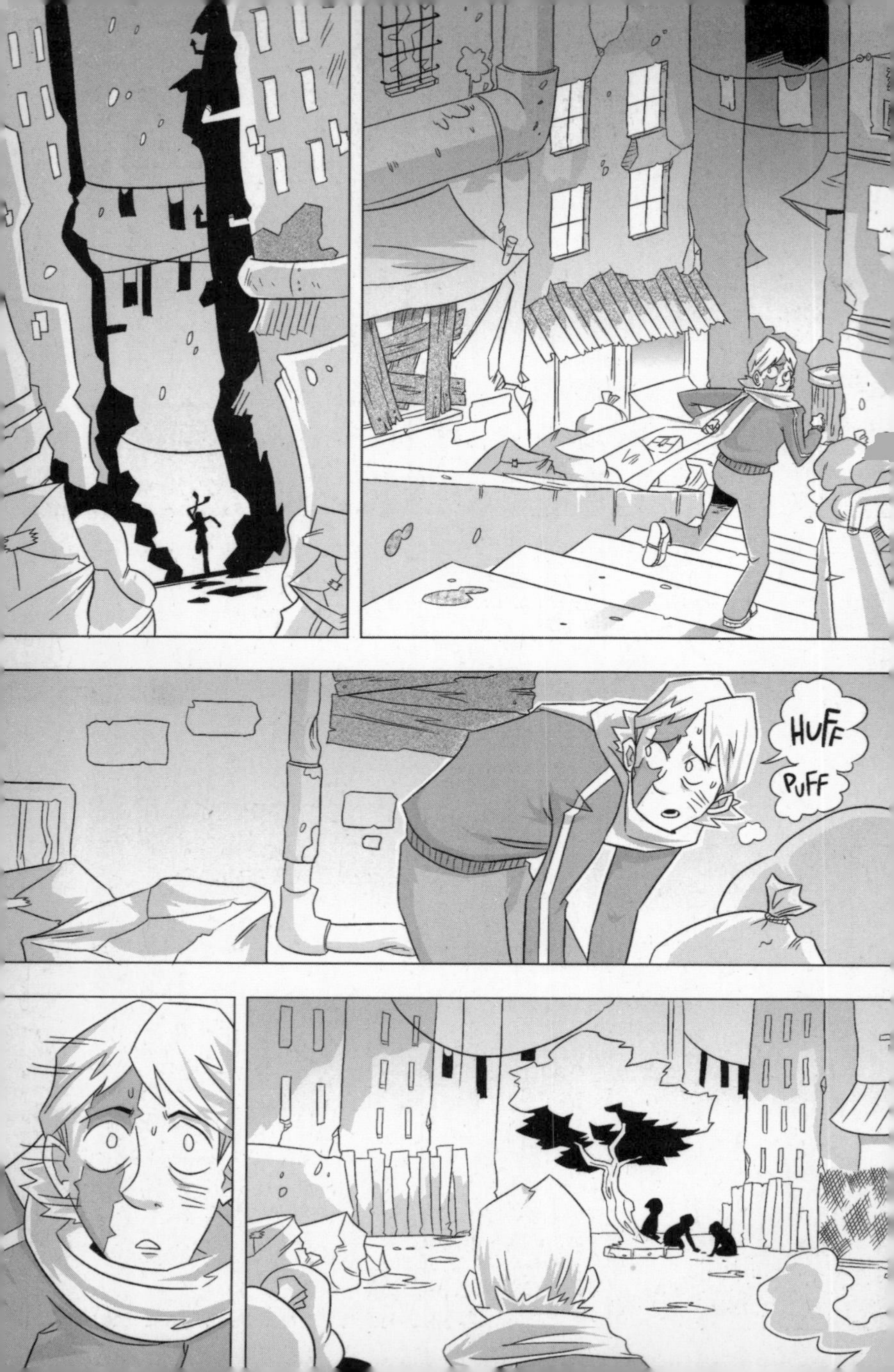
HUFF
PUFF

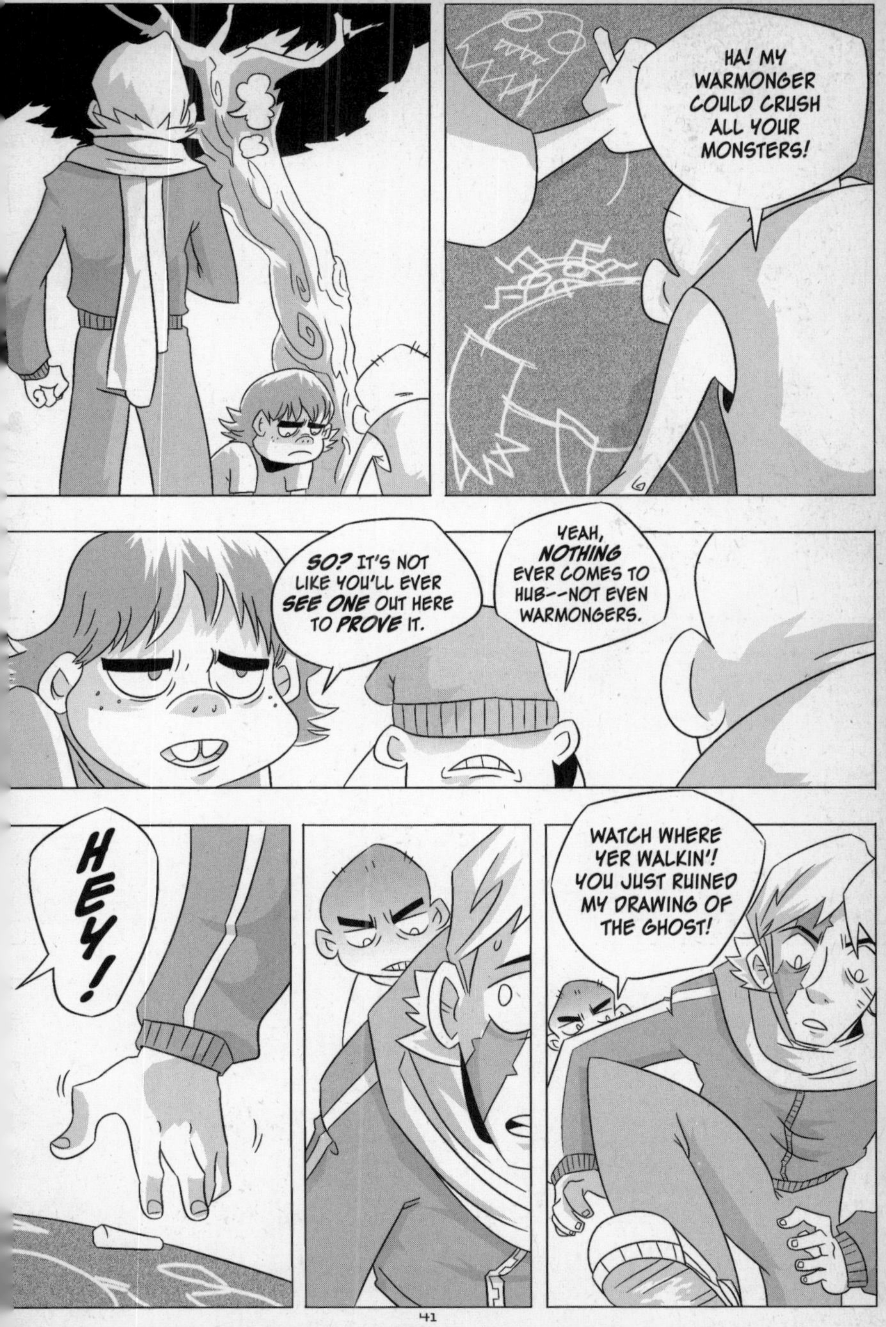
HA! MY WARMONGER COULD CRUSH ALL YOUR MONSTERS!
SO? IT'S NOT LIKE YOU'LL EVER SEE ONE OUT HERE TO PROVE IT.
YEAH, NOTHING EVER COMES TO HUB--NOT EVEN WARMONGERS.
HEY!
WATCH WHERE YER WALKIN'! YOU JUST RUINED MY DRAWING OF THE GHOST!

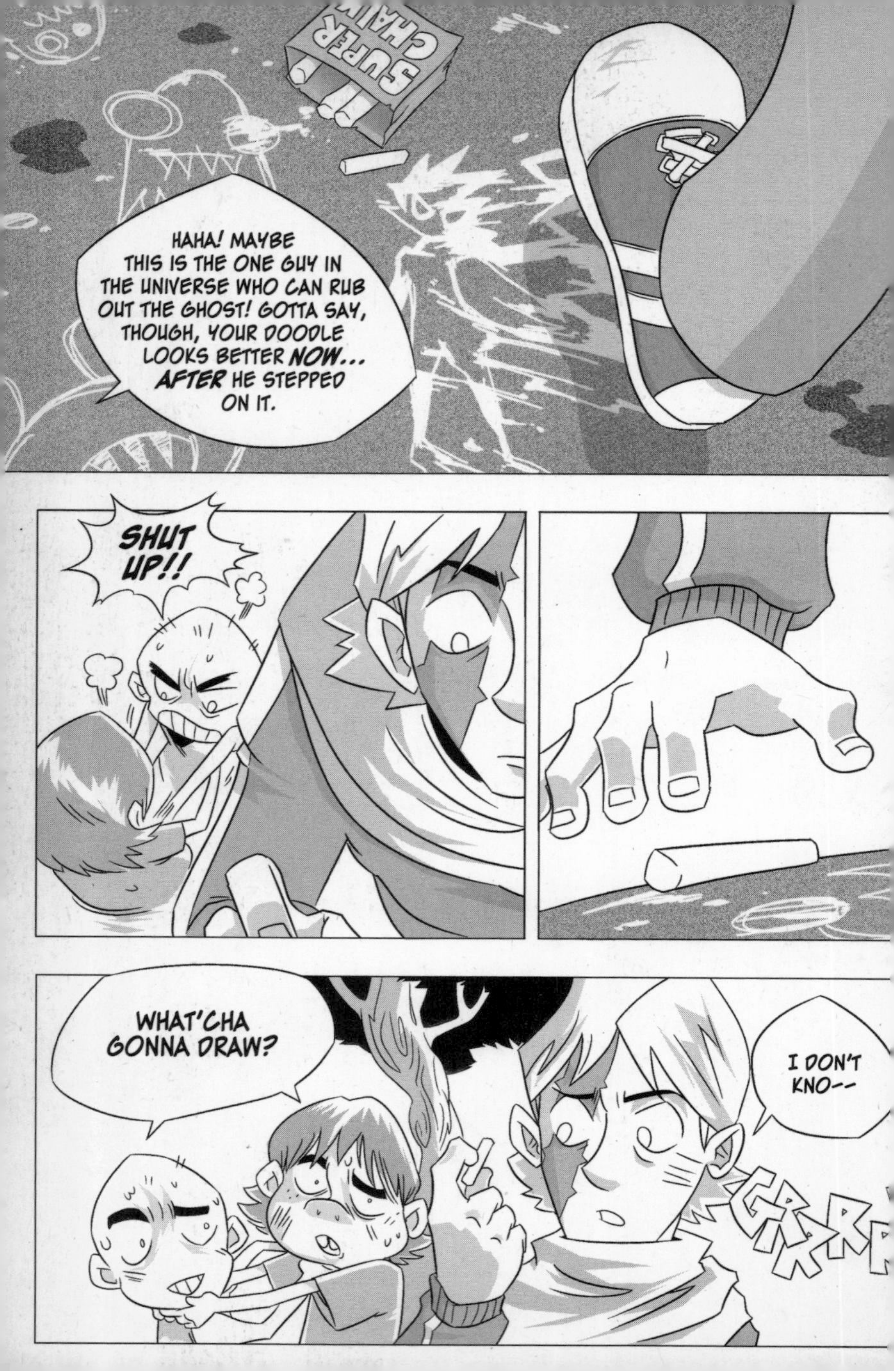
HAHA! MAYBE THIS IS THE ONE GUY IN THE UNIVERSE WHO CAN RUB OUT THE GHOST! GOTTA SAY, THOUGH, YOUR DOODLE LOOKS BETTER **NOW**... **AFTER** HE STEPPED ON IT.
SHUT UP!!
WHAT'CHA GONNA DRAW?
I DON'T KNO--
GRRR

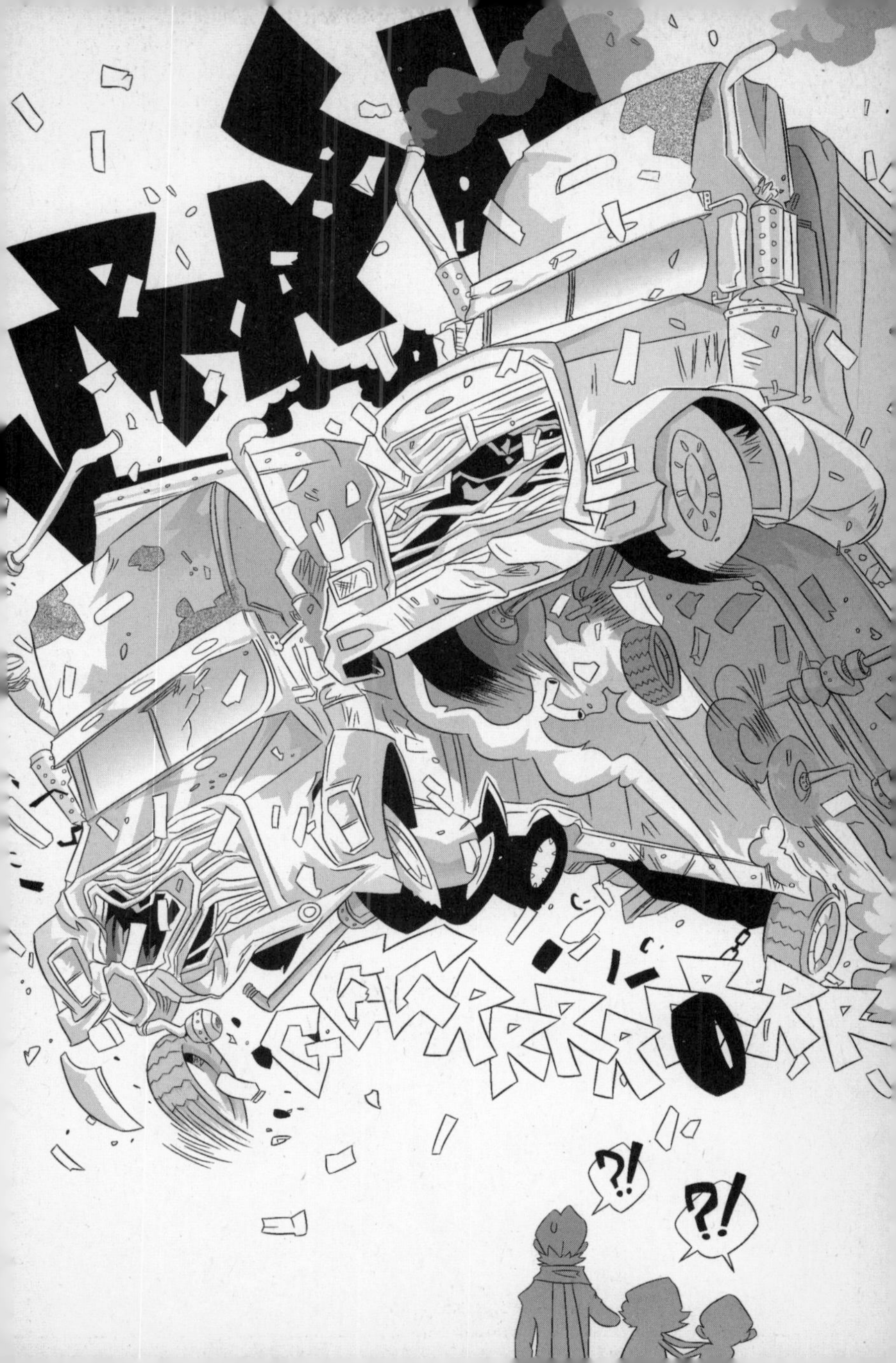
?!
?!

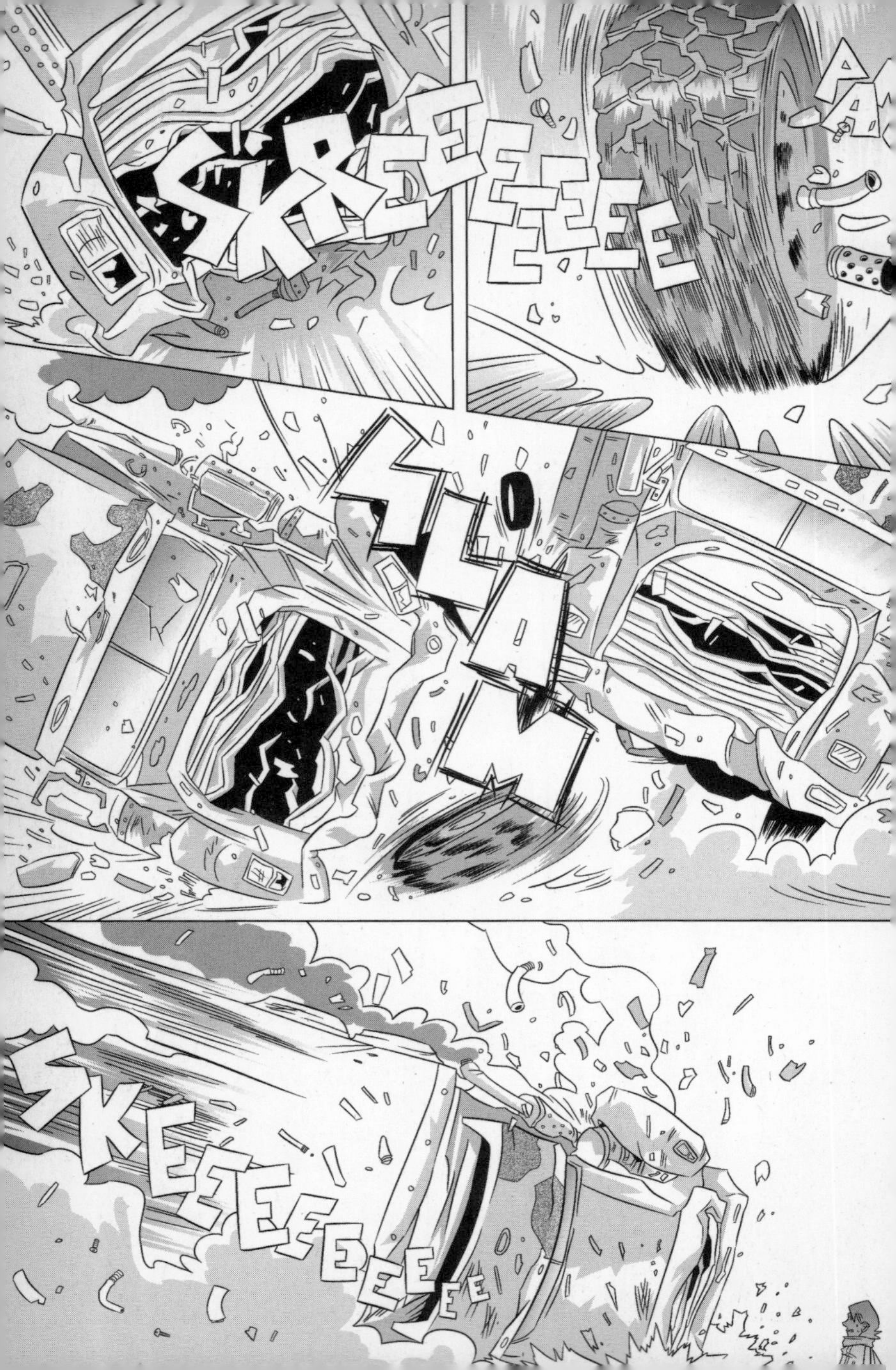
PA
SKREEEEEEEE
SLAM
SKEEEEEEEEEE

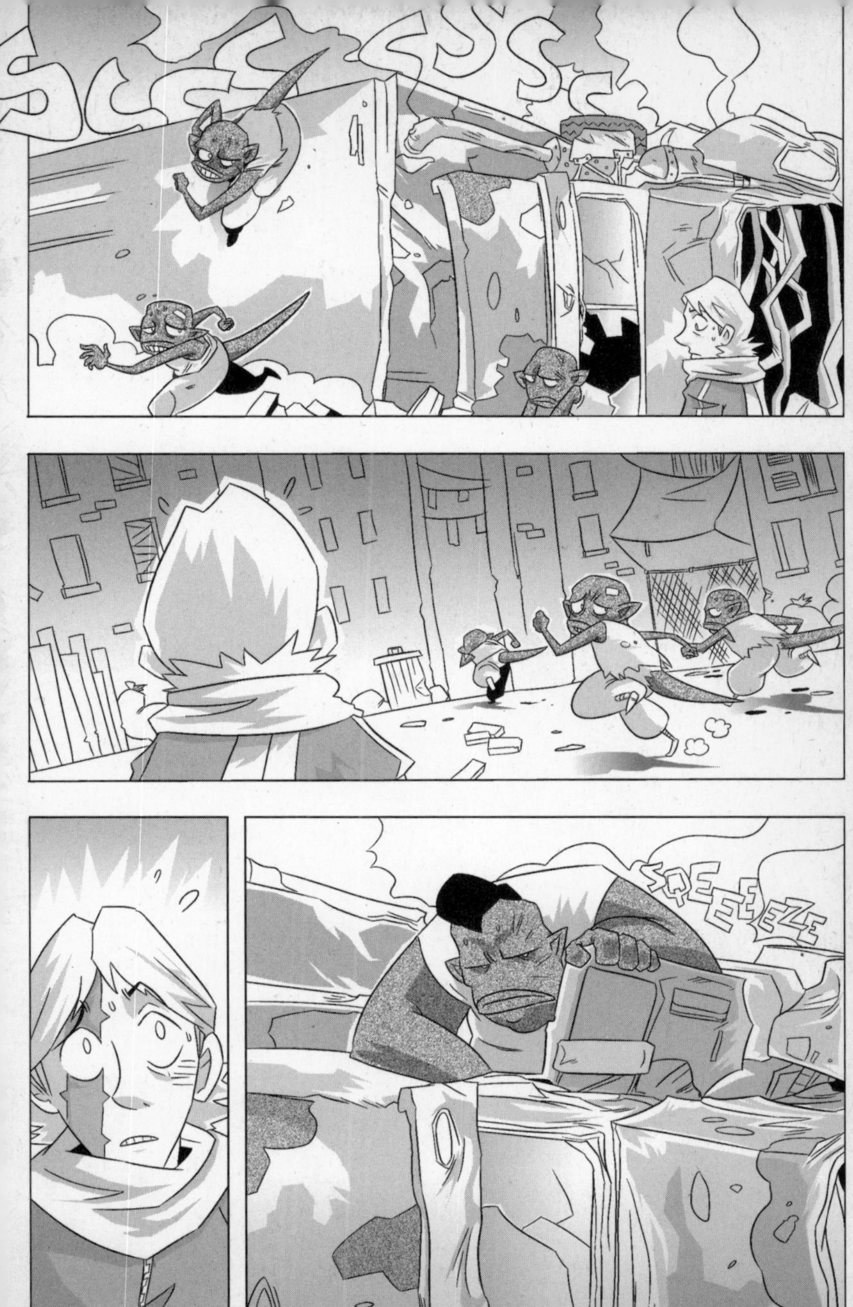
SQEEEEZE

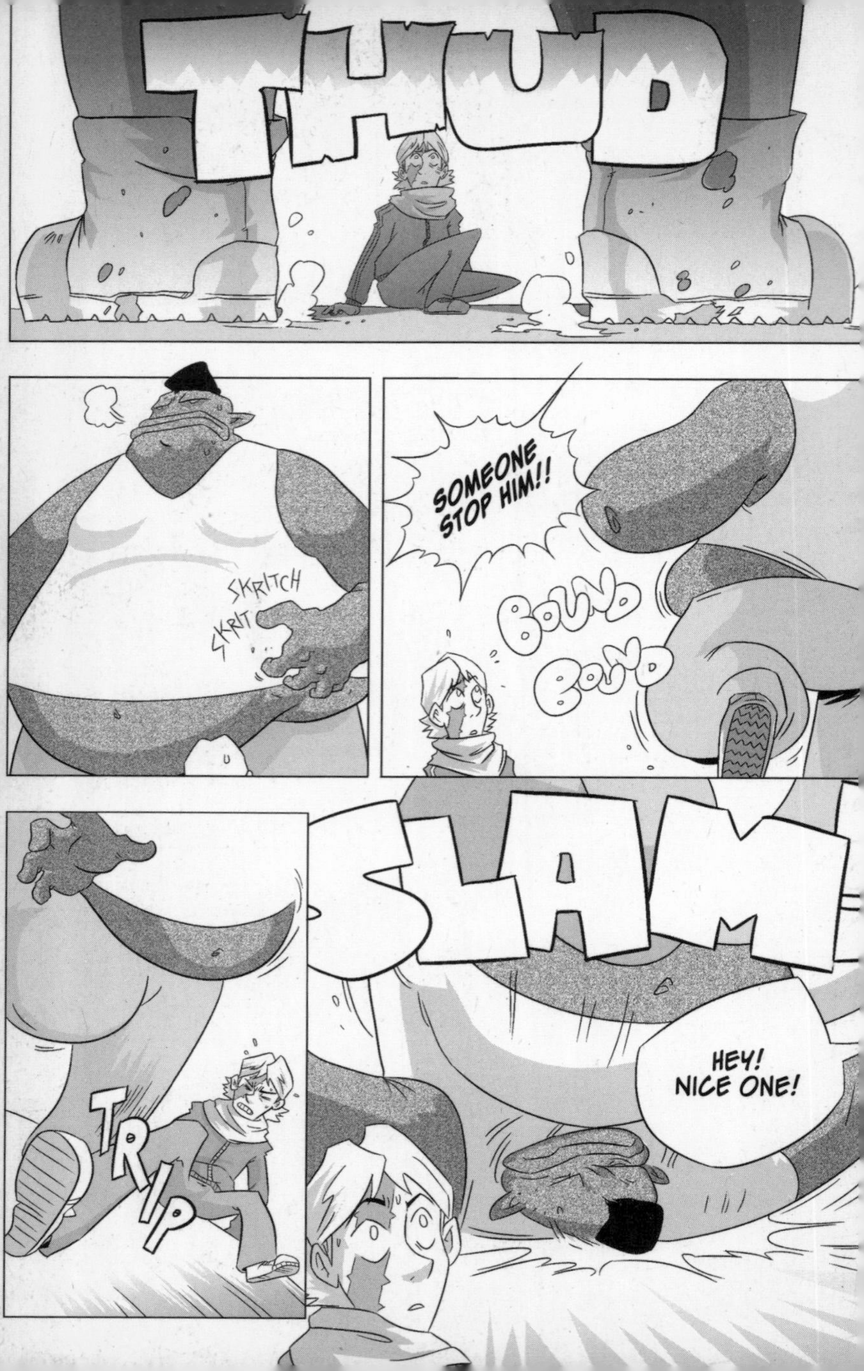
THUD
SKRITCH
SKRIT
SOMEONE STOP HIM!!
BOUND
BOUND
TRIP
SLAM
HEY! NICE ONE!

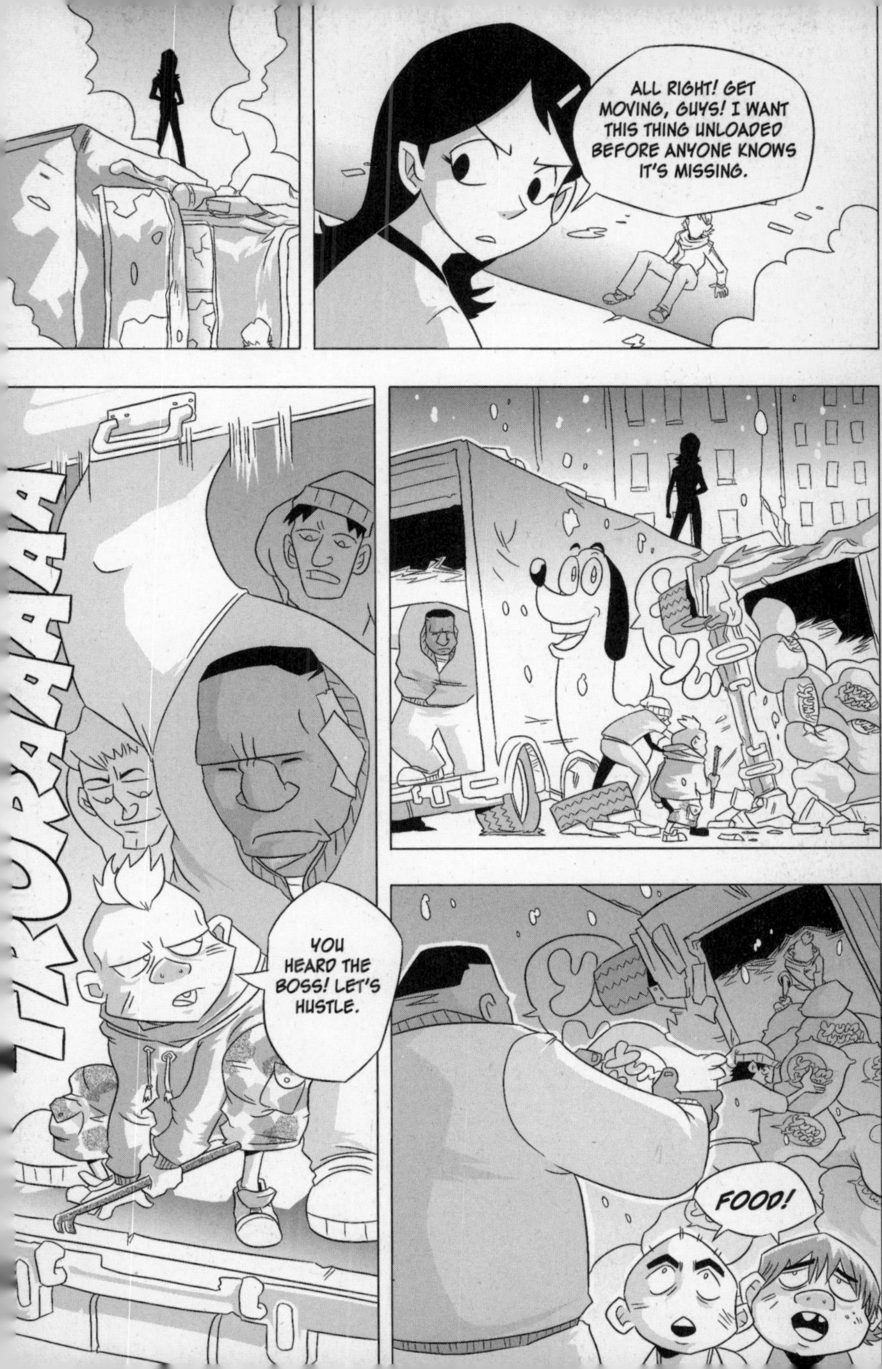
ALL RIGHT! GET MOVING, GUYS! I WANT THIS THING UNLOADED BEFORE ANYONE KNOWS IT'S MISSING.
YOU HEARD THE BOSS! LET'S HUSTLE.
FOOD!

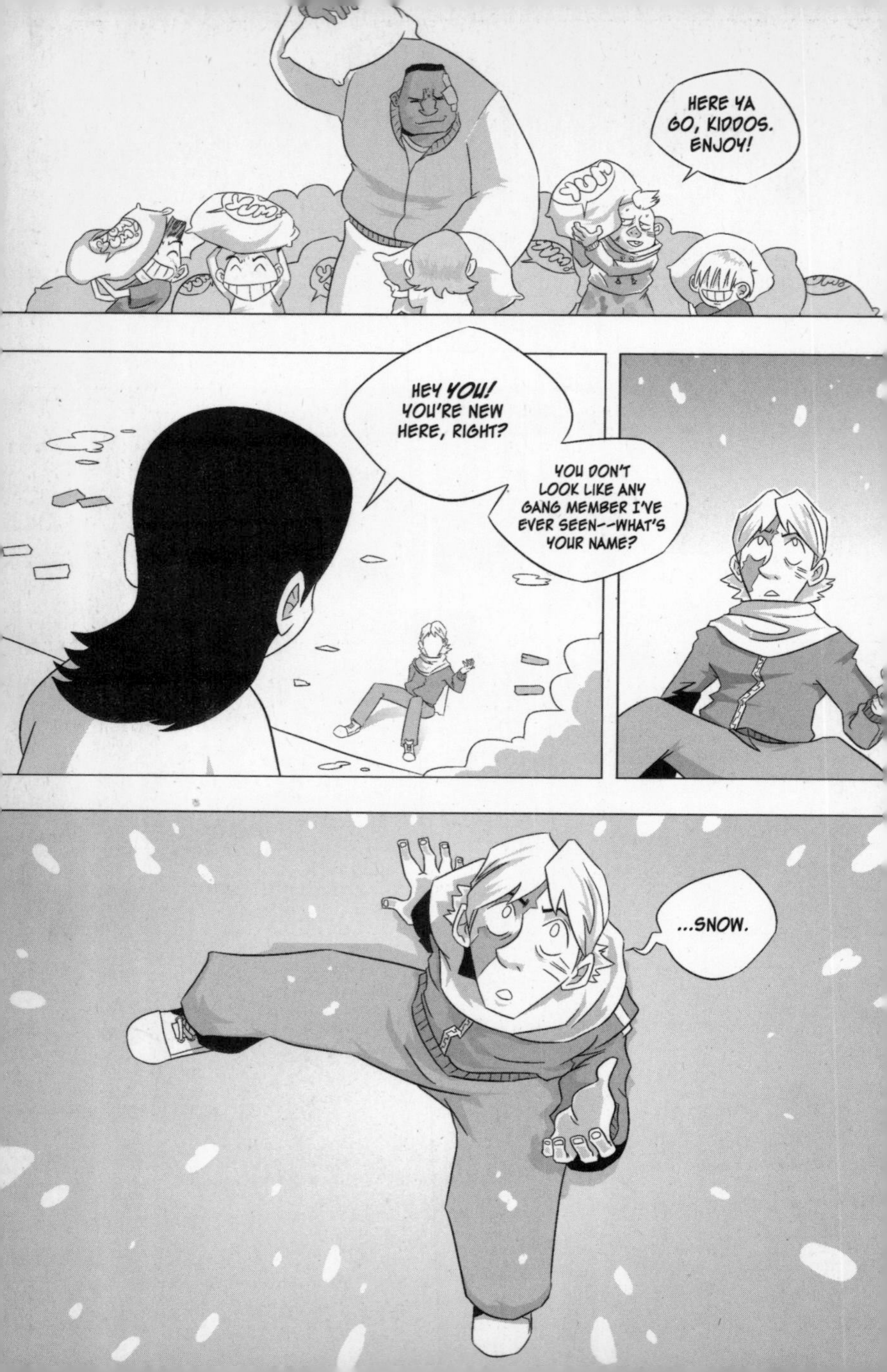
HERE YA GO, KIDDOS. ENJOY!
HEY YOU! YOU'RE NEW HERE, RIGHT?
YOU DON'T LOOK LIKE ANY GANG MEMBER I'VE EVER SEEN--WHAT'S YOUR NAME?
...SNOW.

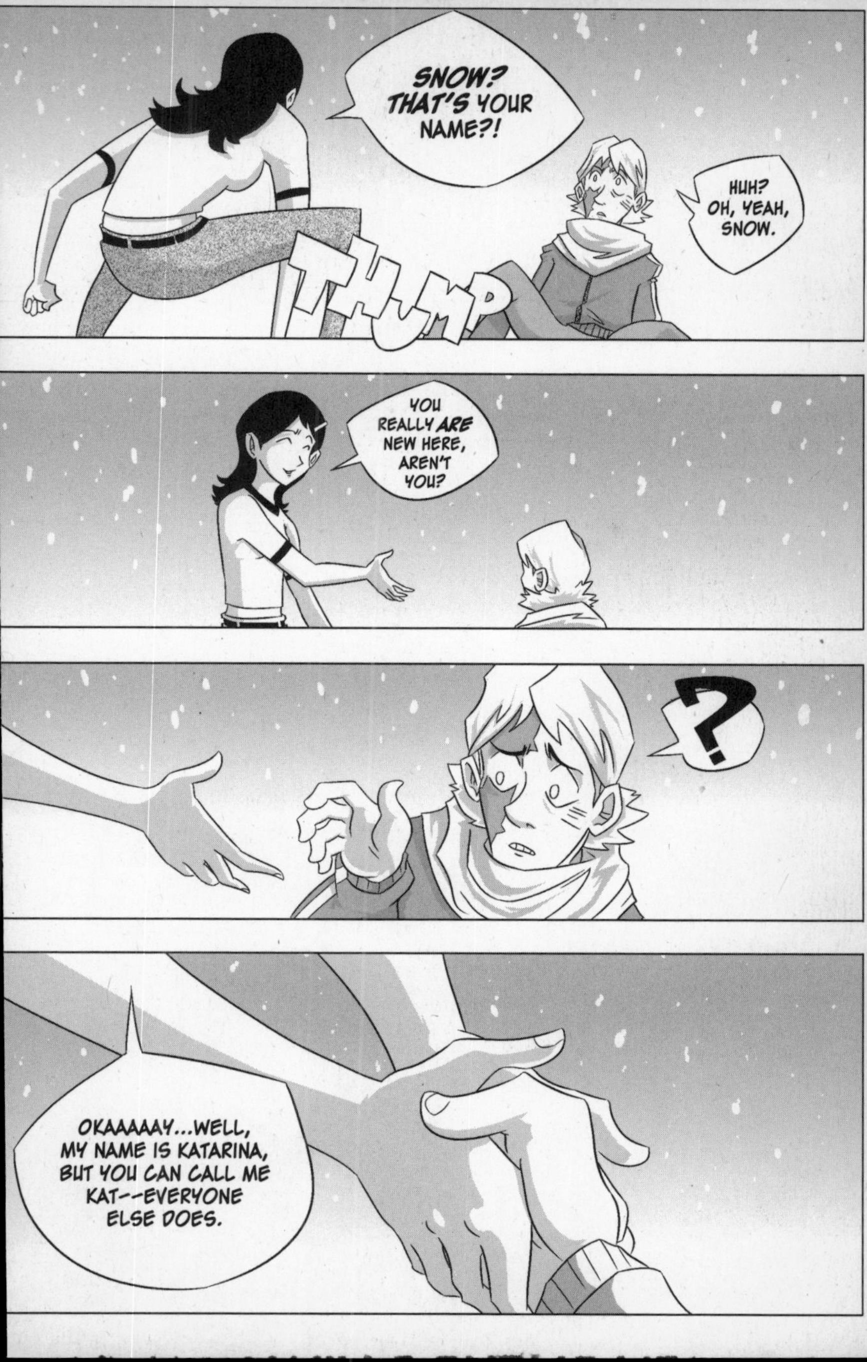
SNOW? THAT'S YOUR NAME?!
HUH? OH, YEAH, SNOW.
THUMP
YOU REALLY ARE NEW HERE, AREN'T YOU?
?
OKAAAAAY...WELL, MY NAME IS KATARINA, BUT YOU CAN CALL ME KAT--EVERYONE ELSE DOES.

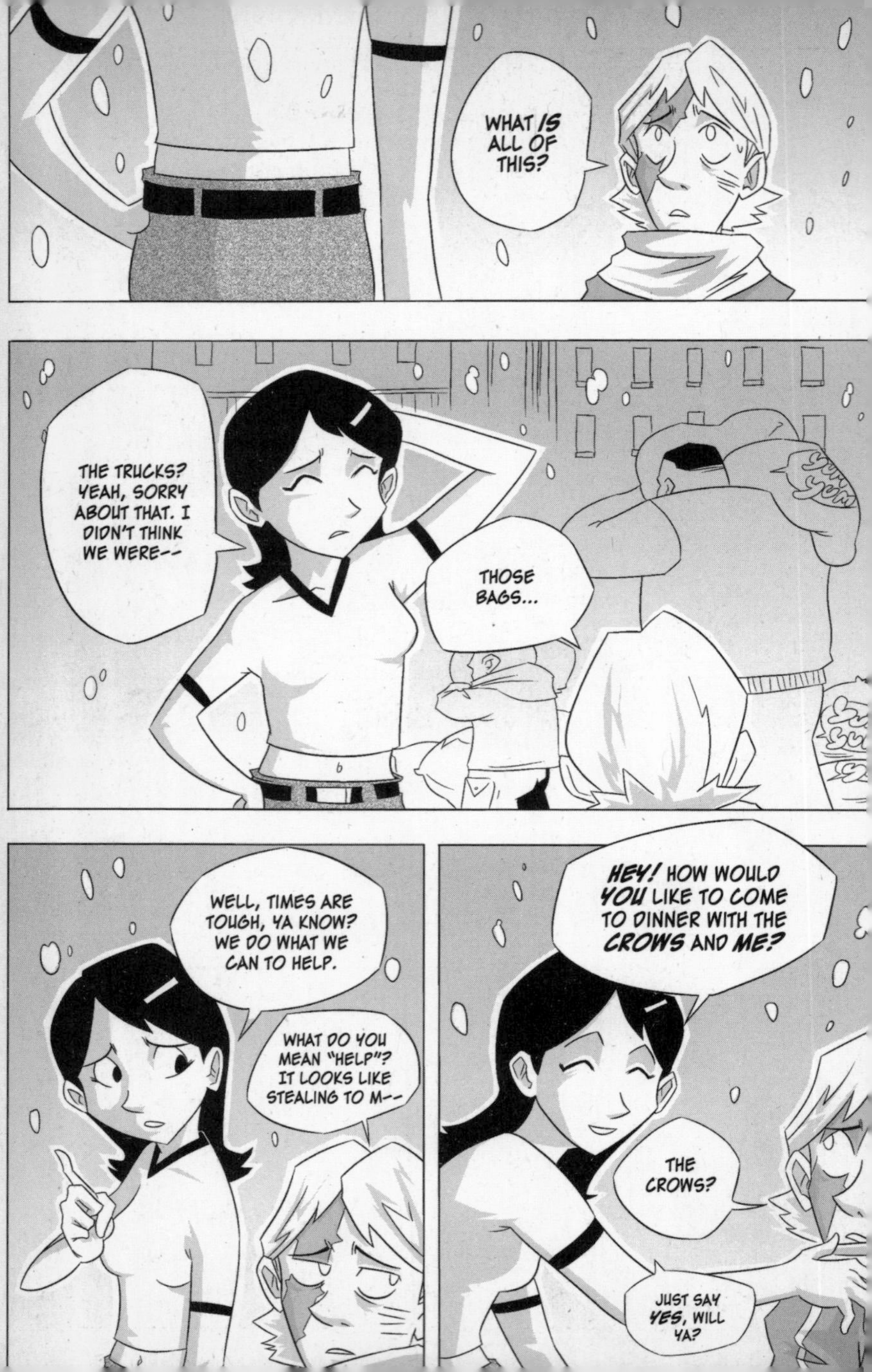
WHAT *IS* ALL OF THIS?
THE TRUCKS? YEAH, SORRY ABOUT THAT. I DIDN'T THINK WE WERE--
THOSE BAGS...
WELL, TIMES ARE TOUGH, YA KNOW? WE DO WHAT WE CAN TO HELP.
WHAT DO YOU MEAN "HELP"? IT LOOKS LIKE STEALING TO M--
HEY! HOW WOULD ***YOU*** LIKE TO COME TO DINNER WITH THE ***CROWS*** AND ***ME?***
THE CROWS?
JUST SAY ***YES***, WILL YA?

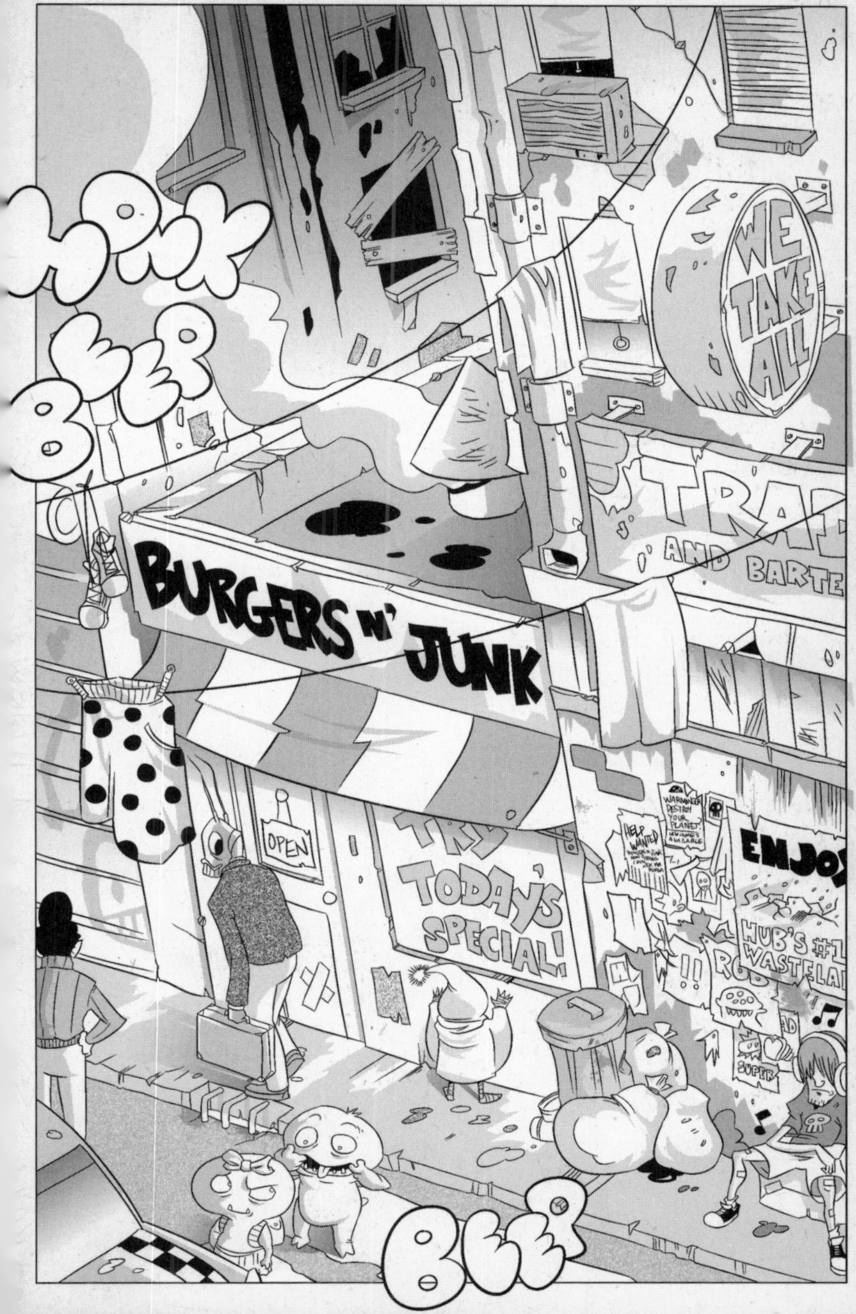
HONK
BEEP
WE TAKE ALL
BURGERS N' JUNK
TRA
AND BARTE
OPEN
TRY TODAY'S SPECIAL!
HELP WANTED
WARMONGER DESTROY YOUR PLANET
ENJO
HUB'S #1 WASTELA
SUPER
BEEP

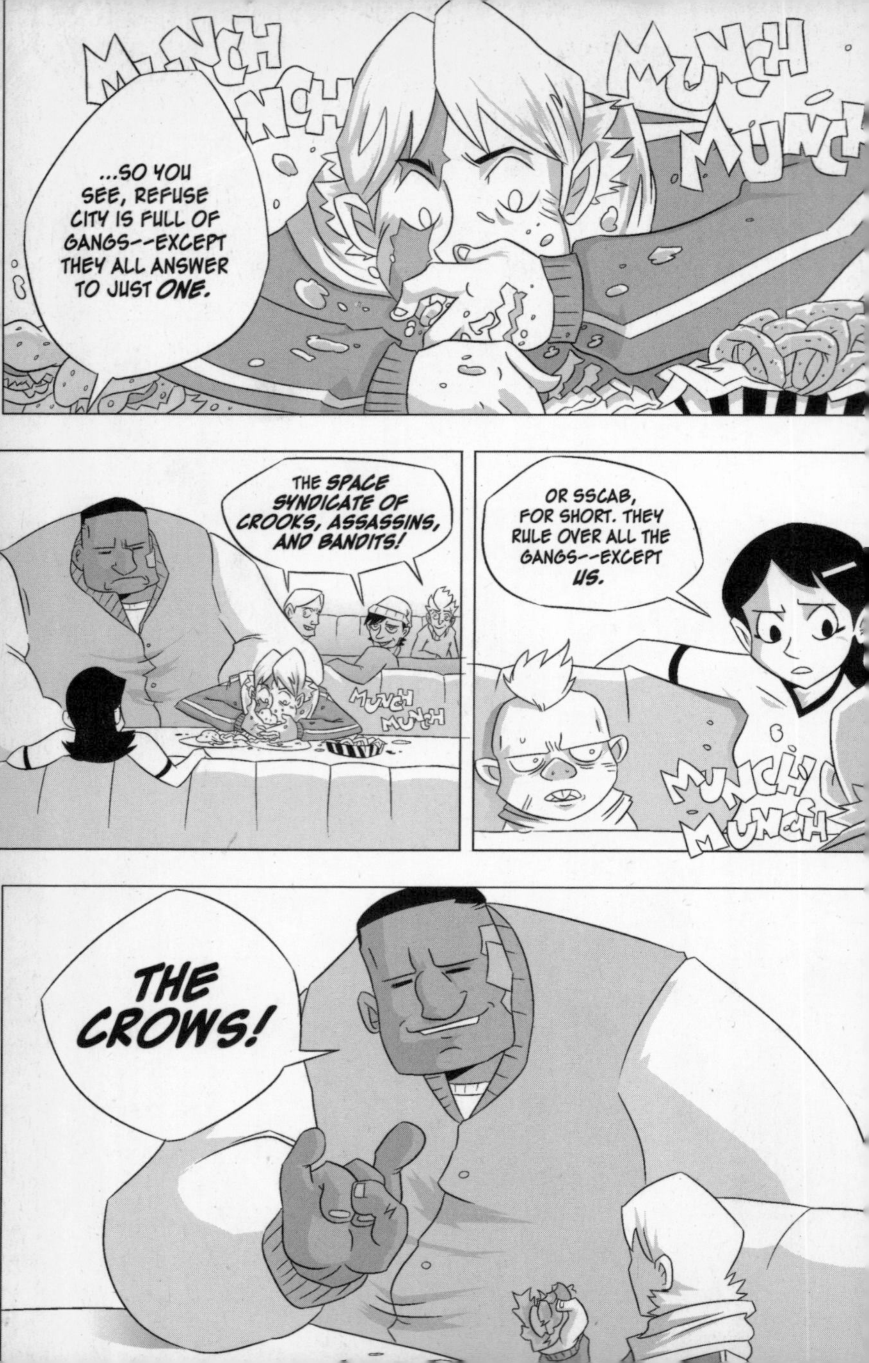
...SO YOU SEE, REFUSE CITY IS FULL OF GANGS--EXCEPT THEY ALL ANSWER TO JUST *ONE.*
MUNCH MUNCH
MUNCH MUNCH
THE *SPACE SYNDICATE OF CROOKS, ASSASSINS, AND BANDITS!*
MUNCH MUNCH
OR SSCAB, FOR SHORT. THEY RULE OVER ALL THE GANGS--EXCEPT *US.*
MUNCH MUNCH
THE CROWS!

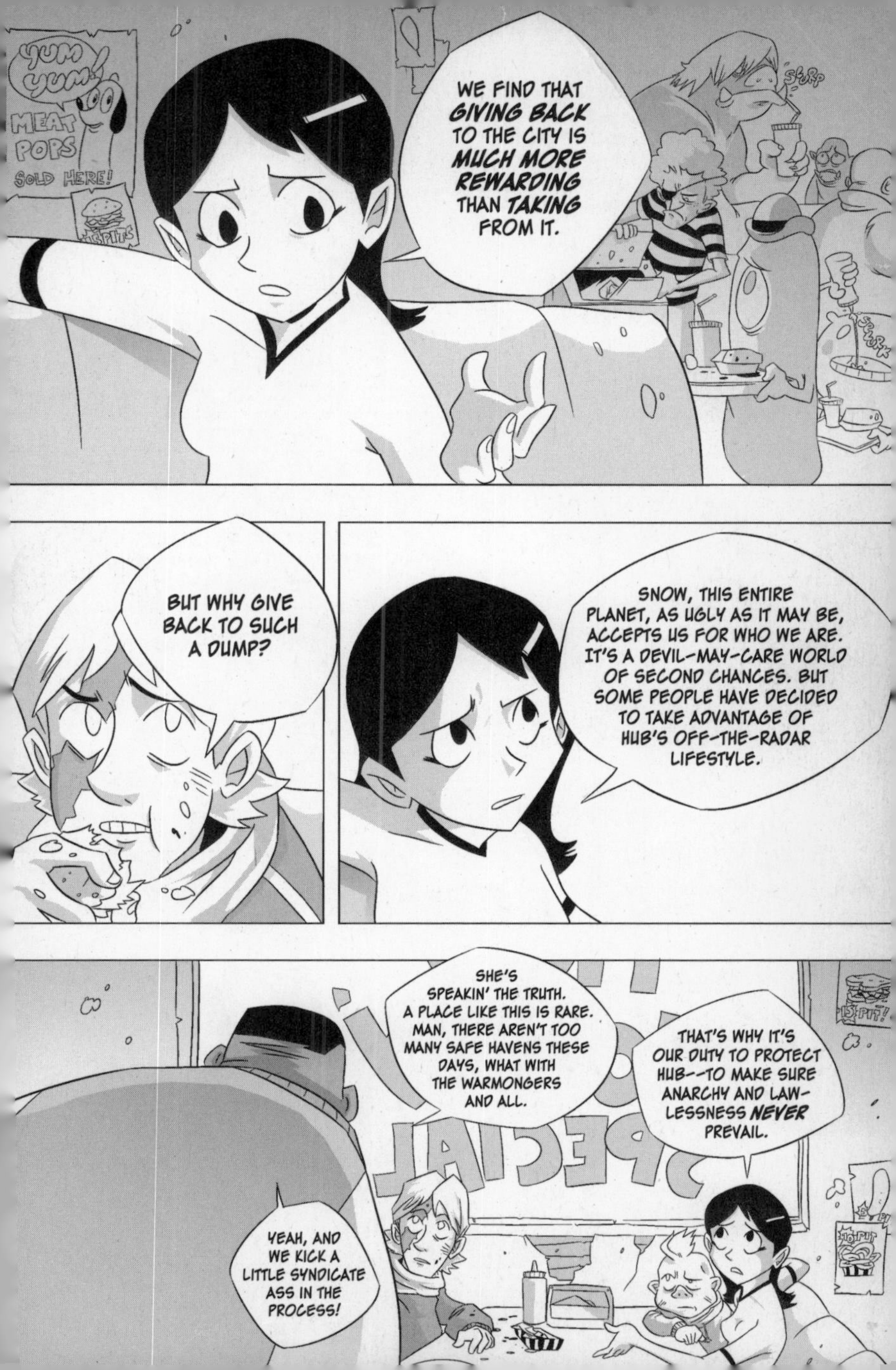
YUM YUM! MEAT POPS SOLD HERE!
15 PITS
WE FIND THAT *GIVING BACK* TO THE CITY IS *MUCH MORE REWARDING* THAN *TAKING* FROM IT.
BUT WHY GIVE BACK TO SUCH A DUMP?
SNOW, THIS ENTIRE PLANET, AS UGLY AS IT MAY BE, ACCEPTS US FOR WHO WE ARE. IT'S A DEVIL-MAY-CARE WORLD OF SECOND CHANCES. BUT SOME PEOPLE HAVE DECIDED TO TAKE ADVANTAGE OF HUB'S OFF-THE-RADAR LIFESTYLE.
SHE'S SPEAKIN' THE TRUTH. A PLACE LIKE THIS IS RARE. MAN, THERE AREN'T TOO MANY SAFE HAVENS THESE DAYS, WHAT WITH THE WARMONGERS AND ALL.
THAT'S WHY IT'S OUR DUTY TO PROTECT HUB--TO MAKE SURE ANARCHY AND LAWLESSNESS *NEVER* PREVAIL.
YEAH, AND WE KICK A LITTLE SYNDICATE ASS IN THE PROCESS!

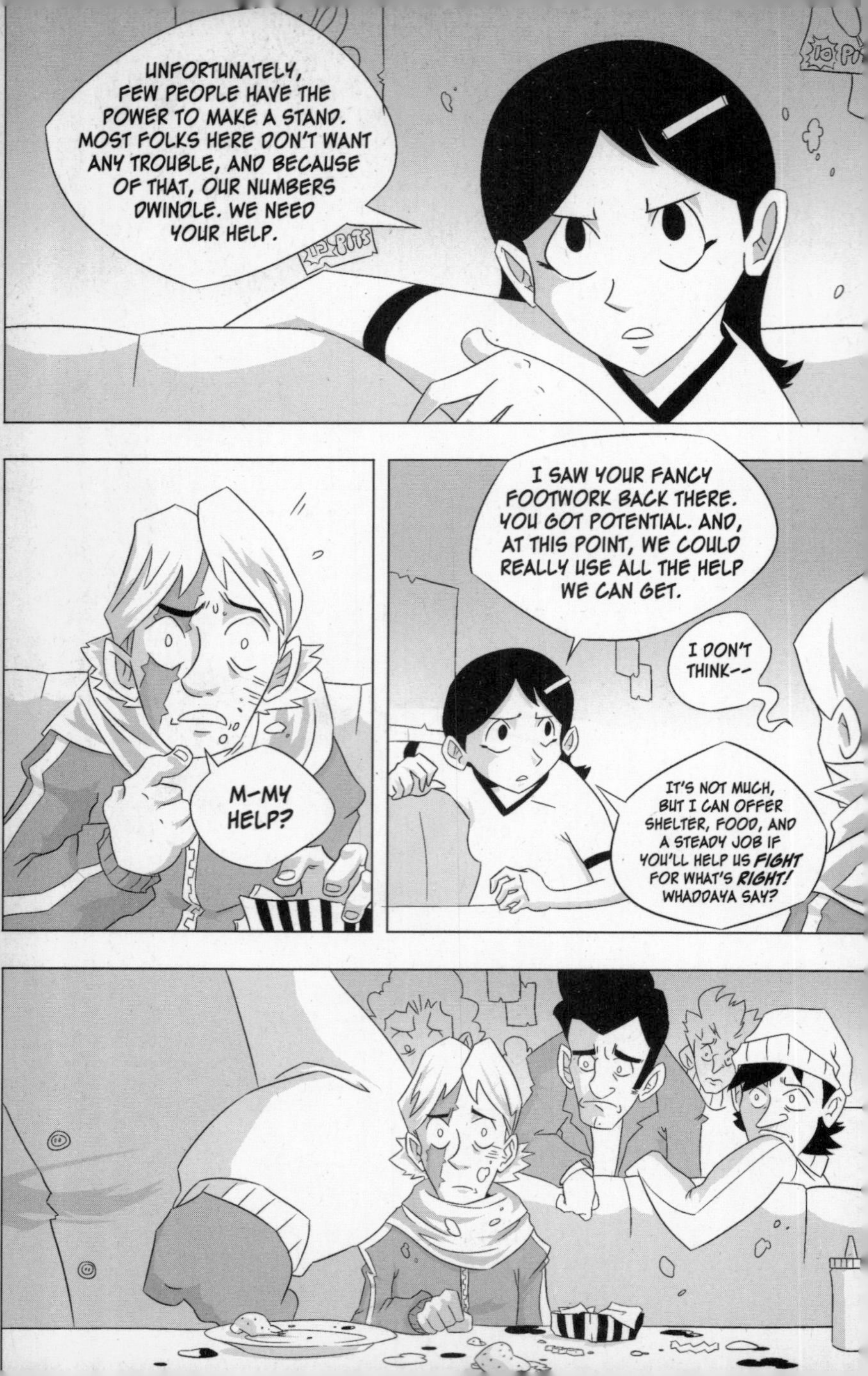
UNFORTUNATELY, FEW PEOPLE HAVE THE POWER TO MAKE A STAND. MOST FOLKS HERE DON'T WANT ANY TROUBLE, AND BECAUSE OF THAT, OUR NUMBERS DWINDLE. WE NEED YOUR HELP.
M-MY HELP?
I SAW YOUR FANCY FOOTWORK BACK THERE. YOU GOT POTENTIAL. AND, AT THIS POINT, WE COULD REALLY USE ALL THE HELP WE CAN GET.
I DON'T THINK--
IT'S NOT MUCH, BUT I CAN OFFER SHELTER, FOOD, AND A STEADY JOB IF YOU'LL HELP US *FIGHT* FOR WHAT'S *RIGHT!* WHADDAYA SAY?

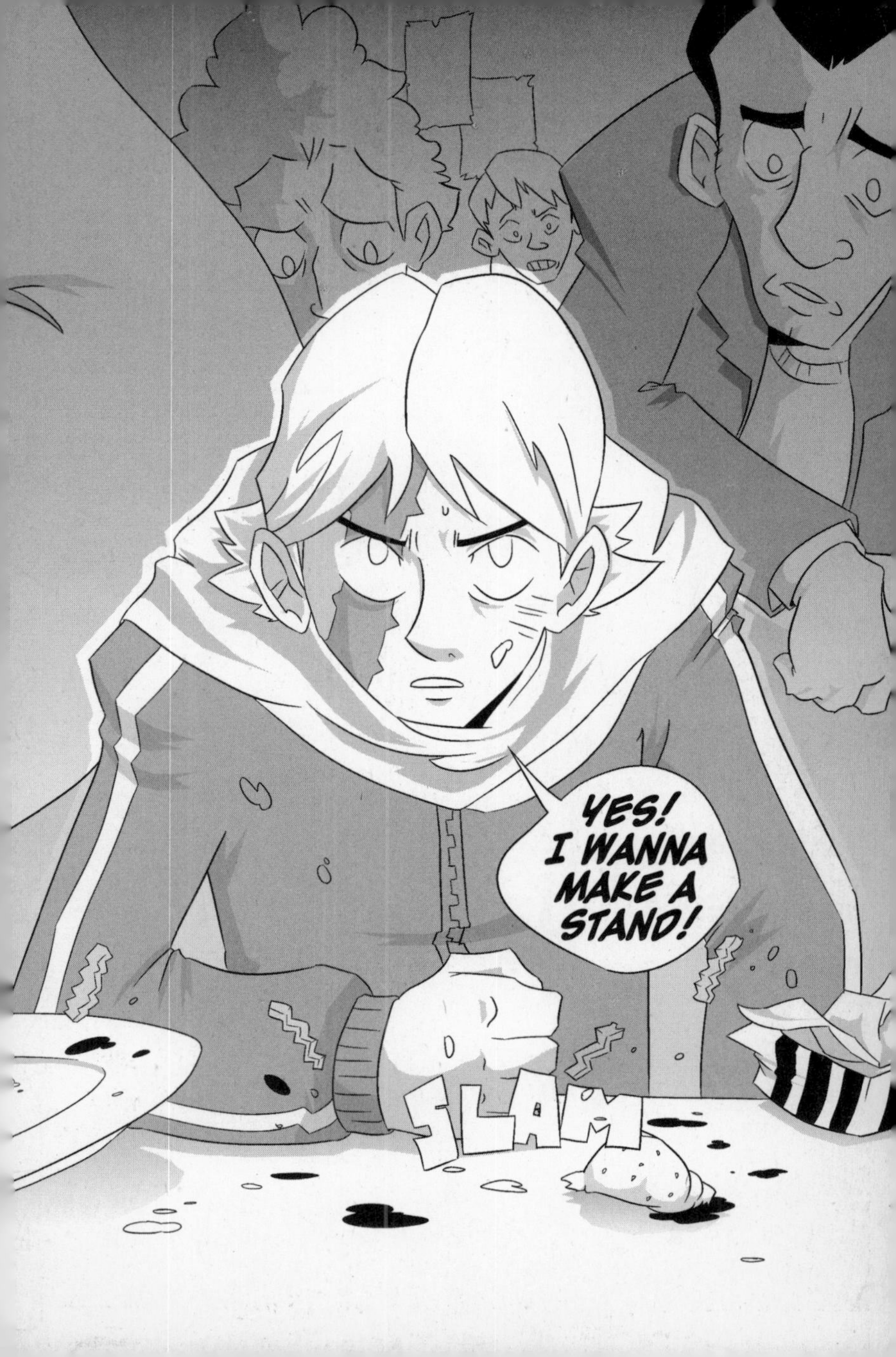
YES! I WANNA MAKE A STAND!
SLAM

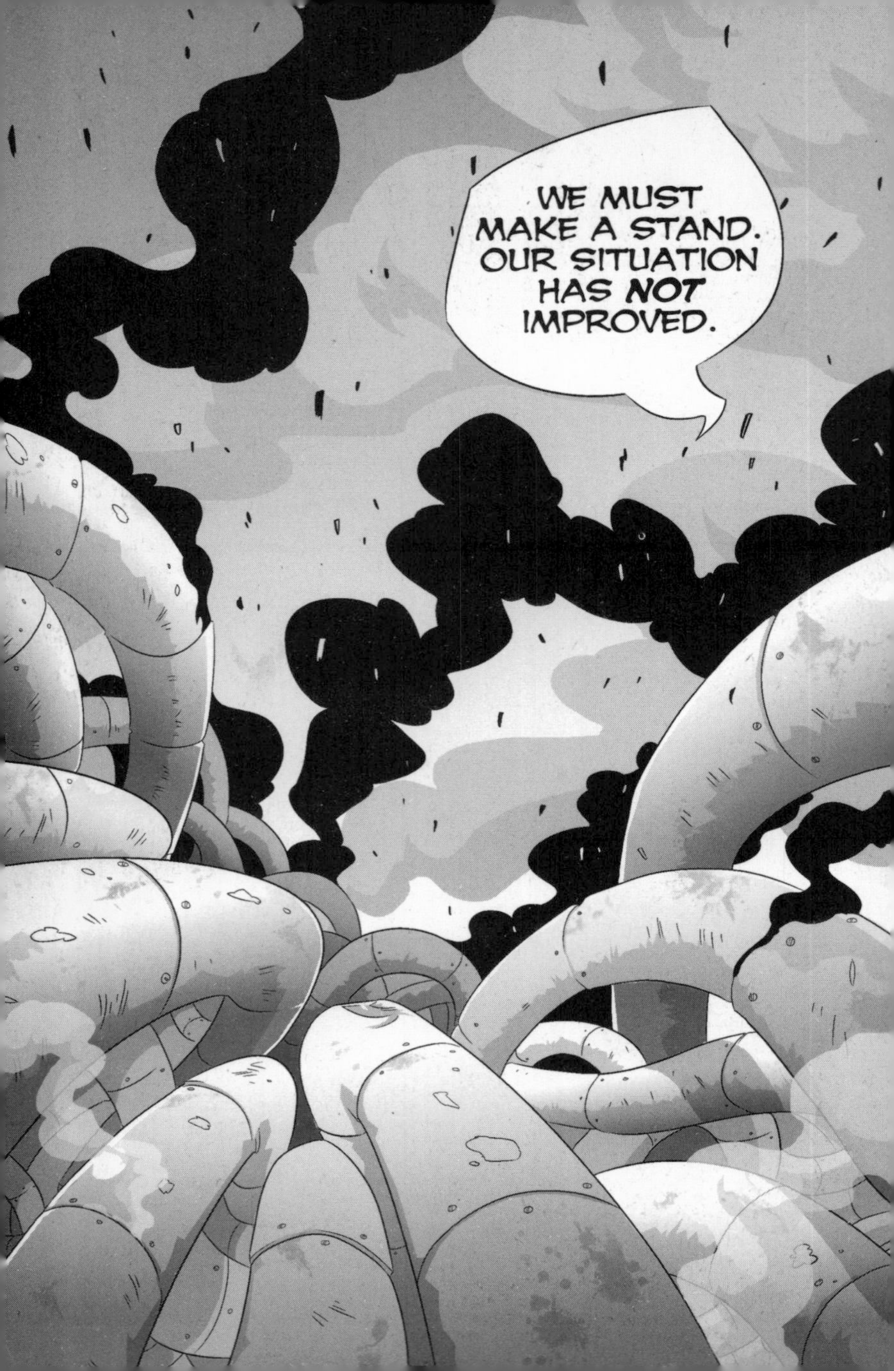
WE MUST MAKE A STAND. OUR SITUATION HAS NOT IMPROVED.

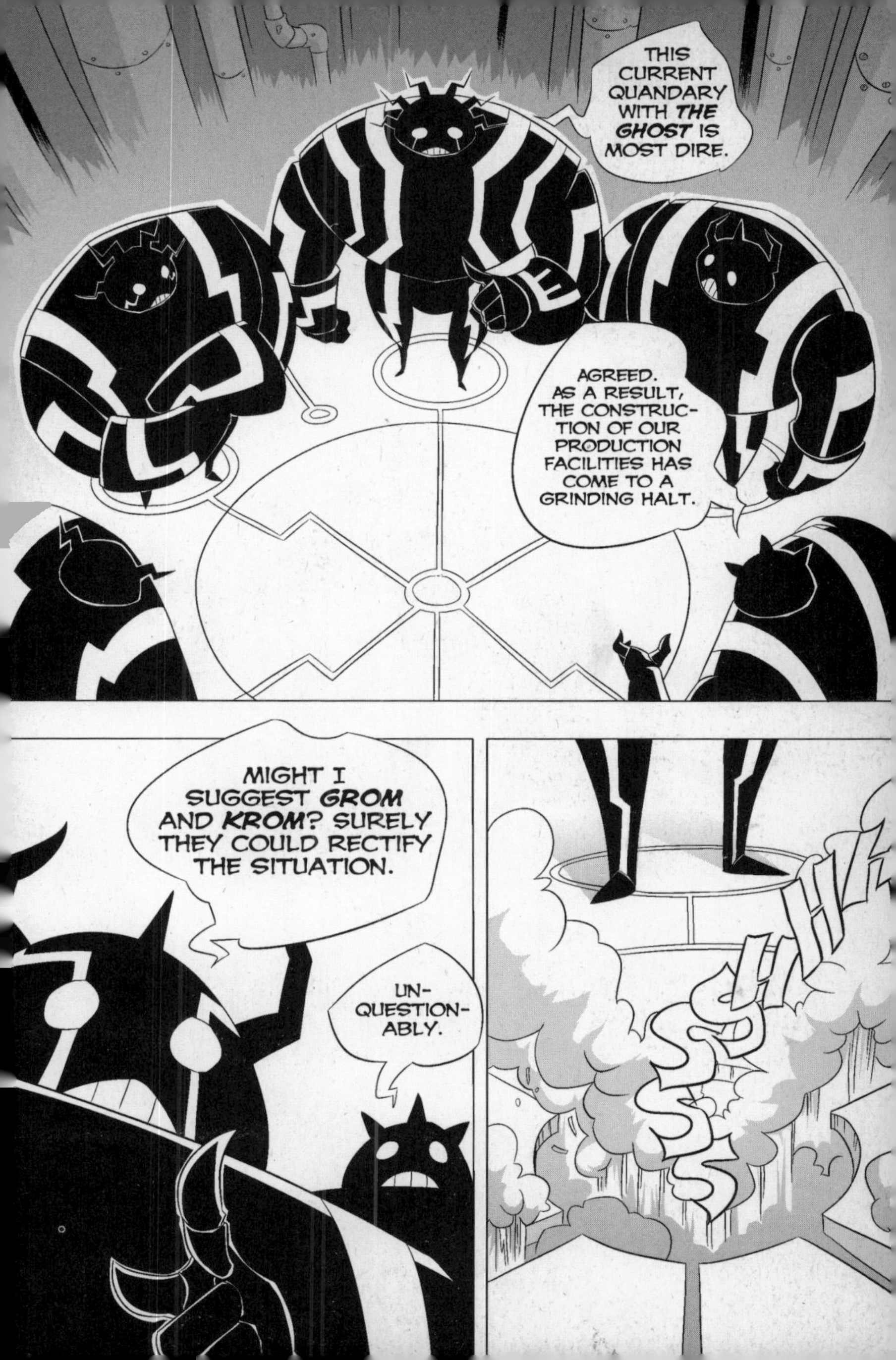
THIS CURRENT QUANDARY WITH THE GHOST IS MOST DIRE.
AGREED. AS A RESULT, THE CONSTRUCTION OF OUR PRODUCTION FACILITIES HAS COME TO A GRINDING HALT.
MIGHT I SUGGEST GROM AND KROM? SURELY THEY COULD RECTIFY THE SITUATION.
UNQUESTIONABLY.

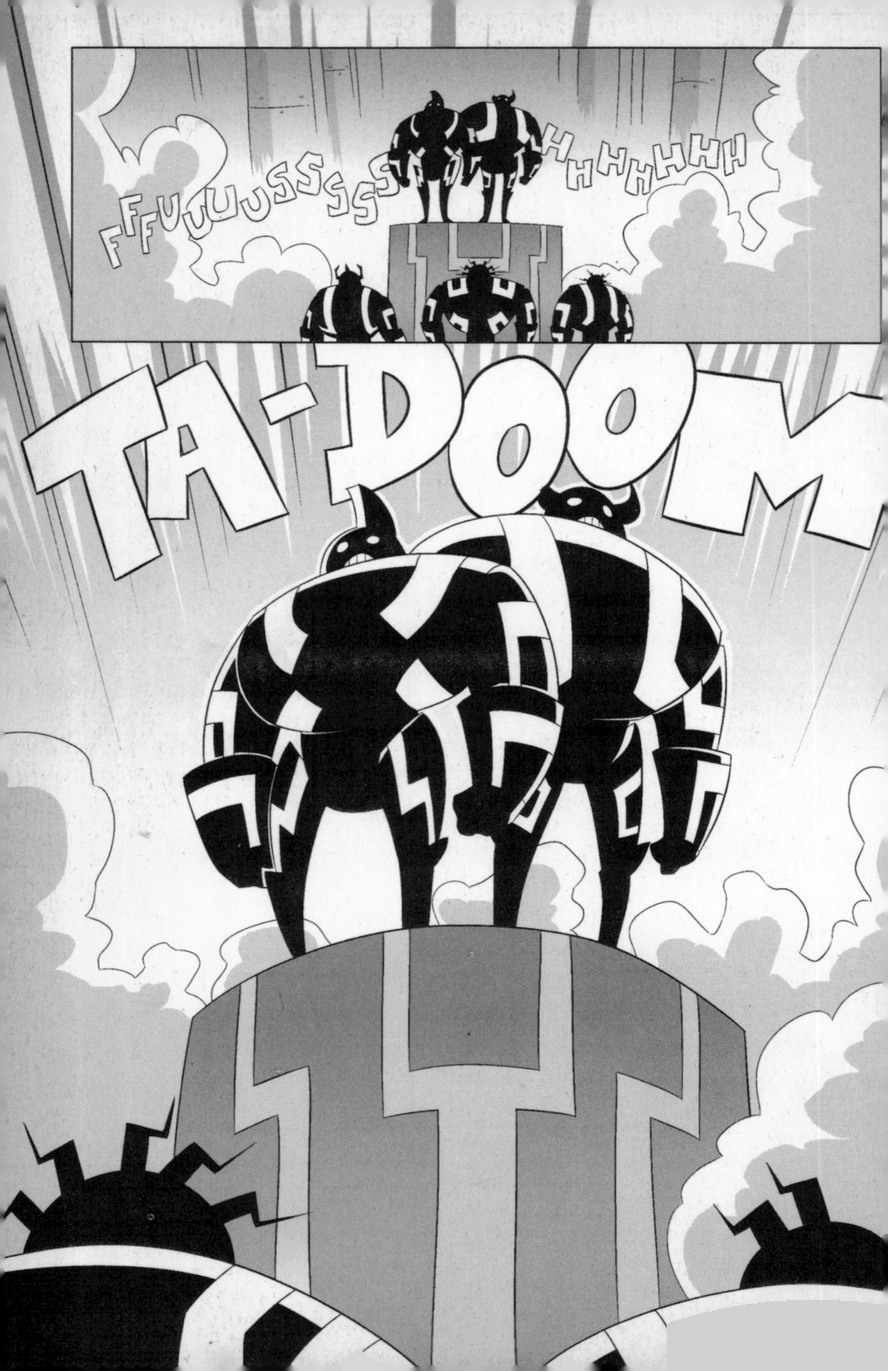
FFFUUUUSSSSSHHHHHHHH
TA-DOOM

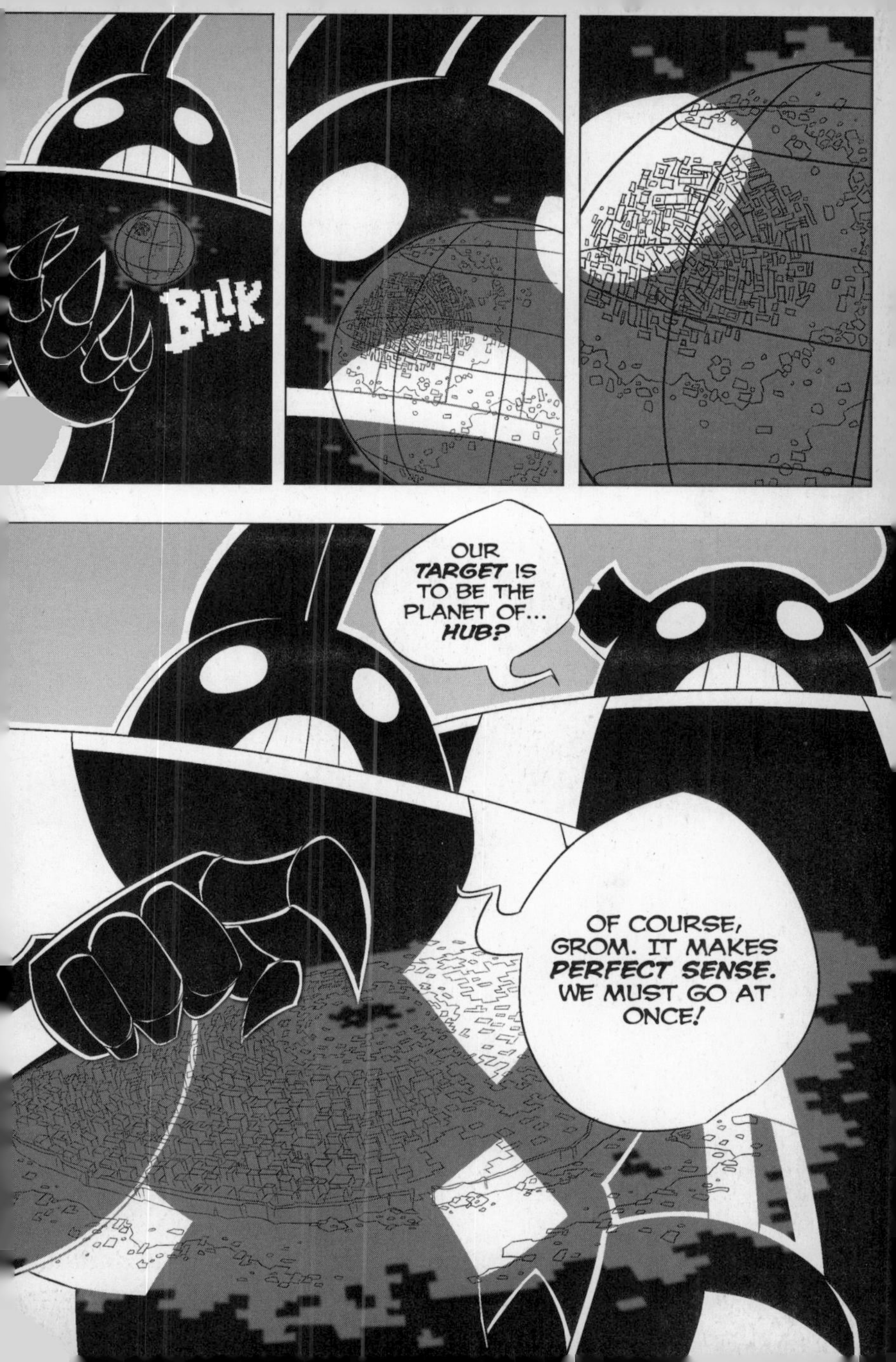
BLIK
OUR *TARGET* IS TO BE THE PLANET OF... *HUB?*
OF COURSE, GROM. IT MAKES *PERFECT SENSE.* WE MUST GO AT ONCE!

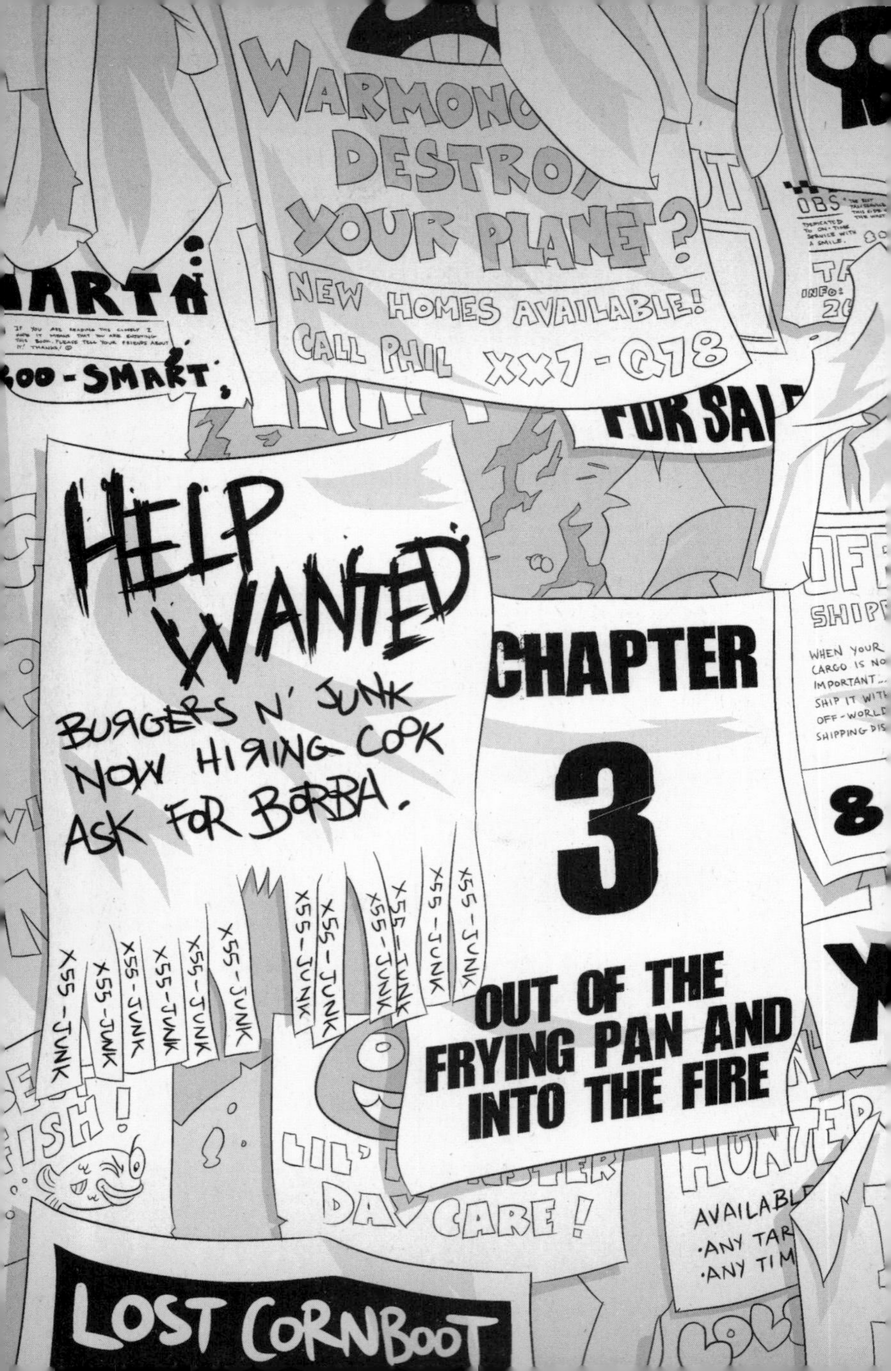
YOUR PLANET?
NEW HOMES AVAILABLE!
CALL PHIL XX7-Q78
FOR SAL
HELP WANTED
BURGERS N' JUNK
NOW HIRING COOK
ASK FOR BORBA.
X55-JUNK
CHAPTER
3
OUT OF THE
FRYING PAN AND
INTO THE FIRE
SHIPP
WHEN YOUR
CARGO IS NO
IMPORTANT...
SHIP IT WITH
OFF-WORLD
SHIPPING DIS
DAY CARE!
AVAILABL
·ANY TAR
·ANY TIM
LOST CORNBOOT

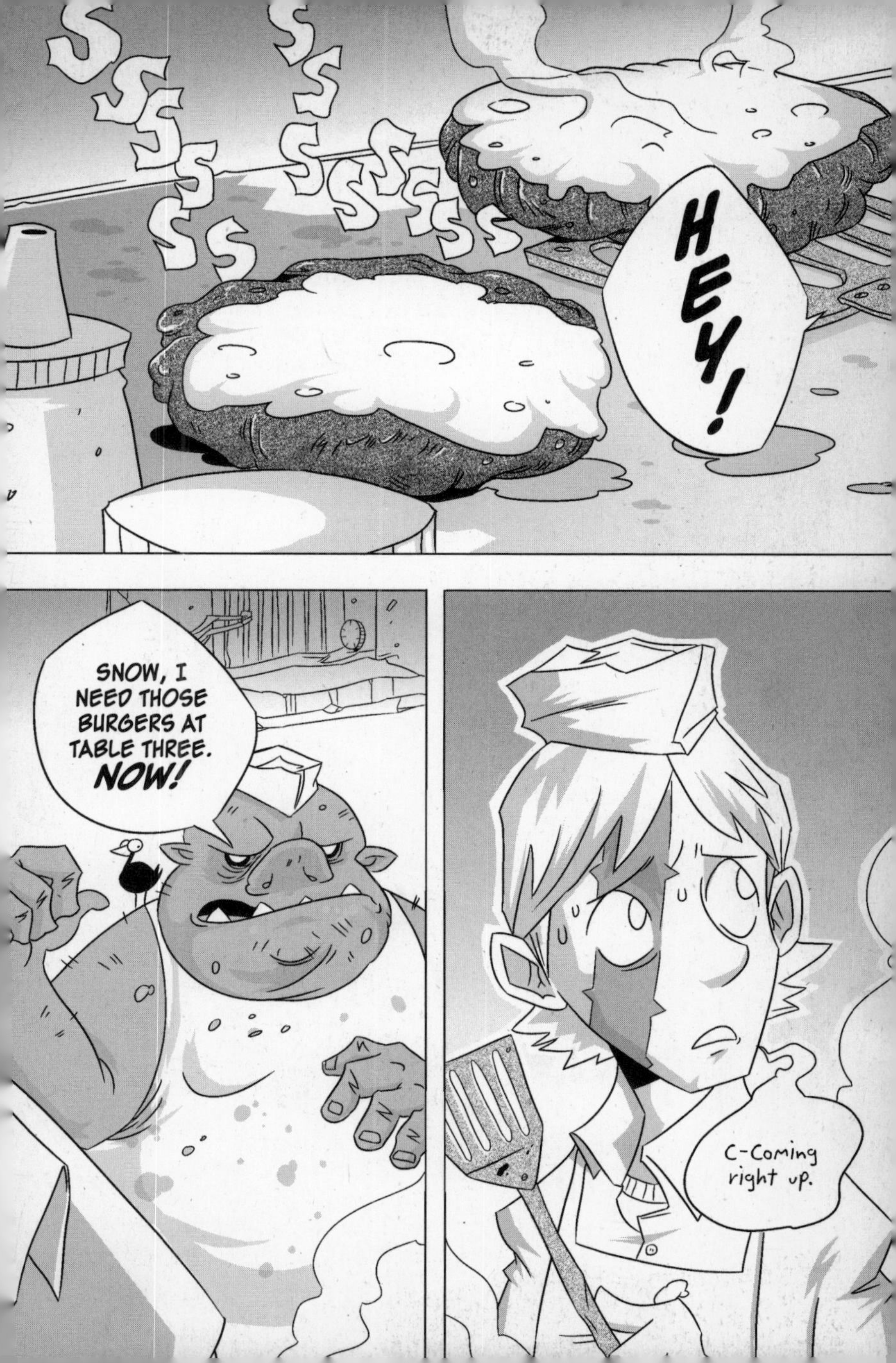
SSSSSS
SSSSSSSSS
HEY!
SNOW, I NEED THOSE BURGERS AT TABLE THREE. NOW!
C-Coming right up.

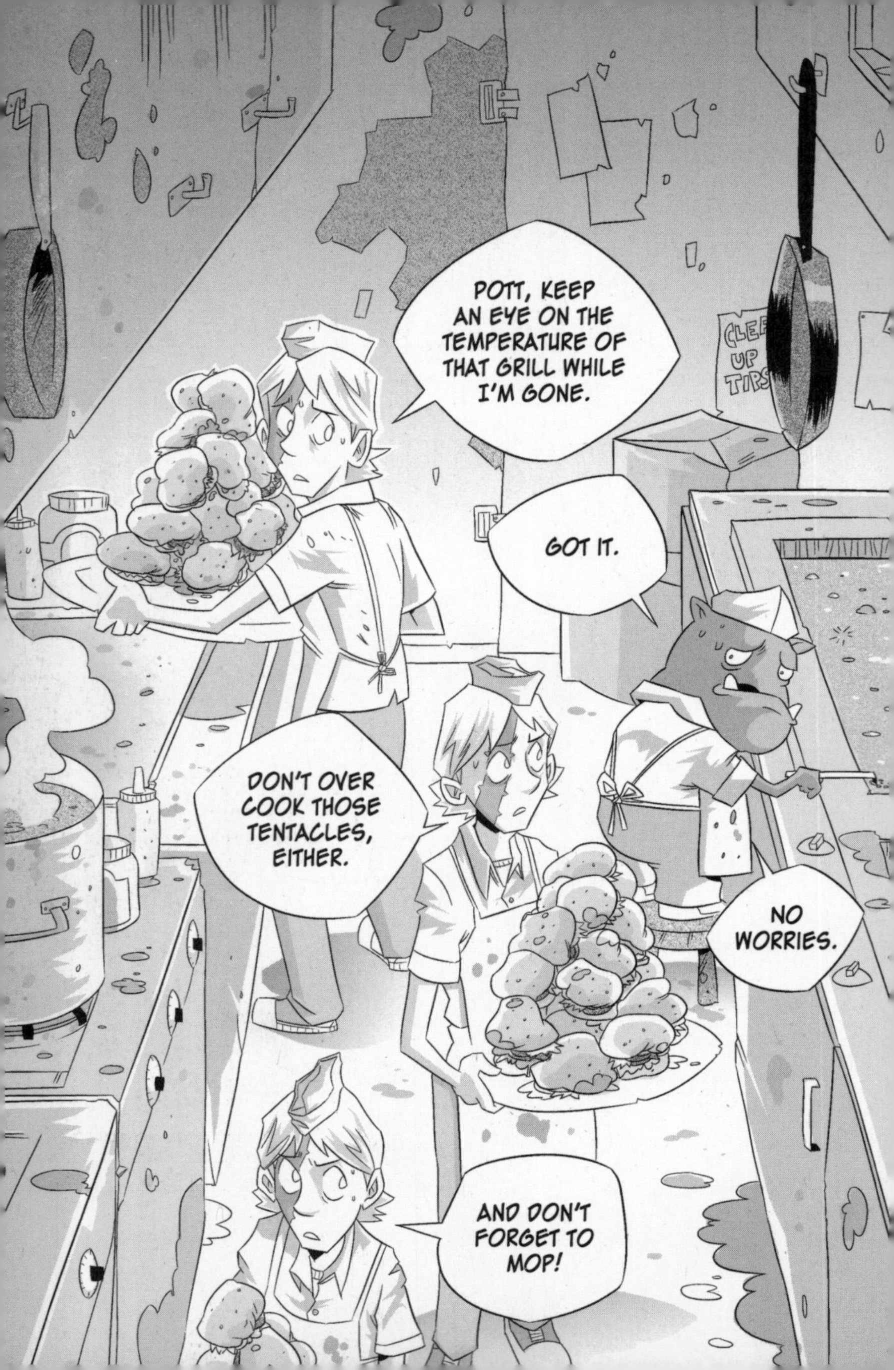
POTT, KEEP AN EYE ON THE TEMPERATURE OF THAT GRILL WHILE I'M GONE.
GOT IT.
DON'T OVER COOK THOSE TENTACLES, EITHER.
NO WORRIES.
AND DON'T FORGET TO MOP!

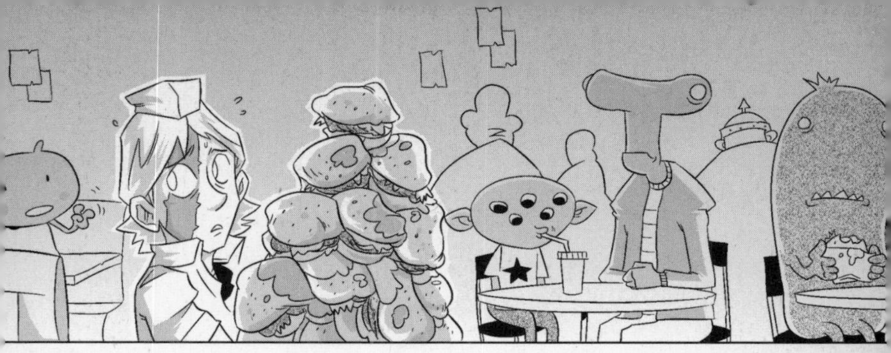
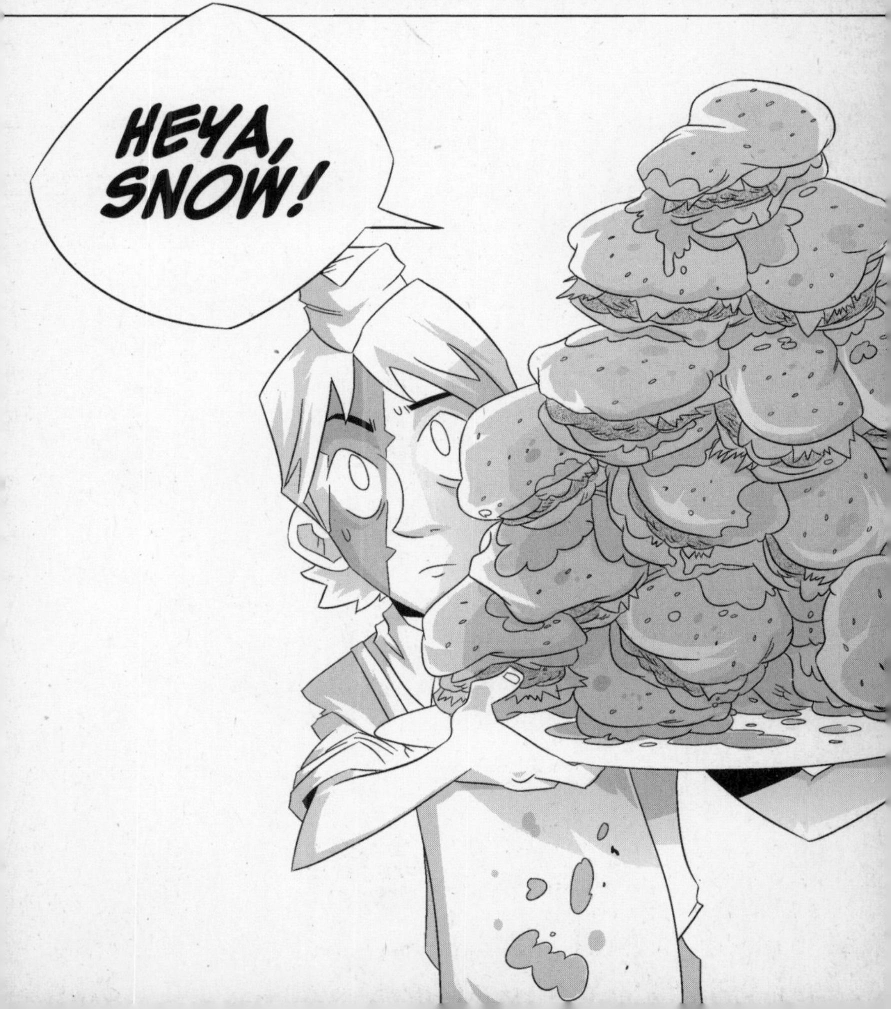
HEYA, SNOW!

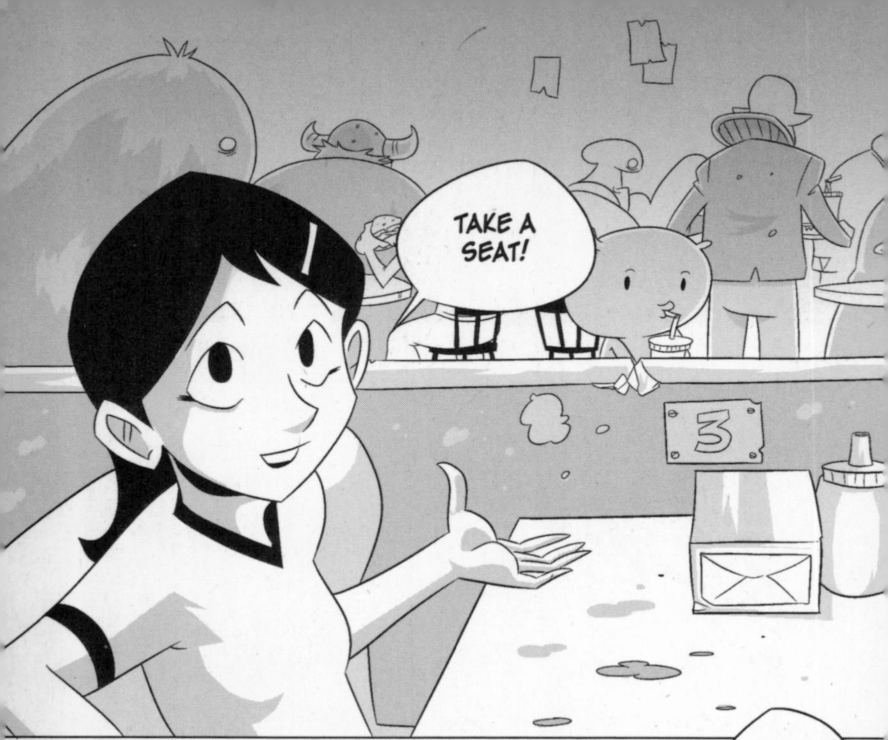
TAKE A SEAT!

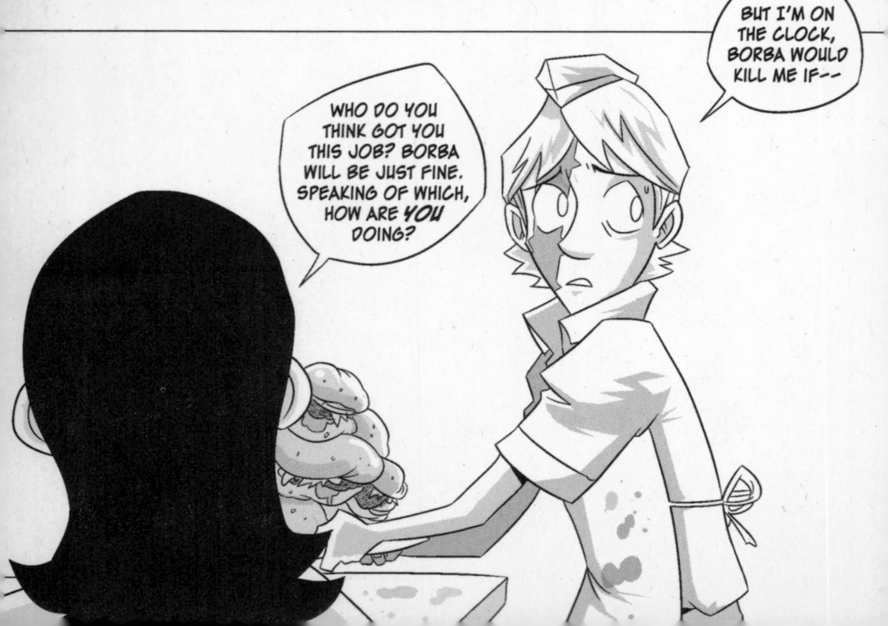
BUT I'M ON THE CLOCK, BORBA WOULD KILL ME IF--
WHO DO YOU THINK GOT YOU THIS JOB? BORBA WILL BE JUST FINE. SPEAKING OF WHICH, HOW ARE *YOU* DOING?

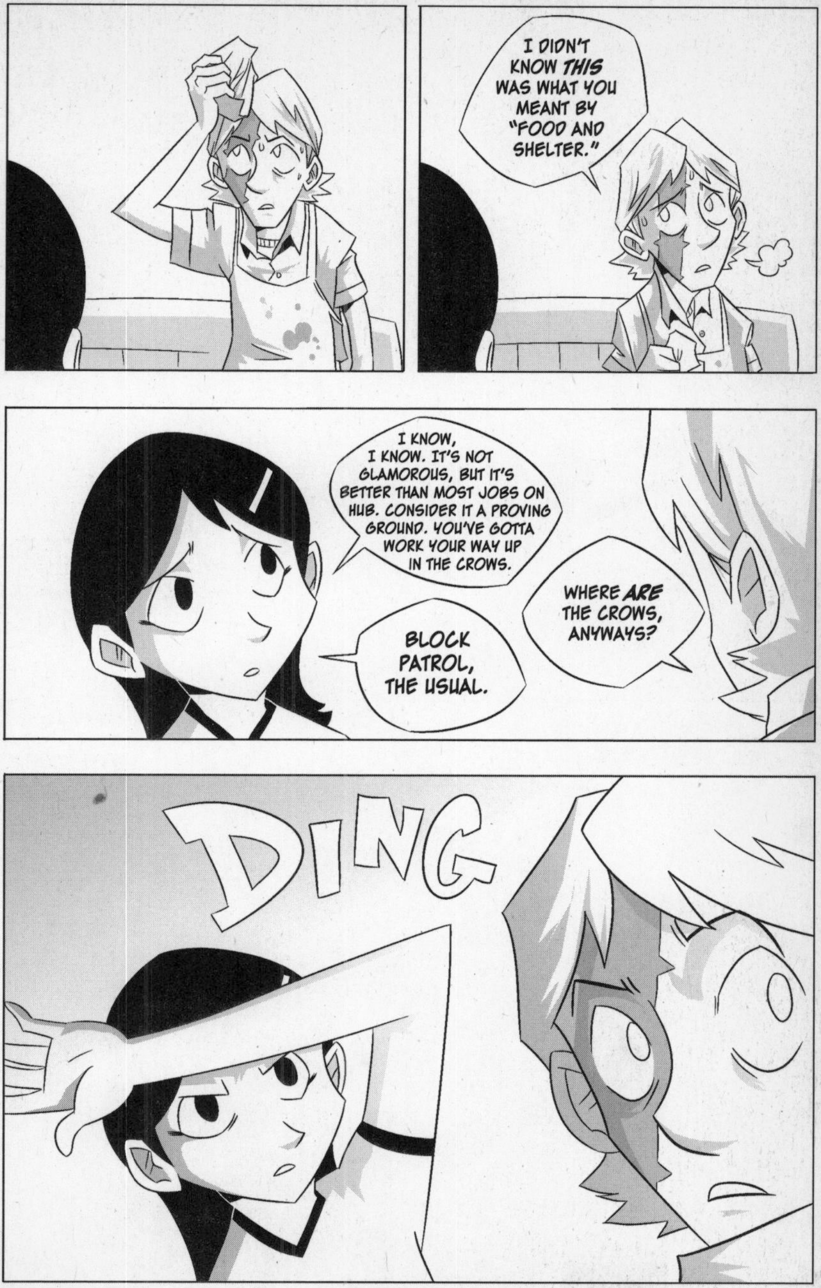
I DIDN'T KNOW THIS WAS WHAT YOU MEANT BY "FOOD AND SHELTER."
I KNOW, I KNOW. IT'S NOT GLAMOROUS, BUT IT'S BETTER THAN MOST JOBS ON HUB. CONSIDER IT A PROVING GROUND. YOU'VE GOTTA WORK YOUR WAY UP IN THE CROWS.
WHERE ARE THE CROWS, ANYWAYS?
BLOCK PATROL, THE USUAL.
DING

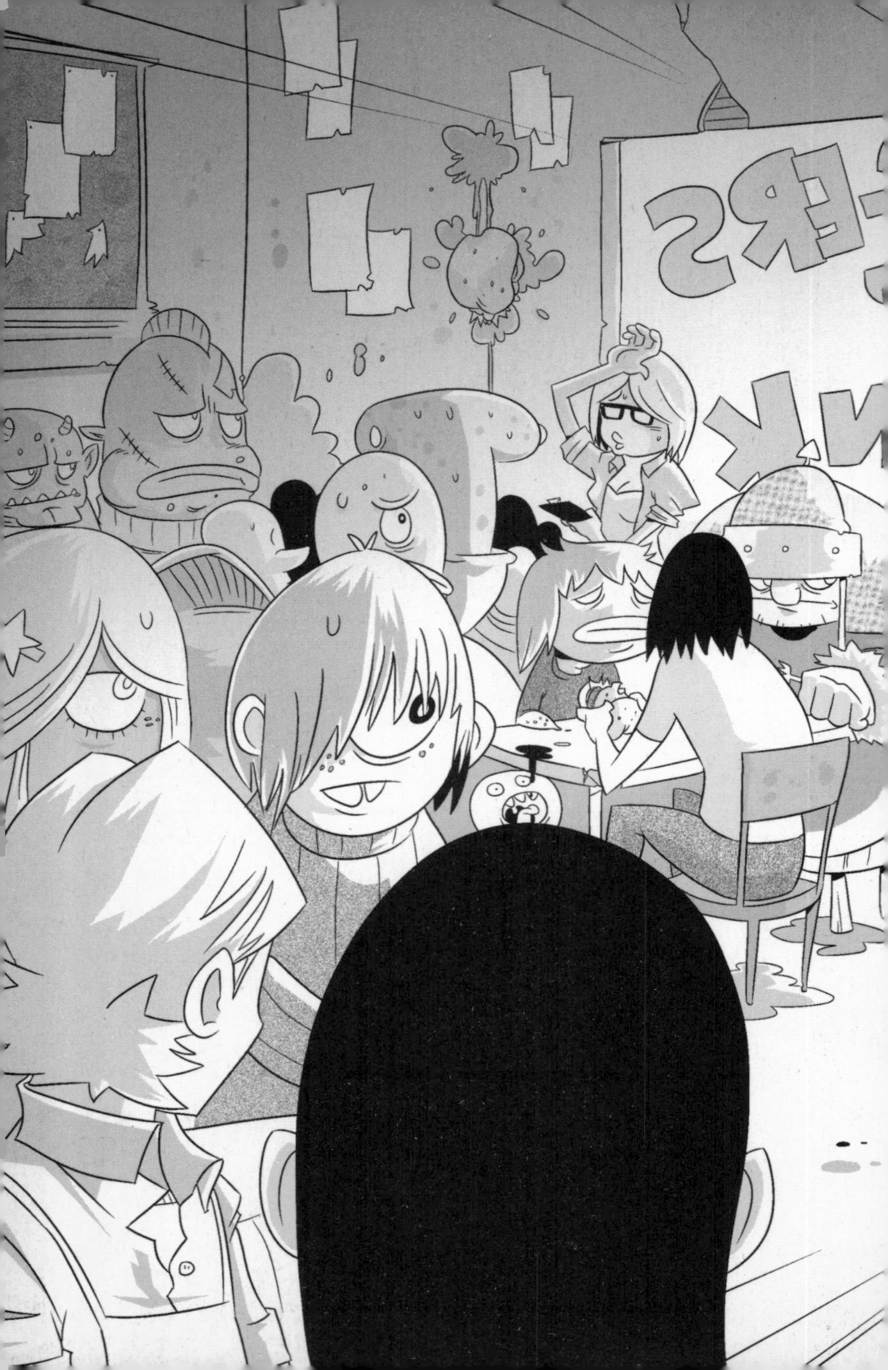

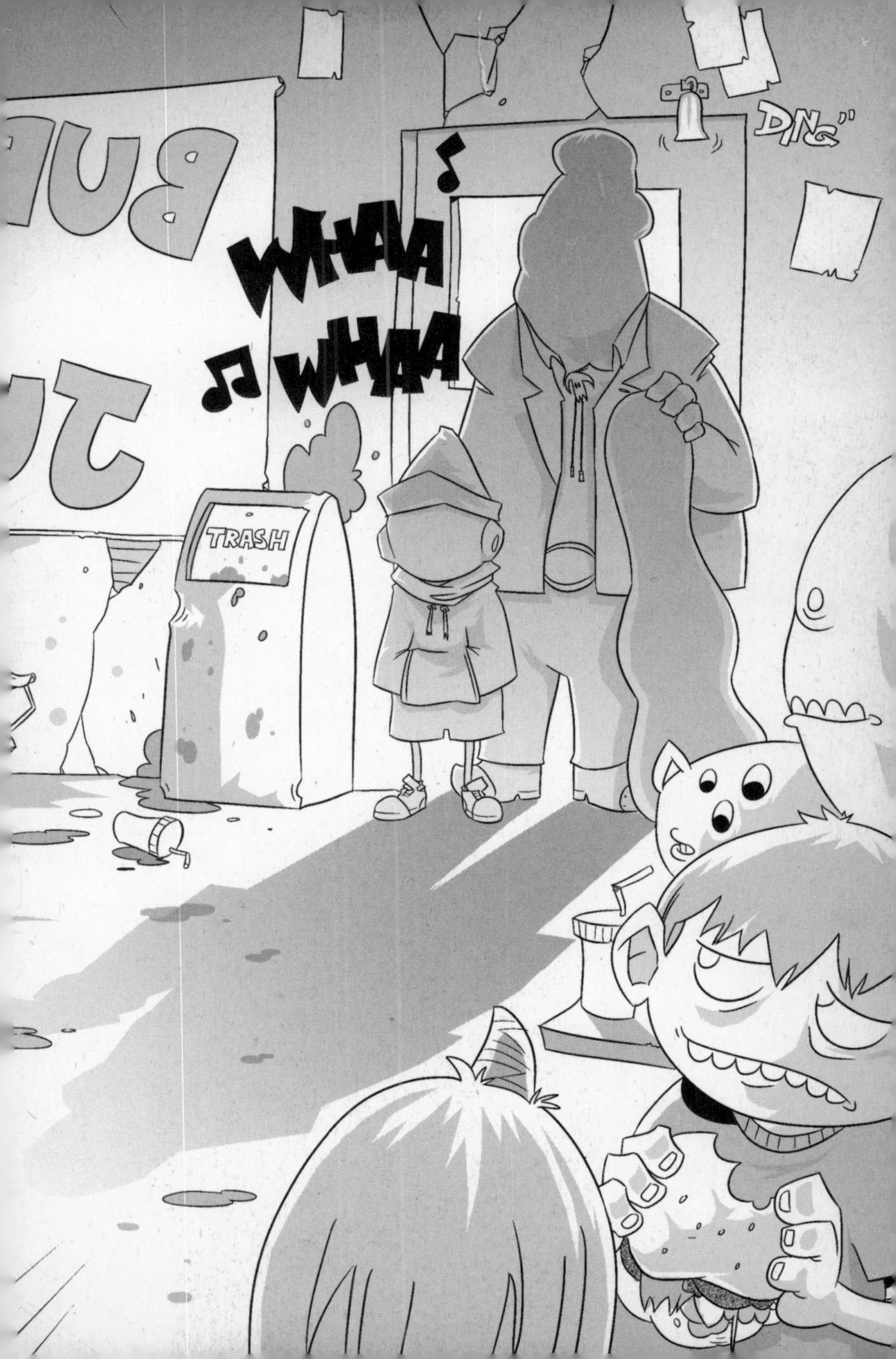
DING"
WHAA
WHAA
TRASH

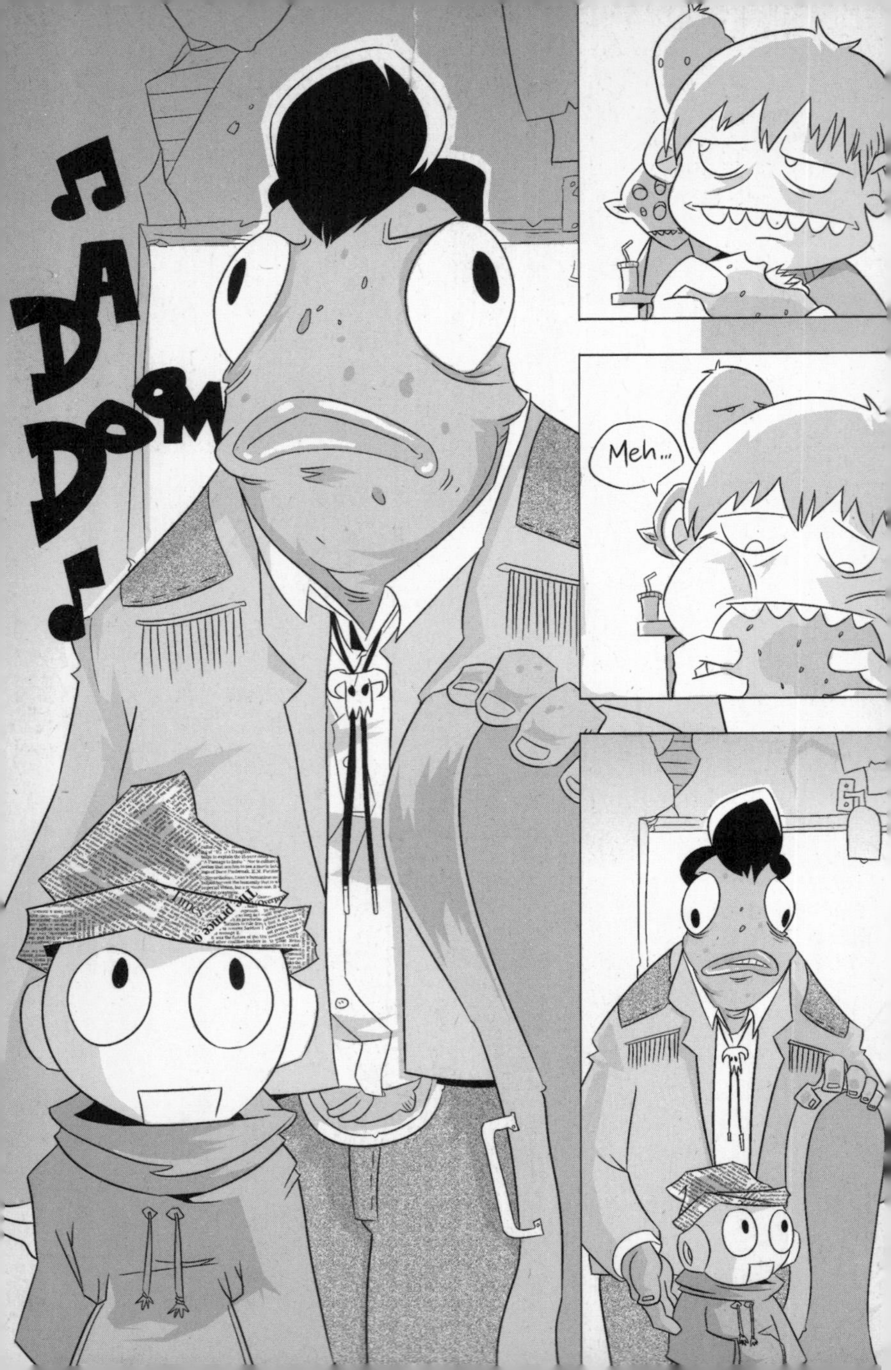
Meh...
DA DOOM D

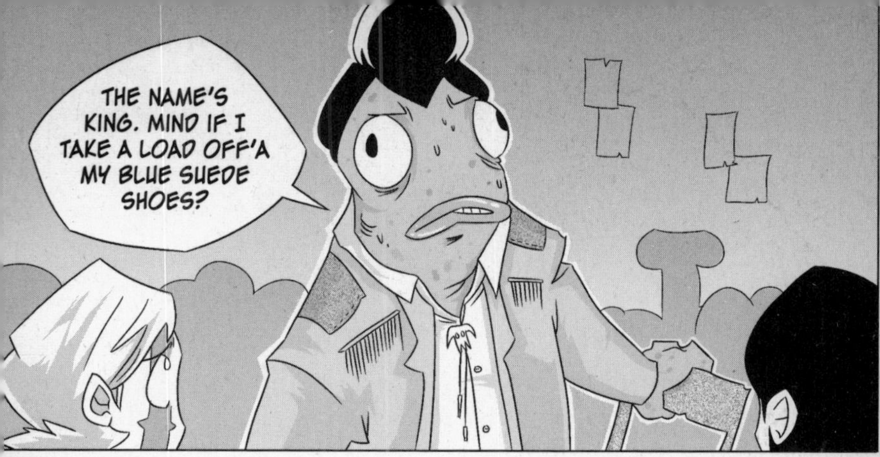
THE NAME'S KING. MIND IF I TAKE A LOAD OFF'A MY BLUE SUEDE SHOES?
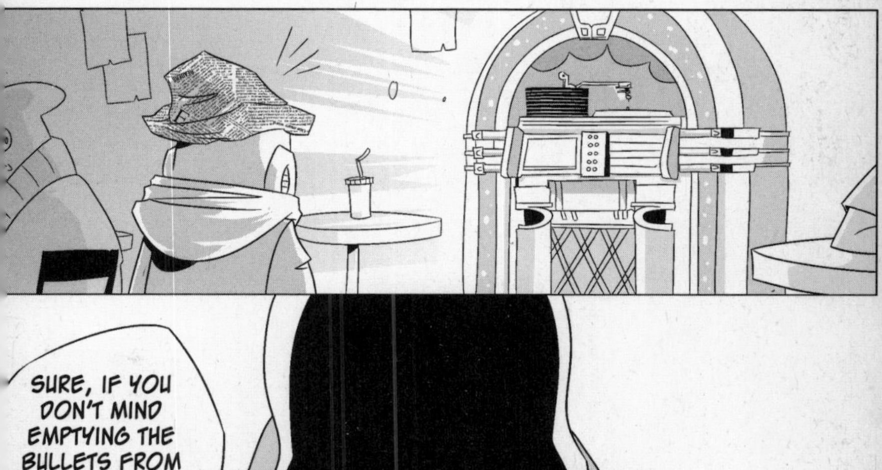
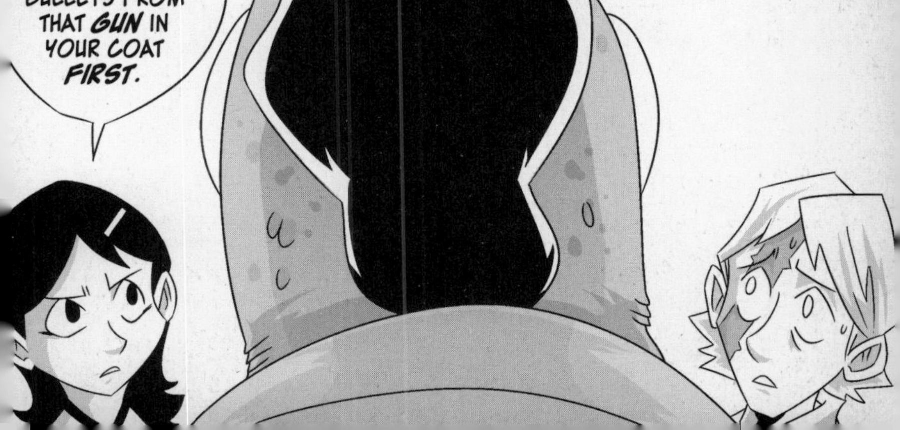
SURE, IF YOU DON'T MIND EMPTYING THE BULLETS FROM THAT GUN IN YOUR COAT FIRST.

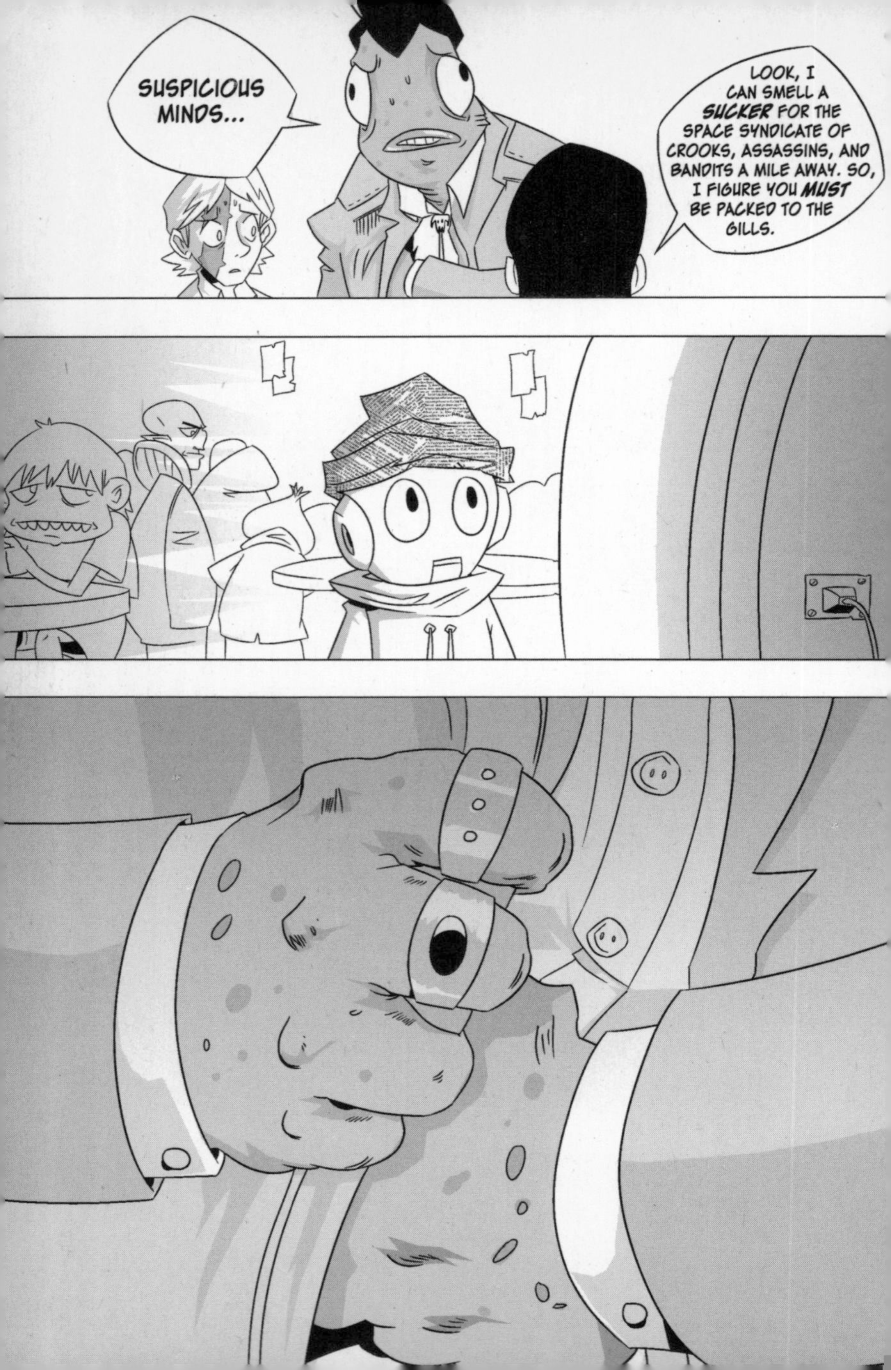
SUSPICIOUS MINDS...
LOOK, I CAN SMELL A **SUCKER** FOR THE SPACE SYNDICATE OF CROOKS, ASSASSINS, AND BANDITS A MILE AWAY. SO, I FIGURE YOU **MUST** BE PACKED TO THE GILLS.

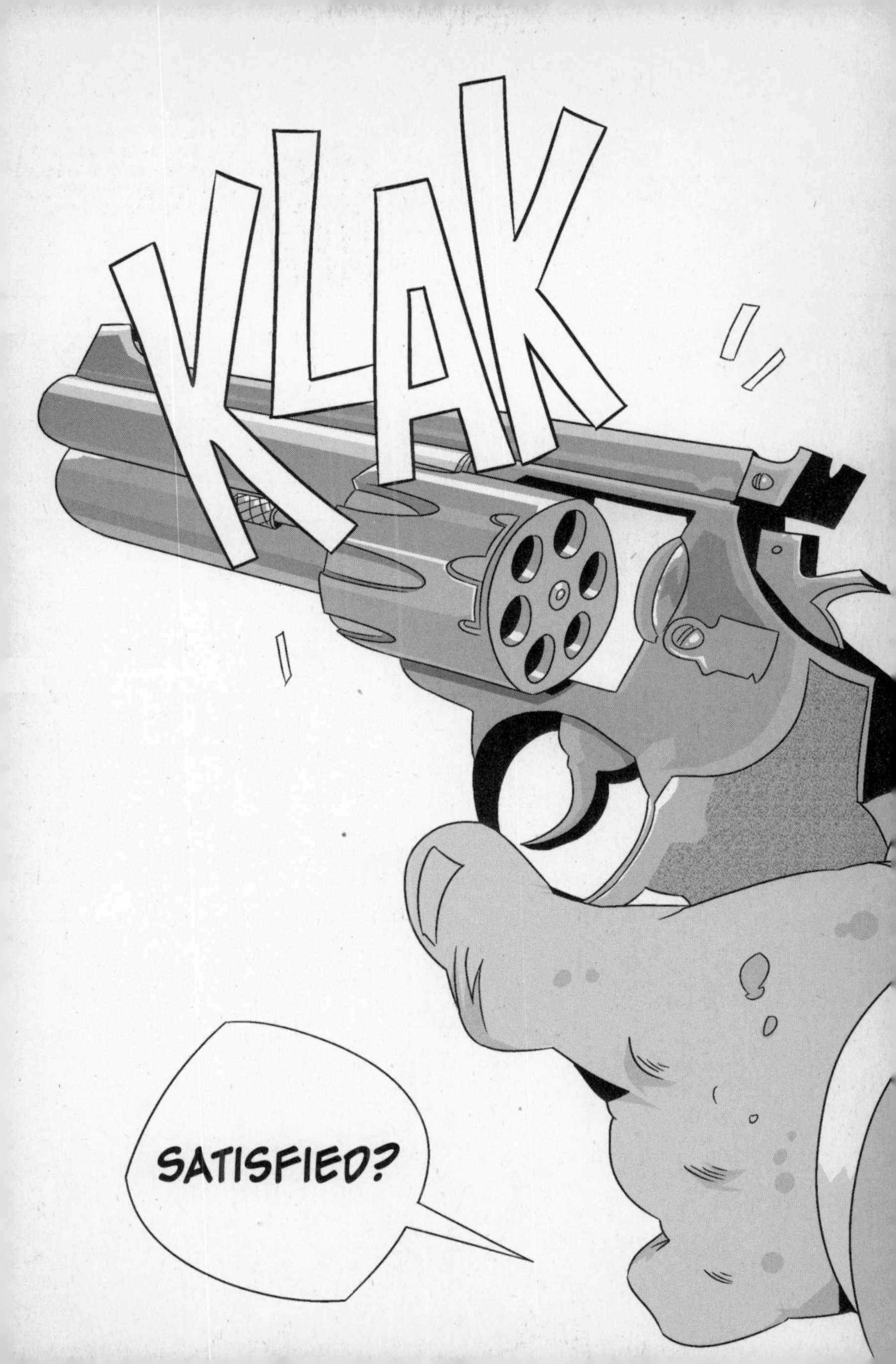
KLAK
SATISFIED?

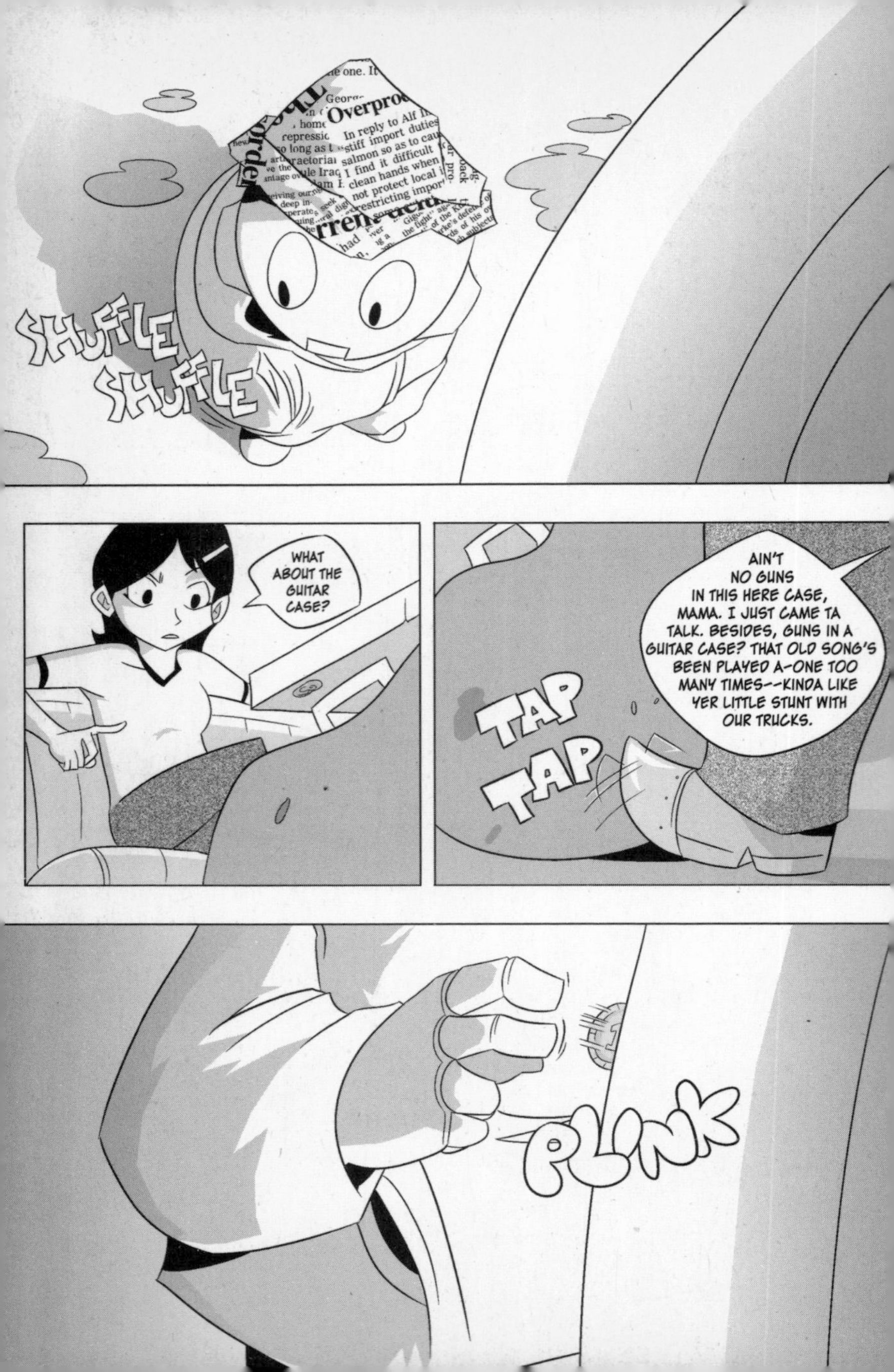
SHUFFLE SHUFFLE
WHAT ABOUT THE GUITAR CASE?
AIN'T NO GUNS IN THIS HERE CASE, MAMA. I JUST CAME TA TALK. BESIDES, GUNS IN A GUITAR CASE? THAT OLD SONG'S BEEN PLAYED A-ONE TOO MANY TIMES--KINDA LIKE YER LITTLE STUNT WITH OUR TRUCKS.
TAP TAP
PLINK

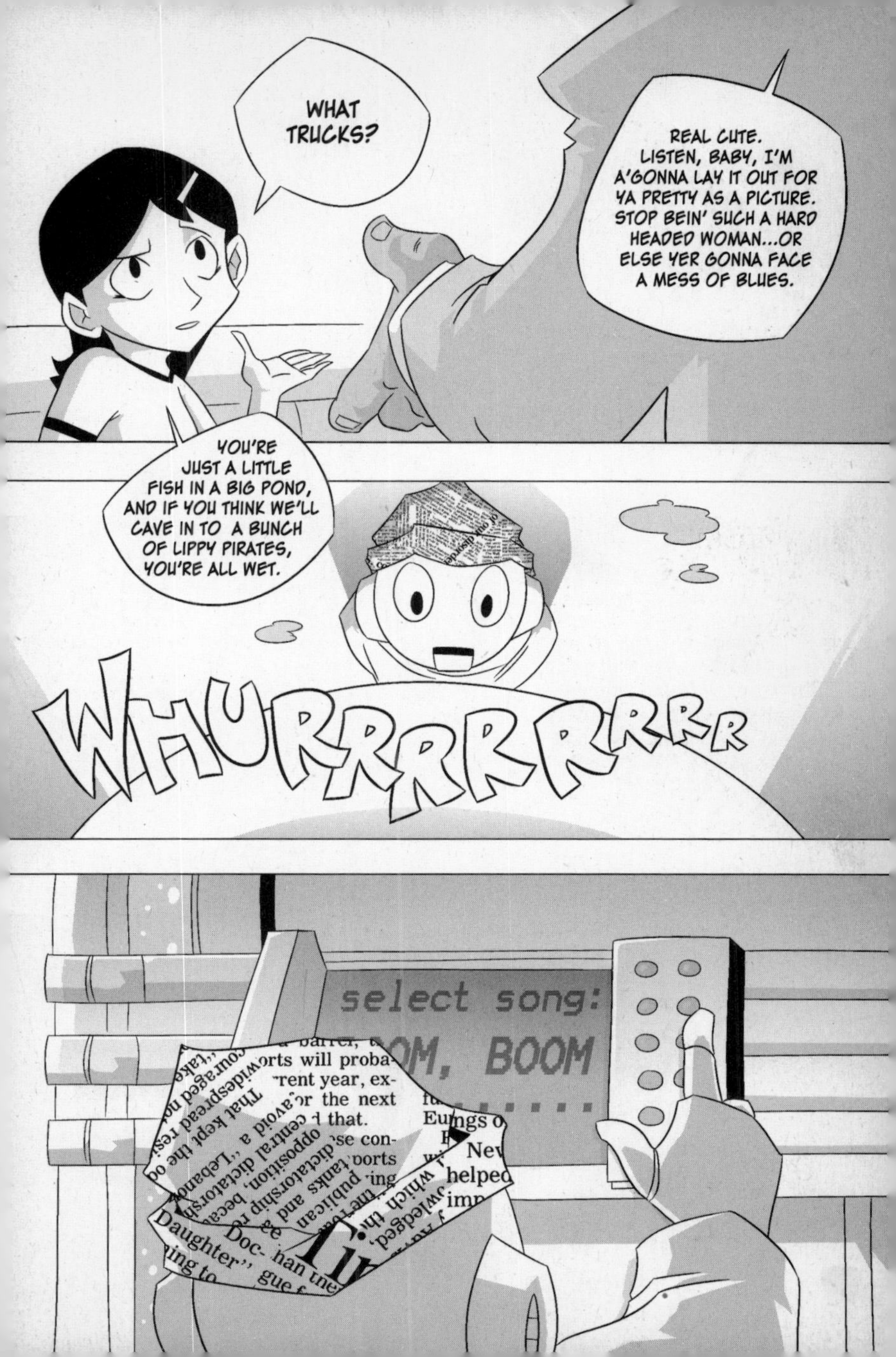
WHAT TRUCKS?
REAL CUTE. LISTEN, BABY, I'M A'GONNA LAY IT OUT FOR YA PRETTY AS A PICTURE. STOP BEIN' SUCH A HARD HEADED WOMAN...OR ELSE YER GONNA FACE A MESS OF BLUES.
YOU'RE JUST A LITTLE FISH IN A BIG POND, AND IF YOU THINK WE'LL CAVE IN TO A BUNCH OF LIPPY PIRATES, YOU'RE ALL WET.
WHURRRRRRRR
select song:
OM, BOOM

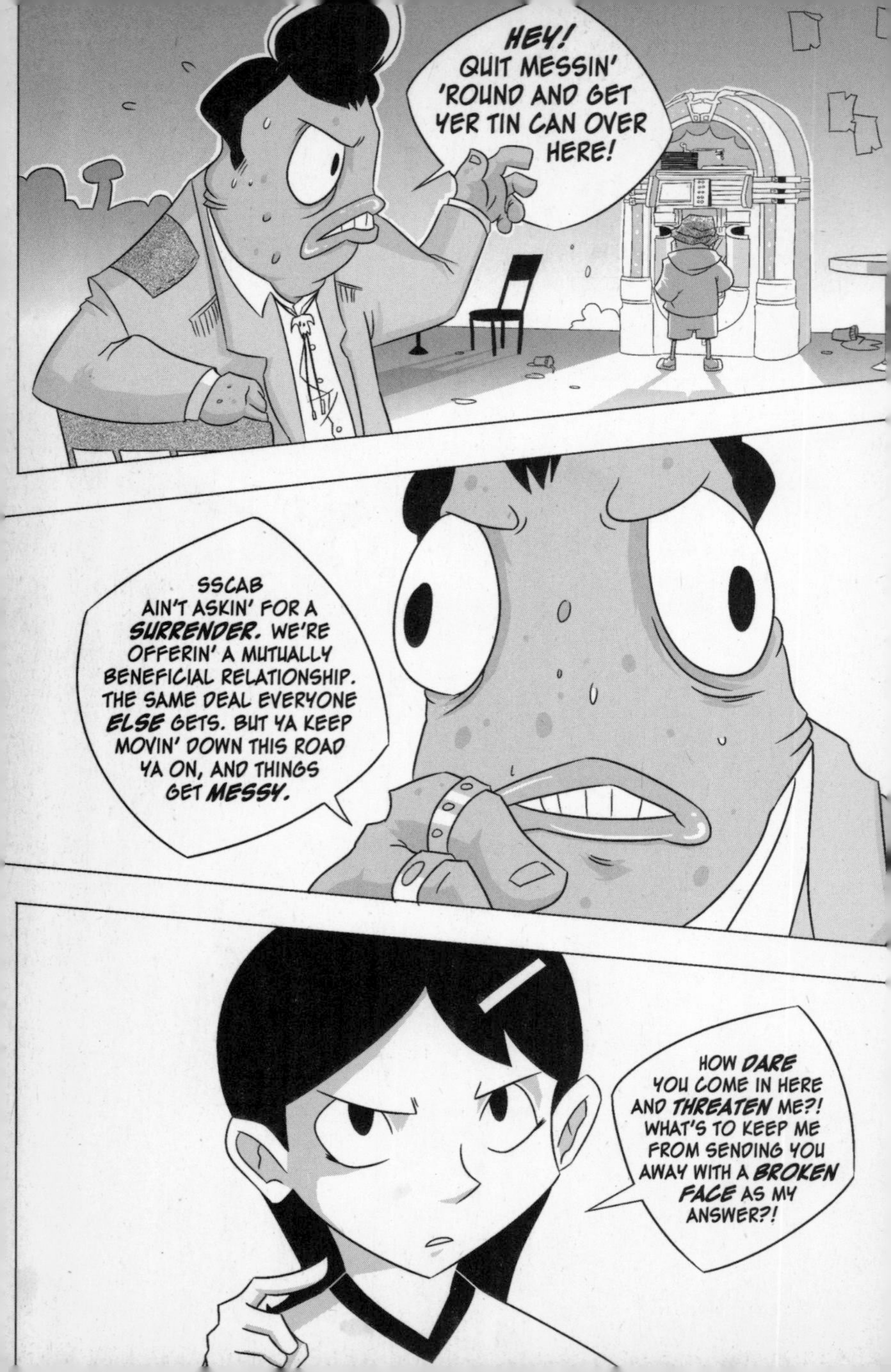
HEY! QUIT MESSIN' 'ROUND AND GET YER TIN CAN OVER HERE!
SSCAB AIN'T ASKIN' FOR A SURRENDER. WE'RE OFFERIN' A MUTUALLY BENEFICIAL RELATIONSHIP. THE SAME DEAL EVERYONE ELSE GETS. BUT YA KEEP MOVIN' DOWN THIS ROAD YA ON, AND THINGS GET MESSY.
HOW DARE YOU COME IN HERE AND THREATEN ME?! WHAT'S TO KEEP ME FROM SENDING YOU AWAY WITH A BROKEN FACE AS MY ANSWER?!

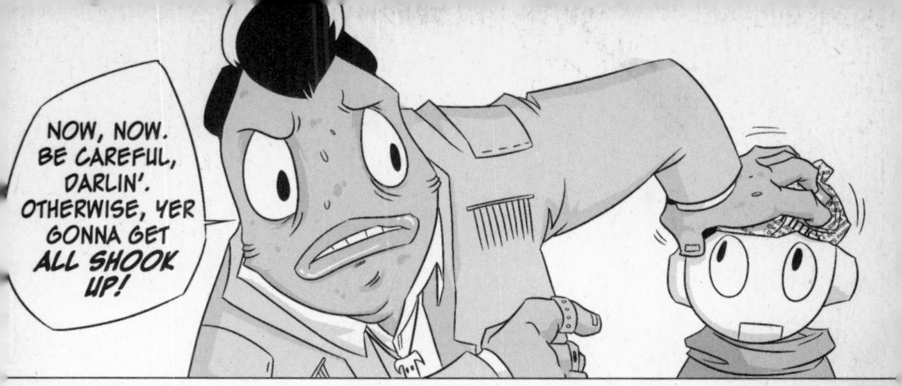
NOW, NOW. BE CAREFUL, DARLIN'. OTHERWISE, YER GONNA GET ALL SHOOK UP!

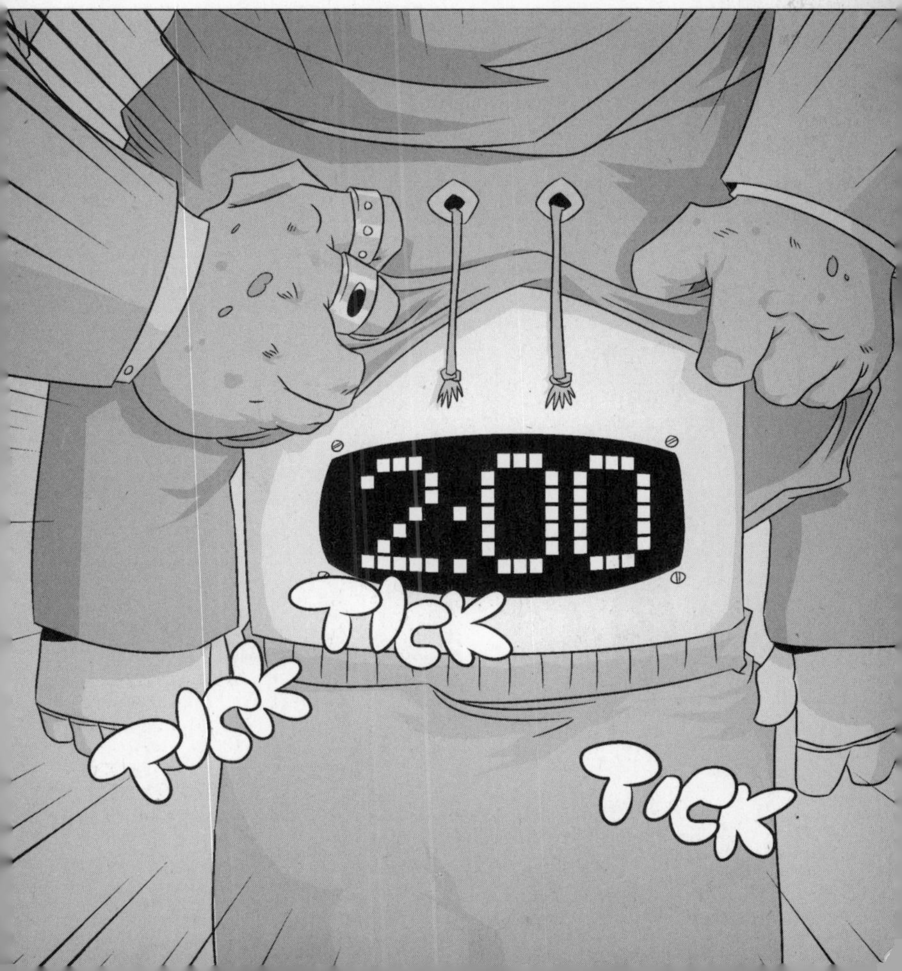
2:00
TICK
TICK
TICK

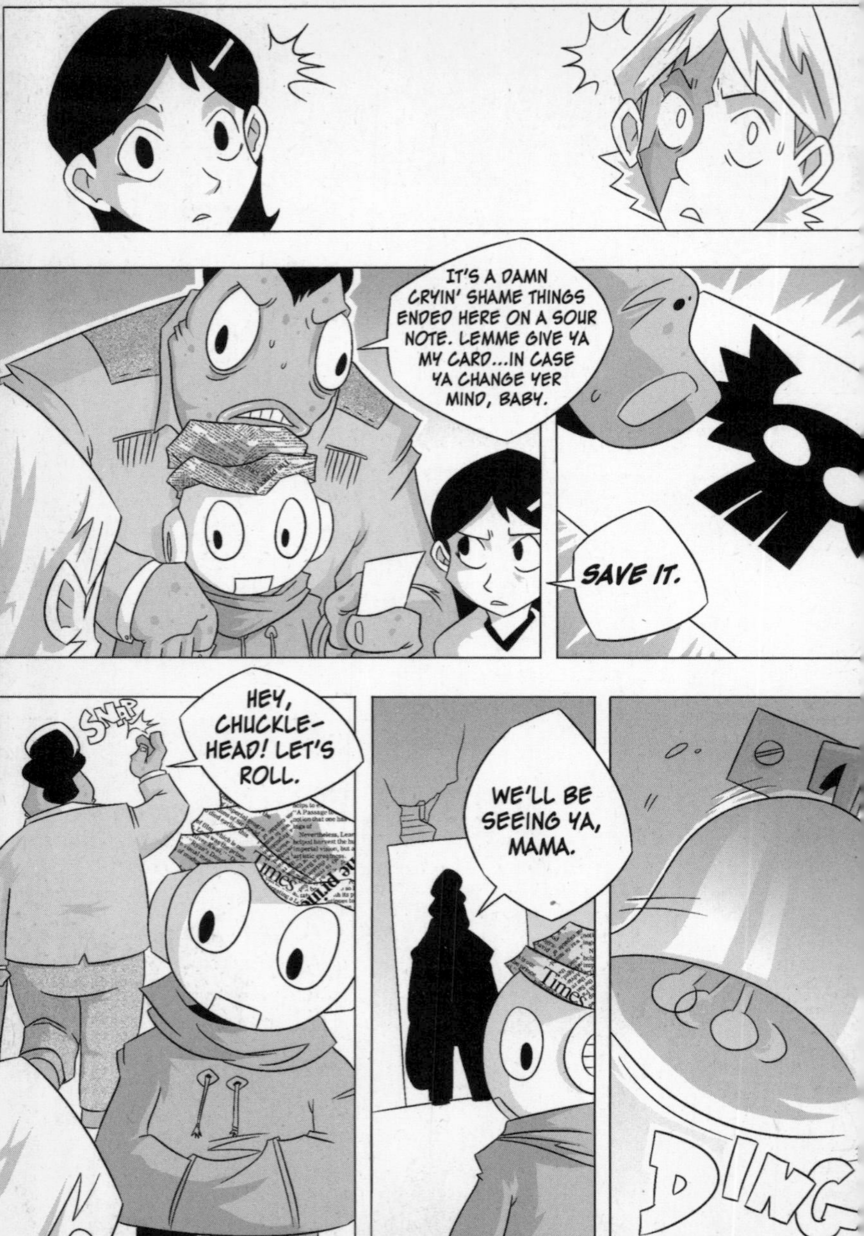
IT'S A DAMN CRYIN' SHAME THINGS ENDED HERE ON A SOUR NOTE. LEMME GIVE YA MY CARD...IN CASE YA CHANGE YER MIND, BABY.
SAVE IT.
SNAP
HEY, CHUCKLE-HEAD! LET'S ROLL.
WE'LL BE SEEING YA, MAMA.
DING

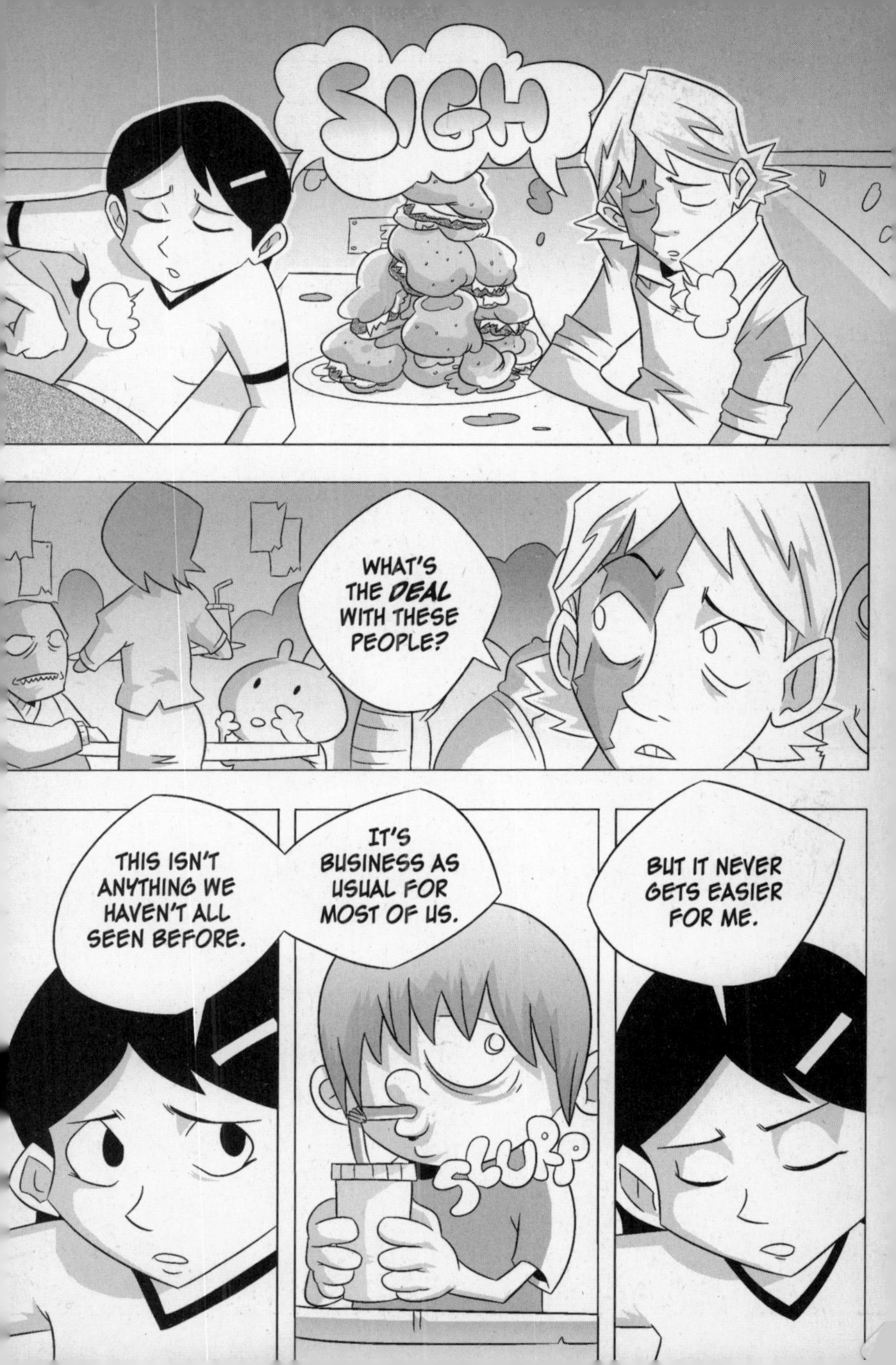
SIGH
WHAT'S THE DEAL WITH THESE PEOPLE?
THIS ISN'T ANYTHING WE HAVEN'T ALL SEEN BEFORE.
IT'S BUSINESS AS USUAL FOR MOST OF US.
SLURP
BUT IT NEVER GETS EASIER FOR ME.

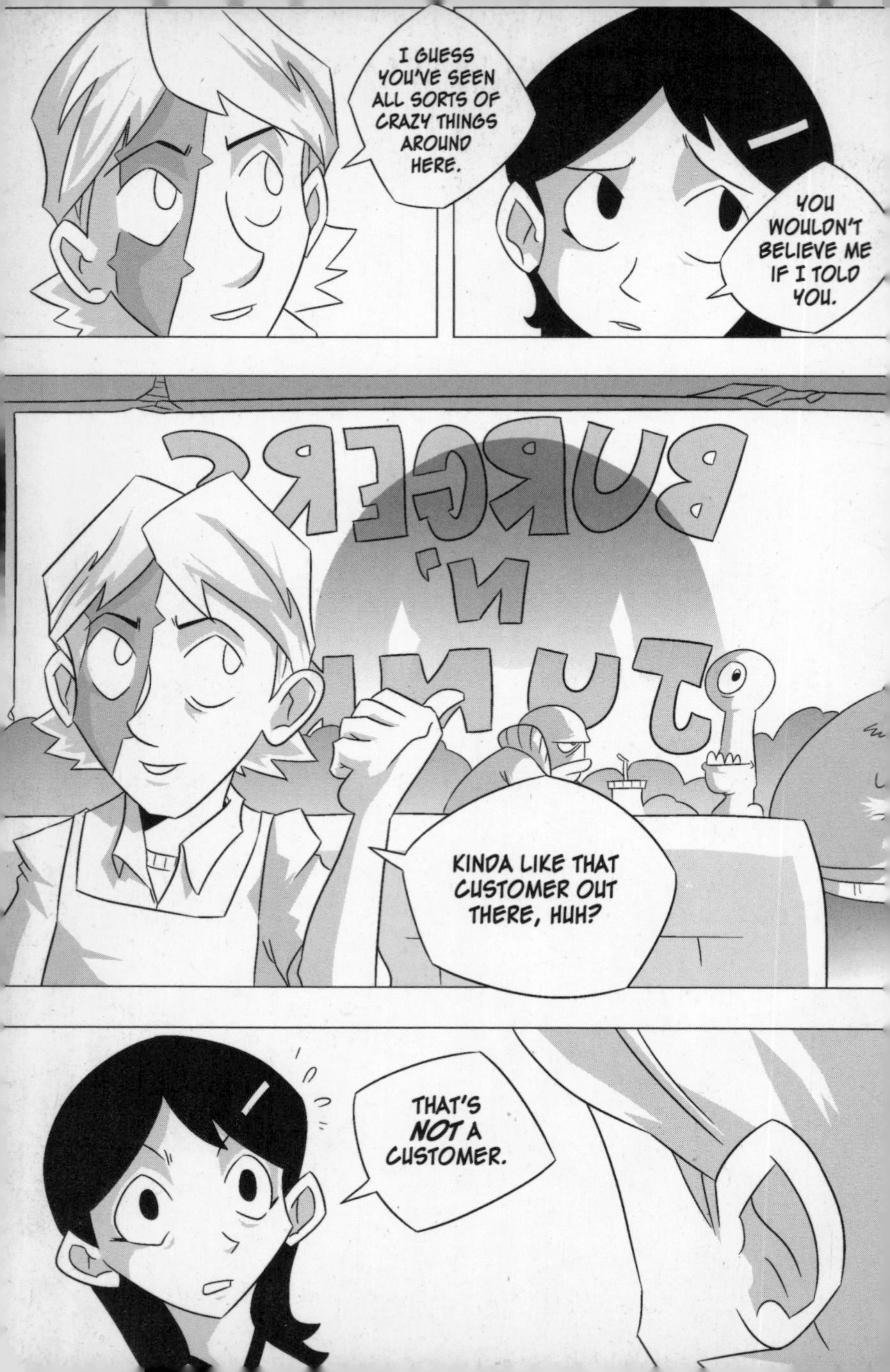
I GUESS YOU'VE SEEN ALL SORTS OF CRAZY THINGS AROUND HERE.
YOU WOULDN'T BELIEVE ME IF I TOLD YOU.
KINDA LIKE THAT CUSTOMER OUT THERE, HUH?
THAT'S *NOT* A CUSTOMER.

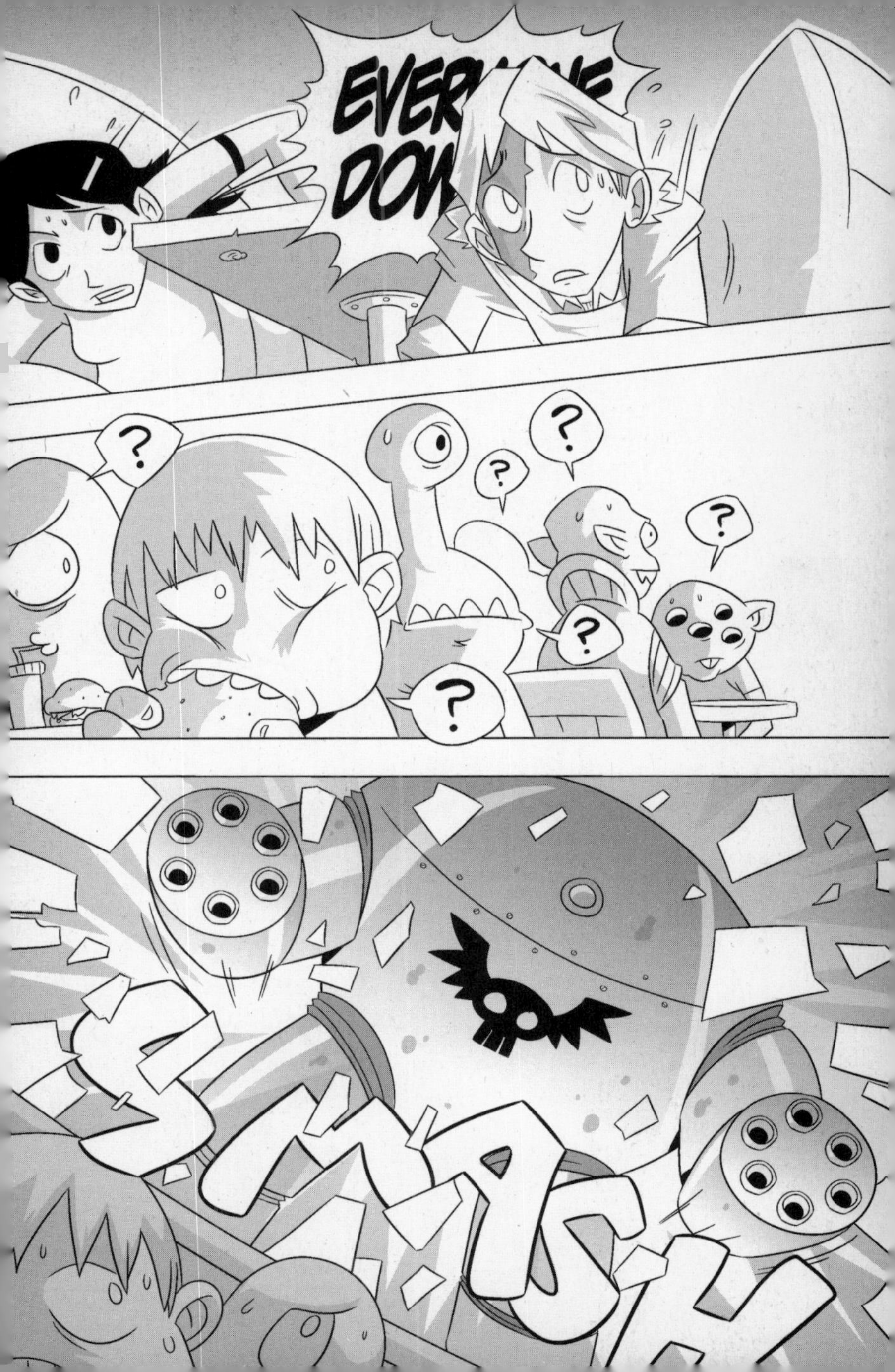
EVER
DOW
?
?
?
?
?
?
?
SMASH

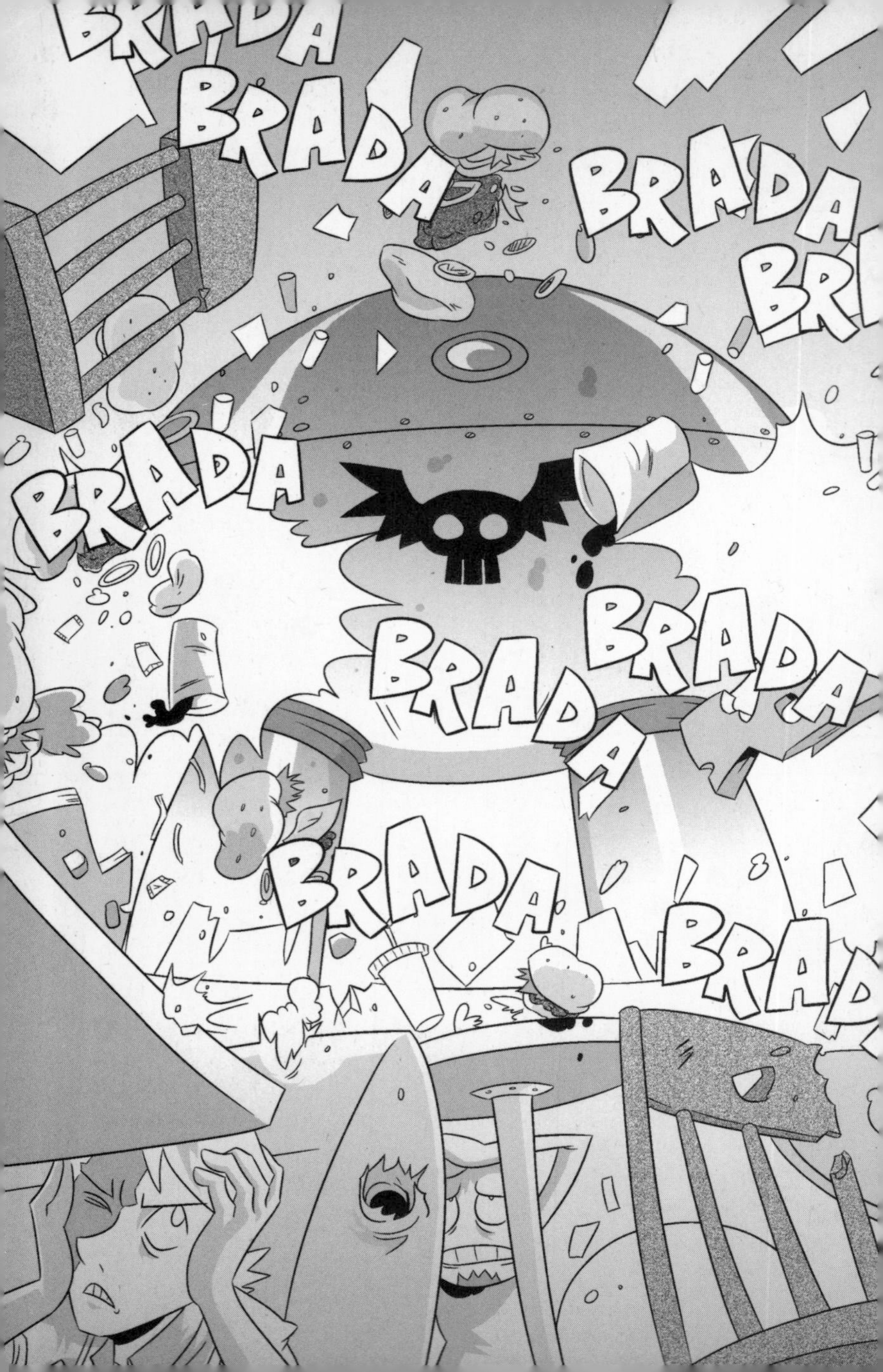
BRADA
BRADA
BRADA
BRADA
BRADA
BRADA
BRADA

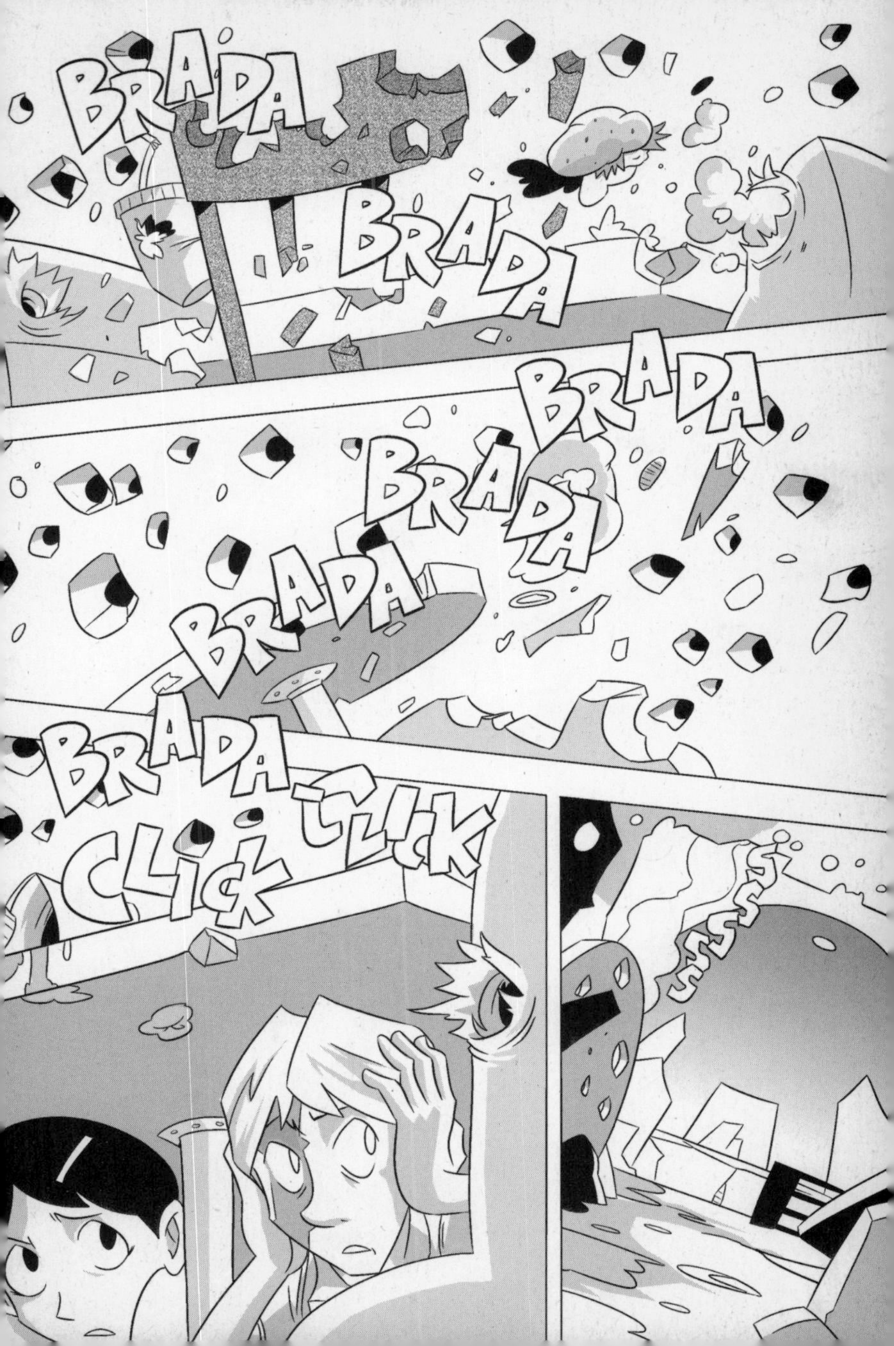
BRADA
BRADA
BRADA
BRADA
BRADA
BRADA-
CLICK
CLICK
SSSSS

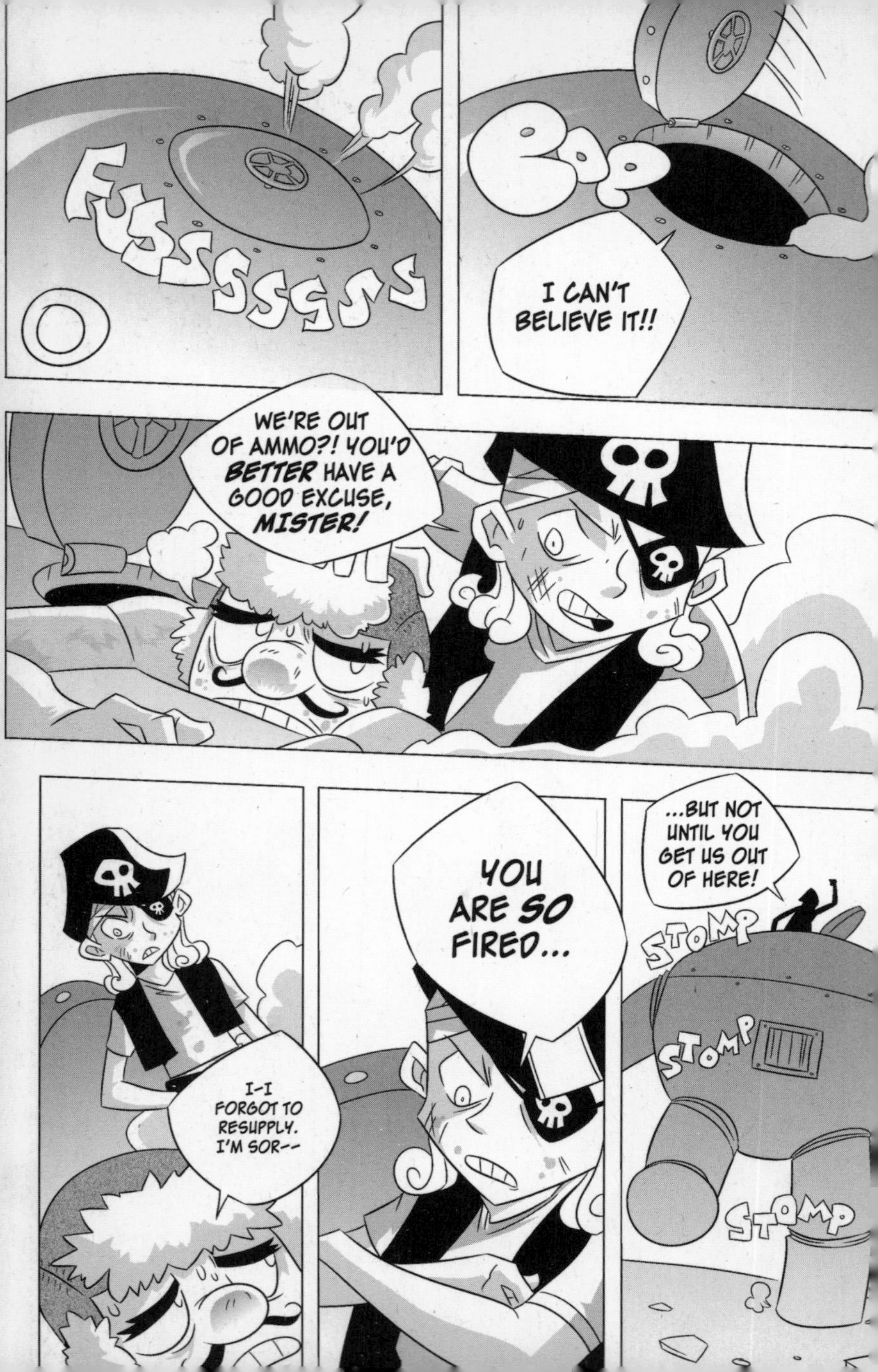
FUSSSSSS
POP
I CAN'T BELIEVE IT!!
WE'RE OUT OF AMMO?! YOU'D BETTER HAVE A GOOD EXCUSE, MISTER!
I-I FORGOT TO RESUPPLY. I'M SOR--
YOU ARE SO FIRED...
...BUT NOT UNTIL YOU GET US OUT OF HERE!
STOMP
STOMP
STOMP

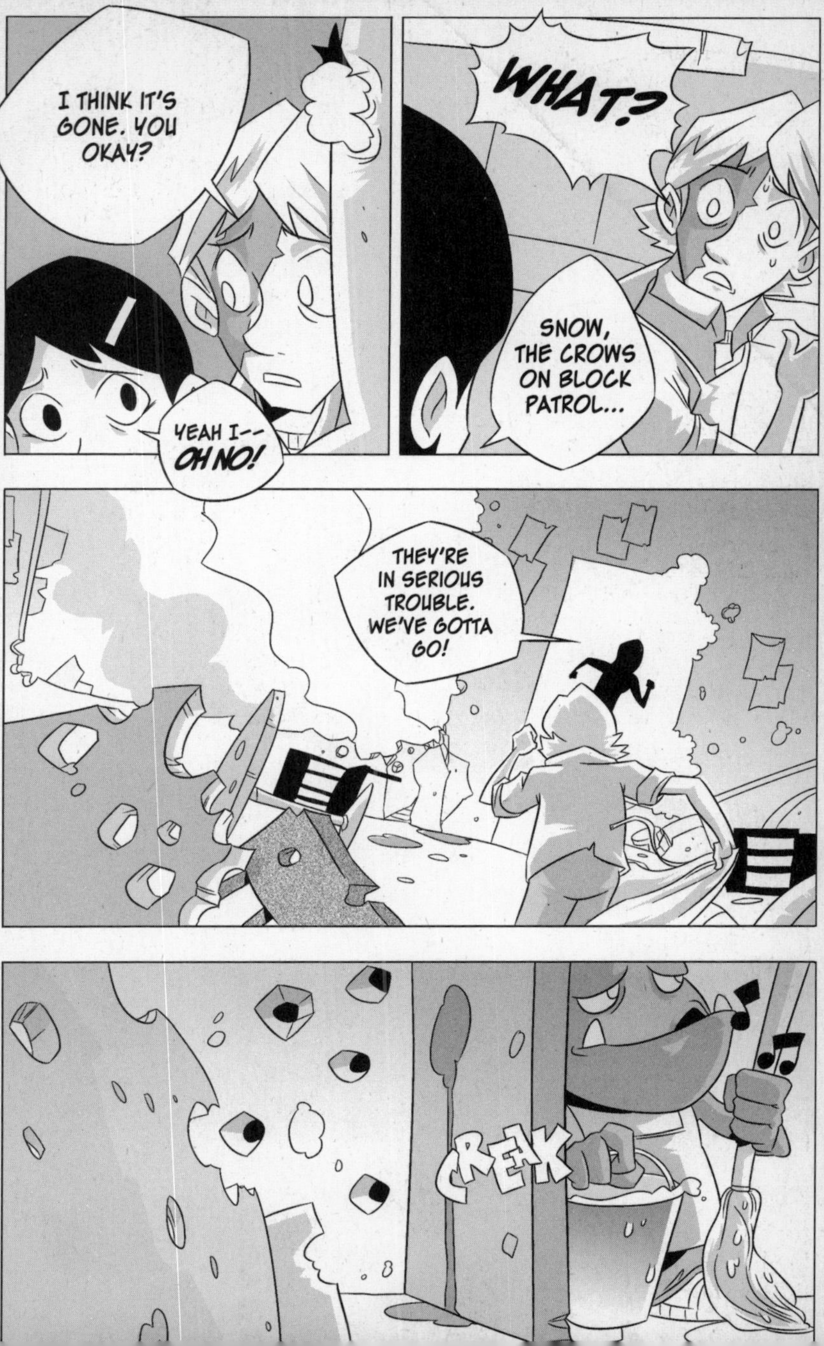
I THINK IT'S GONE. YOU OKAY?
YEAH I-- OH NO!
WHAT?
SNOW, THE CROWS ON BLOCK PATROL...
THEY'RE IN SERIOUS TROUBLE. WE'VE GOTTA GO!
CREAK

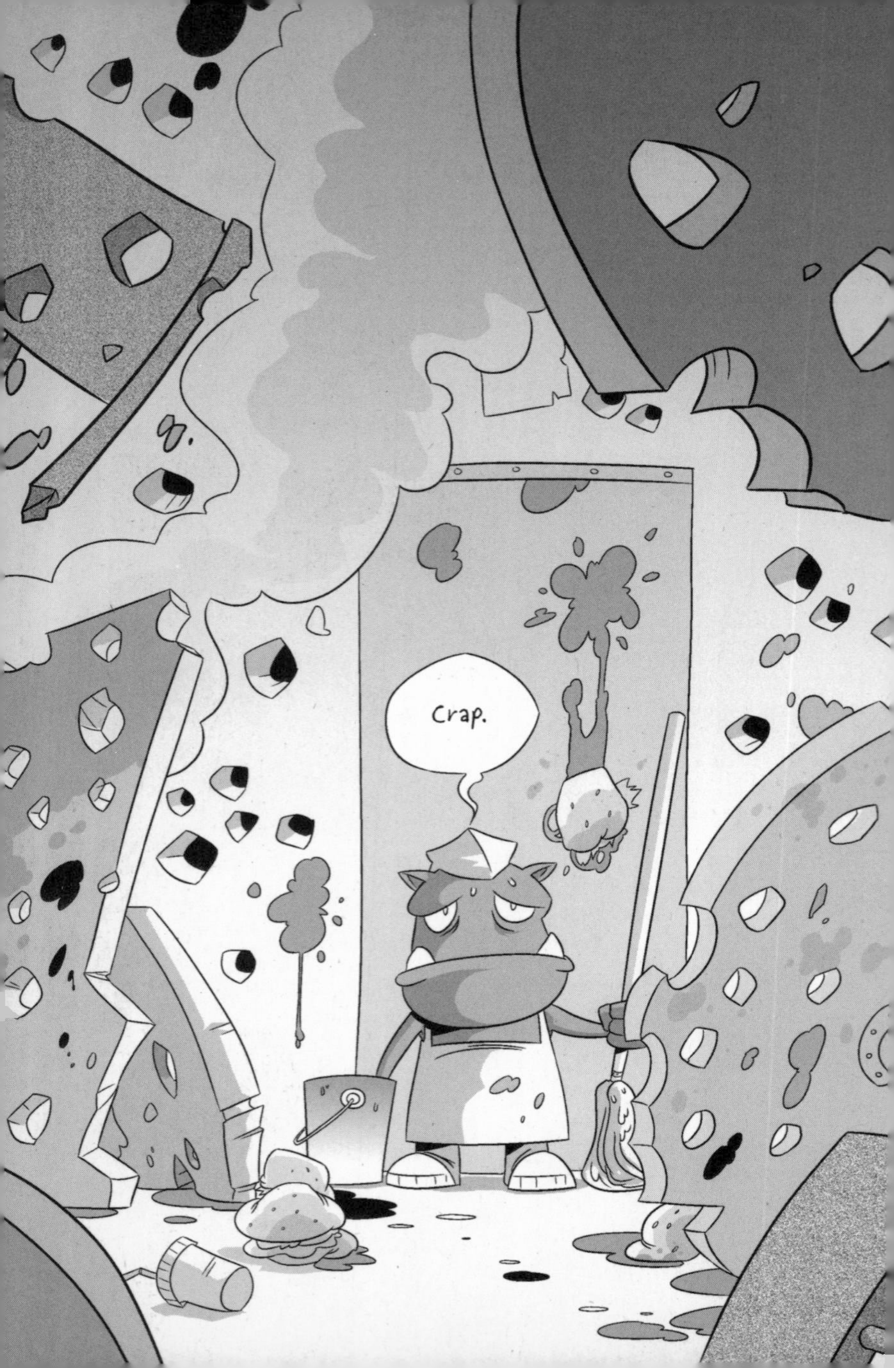
Crap.

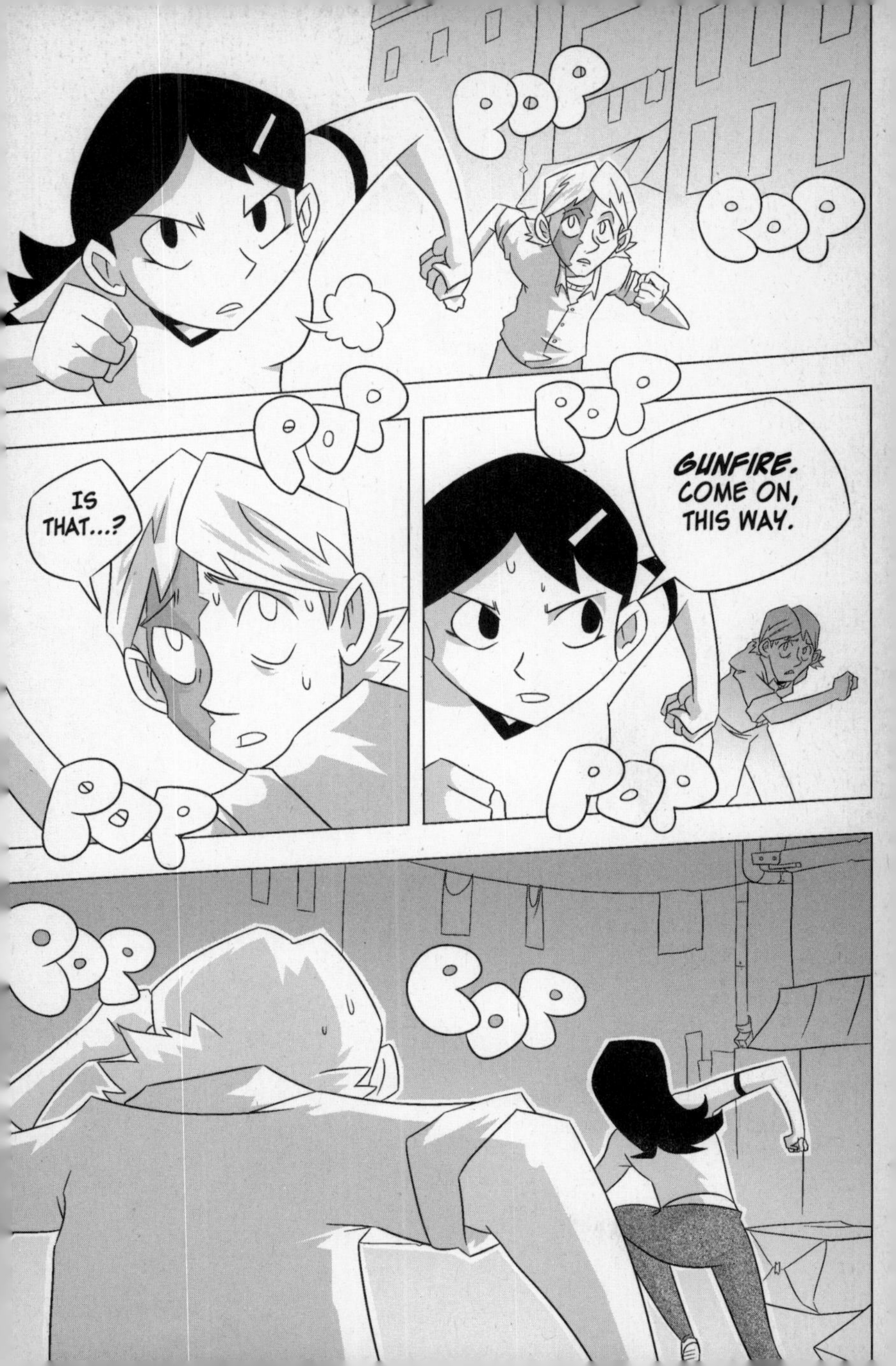
POP
POP
POP
IS THAT...?
POP
POP
GUNFIRE. COME ON, THIS WAY.
POP
POP
POP

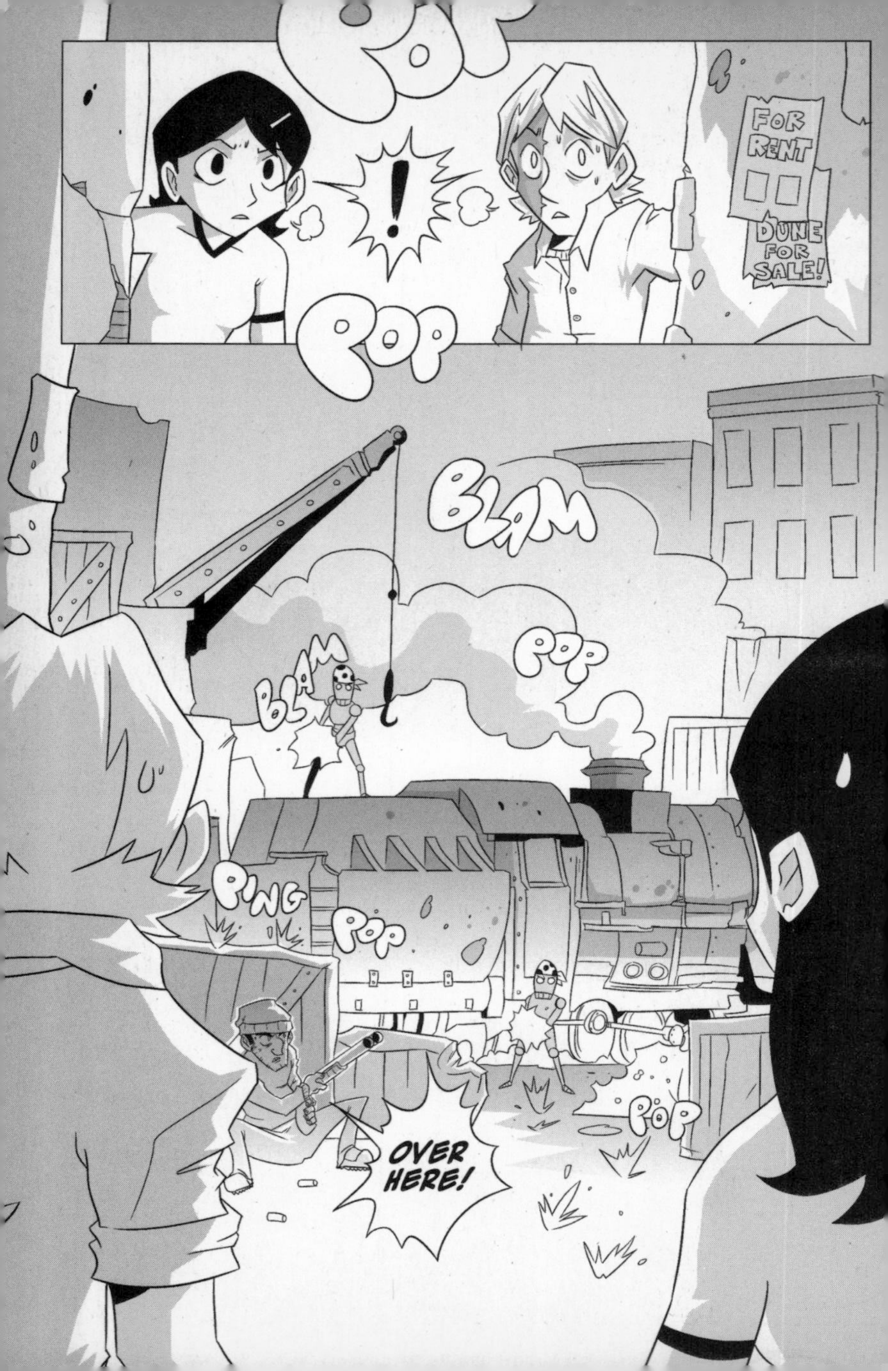
FOR RENT
DUNE FOR SALE!
POP
!
POP
BLAM
POP
BLAM
POP
PING
POP
OVER HERE!

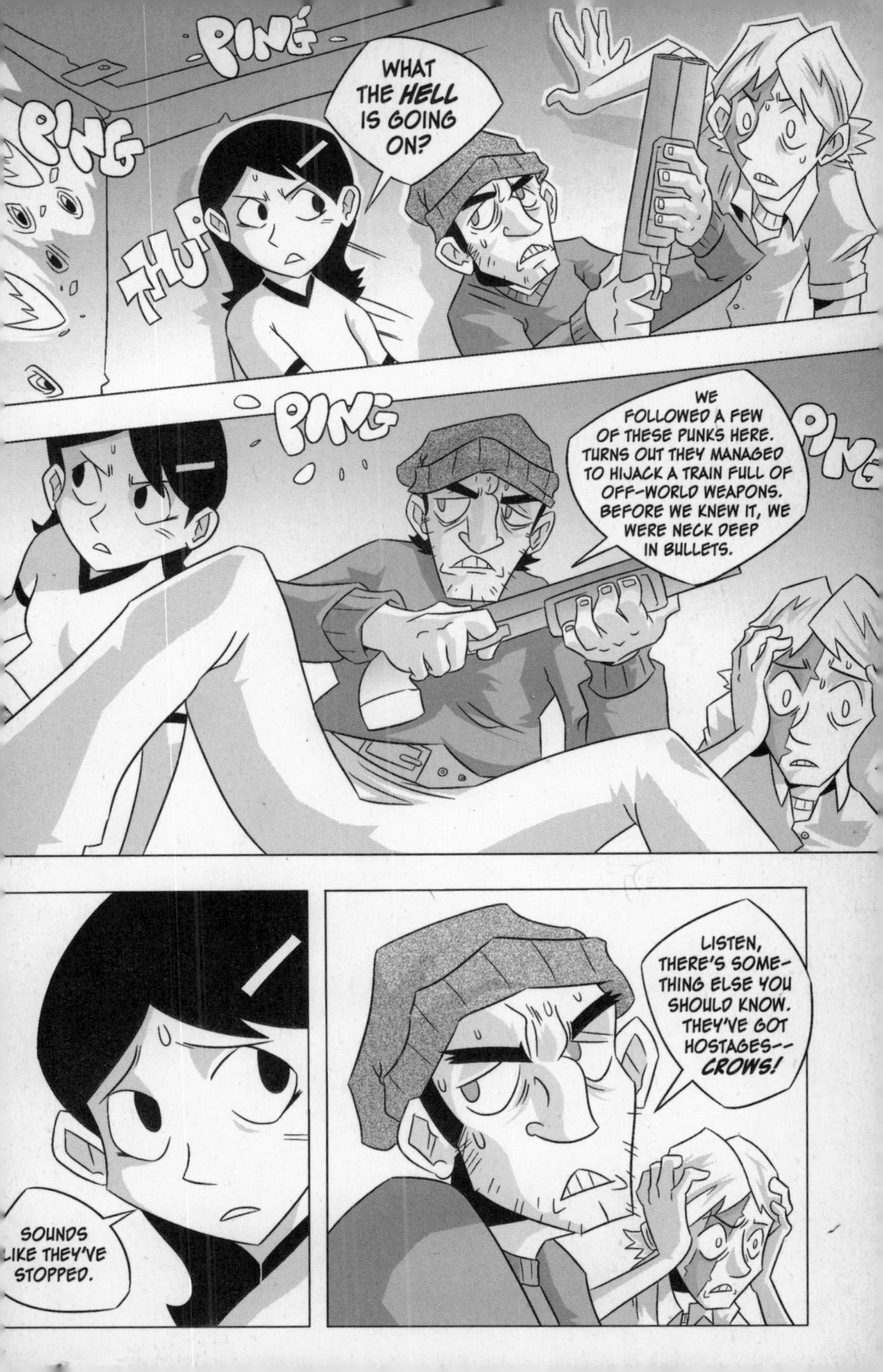
PING
PING
THUP
WHAT THE *HELL* IS GOING ON?
PING
WE FOLLOWED A FEW OF THESE PUNKS HERE. TURNS OUT THEY MANAGED TO HIJACK A TRAIN FULL OF OFF-WORLD WEAPONS. BEFORE WE KNEW IT, WE WERE NECK DEEP IN BULLETS.
PING
SOUNDS LIKE THEY'VE STOPPED.
LISTEN, THERE'S SOME-THING ELSE YOU SHOULD KNOW. THEY'VE GOT HOSTAGES-- *CROWS!*

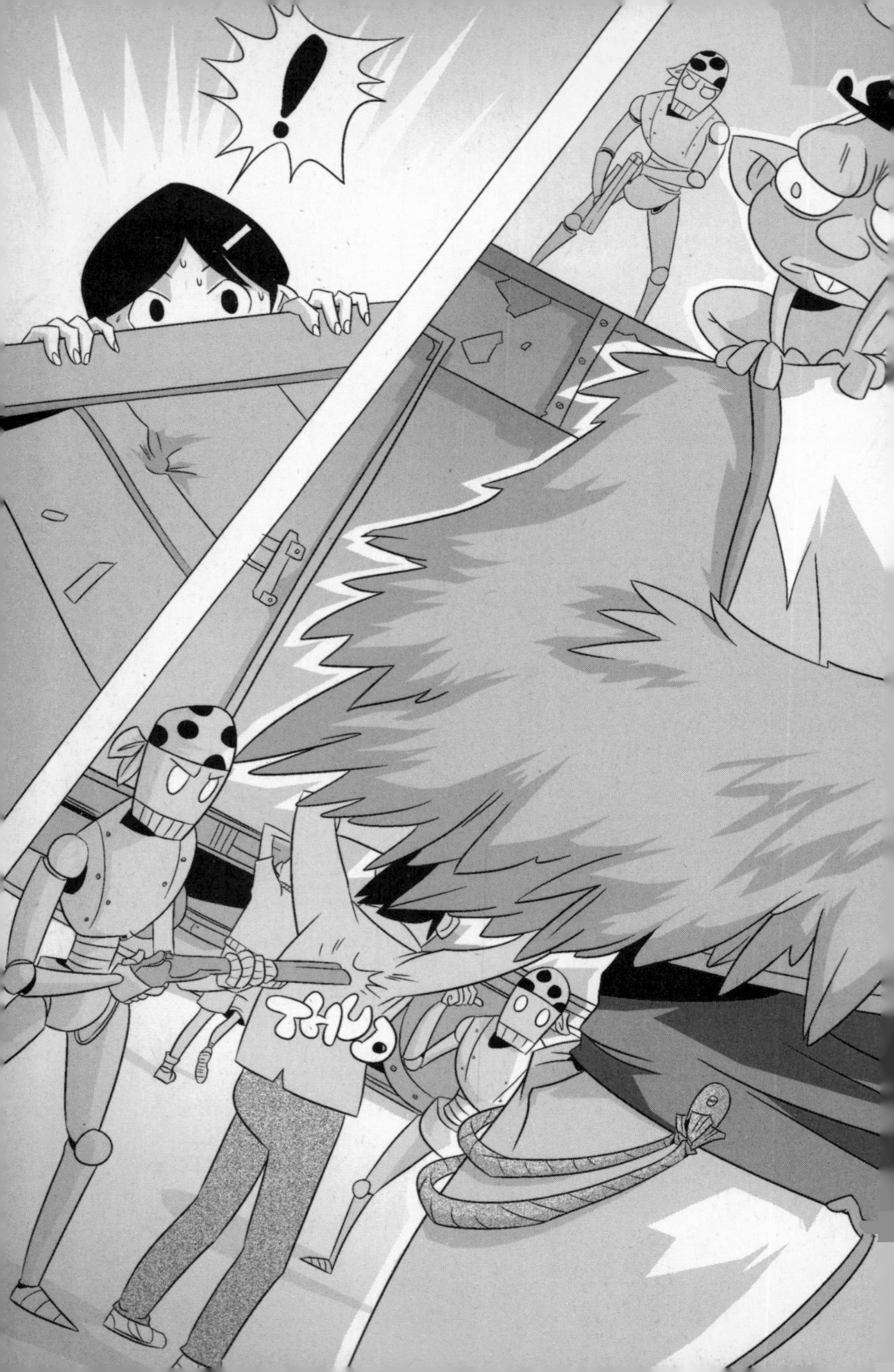
!
THUD

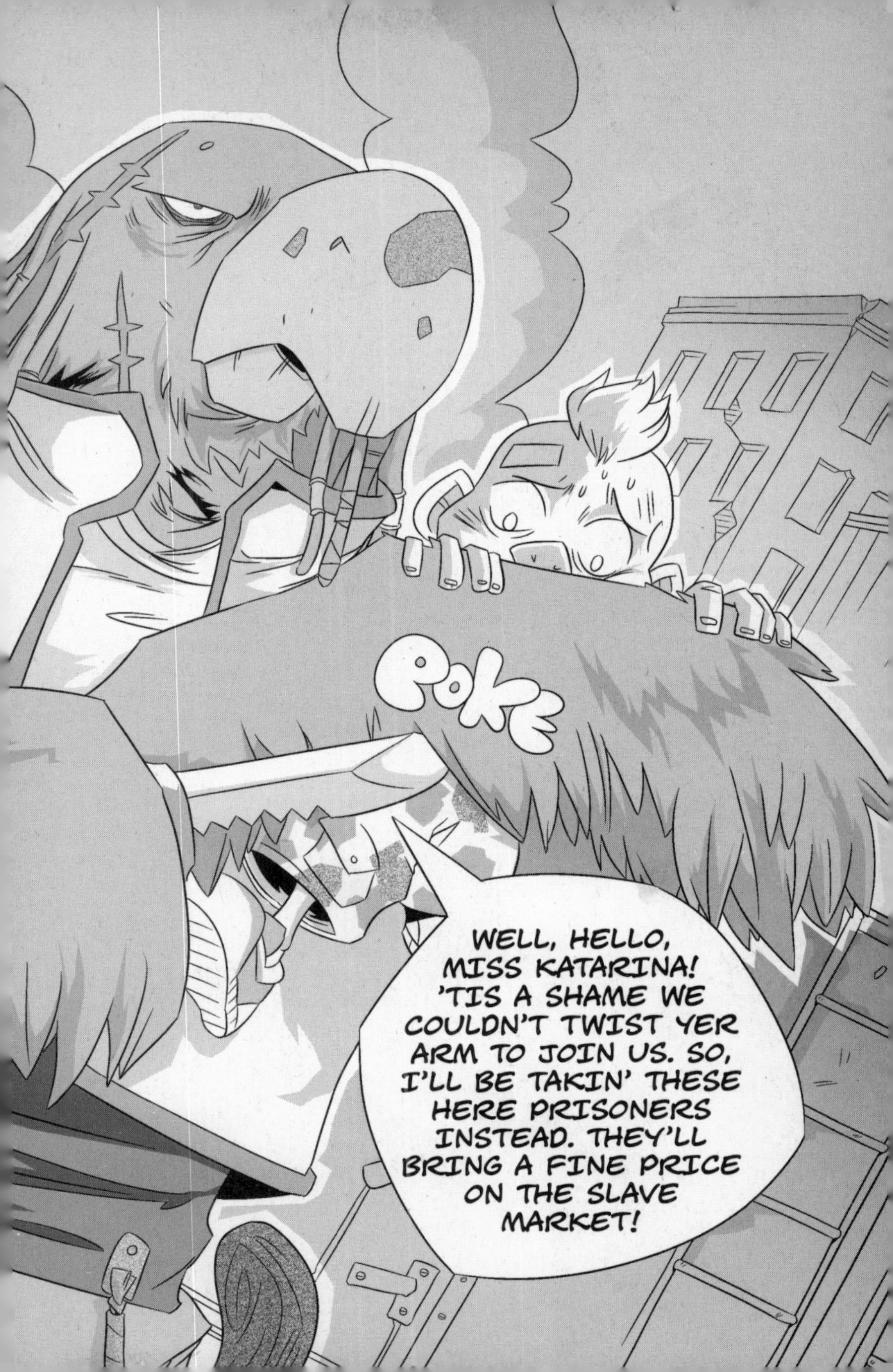
POKE
WELL, HELLO, MISS KATARINA! 'TIS A SHAME WE COULDN'T TWIST YER ARM TO JOIN US. SO, I'LL BE TAKIN' THESE HERE PRISONERS INSTEAD. THEY'LL BRING A FINE PRICE ON THE SLAVE MARKET!

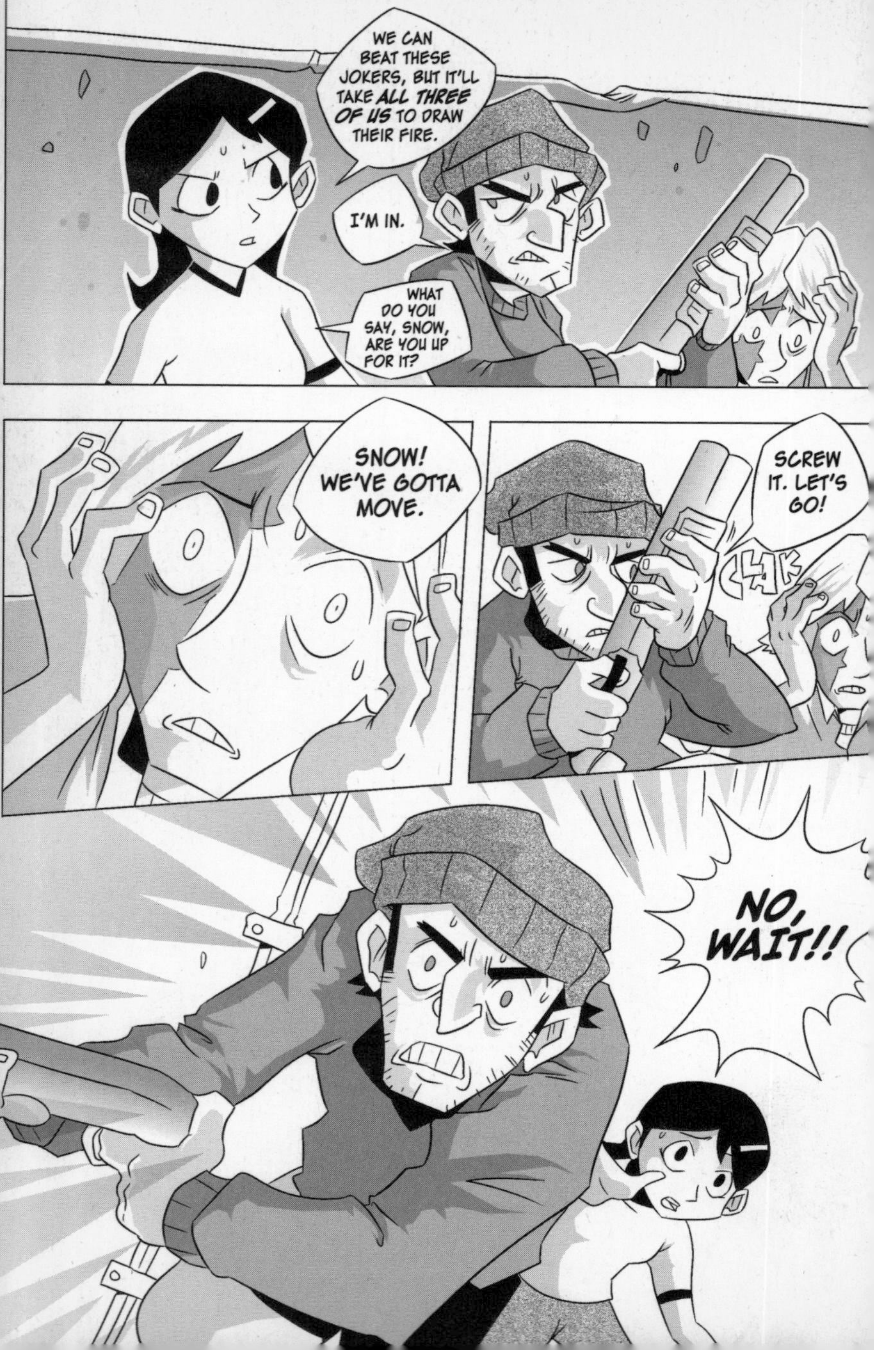
WE CAN BEAT THESE JOKERS, BUT IT'LL TAKE ***ALL THREE OF US*** TO DRAW THEIR FIRE.
I'M IN.
WHAT DO YOU SAY, SNOW, ARE YOU UP FOR IT?
SNOW! WE'VE GOTTA MOVE.
SCREW IT. LET'S GO!
CLAK
NO, WAIT!!

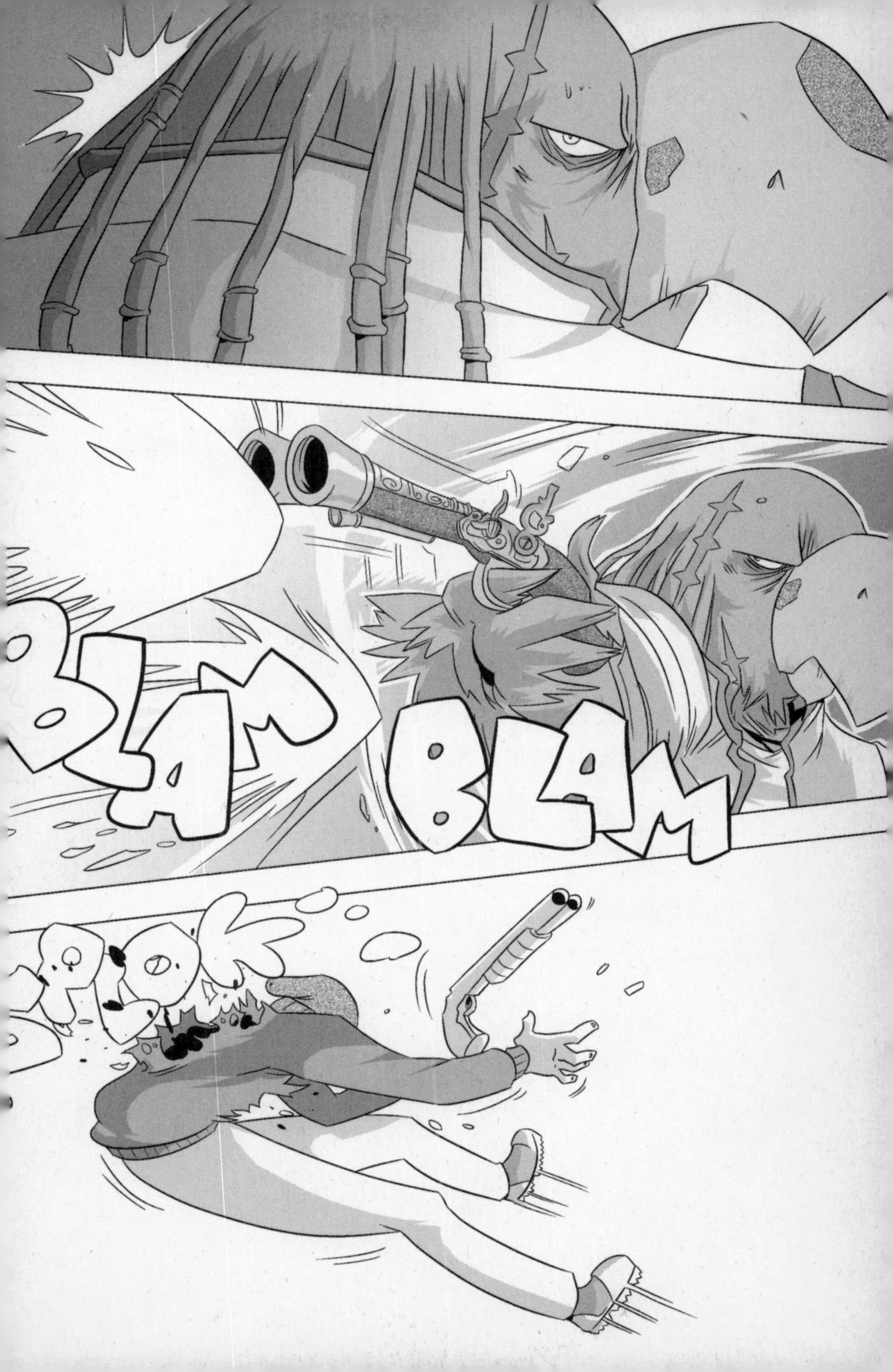
BLAM
BLAM

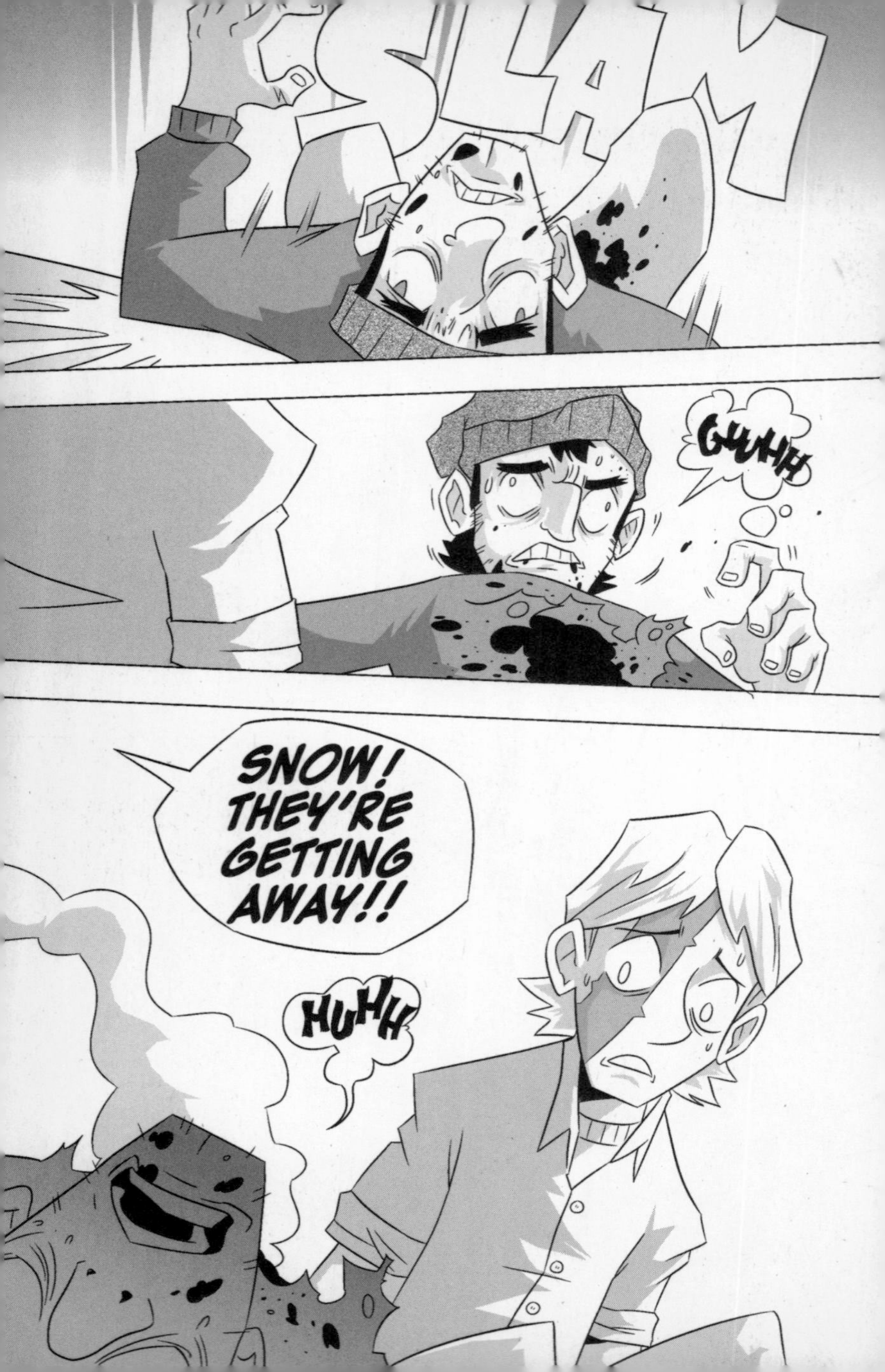
SLAM
GUUHH
SNOW! THEY'RE GETTING AWAY!!
HUHH

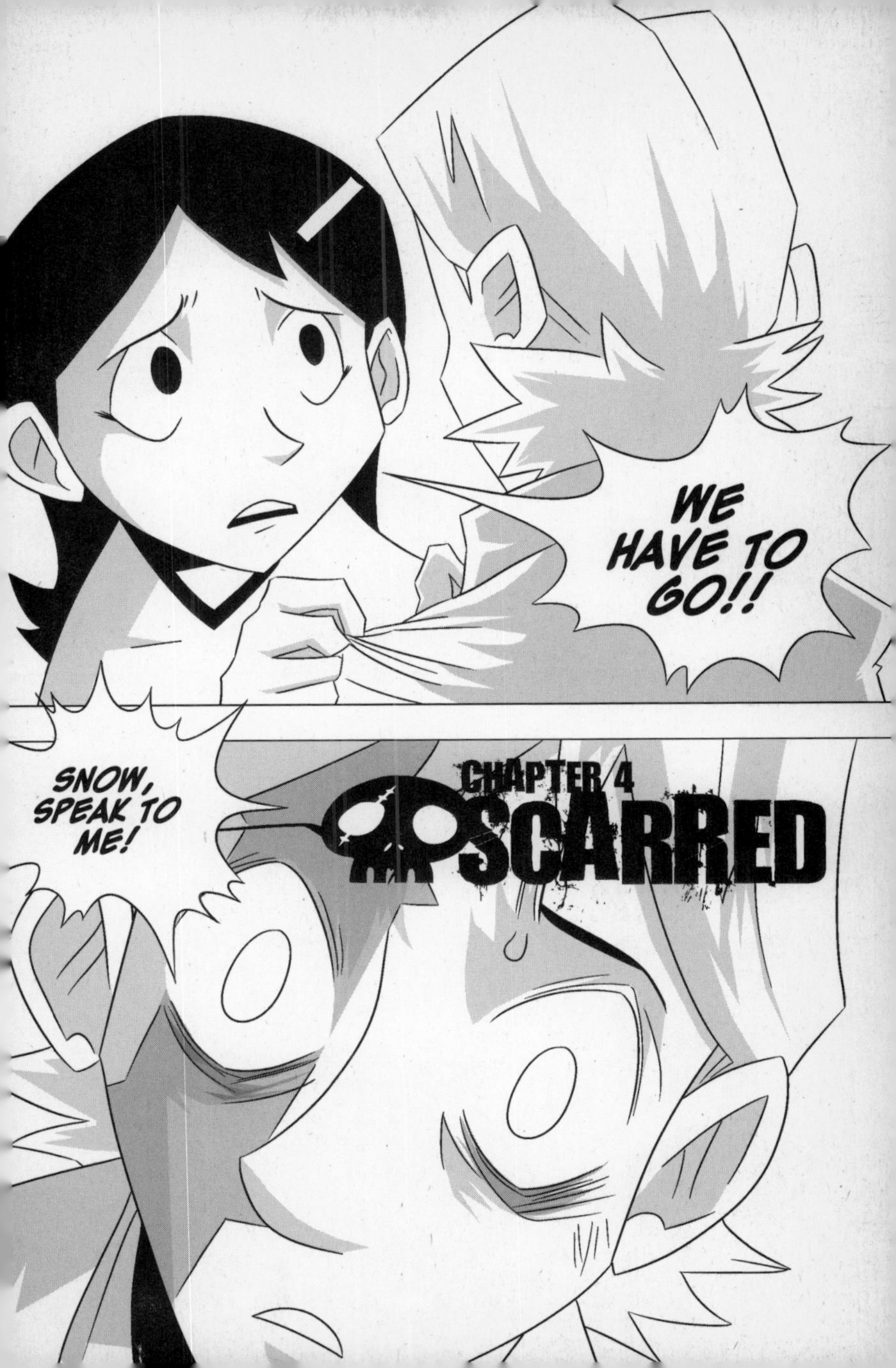
WE HAVE TO GO!!
CHAPTER 4
SCARRED
SNOW, SPEAK TO ME!

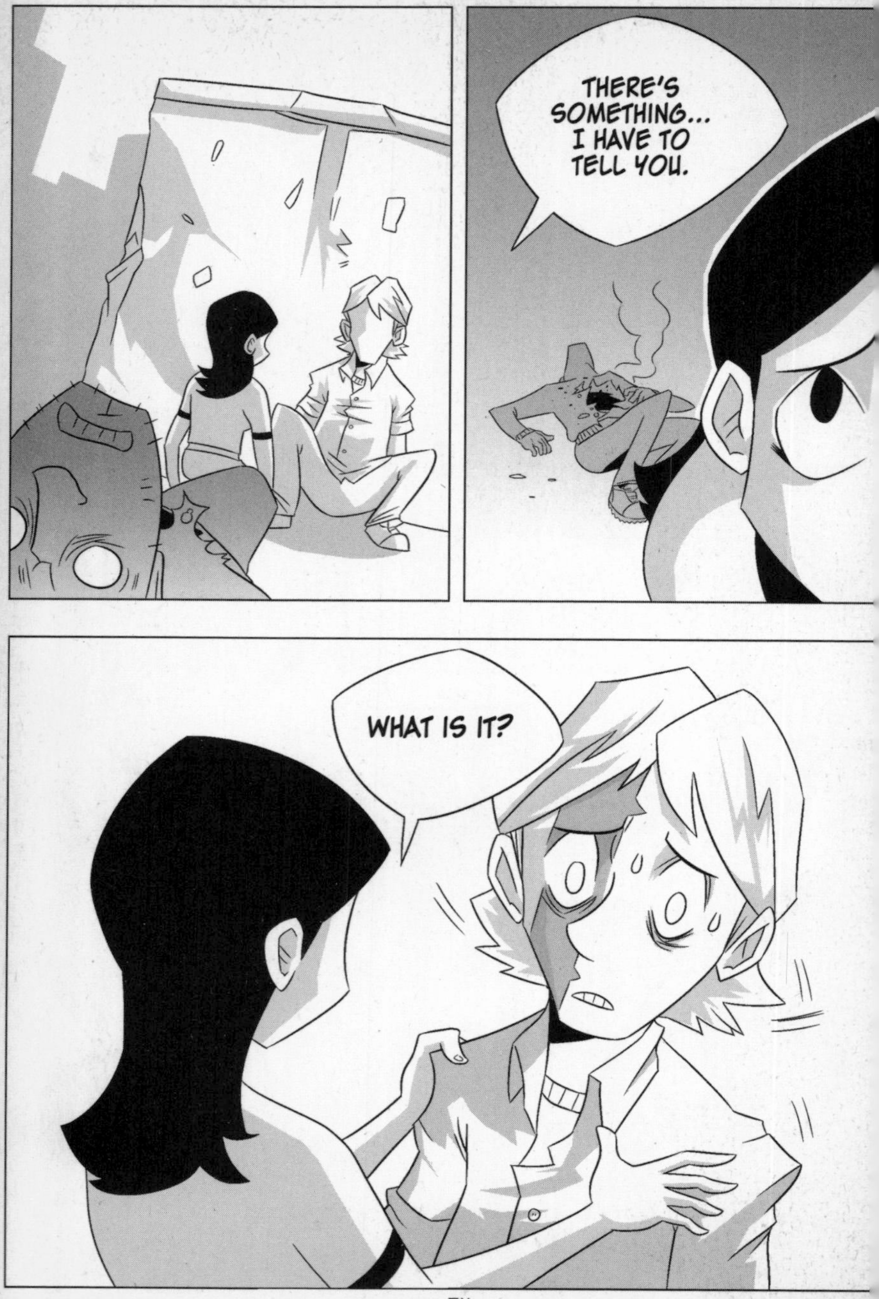
THERE'S SOMETHING... I HAVE TO TELL YOU.
WHAT IS IT?

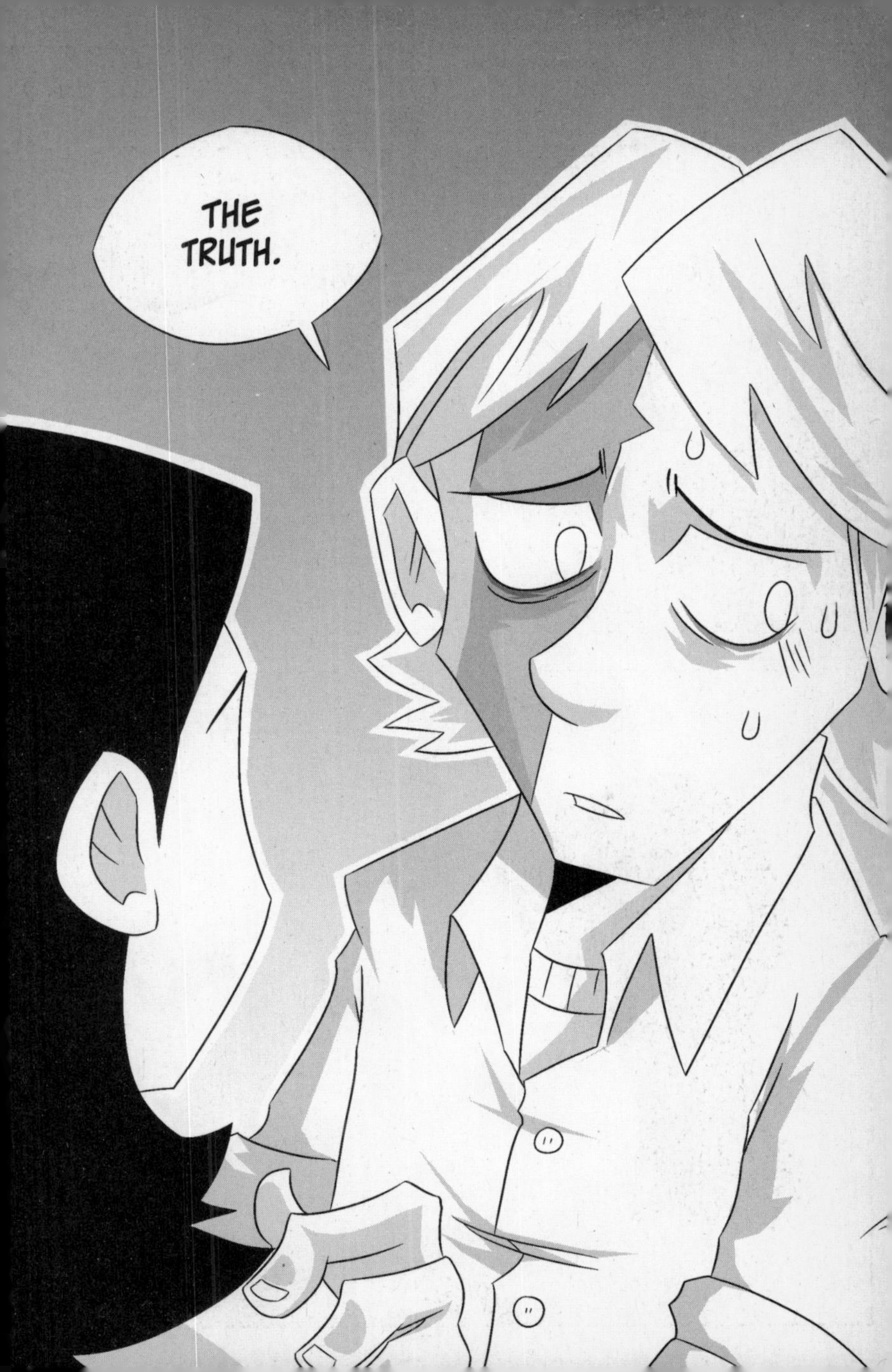
THE TRUTH.

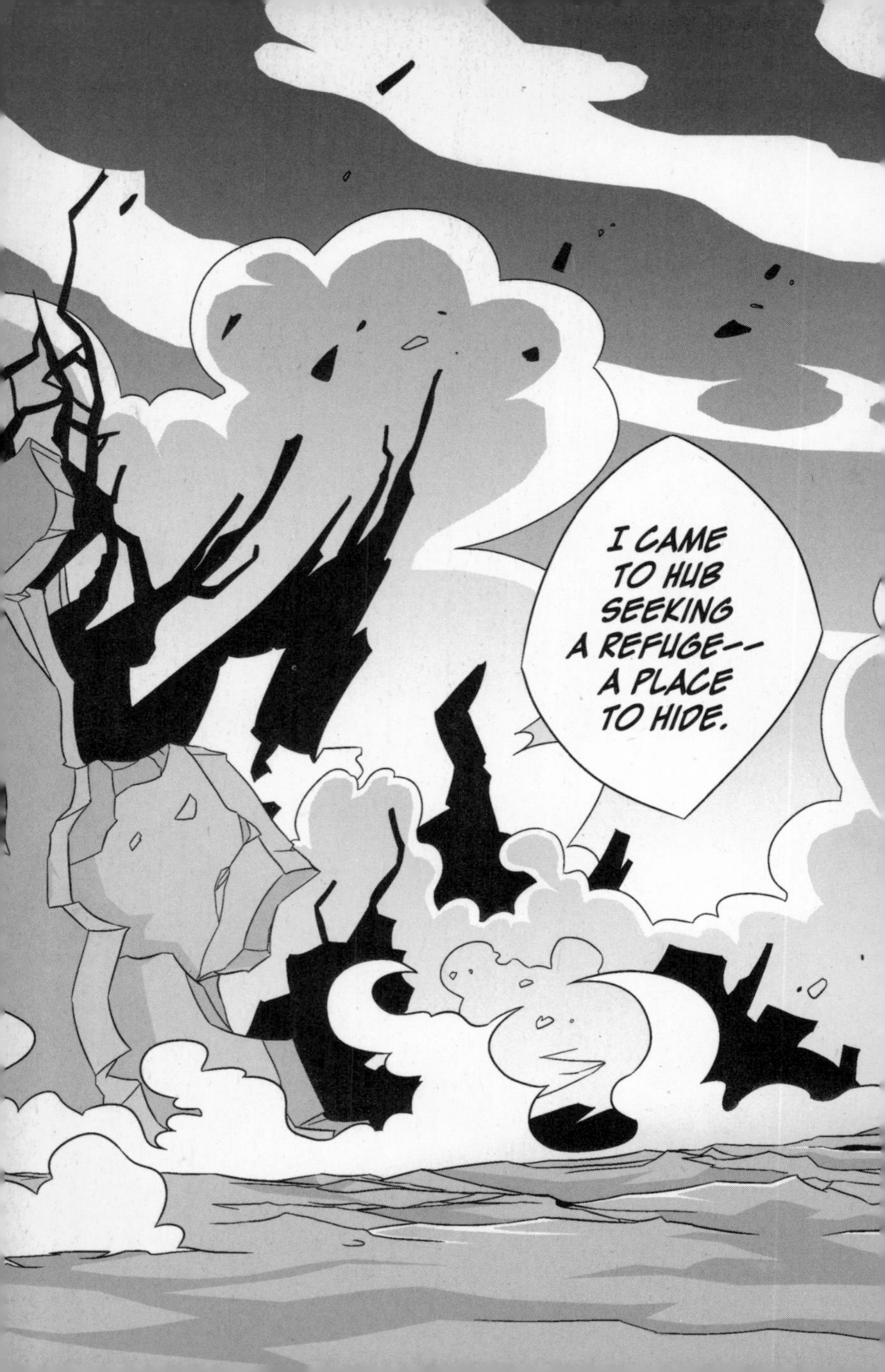
I CAME TO HUB SEEKING A REFUGE-- A PLACE TO HIDE.

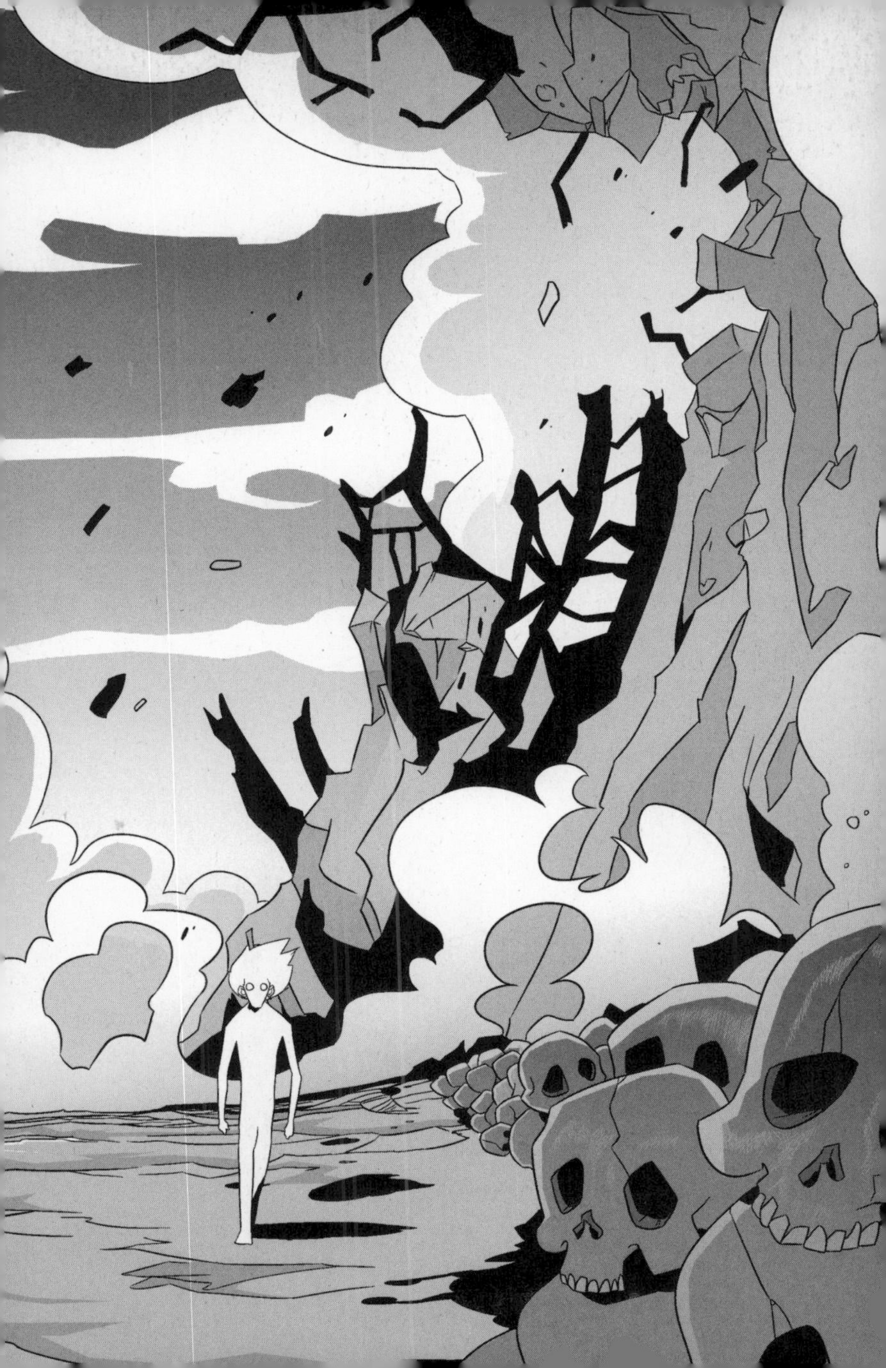

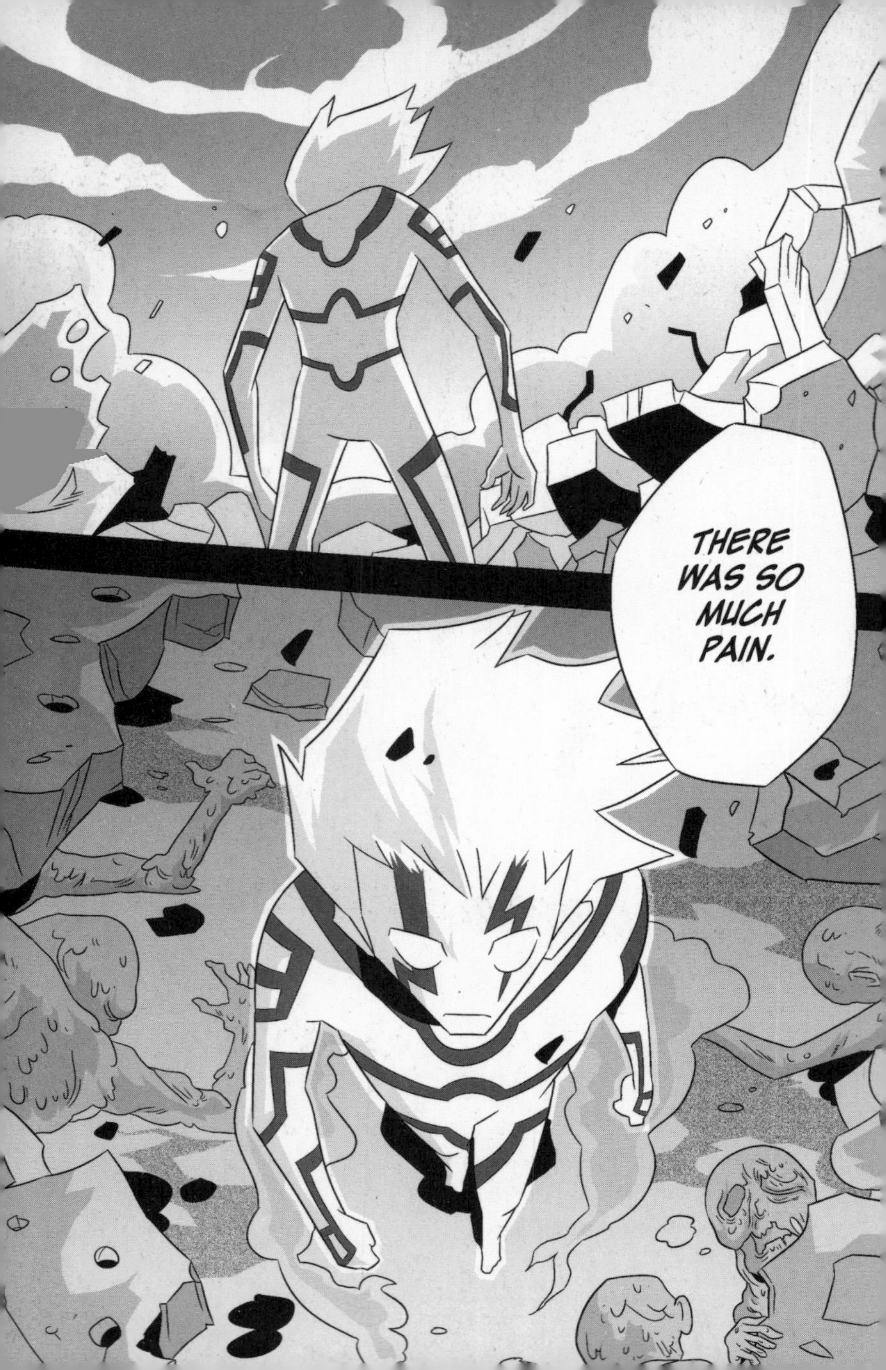
THERE WAS SO MUCH PAIN.

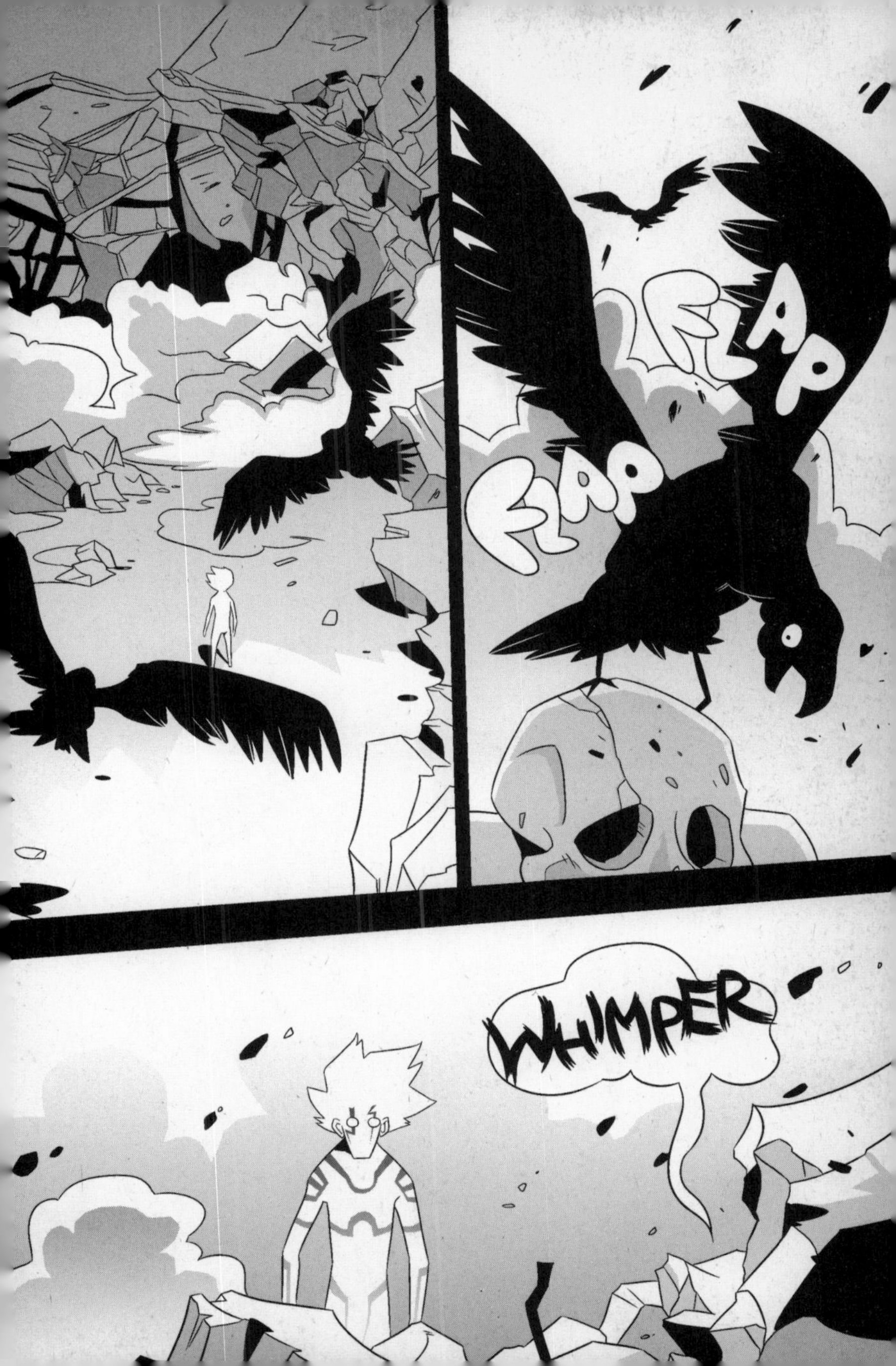
FLAP
FLAP
WHIMPER

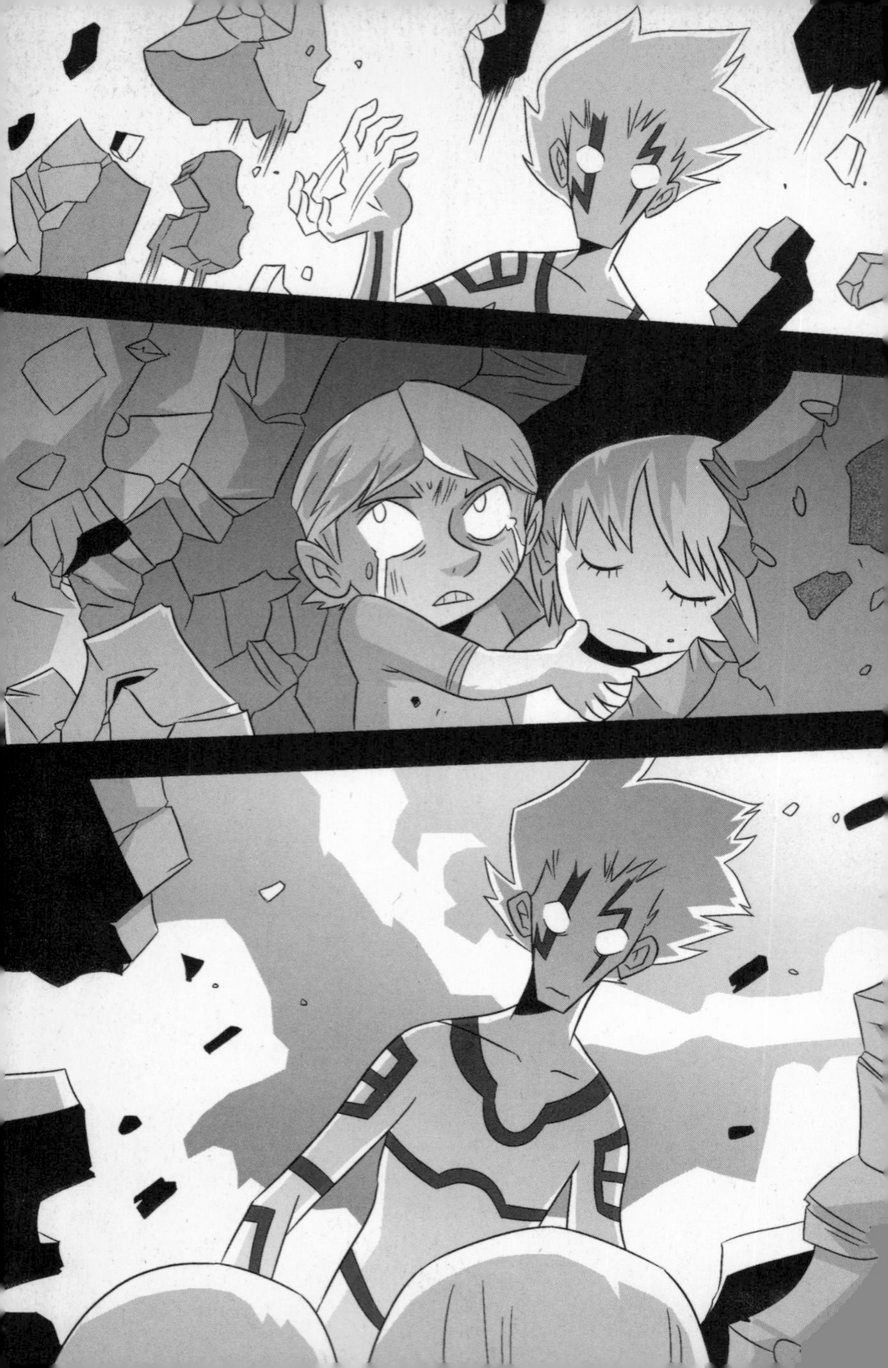

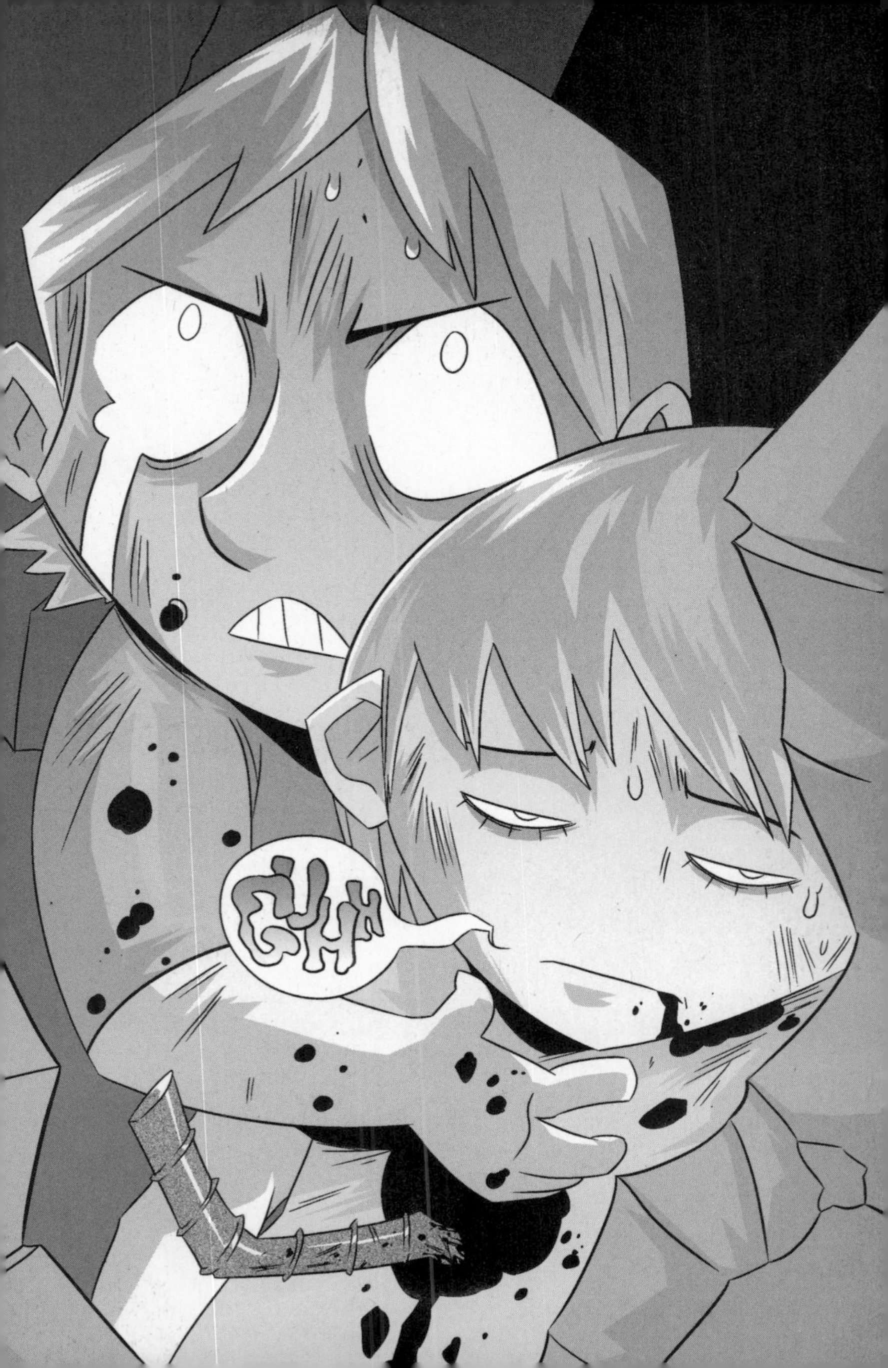
GUH

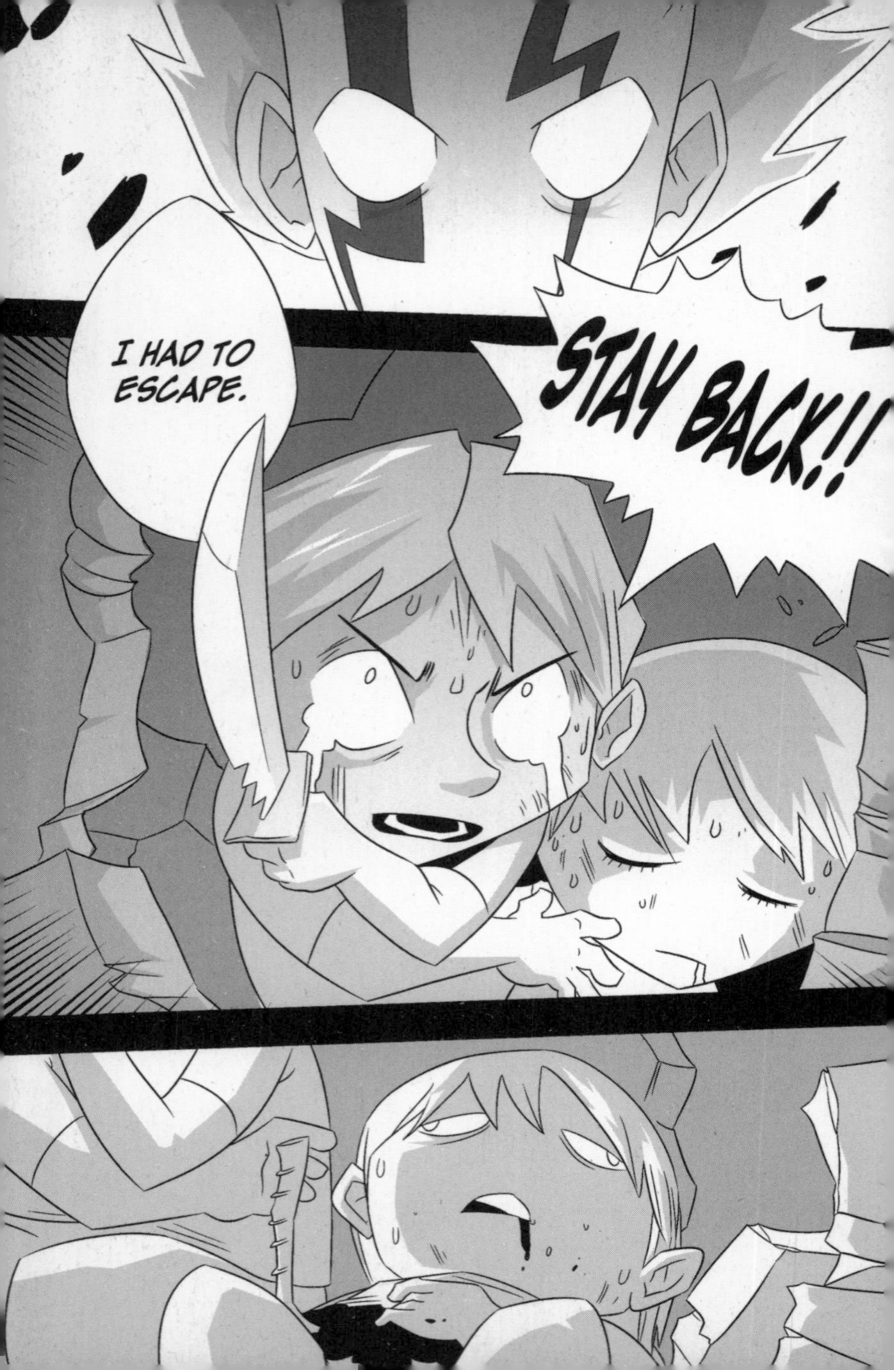
STAY BACK!!
I HAD TO ESCAPE.

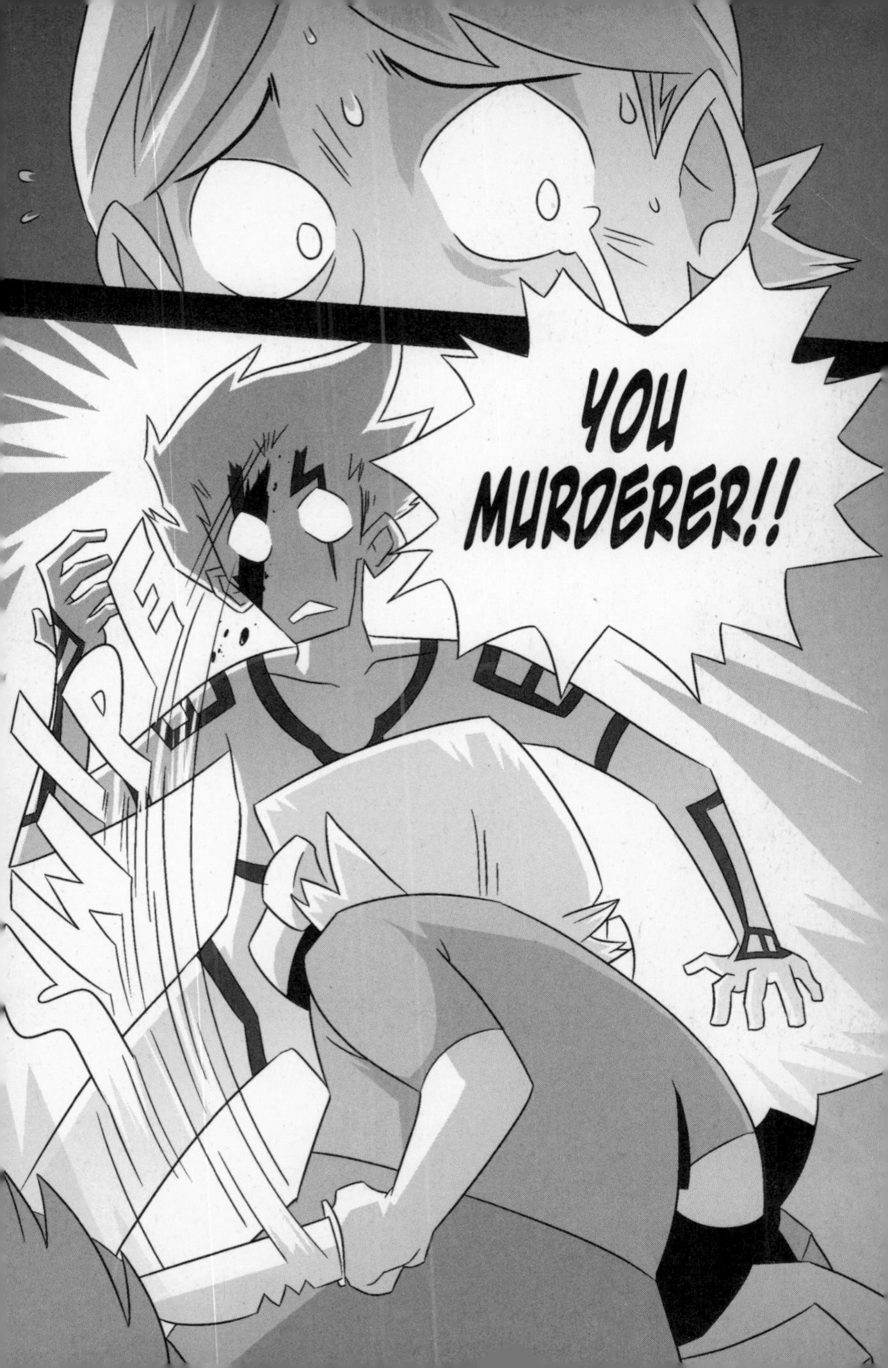
YOU MURDERER!!

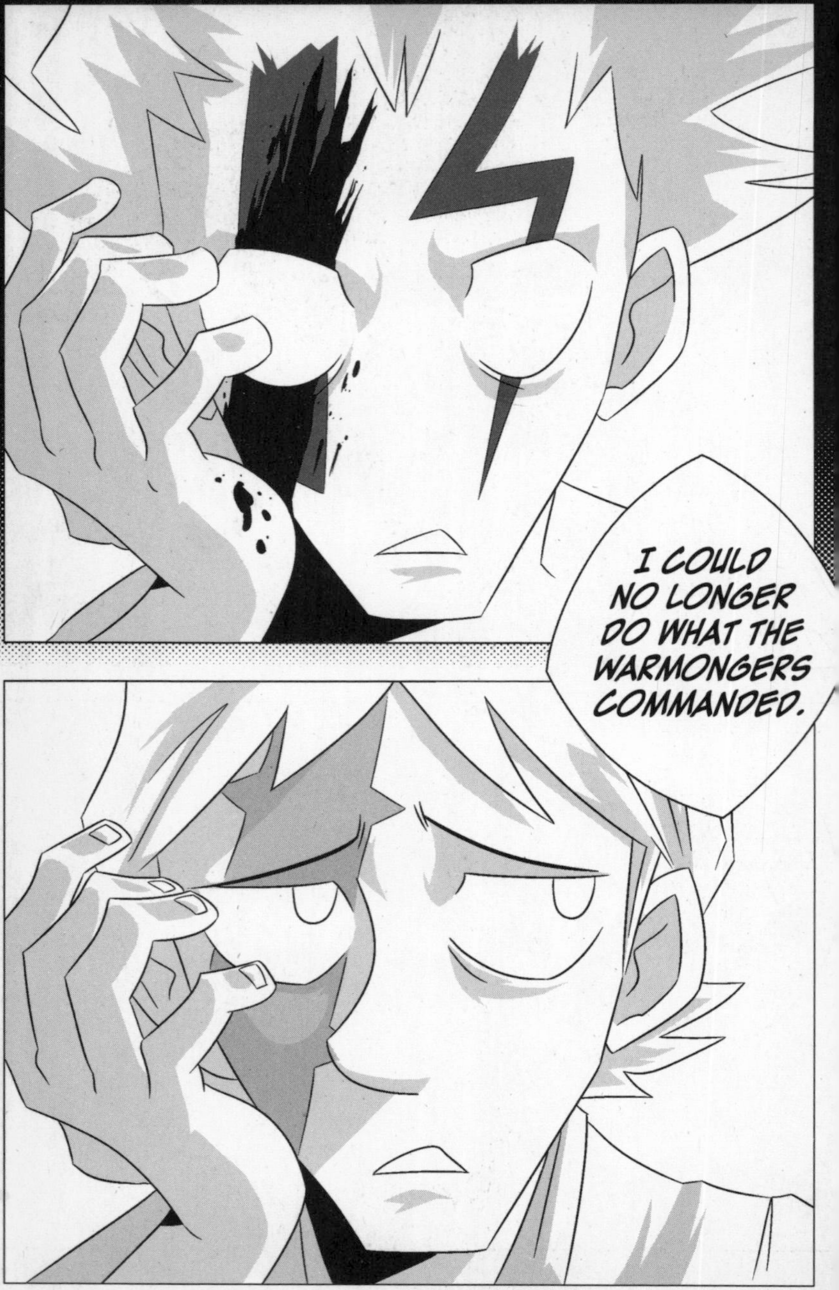
I COULD NO LONGER DO WHAT THE WARMONGERS COMMANDED.

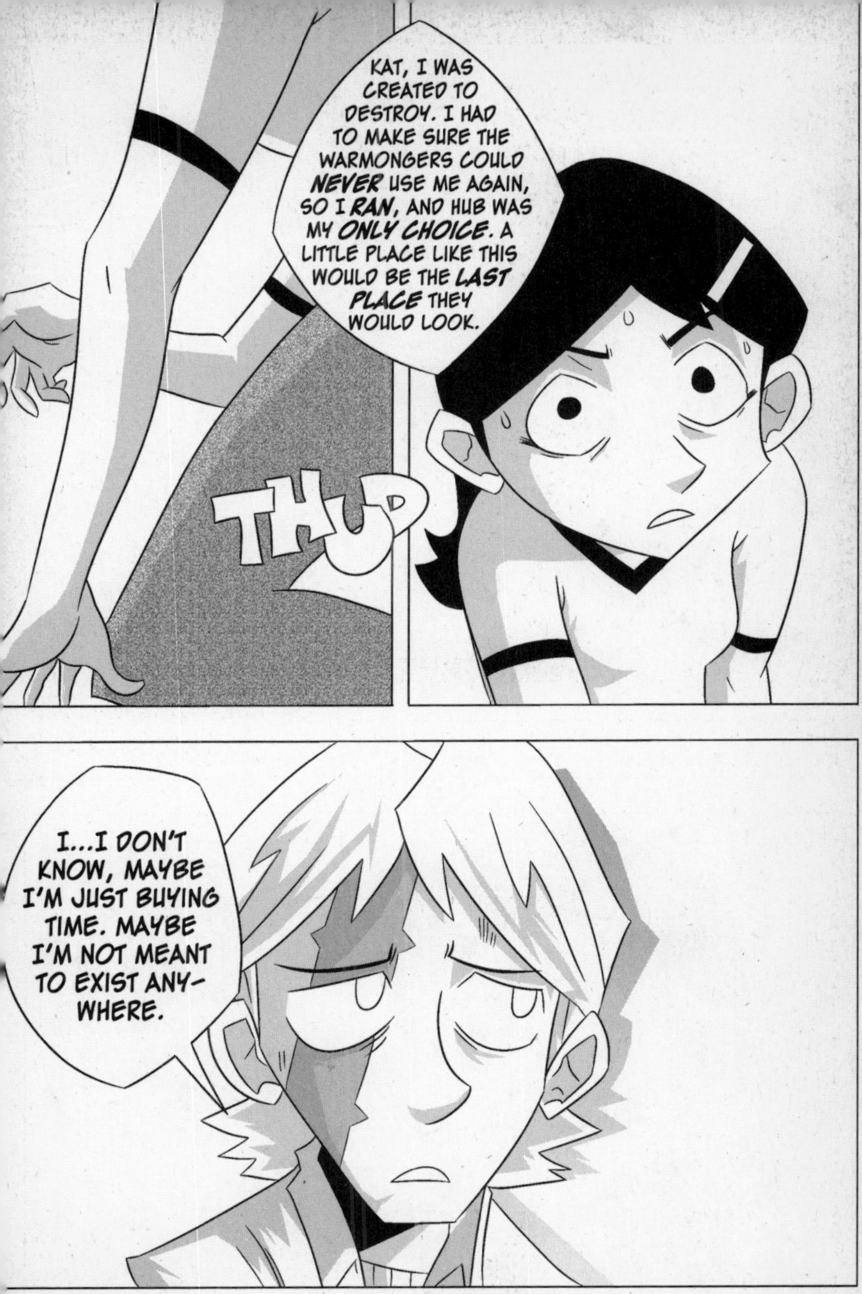
KAT, I WAS CREATED TO DESTROY. I HAD TO MAKE SURE THE WARMONGERS COULD NEVER USE ME AGAIN, SO I RAN, AND HUB WAS MY ONLY CHOICE. A LITTLE PLACE LIKE THIS WOULD BE THE LAST PLACE THEY WOULD LOOK.
THUD
I...I DON'T KNOW, MAYBE I'M JUST BUYING TIME. MAYBE I'M NOT MEANT TO EXIST ANY-WHERE.

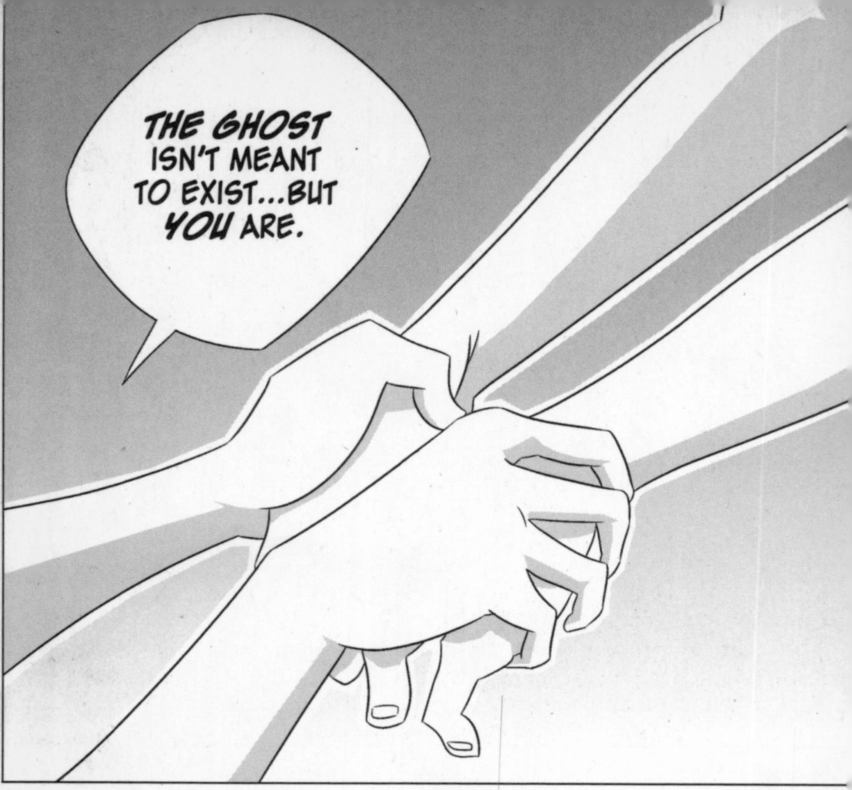
THE GHOST ISN'T MEANT TO EXIST...BUT YOU ARE.
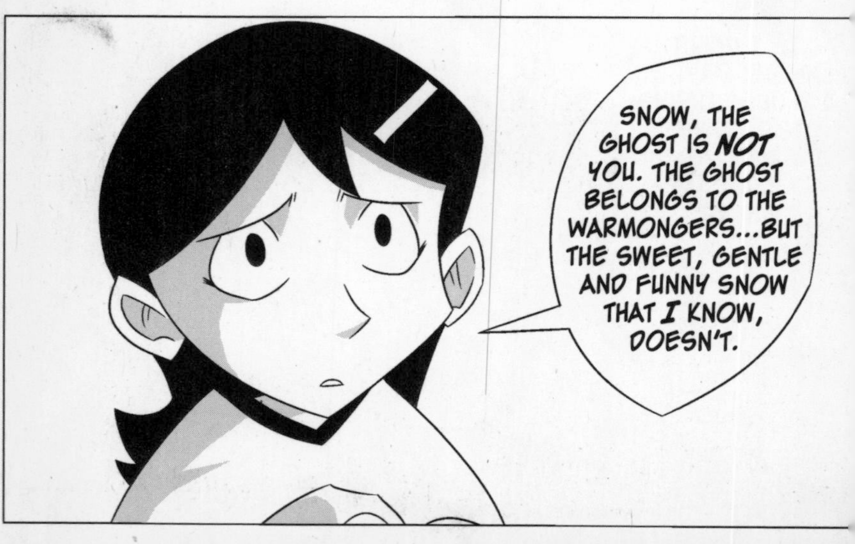
SNOW, THE GHOST IS NOT YOU. THE GHOST BELONGS TO THE WARMONGERS...BUT THE SWEET, GENTLE AND FUNNY SNOW THAT I KNOW, DOESN'T.

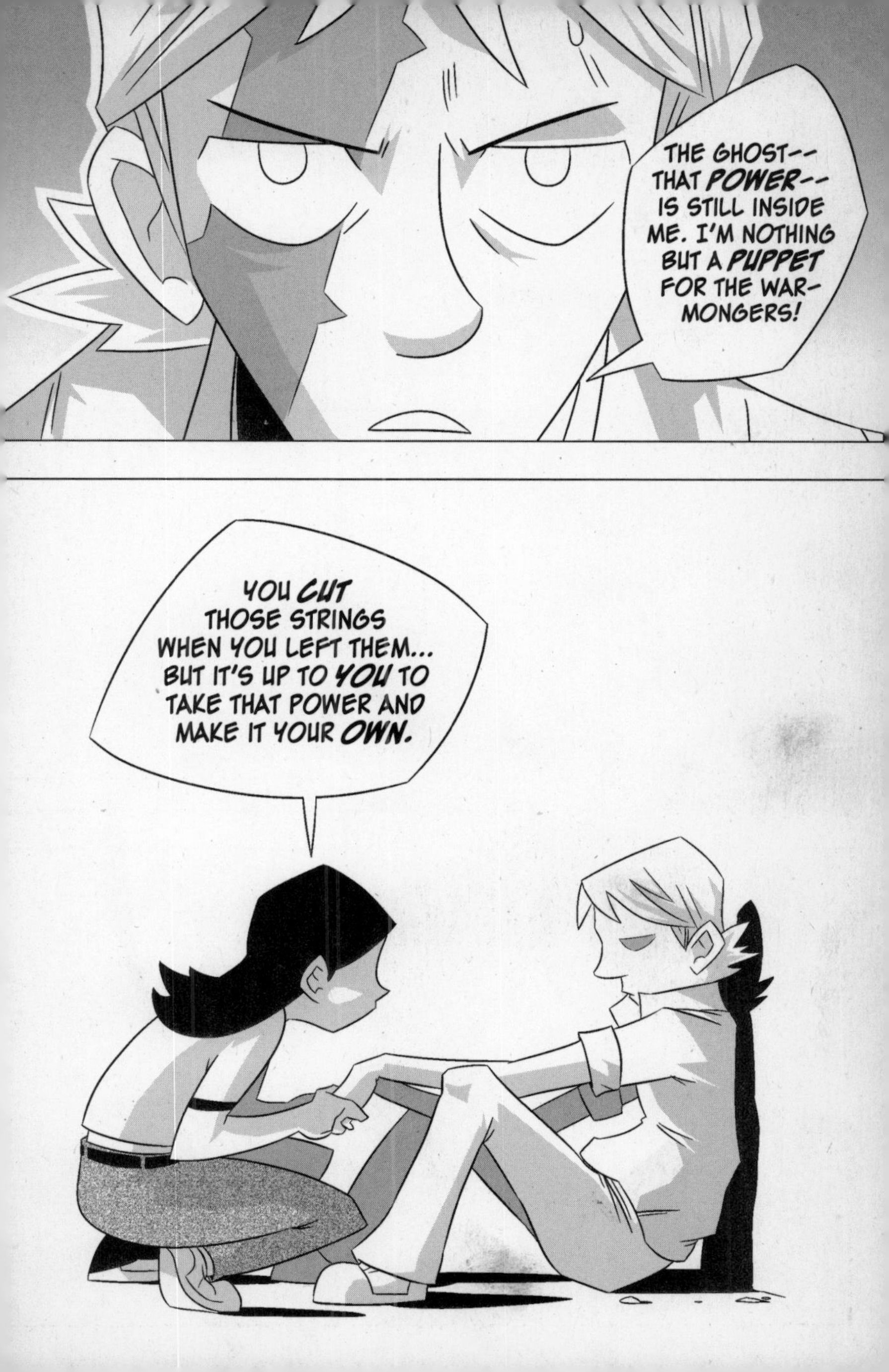
THE GHOST-- THAT POWER-- IS STILL INSIDE ME. I'M NOTHING BUT A PUPPET FOR THE WAR-MONGERS!
YOU CUT THOSE STRINGS WHEN YOU LEFT THEM... BUT IT'S UP TO YOU TO TAKE THAT POWER AND MAKE IT YOUR OWN.

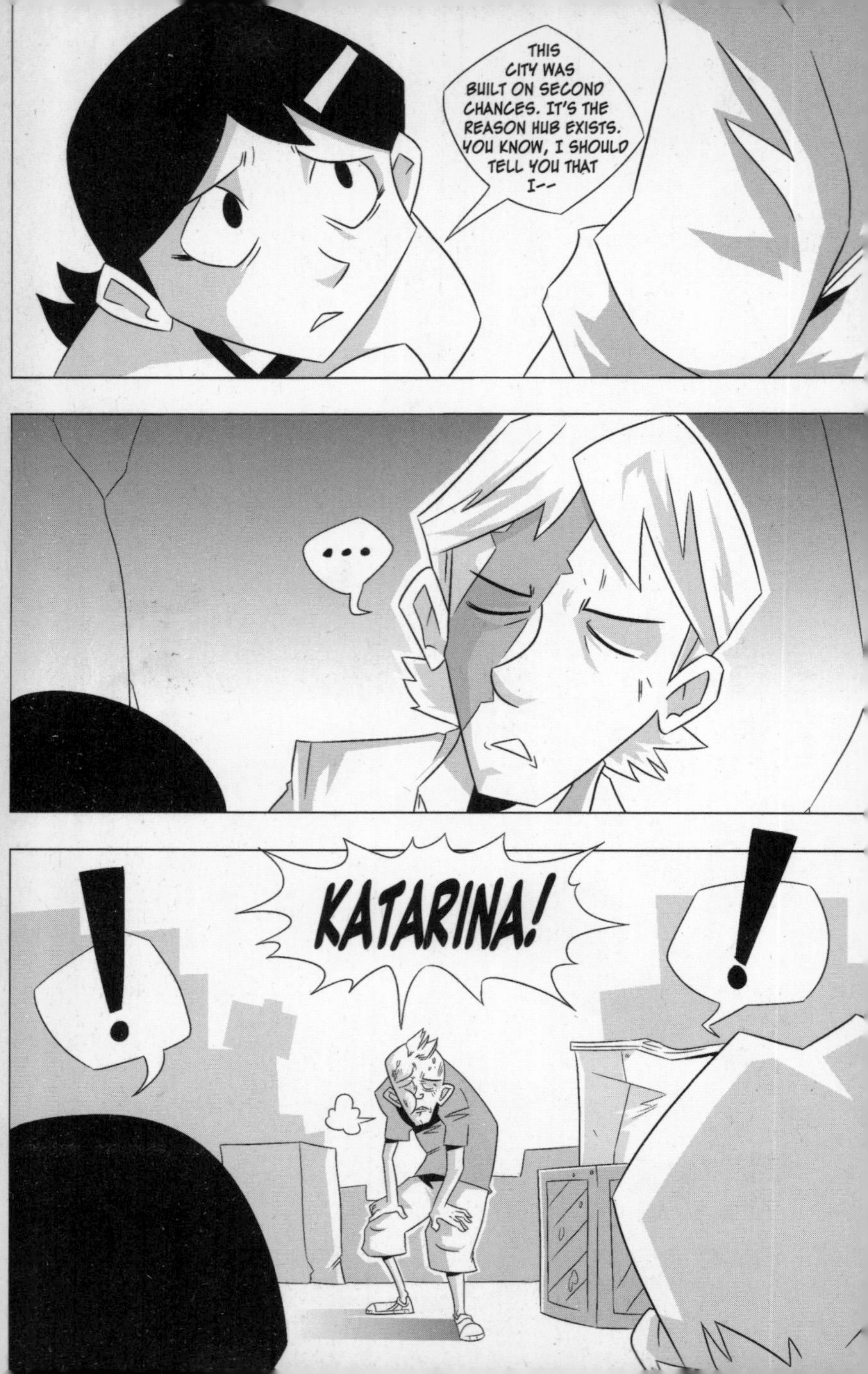
THIS CITY WAS BUILT ON SECOND CHANCES. IT'S THE REASON HUB EXISTS. YOU KNOW, I SHOULD TELL YOU THAT I--
...
!
KATARINA!
!

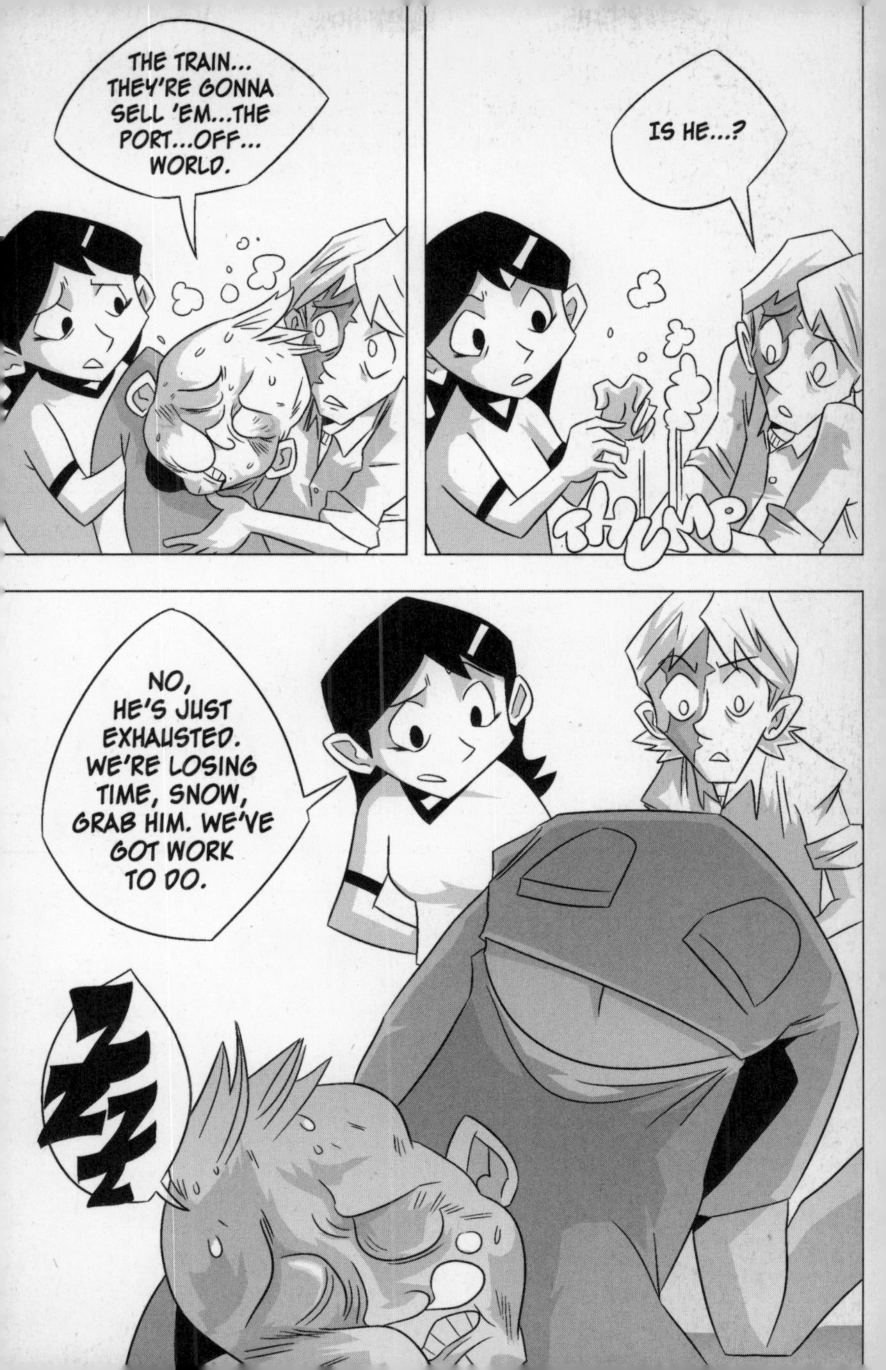
THE TRAIN... THEY'RE GONNA SELL 'EM...THE PORT...OFF... WORLD.
IS HE...?
THUMP
NO, HE'S JUST EXHAUSTED. WE'RE LOSING TIME, SNOW, GRAB HIM. WE'VE GOT WORK TO DO.
ZZZ

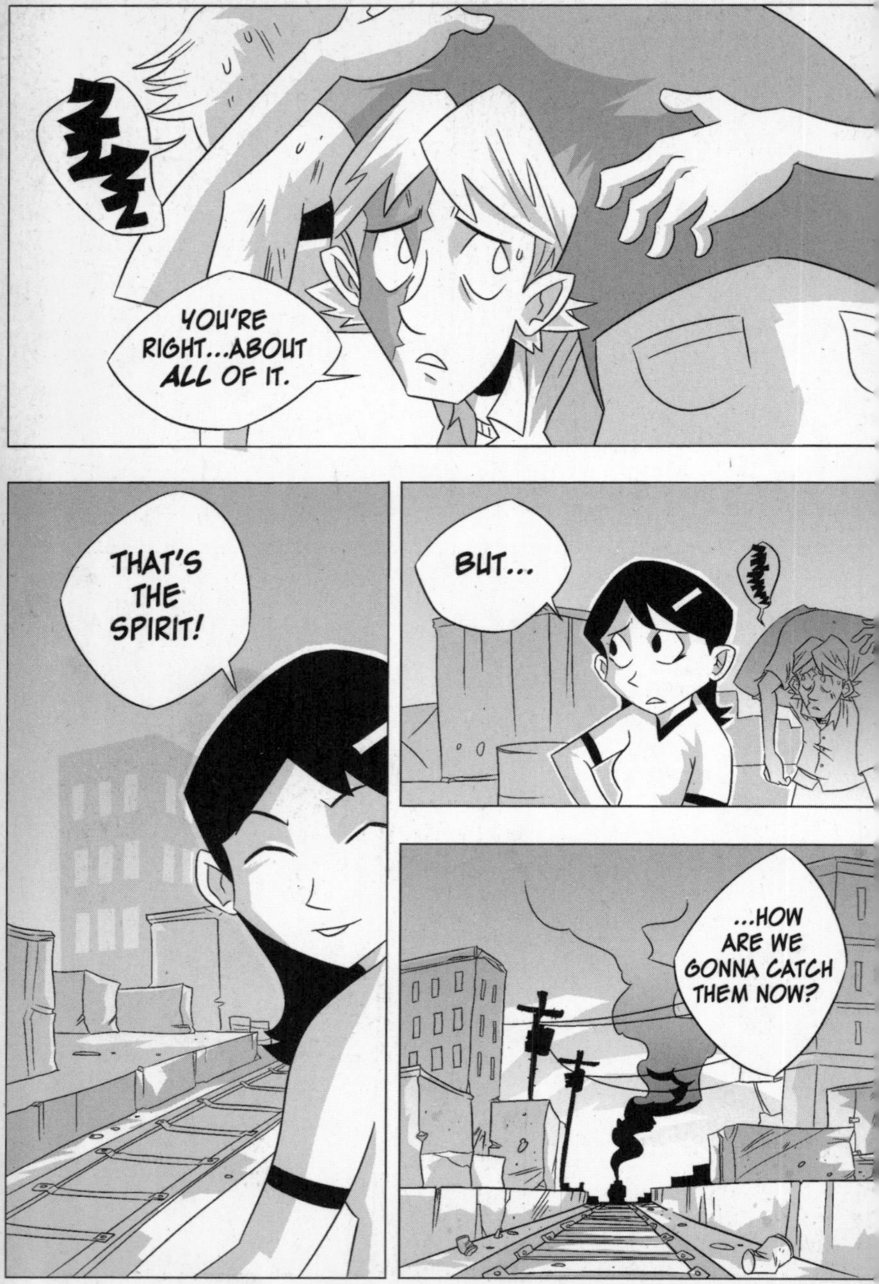
ZZZZ
YOU'RE RIGHT...ABOUT ALL OF IT.
THAT'S THE SPIRIT!
BUT...
...HOW ARE WE GONNA CATCH THEM NOW?

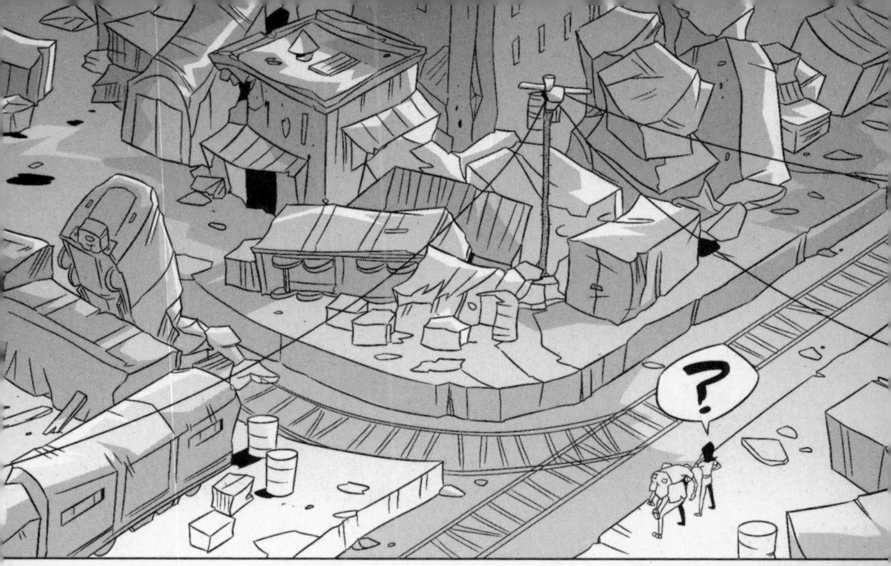
?

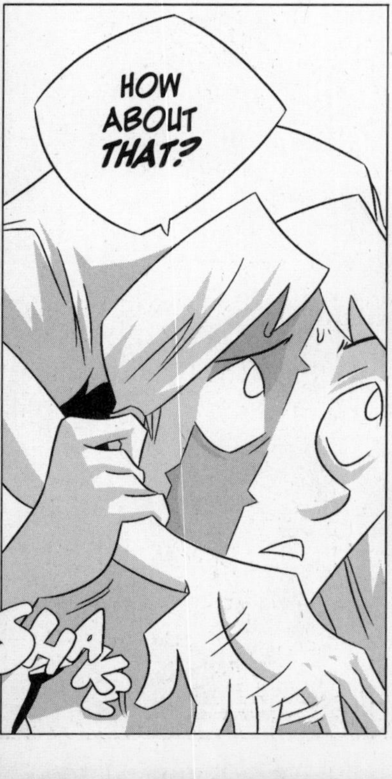
HOW ABOUT *THAT?*
SHAKE

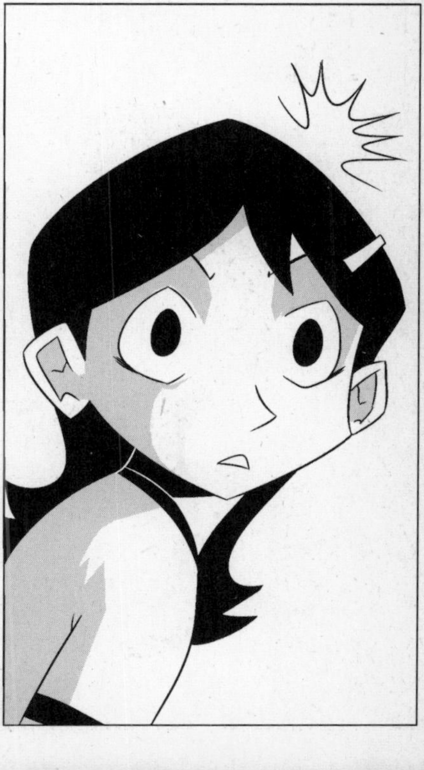

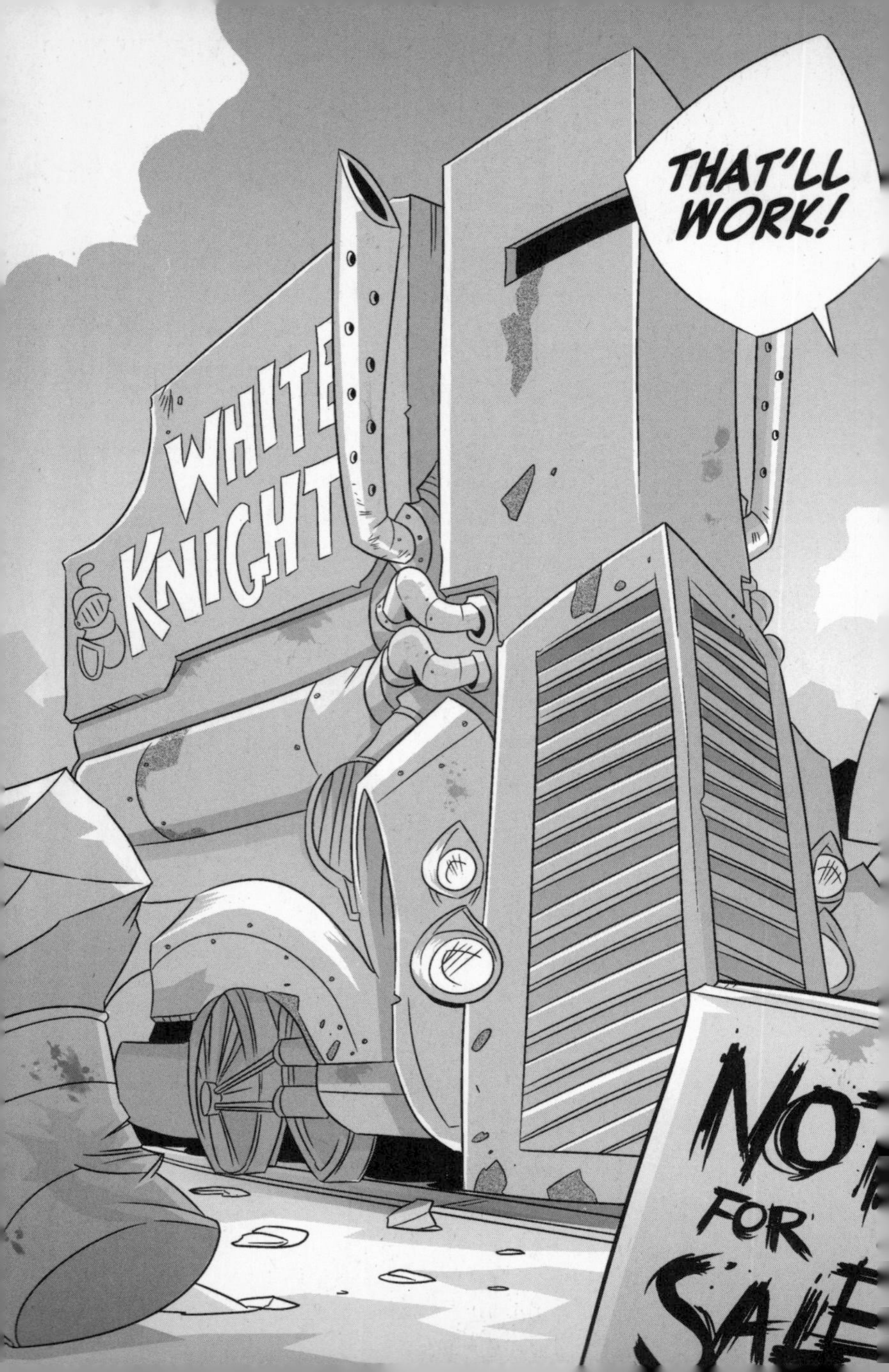
THAT'LL WORK!
WHITE KNIGHT
NO
FOR
SALE

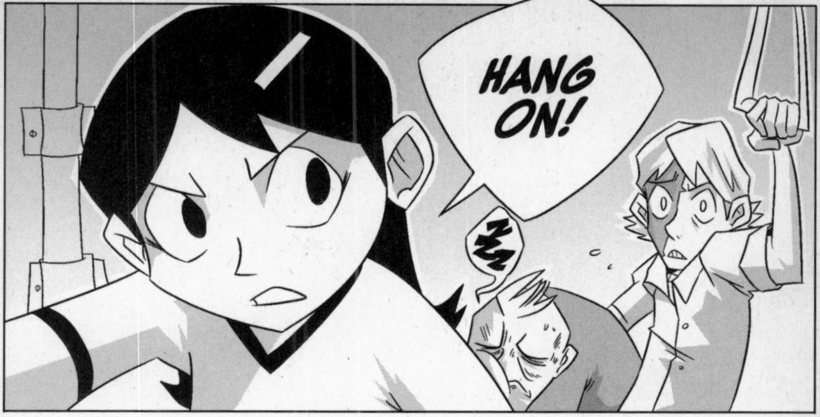
HANG ON!
ZZZ
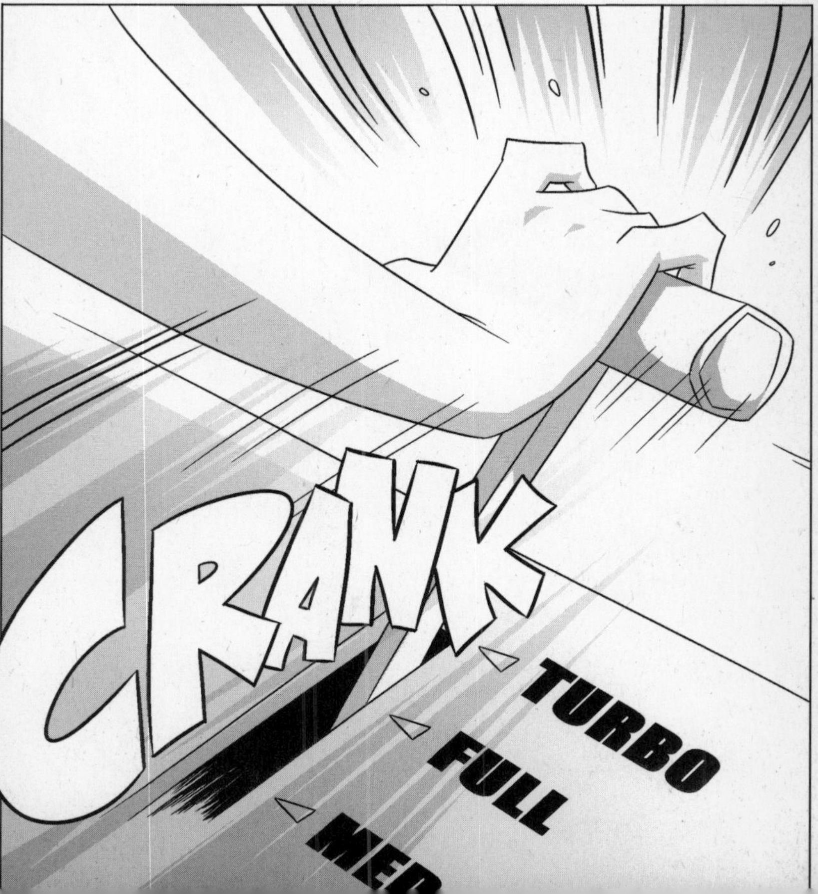
CRANK

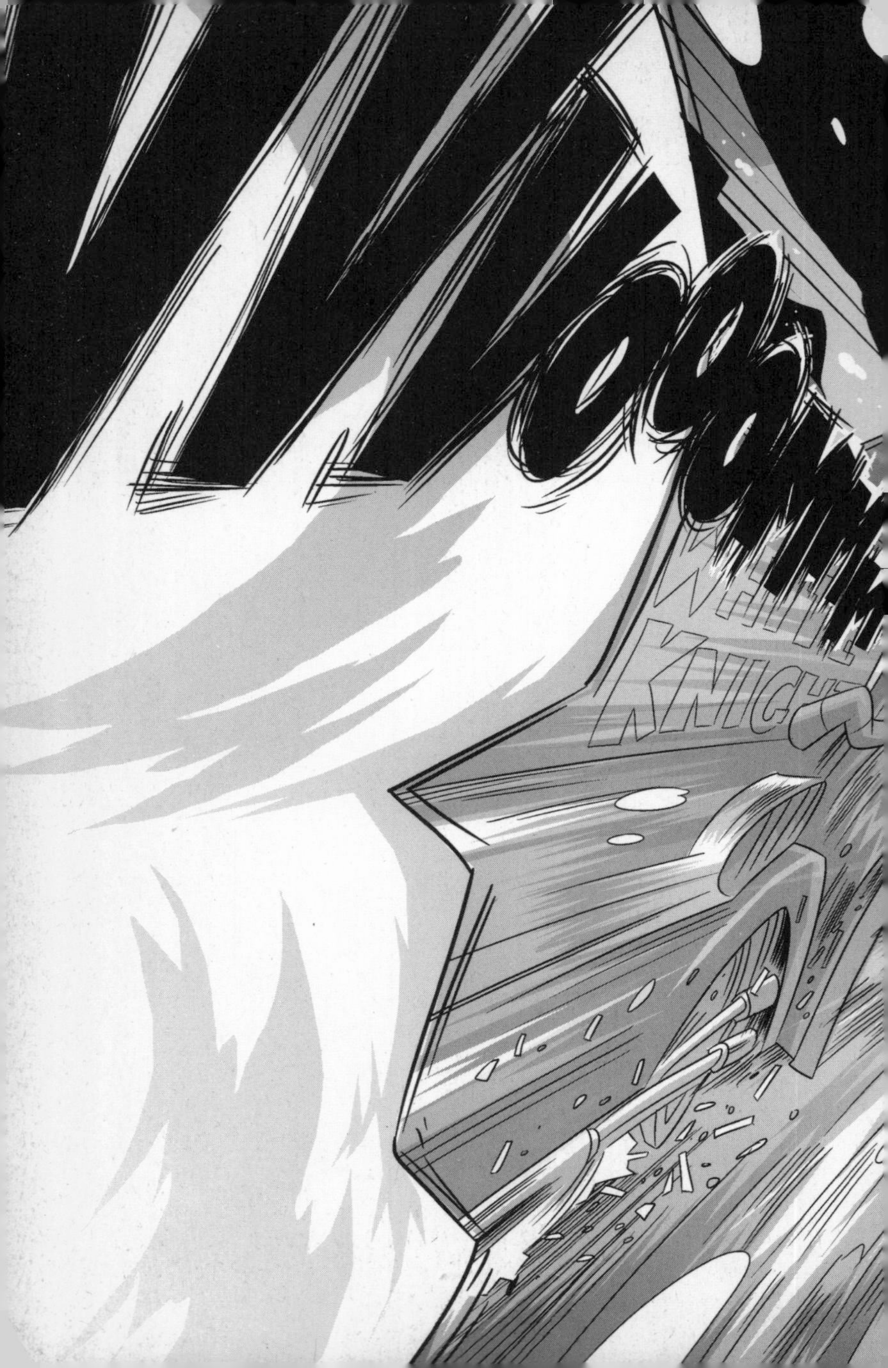

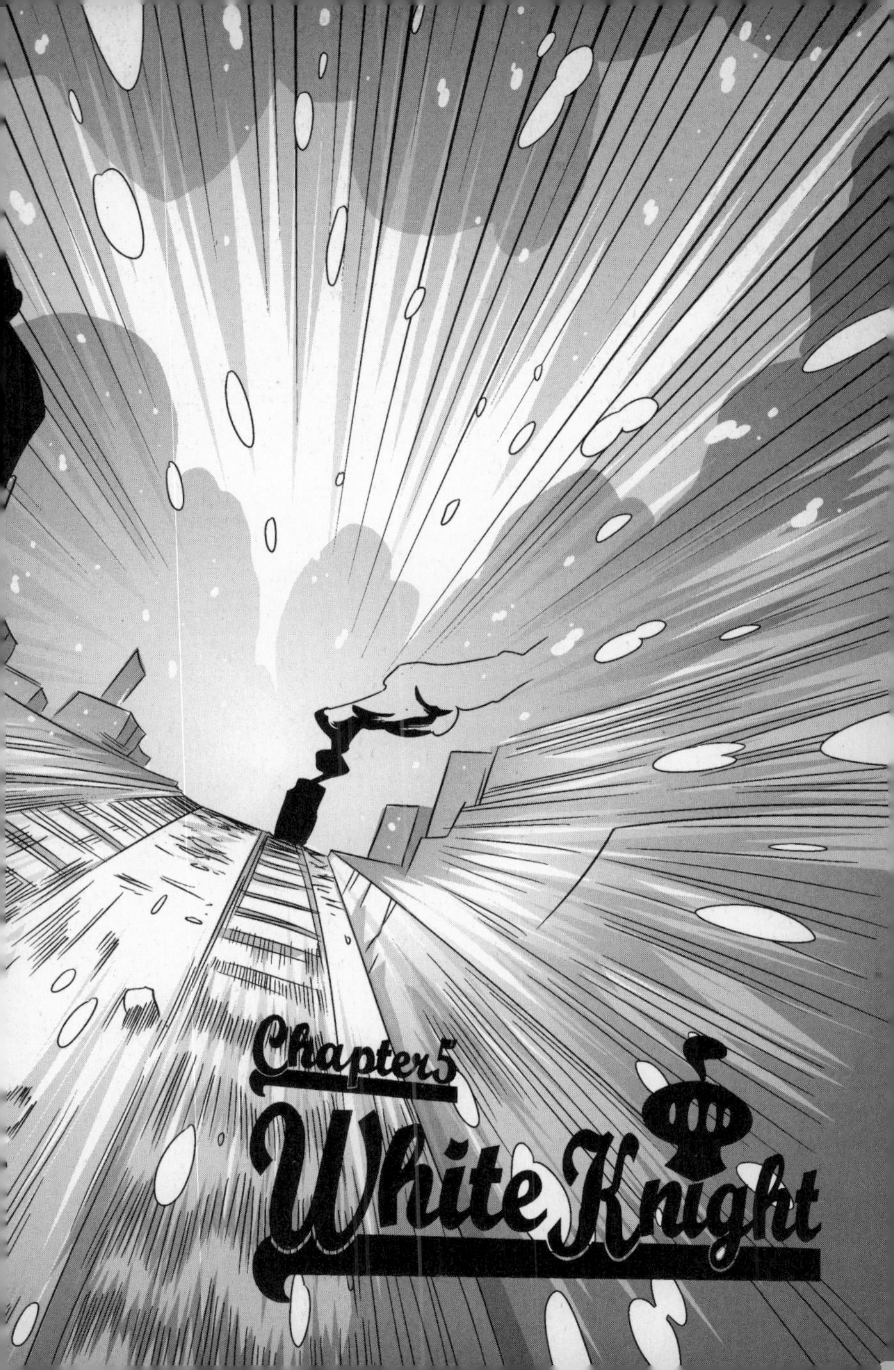
Chapter 5
White Knight

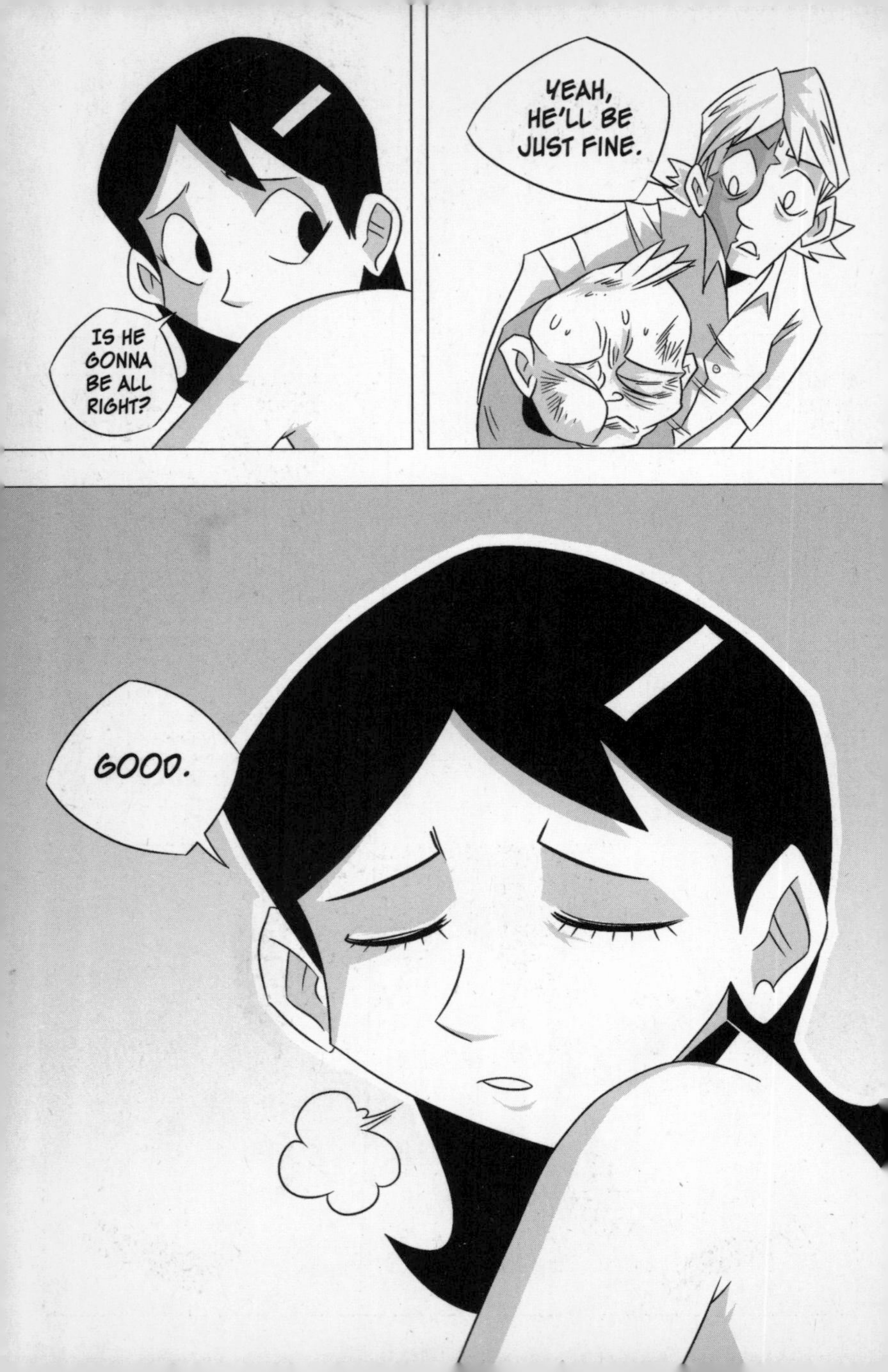
IS HE GONNA BE ALL RIGHT?
YEAH, HE'LL BE JUST FINE.
GOOD.

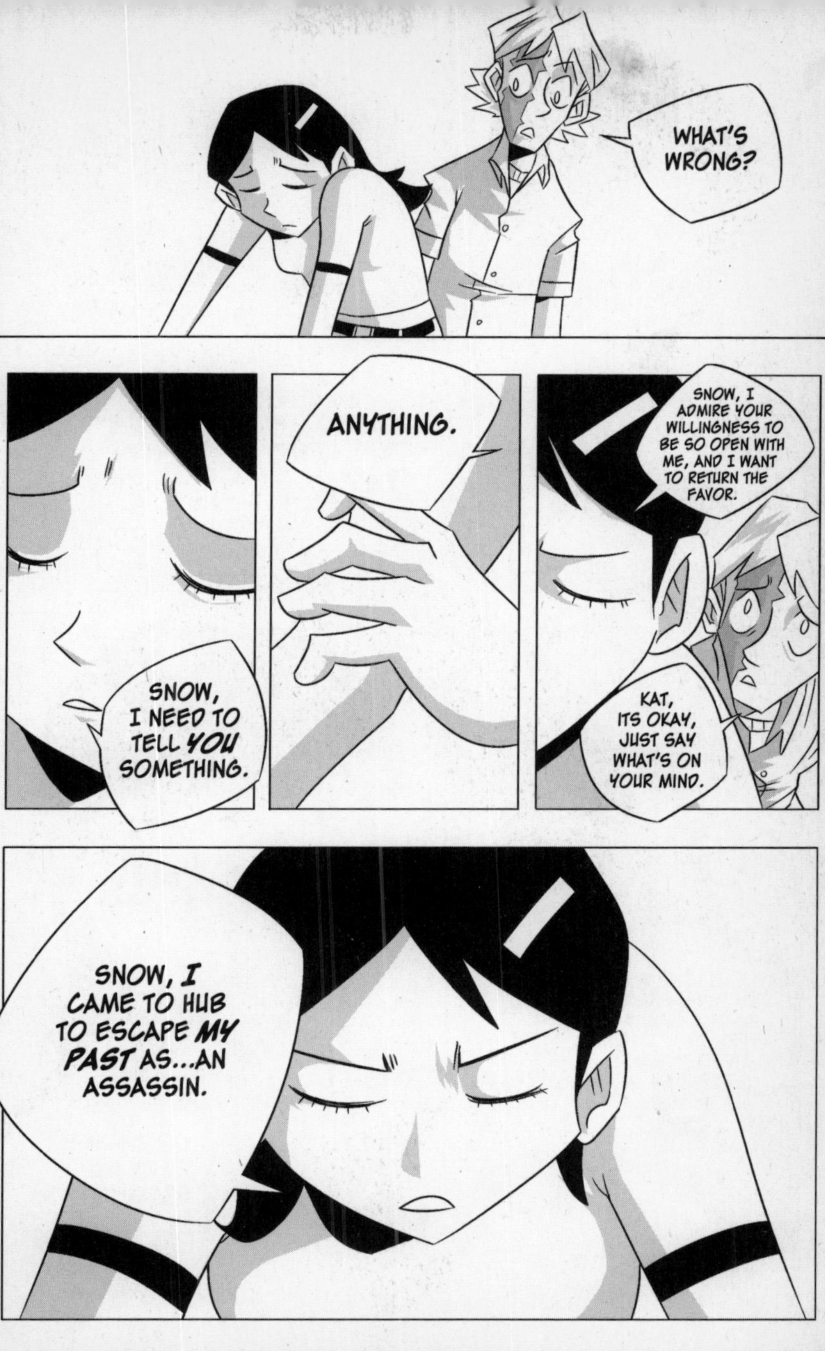
WHAT'S WRONG?
SNOW, I NEED TO TELL YOU SOMETHING.
ANYTHING.
SNOW, I ADMIRE YOUR WILLINGNESS TO BE SO OPEN WITH ME, AND I WANT TO RETURN THE FAVOR.
KAT, ITS OKAY, JUST SAY WHAT'S ON YOUR MIND.
SNOW, I CAME TO HUB TO ESCAPE MY PAST AS...AN ASSASSIN.

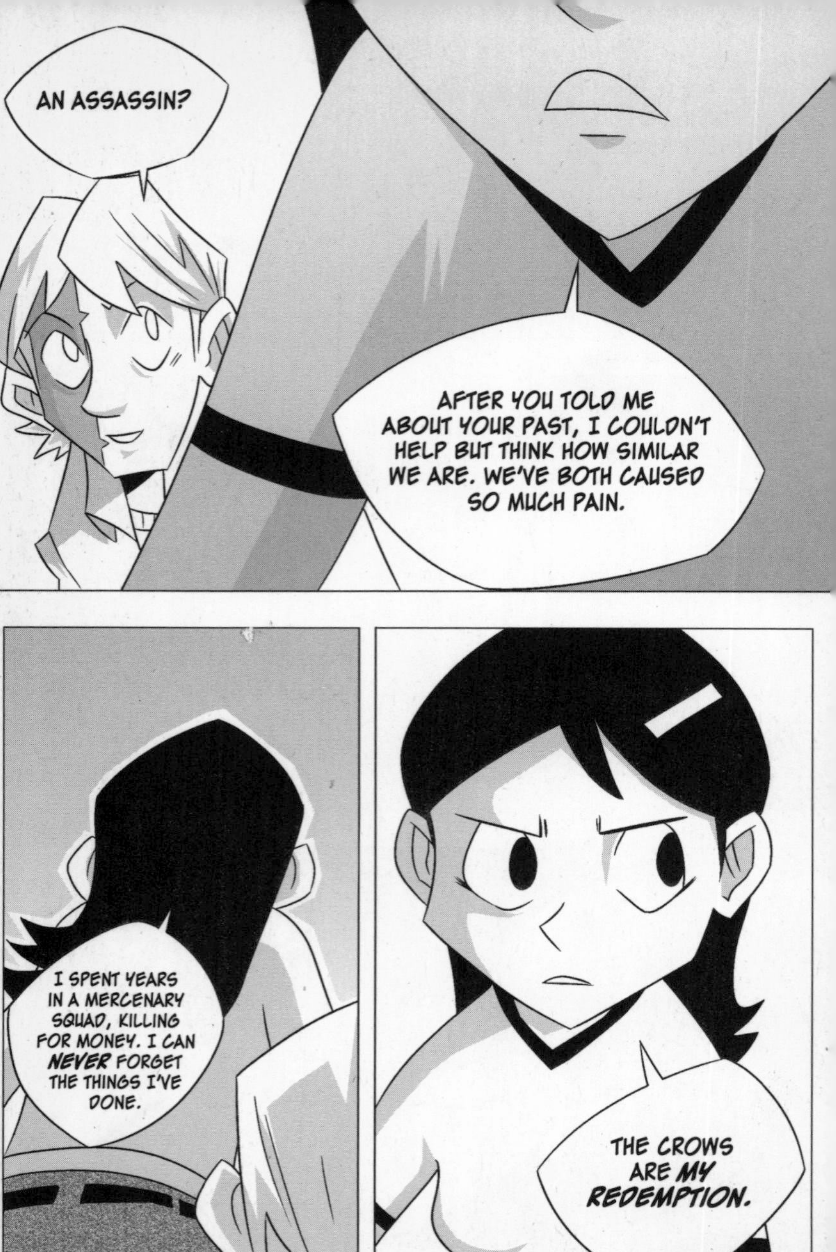
AN ASSASSIN?
AFTER YOU TOLD ME ABOUT YOUR PAST, I COULDN'T HELP BUT THINK HOW SIMILAR WE ARE. WE'VE BOTH CAUSED SO MUCH PAIN.
I SPENT YEARS IN A MERCENARY SQUAD, KILLING FOR MONEY. I CAN *NEVER* FORGET THE THINGS I'VE DONE.
THE CROWS ARE *MY REDEMPTION.*

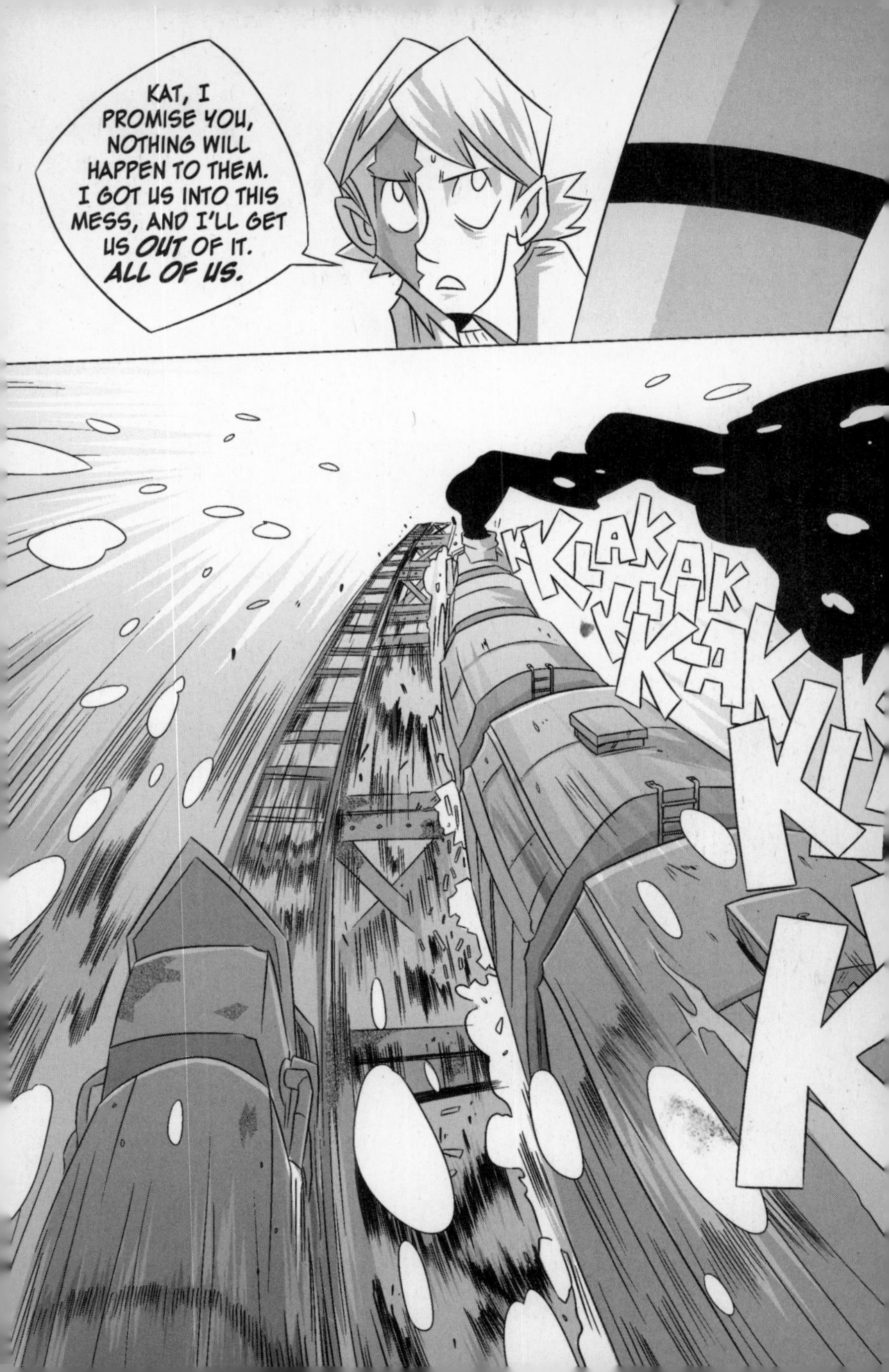
KAT, I PROMISE YOU, NOTHING WILL HAPPEN TO THEM. I GOT US INTO THIS MESS, AND I'LL GET US *OUT* OF IT. ***ALL OF US.***
KLAKAK
KLIK
KLAK
KLIK

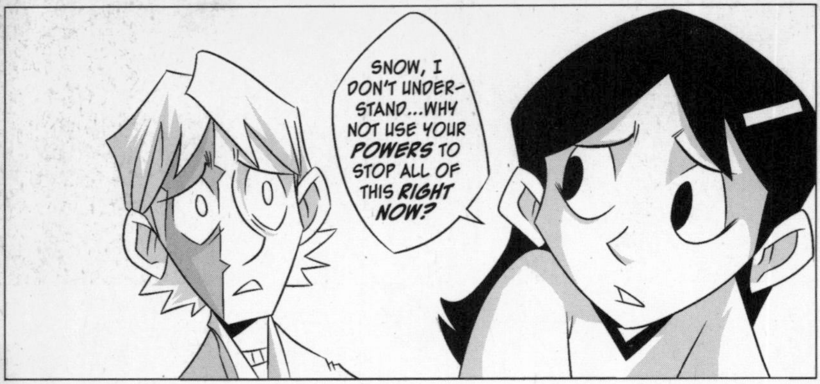
SNOW, I DON'T UNDER-STAND...WHY NOT USE YOUR **POWERS** TO STOP ALL OF THIS **RIGHT NOW?**

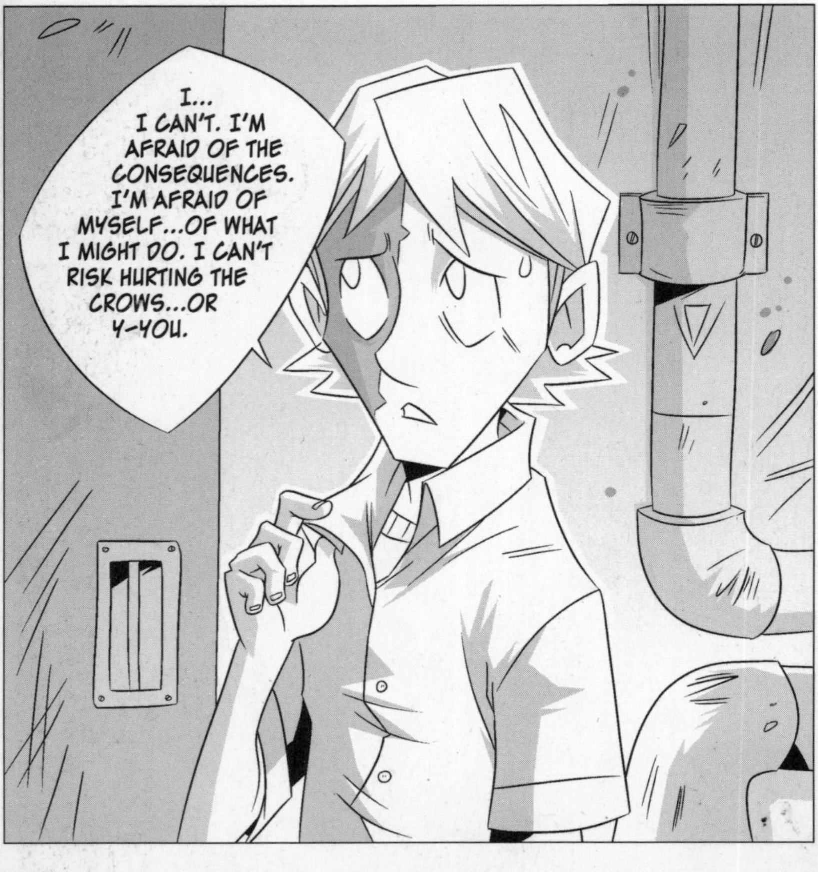
I... I CAN'T. I'M AFRAID OF THE CONSEQUENCES. I'M AFRAID OF MYSELF...OF WHAT I MIGHT DO. I CAN'T RISK HURTING THE CROWS...OR Y-YOU.

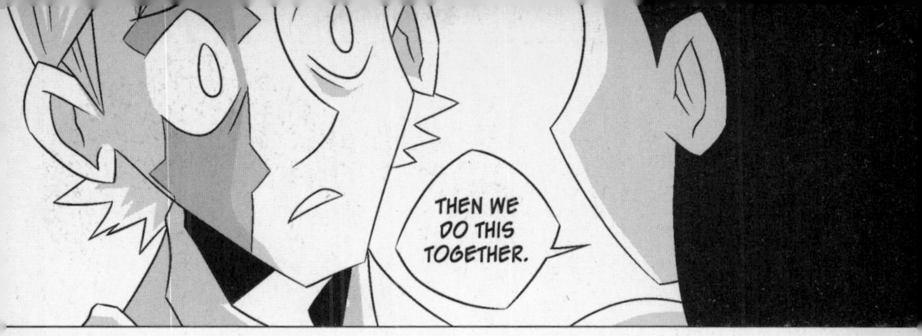
THEN WE DO THIS TOGETHER.
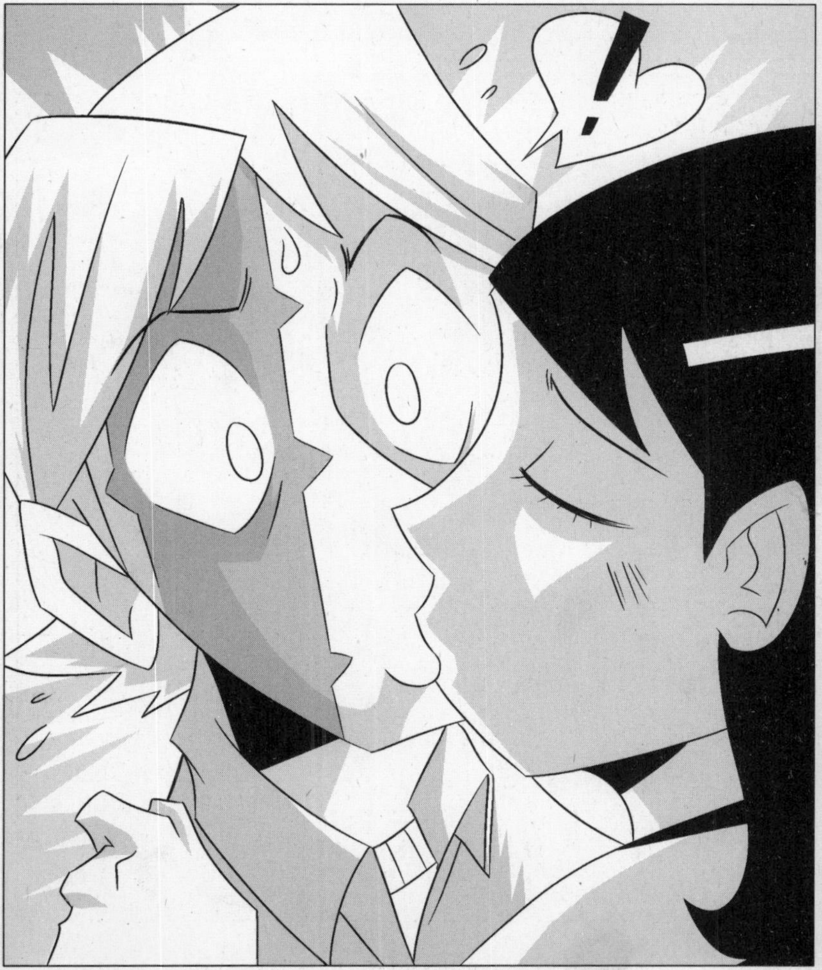
!

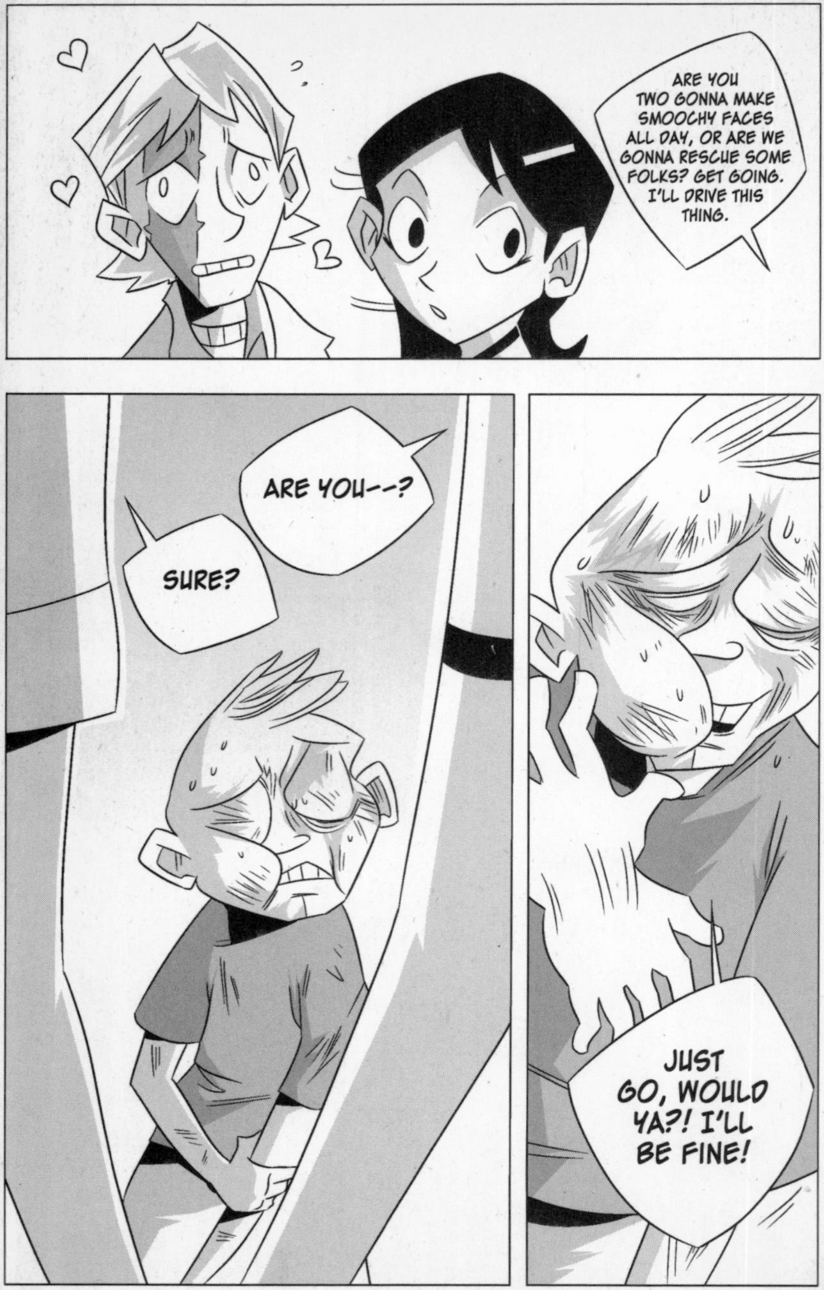
ARE YOU TWO GONNA MAKE SMOOCHY FACES ALL DAY, OR ARE WE GONNA RESCUE SOME FOLKS? GET GOING. I'LL DRIVE THIS THING.
ARE YOU--?
SURE?
JUST GO, WOULD YA?! I'LL BE FINE!

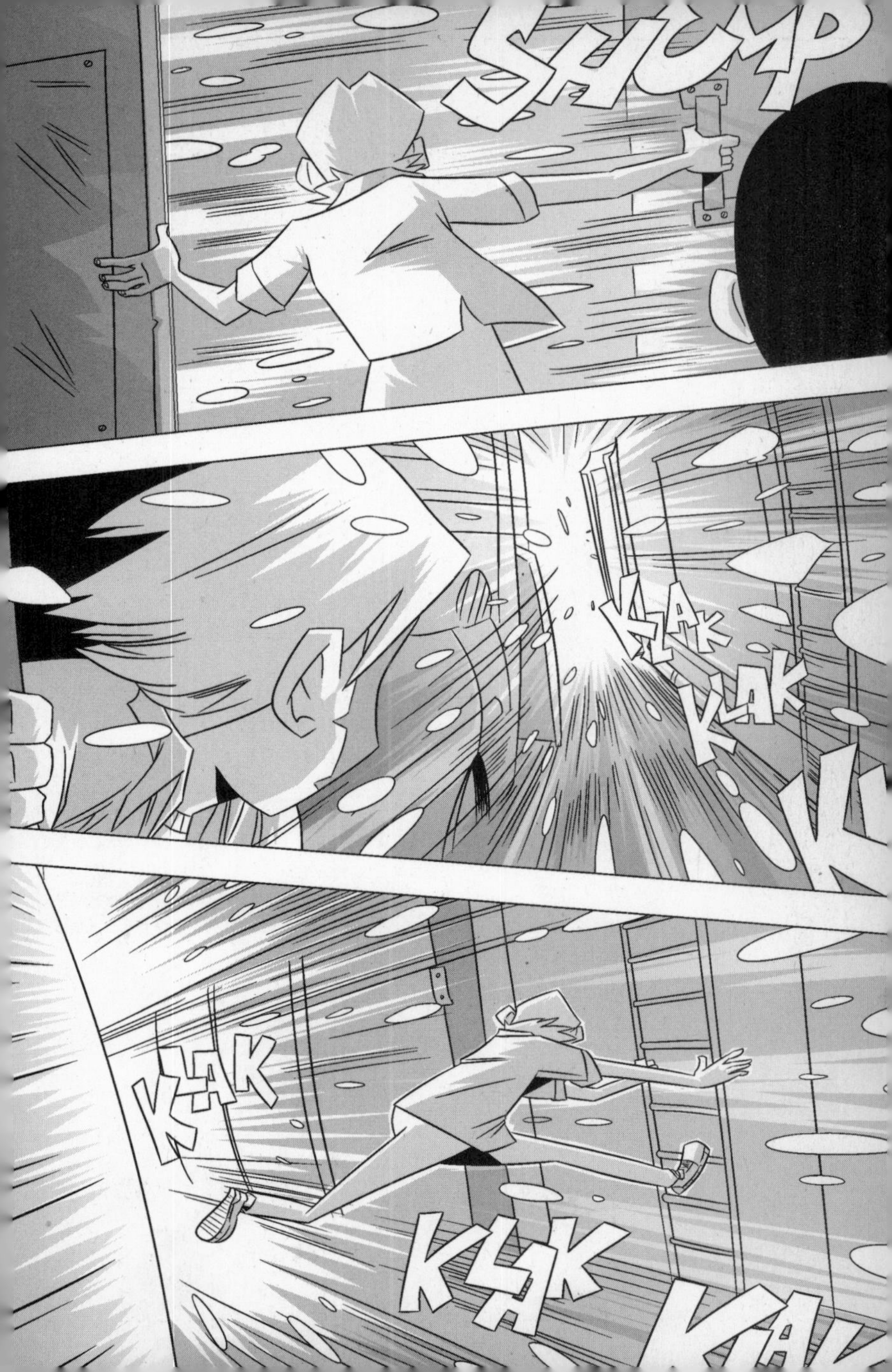
SHUMP
KLAK
KLAK
KLAK
KLAK

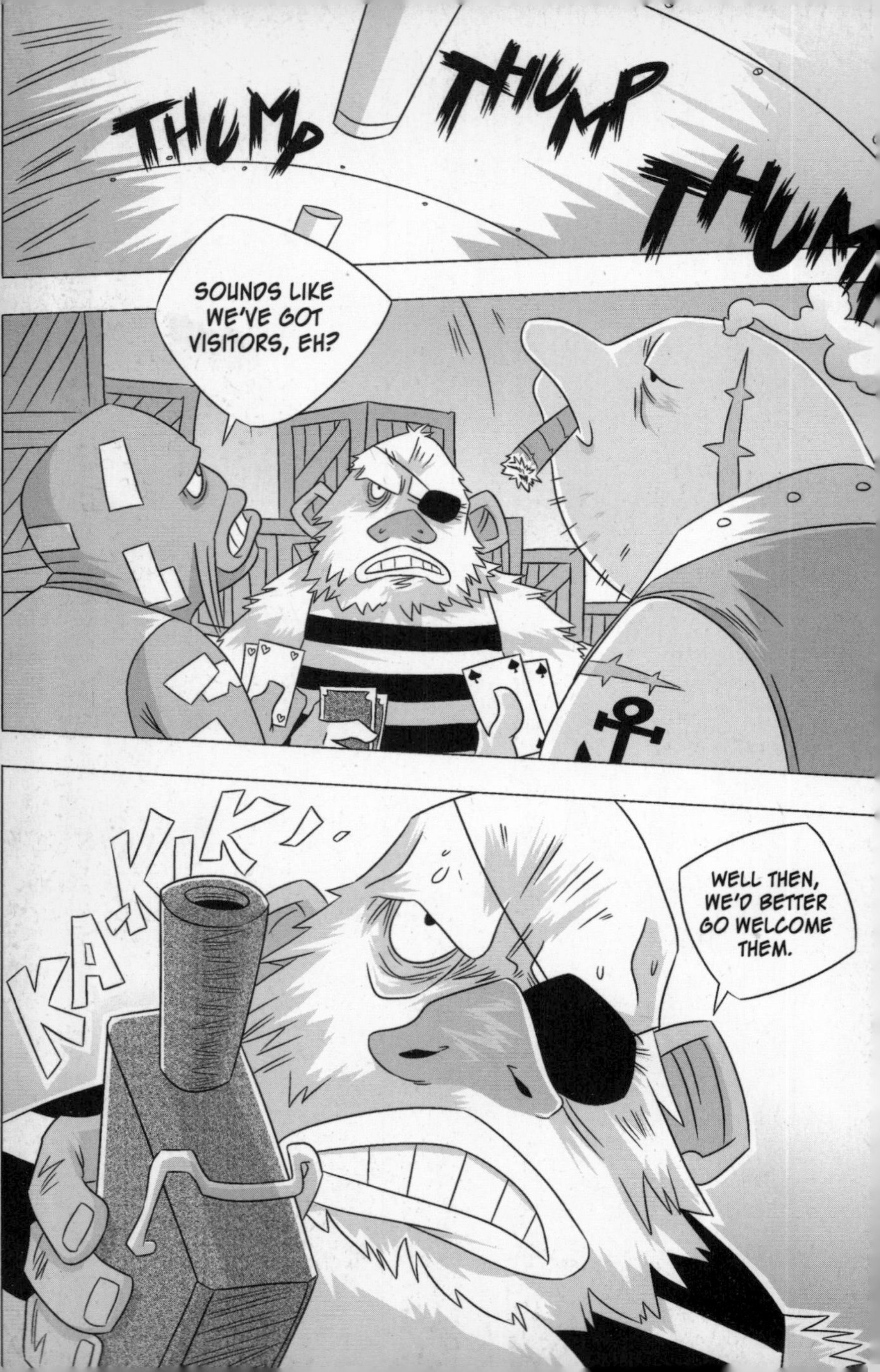
THUMP
THUMP
THUMP
SOUNDS LIKE WE'VE GOT VISITORS, EH?
KA-KLIK!
WELL THEN, WE'D BETTER GO WELCOME THEM.

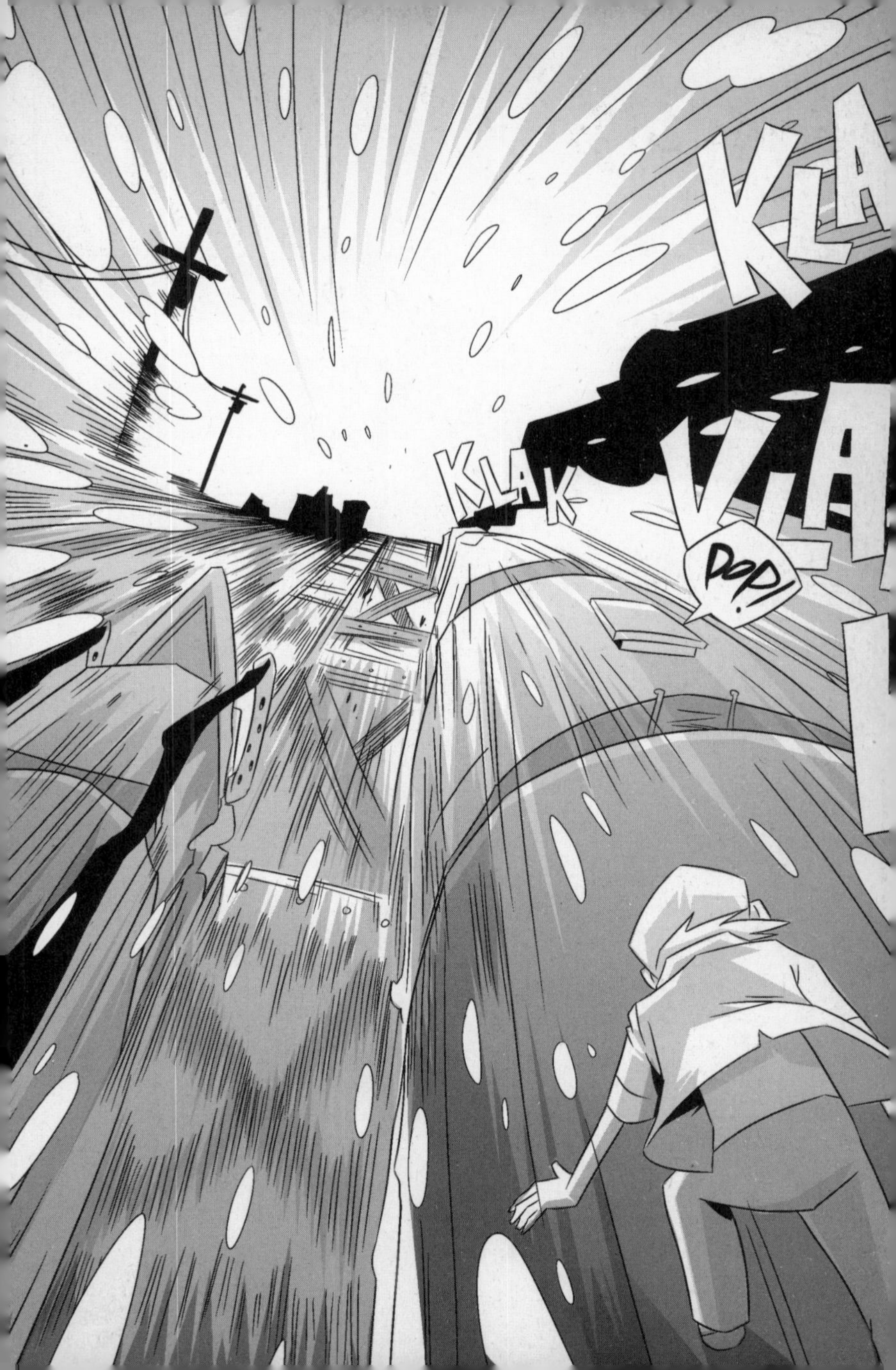
KLA
VLA
DOP!
KLAK

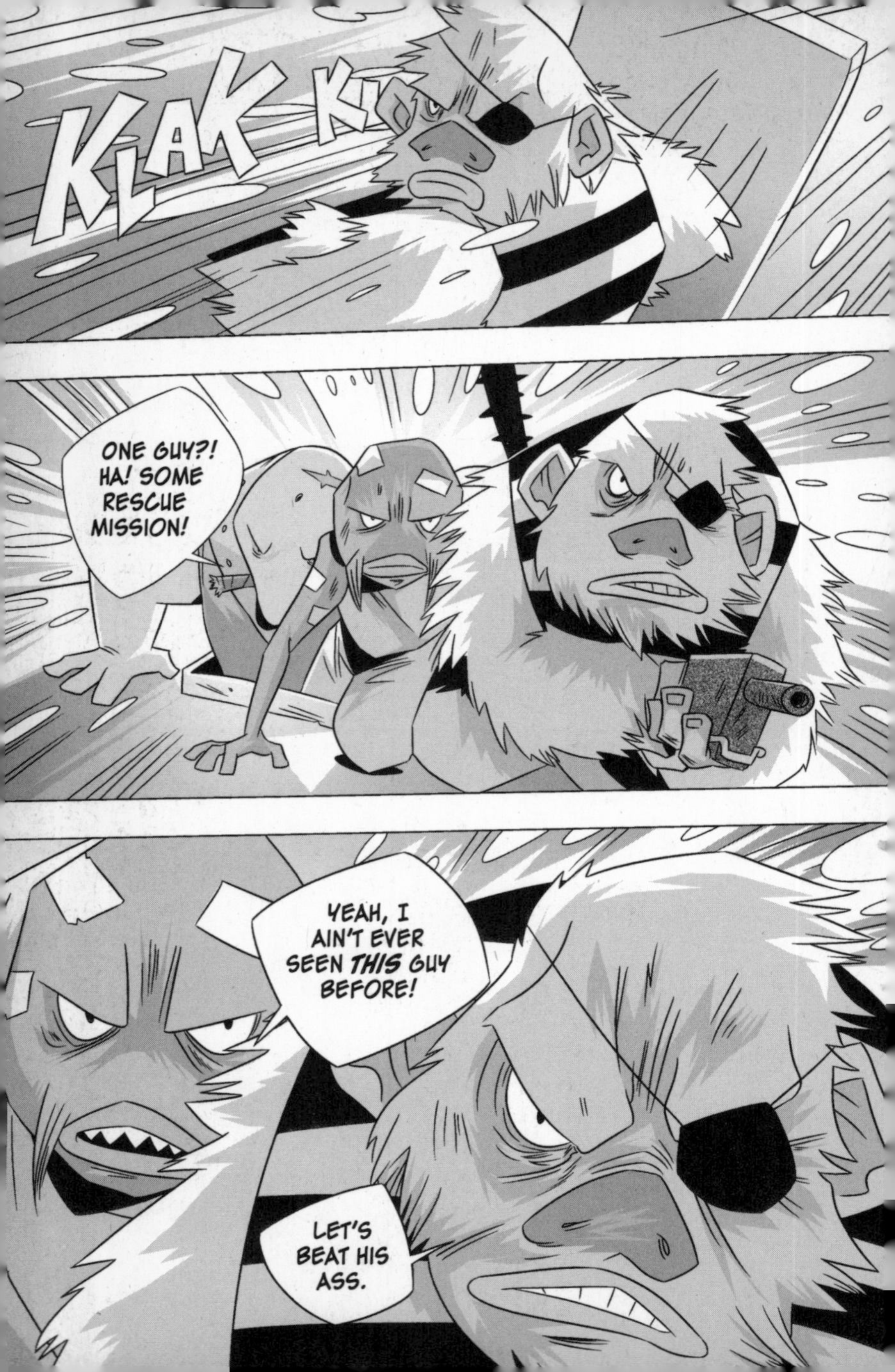
KLAK
ONE GUY?! HA! SOME RESCUE MISSION!
YEAH, I AIN'T EVER SEEN *THIS* GUY BEFORE!
LET'S BEAT HIS ASS.

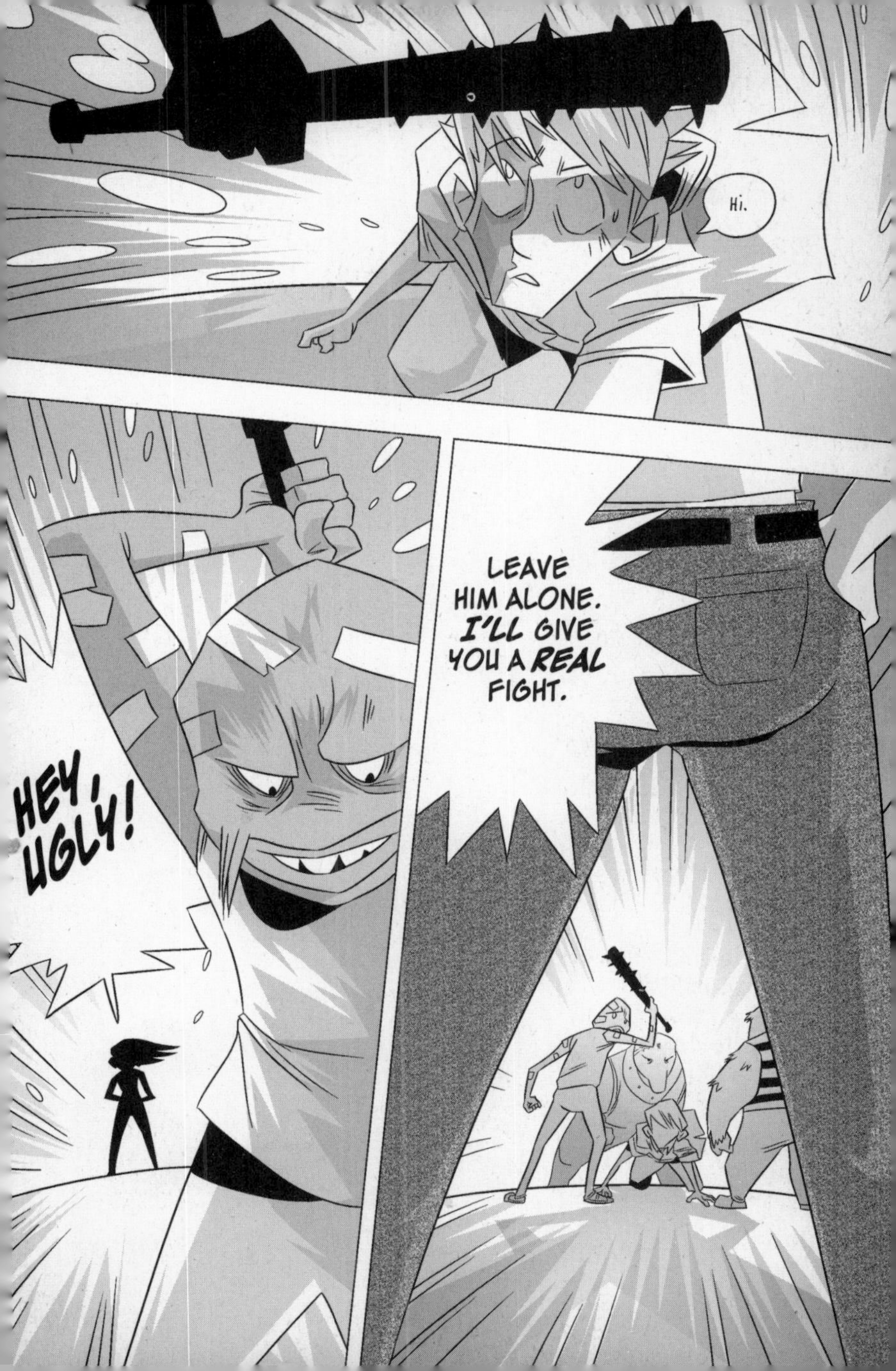
Hi.
HEY, UGLY!
LEAVE HIM ALONE. I'LL GIVE YOU A REAL FIGHT.

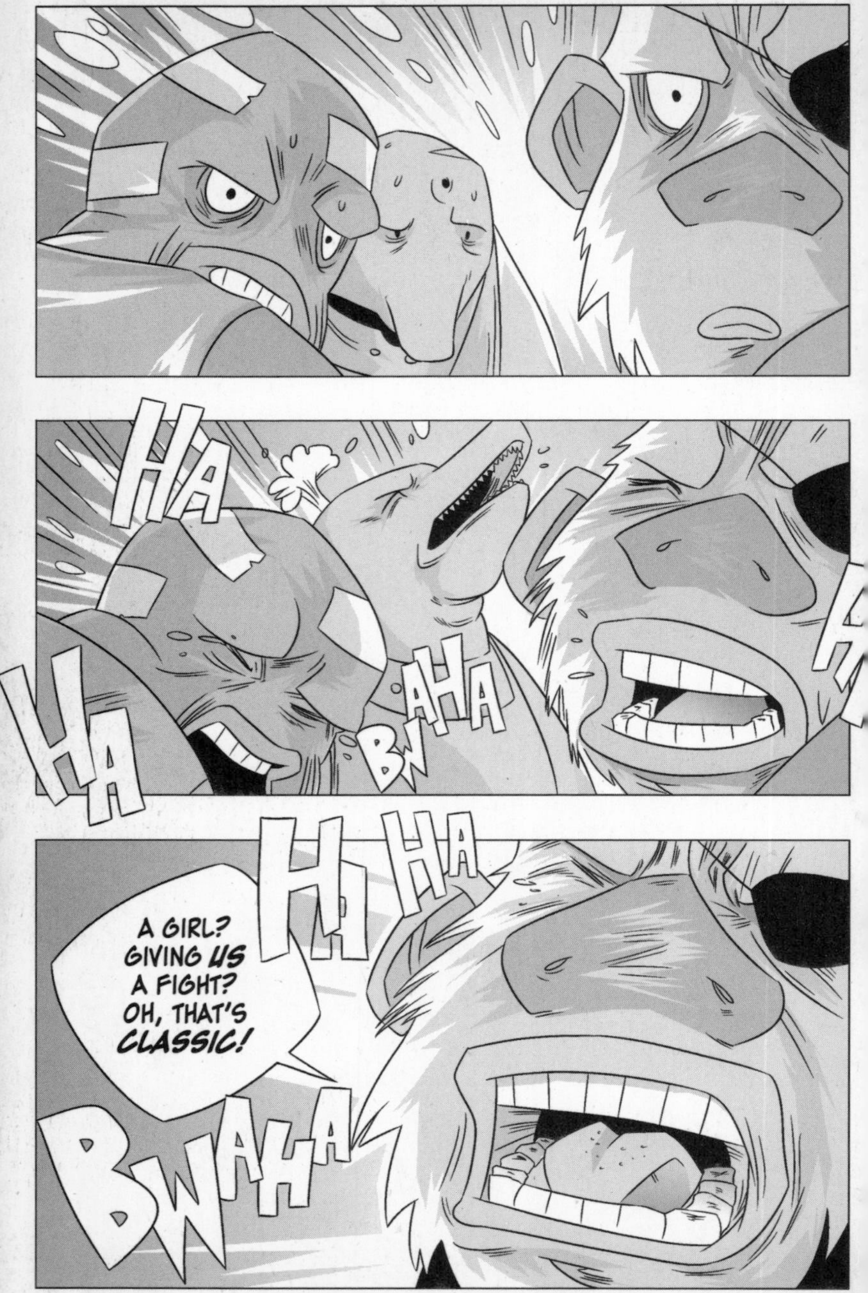
HA HA
BWAHAHA
HA HA
HA HA HA HA
A GIRL? GIVING US A FIGHT? OH, THAT'S CLASSIC!
BWAHAHA

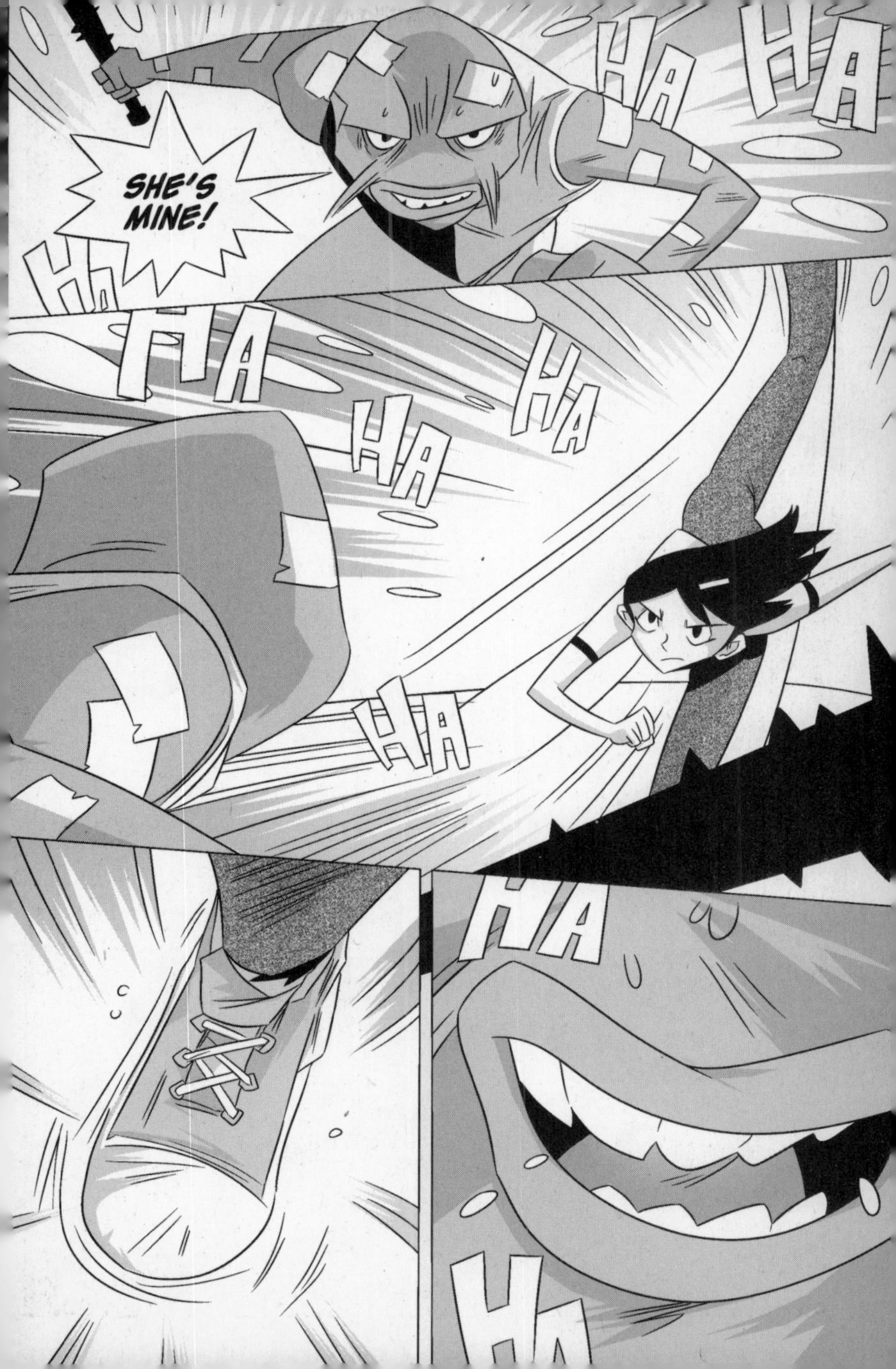
HA HA
SHE'S MINE!
HA
HA HA
HA HA
HA HA
HA HA
HA
HA

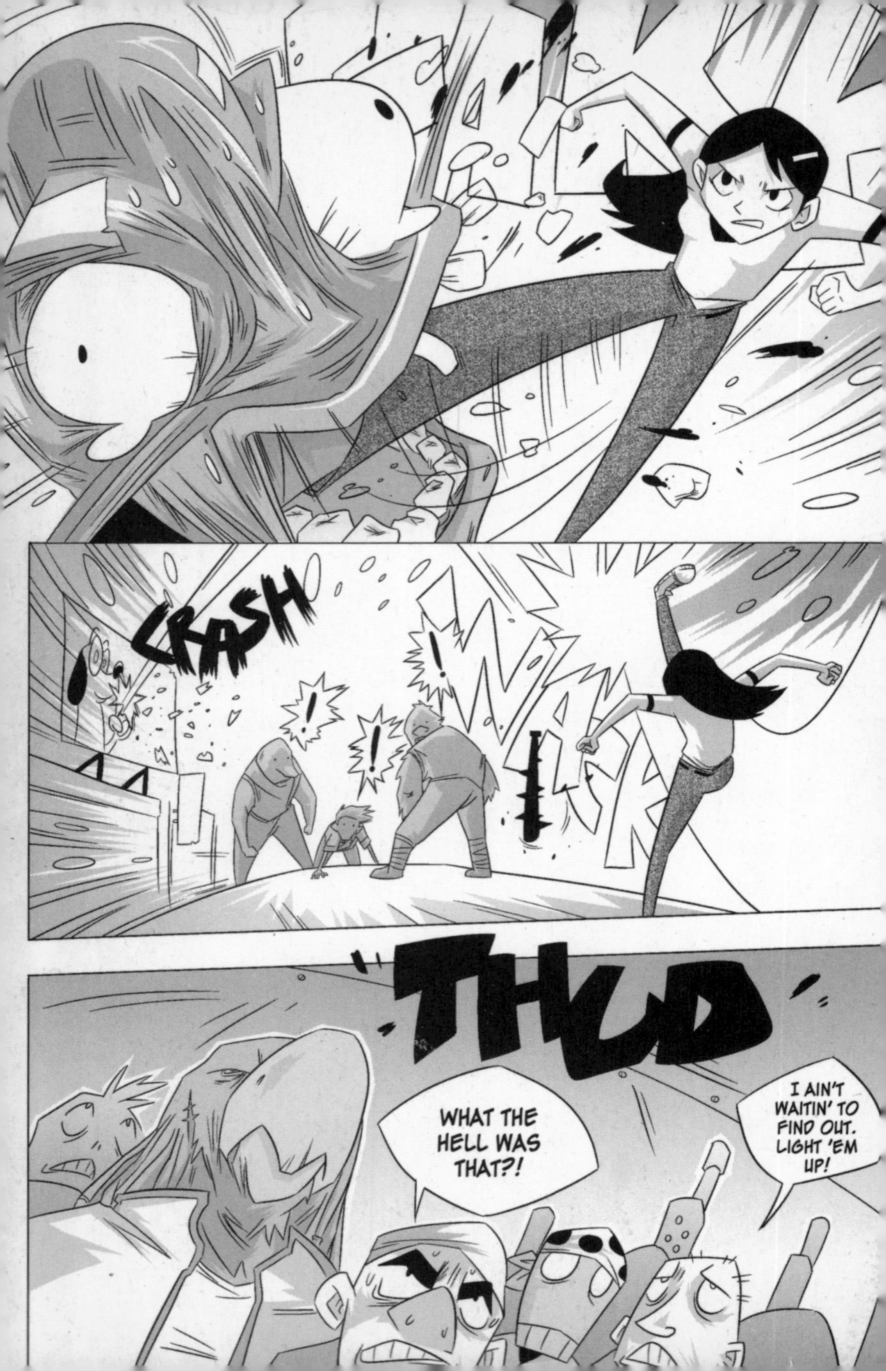

CRASH
!
!
!
THUD
WHAT THE HELL WAS THAT?!
I AIN'T WAITIN' TO FIND OUT. LIGHT 'EM UP!

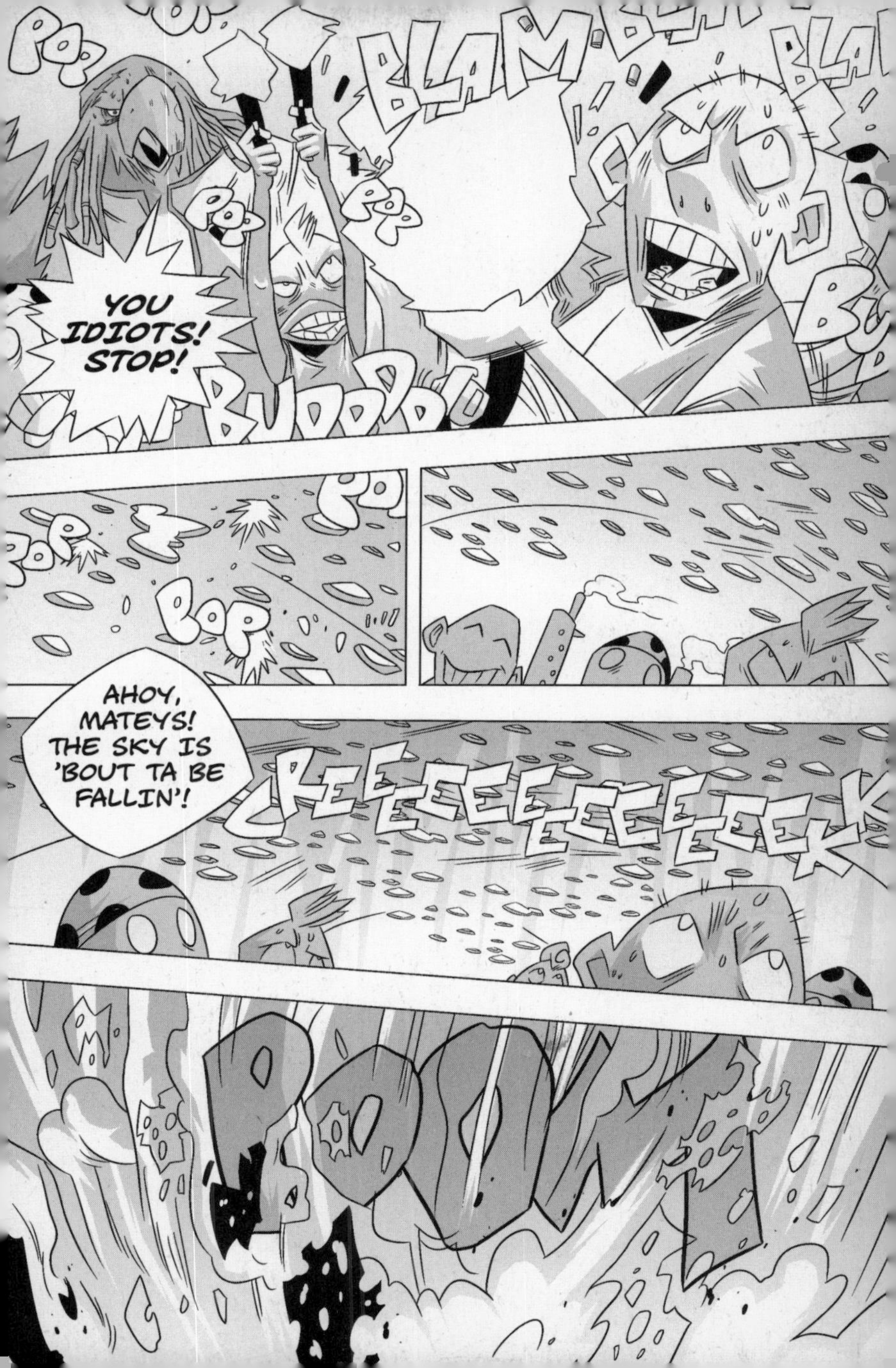
BLAM
POP
POP
YOU IDIOTS! STOP!
POP
POP
AHOY, MATEYS! THE SKY IS 'BOUT TA BE FALLIN'!
BOOM

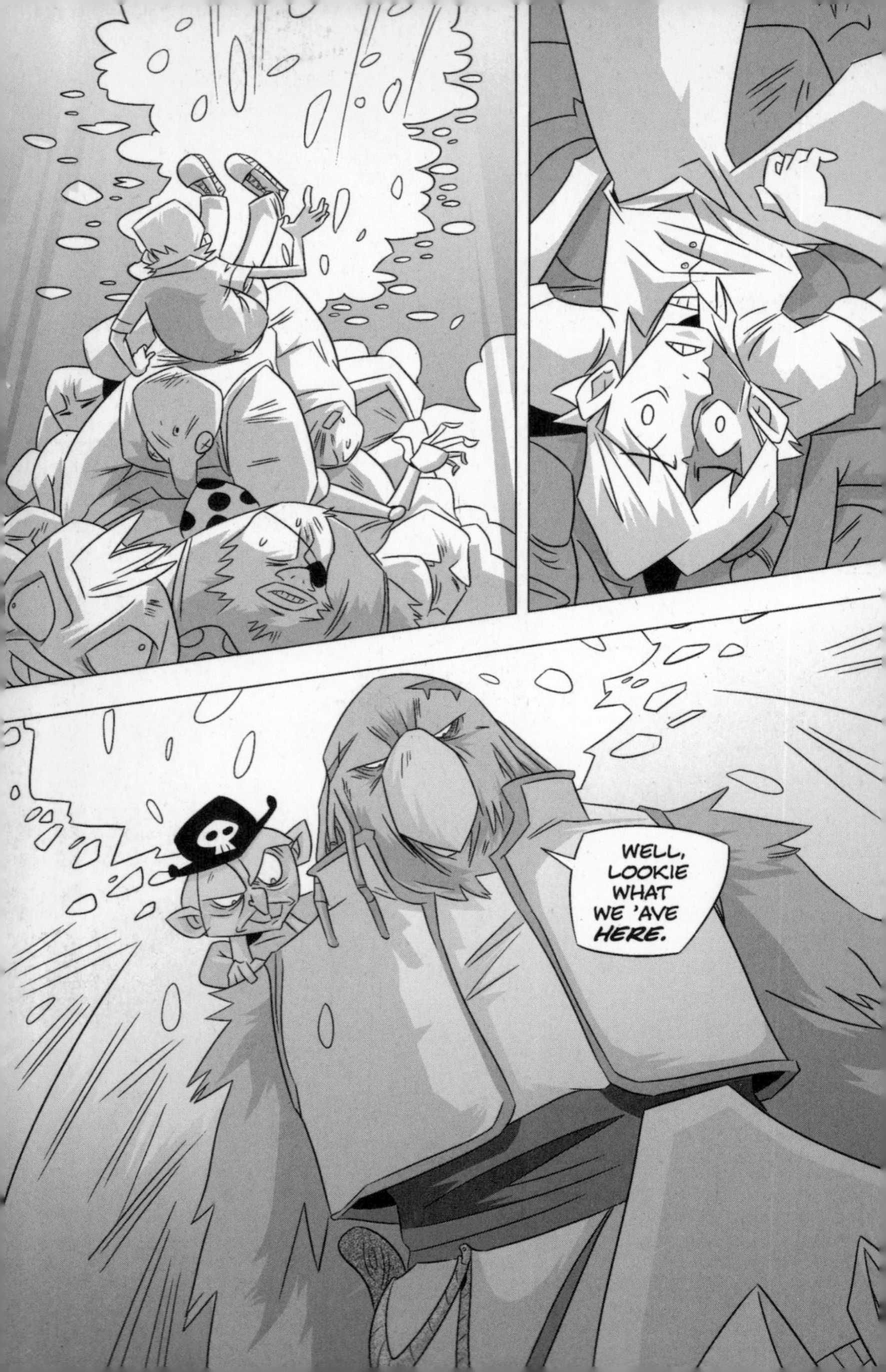
WELL, LOOKIE WHAT WE 'AVE HERE.

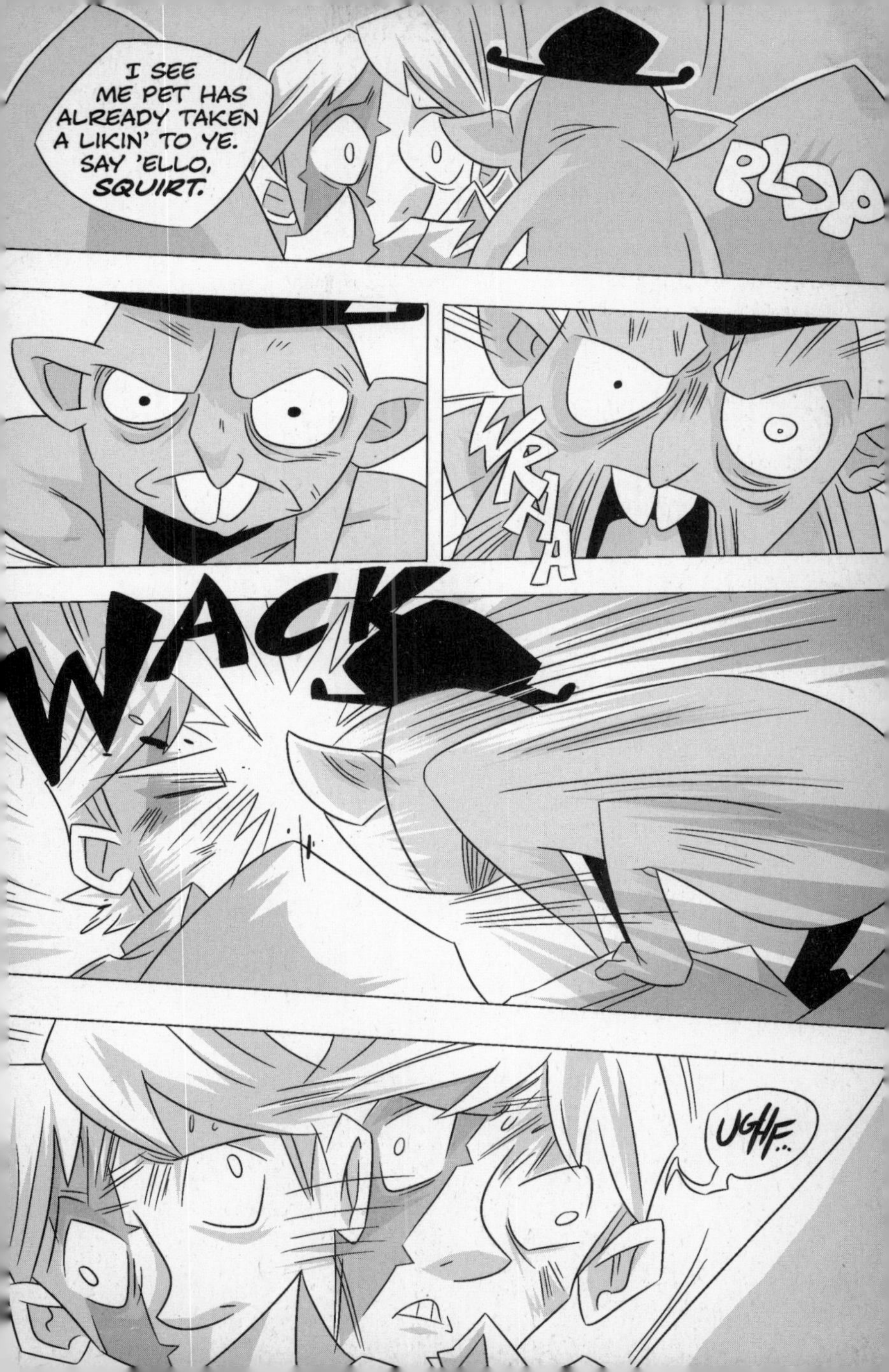
I SEE ME PET HAS ALREADY TAKEN A LIKIN' TO YE. SAY 'ELLO, SQUIRT.
PLOP
WRAAA
WACK
UGHF...

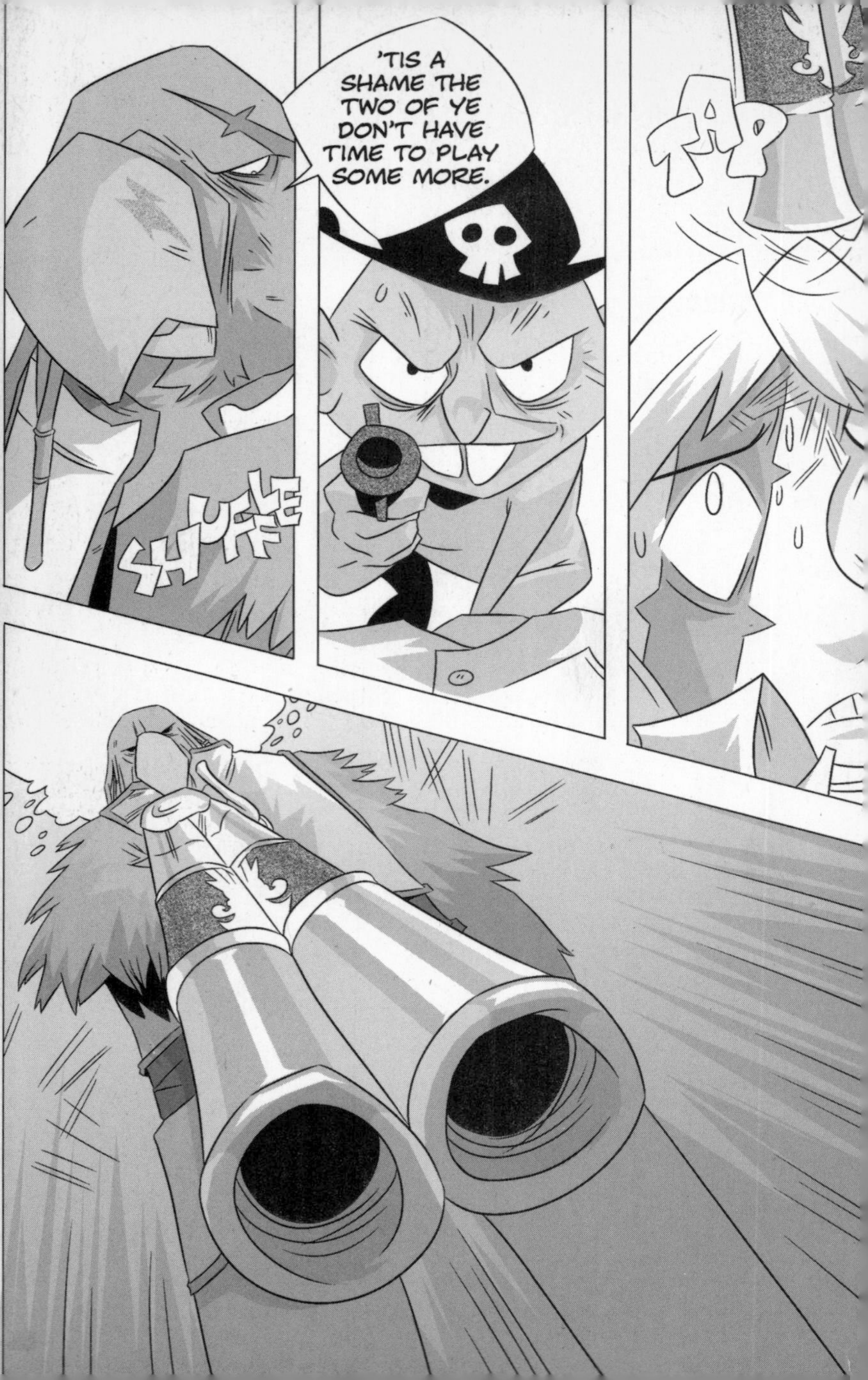
TAP
'TIS A SHAME THE TWO OF YE DON'T HAVE TIME TO PLAY SOME MORE.
SHUFFLE

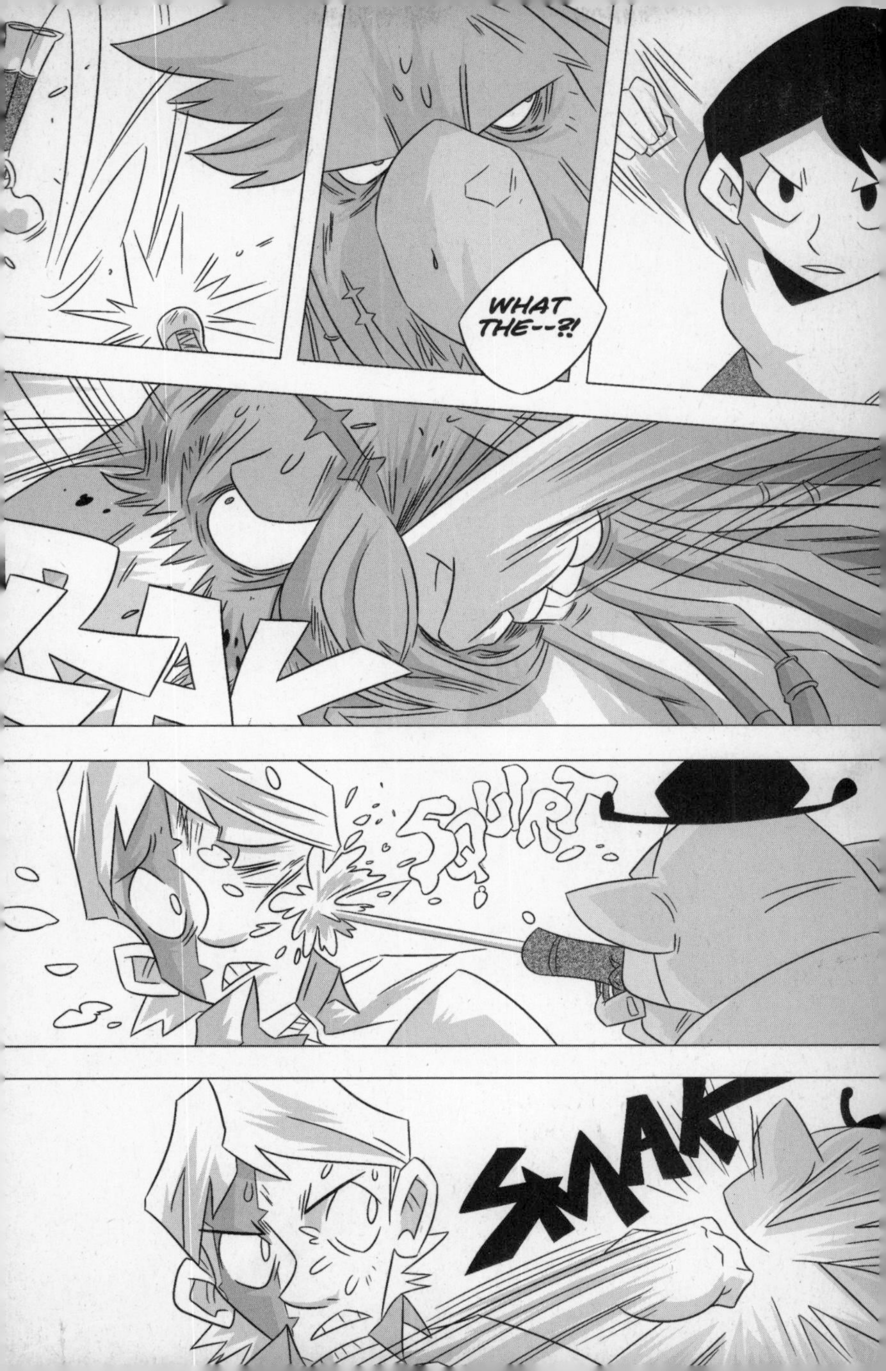
WHAT THE--?!
SMAK
SQUIRT
SMAK

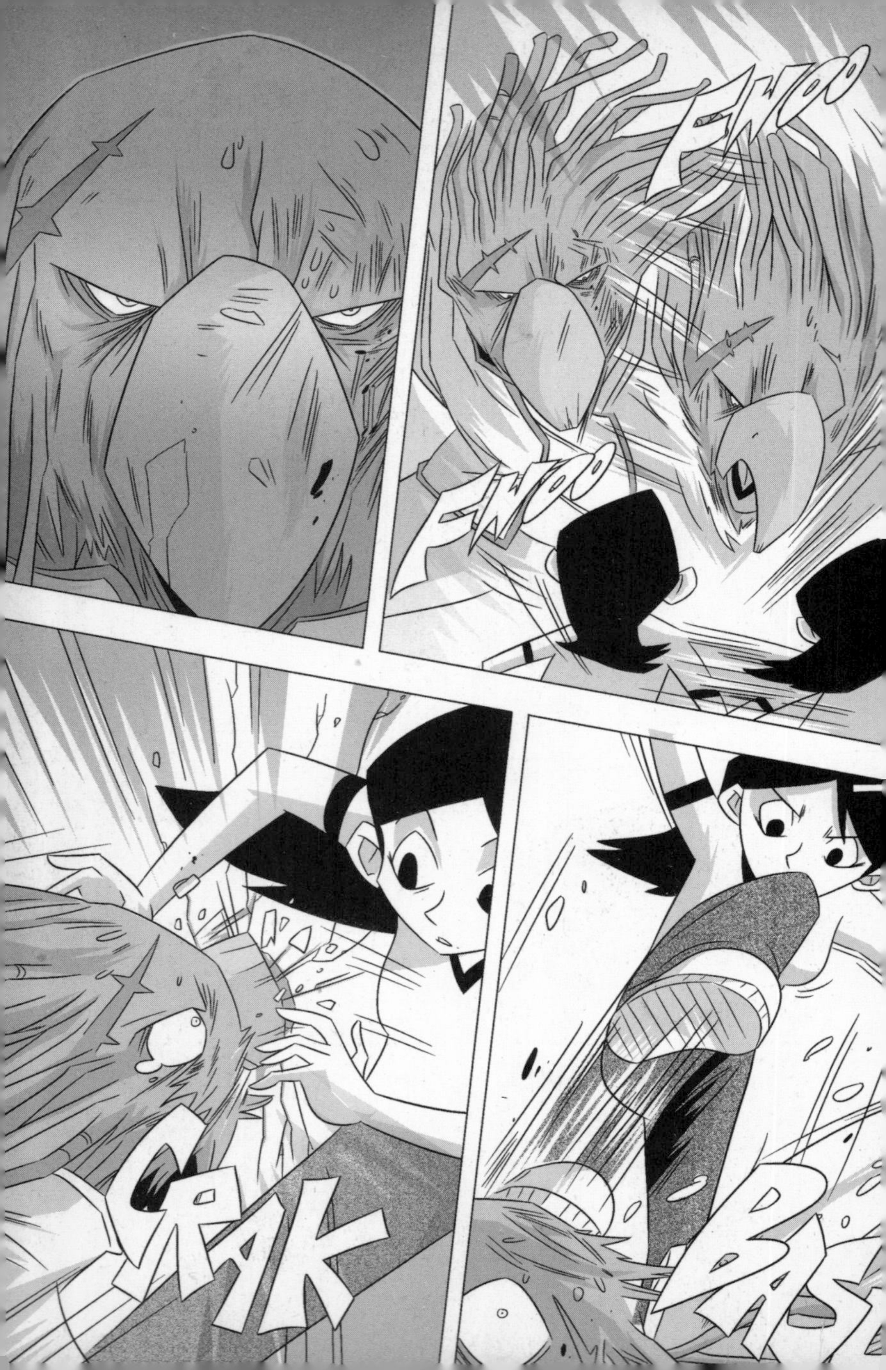
FWOO
FWOO
BAS
CRAK

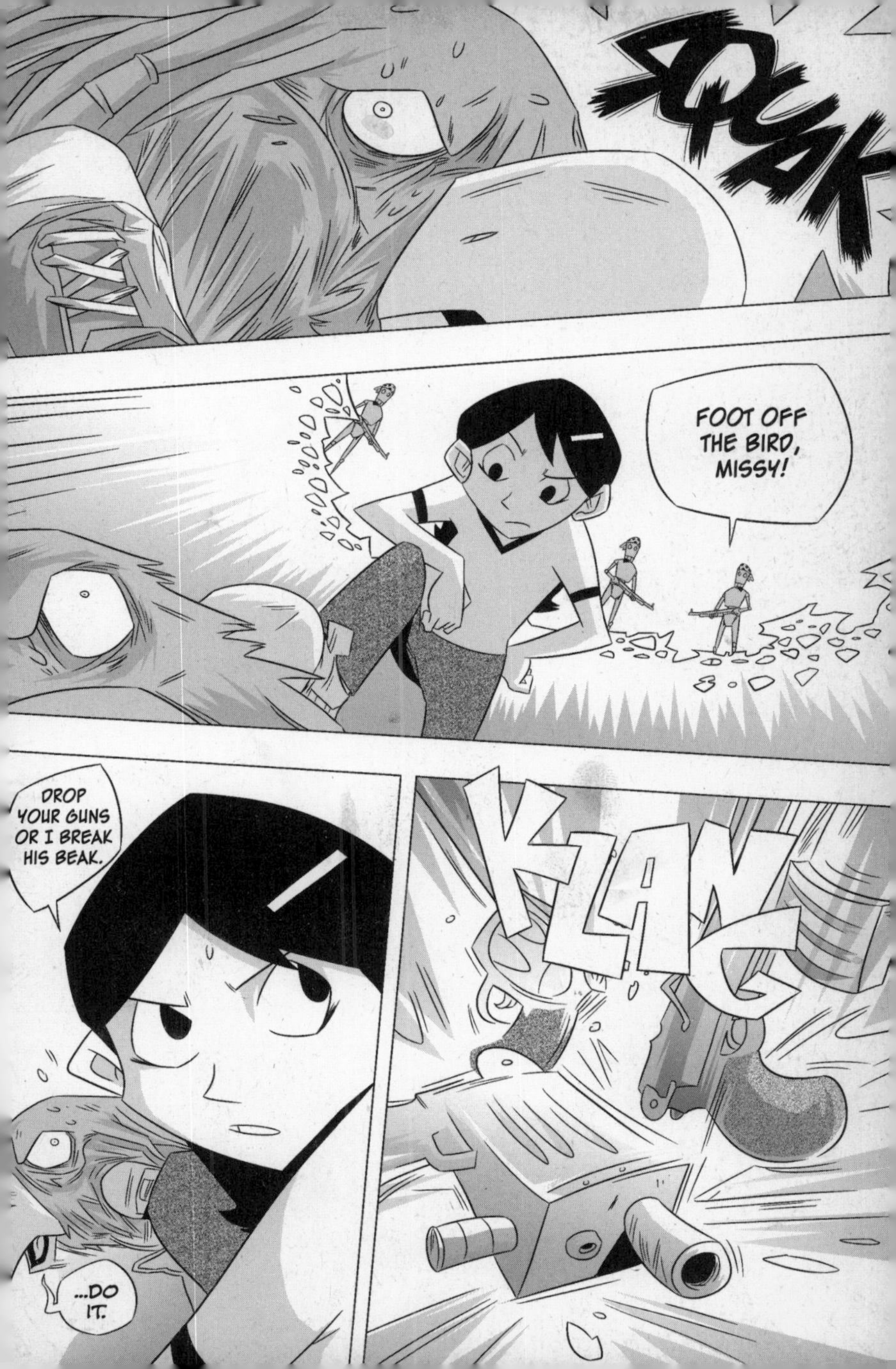
SQUAK
FOOT OFF THE BIRD, MISSY!
DROP YOUR GUNS OR I BREAK HIS BEAK.
...DO IT.
KLANG

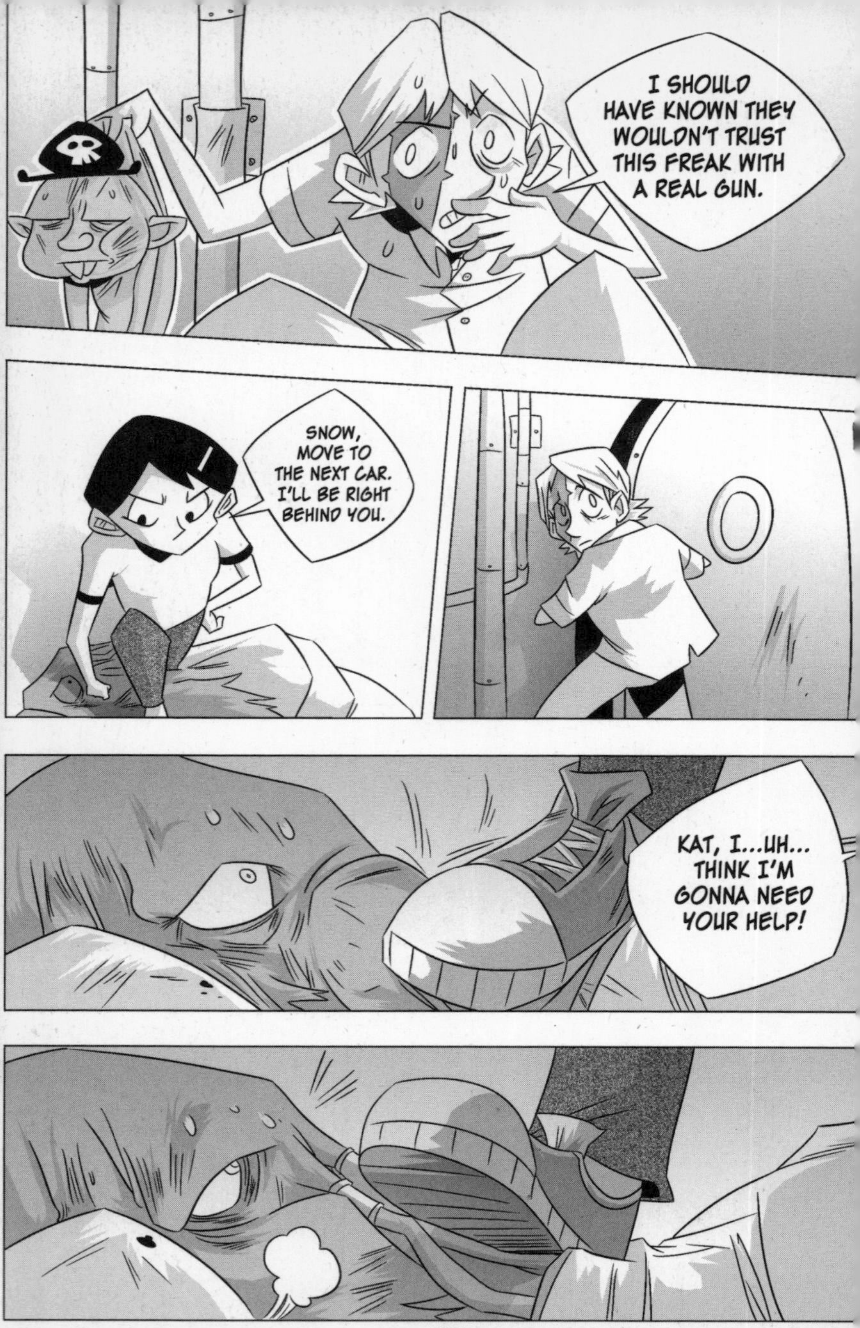
I SHOULD HAVE KNOWN THEY WOULDN'T TRUST THIS FREAK WITH A REAL GUN.
SNOW, MOVE TO THE NEXT CAR. I'LL BE RIGHT BEHIND YOU.
KAT, I...UH... THINK I'M GONNA NEED YOUR HELP!

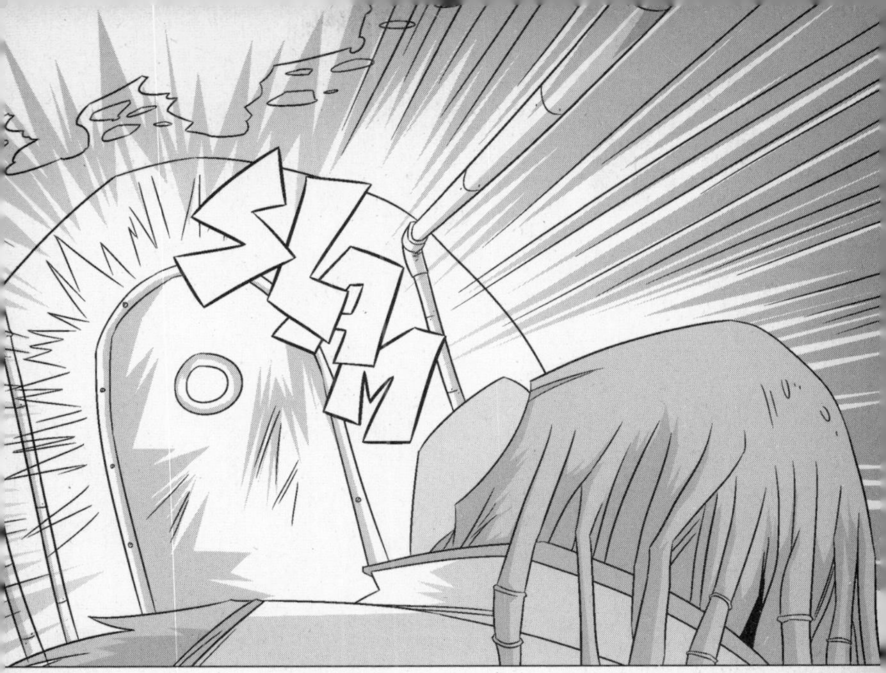
SLAM

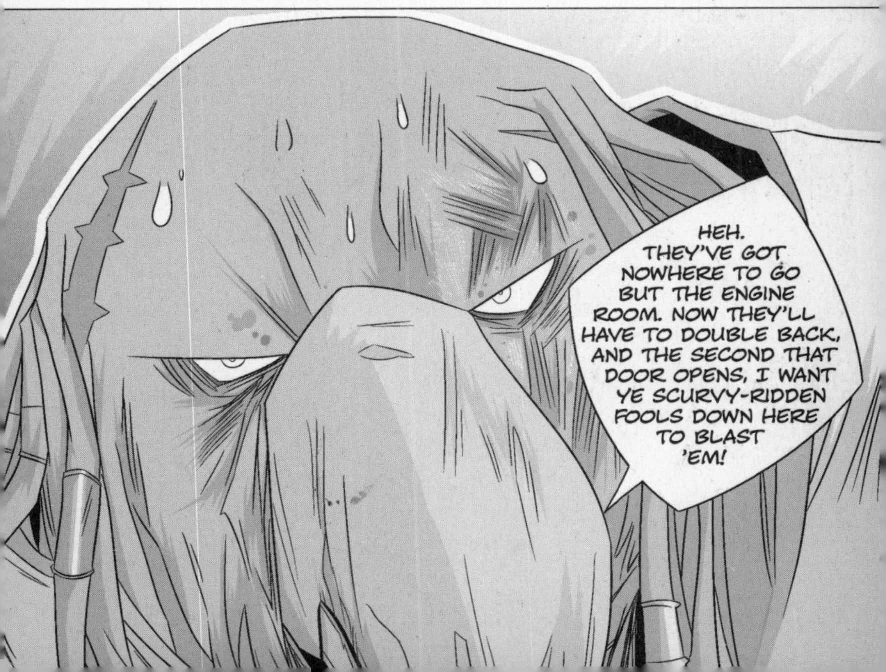
HEH. THEY'VE GOT NOWHERE TO GO BUT THE ENGINE ROOM. NOW THEY'LL HAVE TO DOUBLE BACK, AND THE SECOND THAT DOOR OPENS, I WANT YE SCURVY-RIDDEN FOOLS DOWN HERE TO BLAST 'EM!

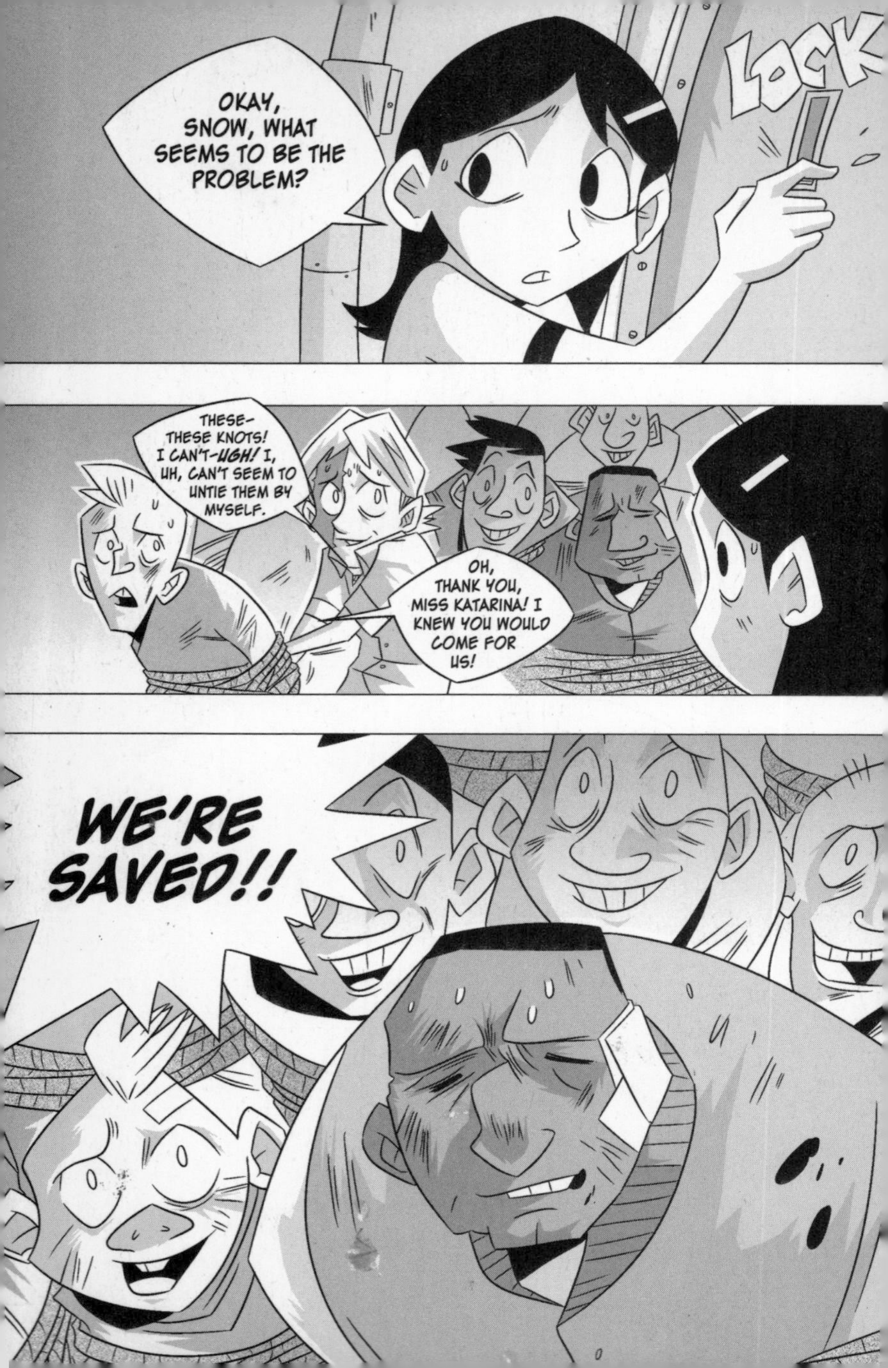
LOCK
OKAY, SNOW, WHAT SEEMS TO BE THE PROBLEM?
THESE- THESE KNOTS! I CAN'T-UGH! I, UH, CAN'T SEEM TO UNTIE THEM BY MYSELF.
OH, THANK YOU, MISS KATARINA! I KNEW YOU WOULD COME FOR US!
WE'RE SAVED!!

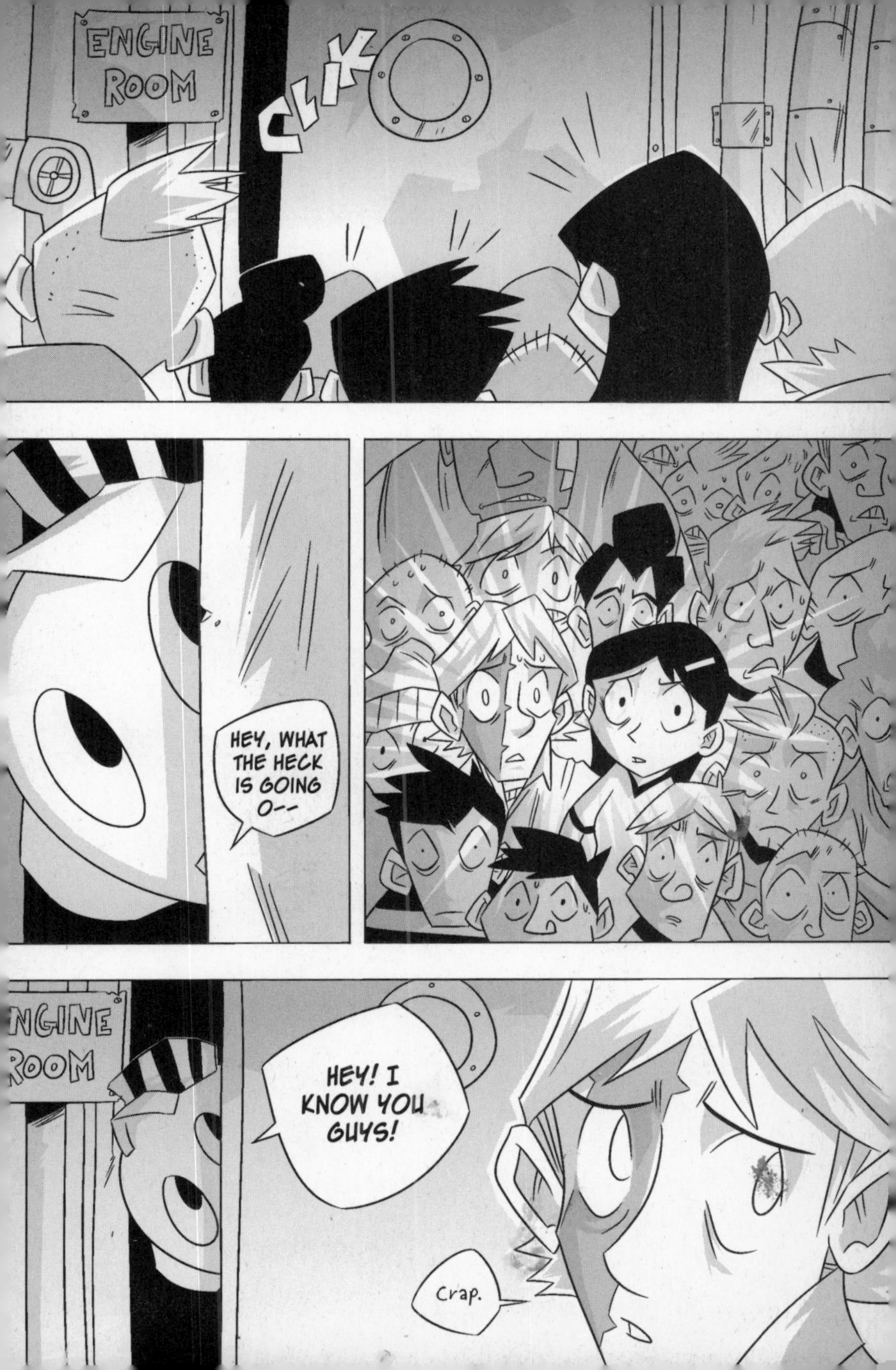
ENGINE ROOM
CLIK
HEY, WHAT THE HECK IS GOING O--
HEY! I KNOW YOU GUYS!
Crap.

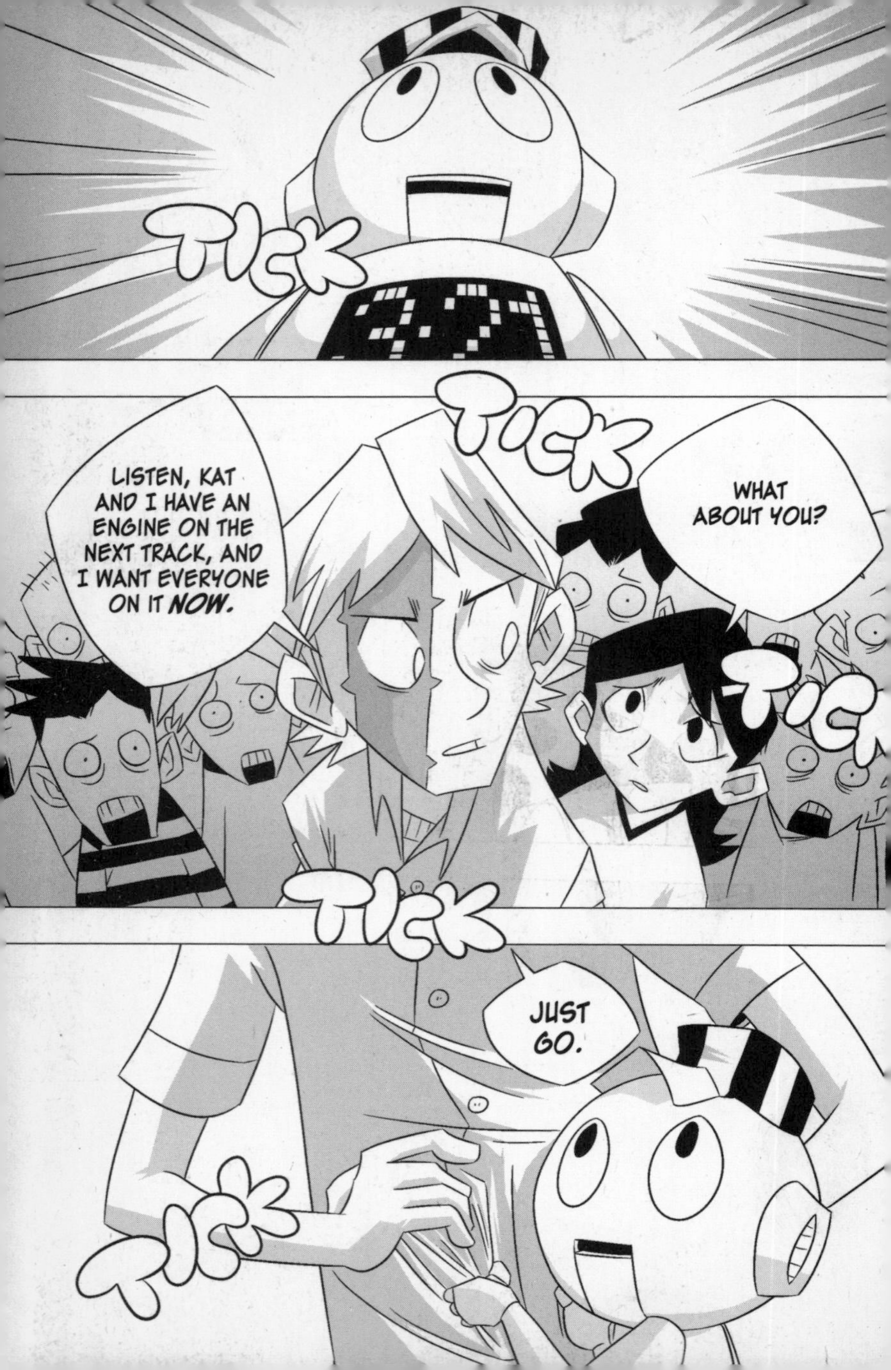
TICK
TICK
LISTEN, KAT AND I HAVE AN ENGINE ON THE NEXT TRACK, AND I WANT EVERYONE ON IT NOW.
WHAT ABOUT YOU?
TICK
TICK
JUST GO.
TICK

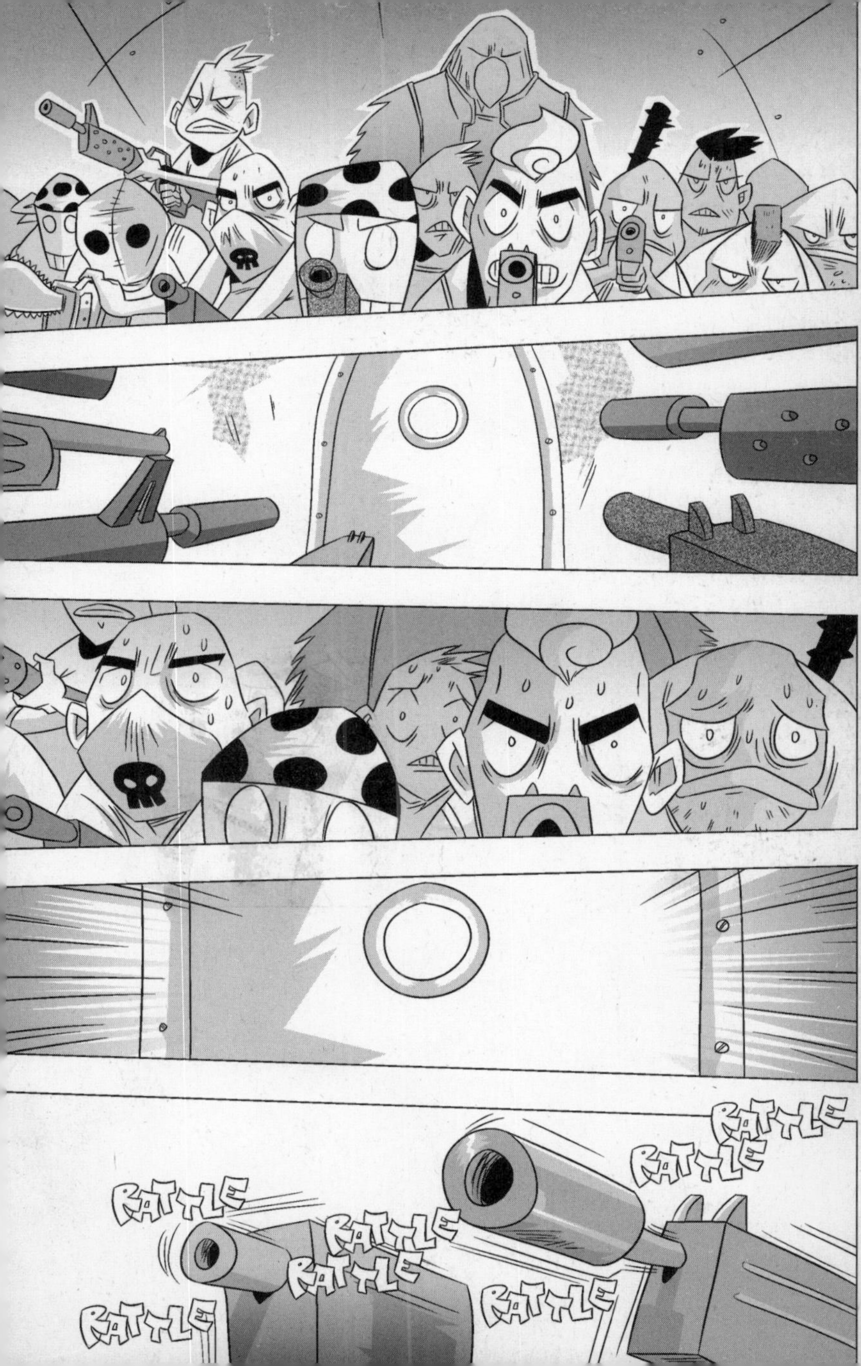
RATTLE
RATTLE
RATTLE
RATTLE
RATTLE
RATTLE
RATTLE

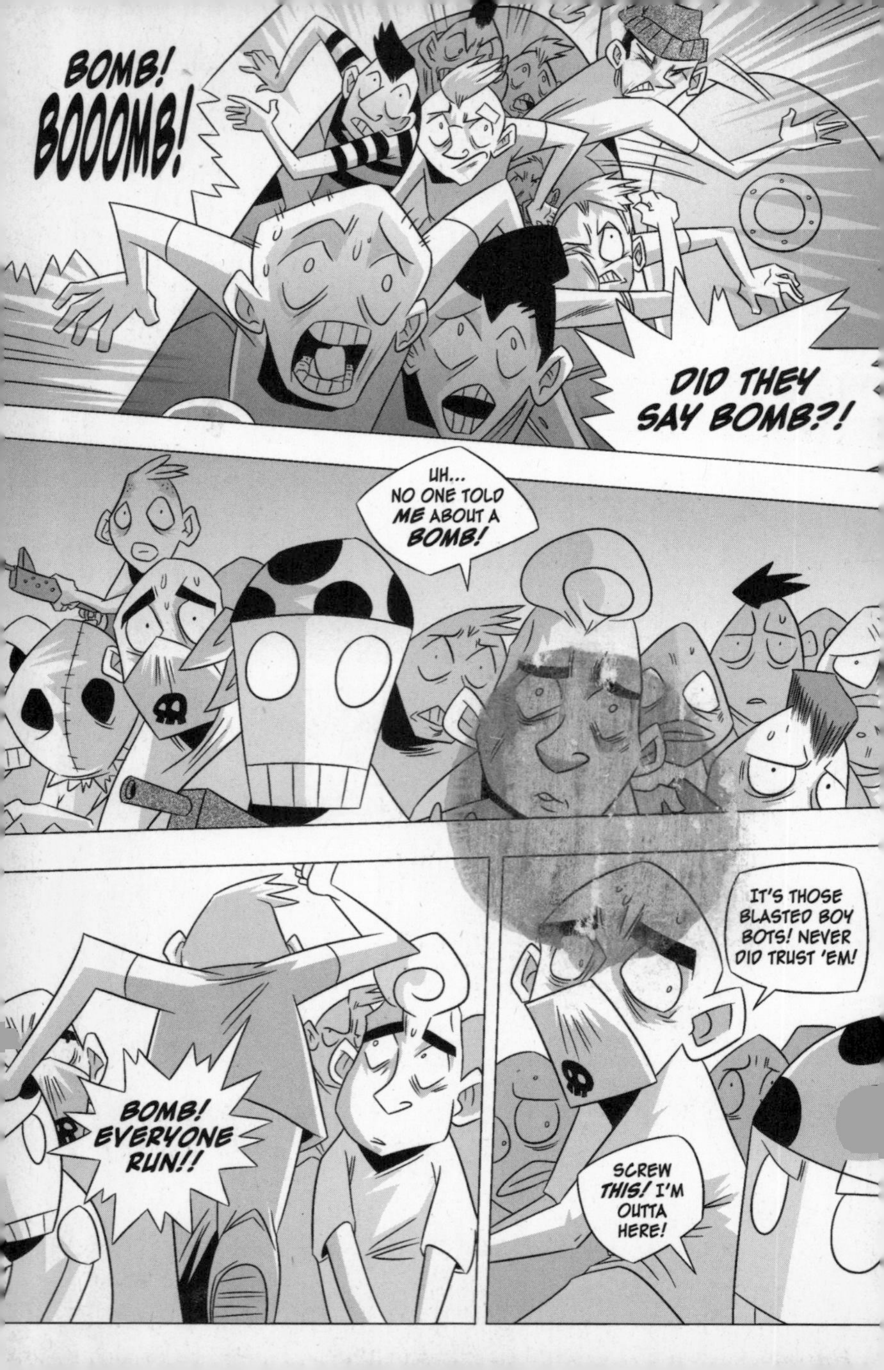
BOMB! BOOOMB!
DID THEY SAY BOMB?!
UH... NO ONE TOLD ME ABOUT A BOMB!
BOMB! EVERYONE RUN!!
IT'S THOSE BLASTED BOY BOTS! NEVER DID TRUST 'EM!
SCREW THIS! I'M OUTTA HERE!

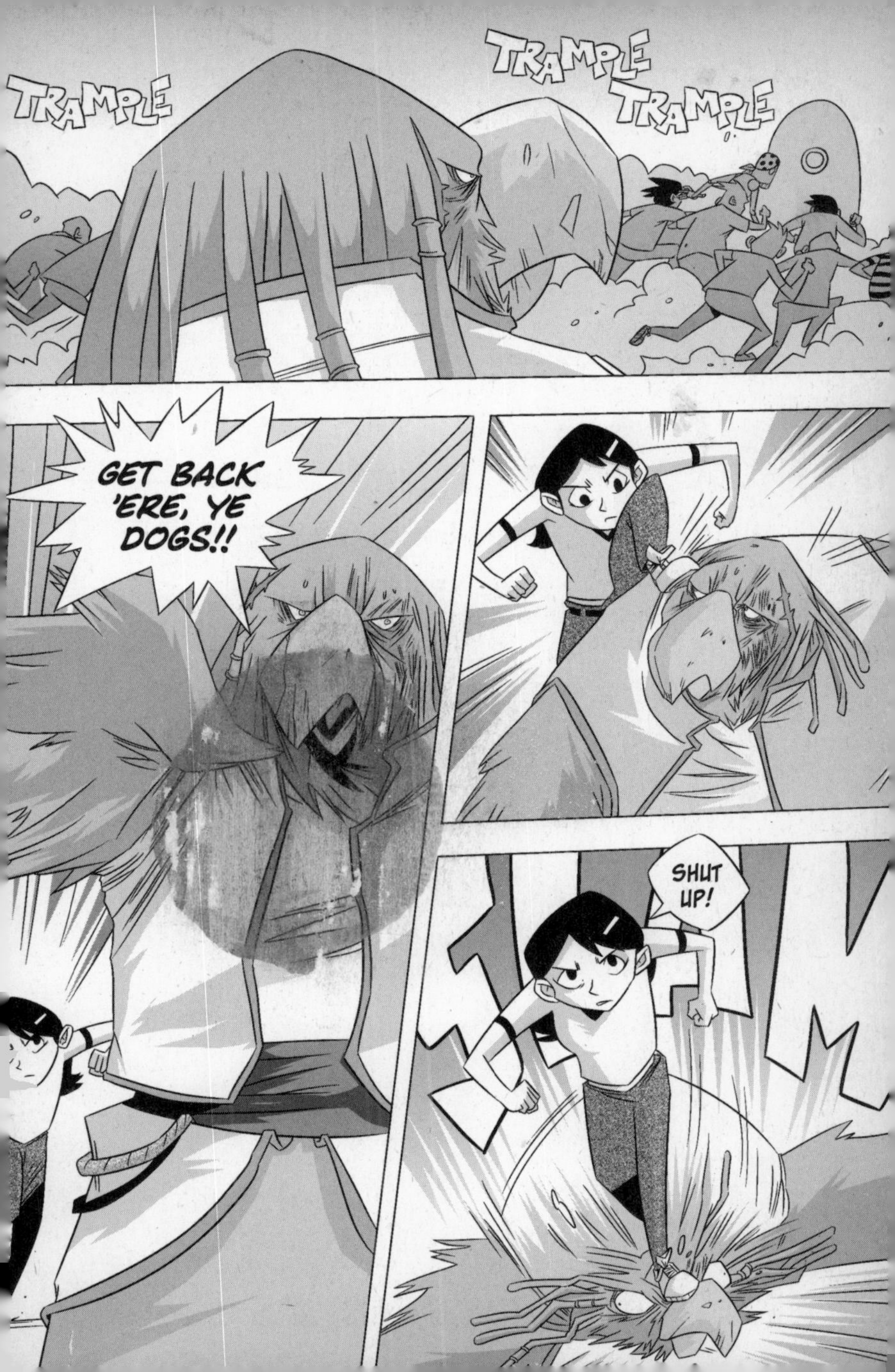
TRAMPLE
TRAMPLE
TRAMPLE
GET BACK 'ERE, YE DOGS!!
SHUT UP!

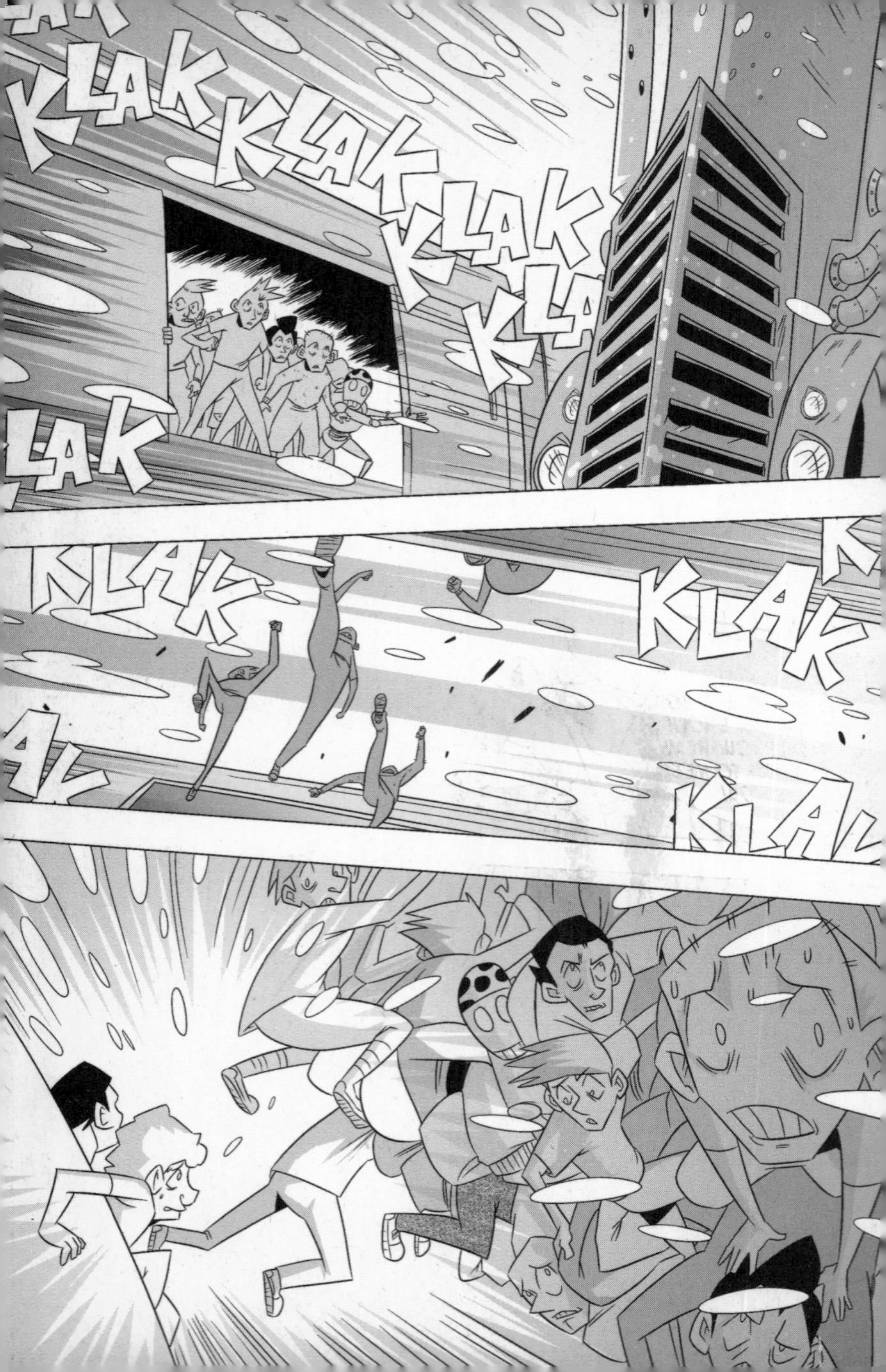
KLAK
KLAK
KLAK
KLAK
KLAK

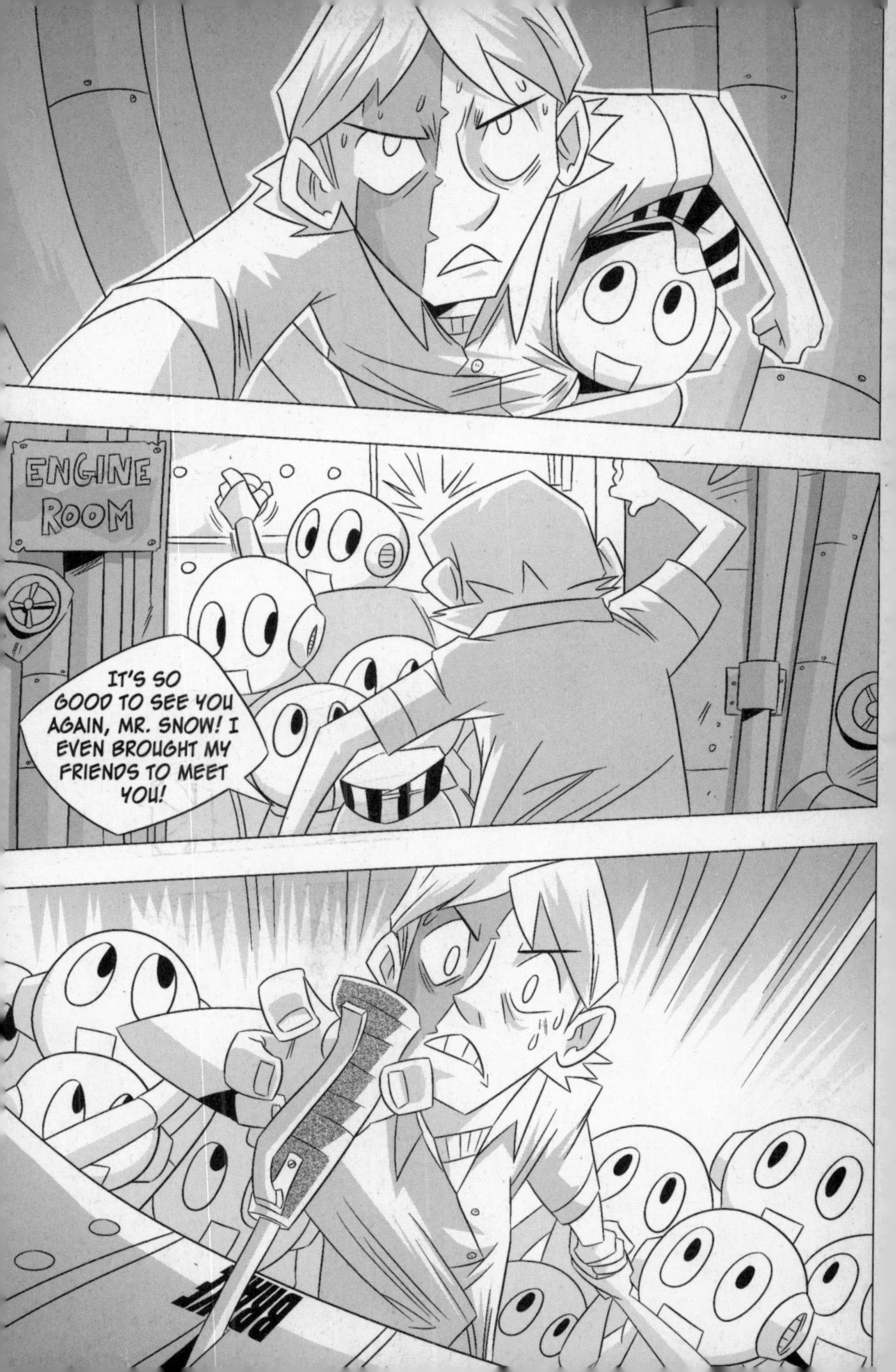
ENGINE ROOM
IT'S SO GOOD TO SEE YOU AGAIN, MR. SNOW! I EVEN BROUGHT MY FRIENDS TO MEET YOU!

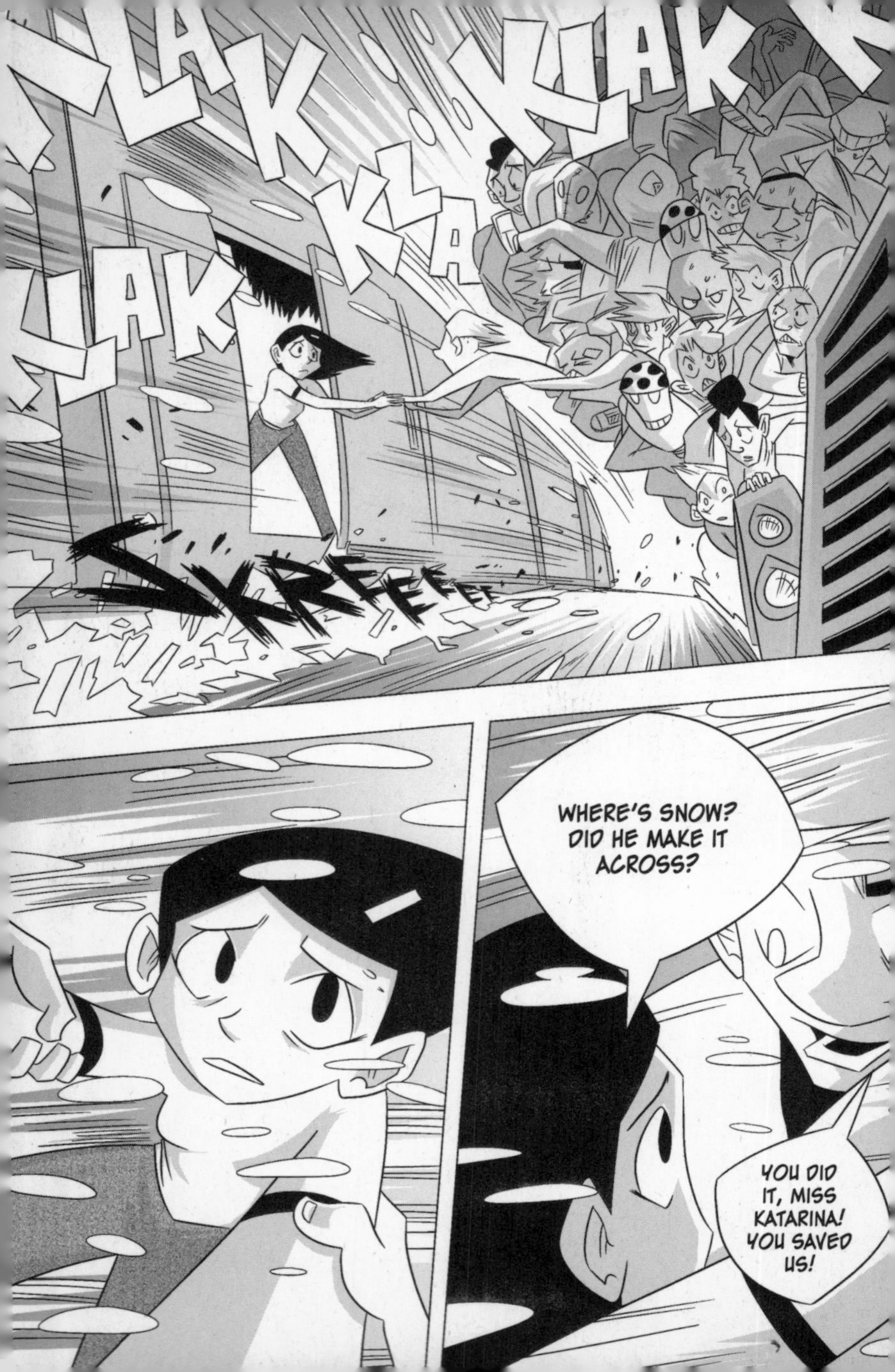
KLAK
KLAK
KLA
SKREEEE
WHERE'S SNOW? DID HE MAKE IT ACROSS?
YOU DID IT, MISS KATARINA! YOU SAVED US!

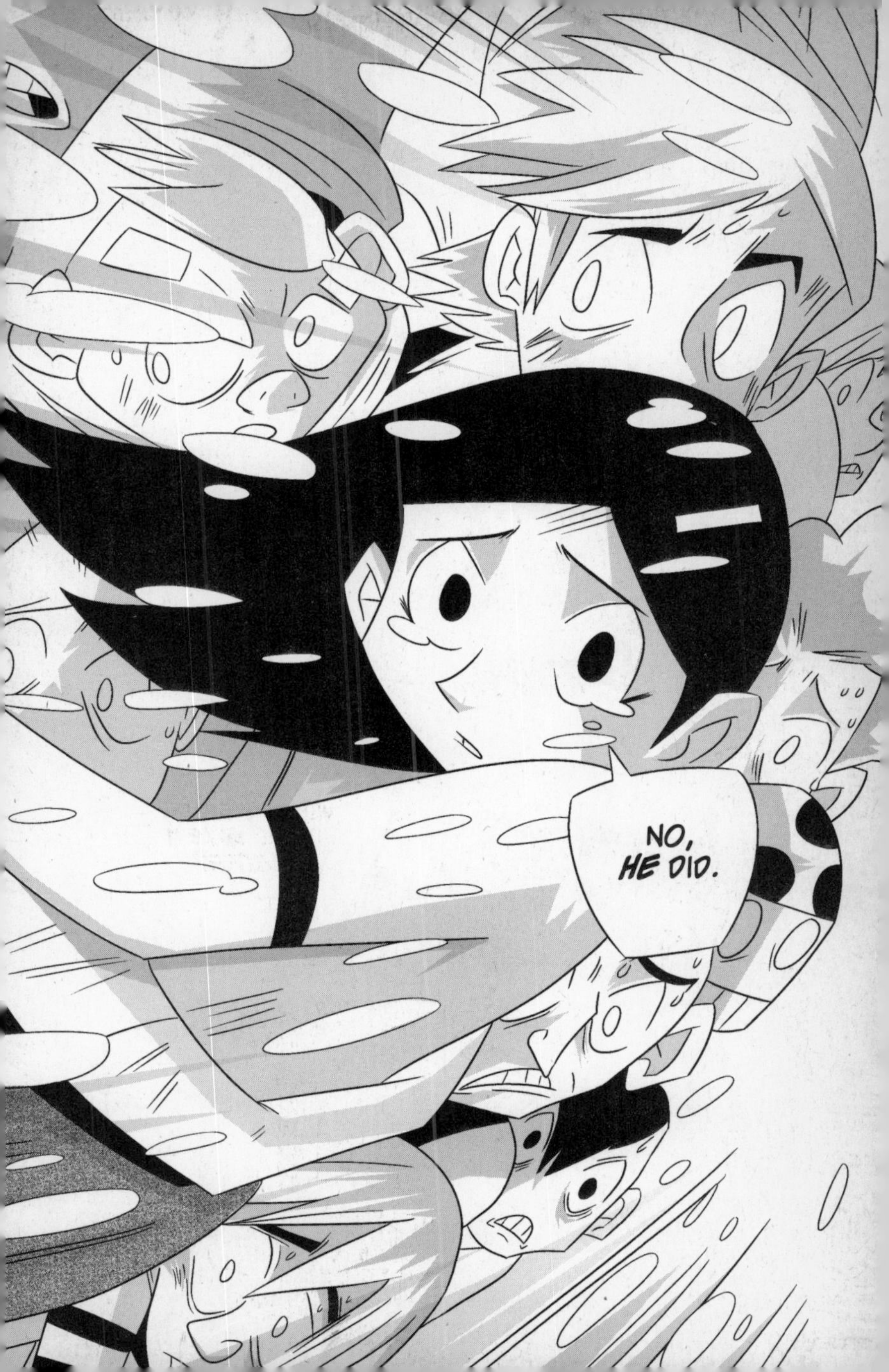
NO, HE DID.

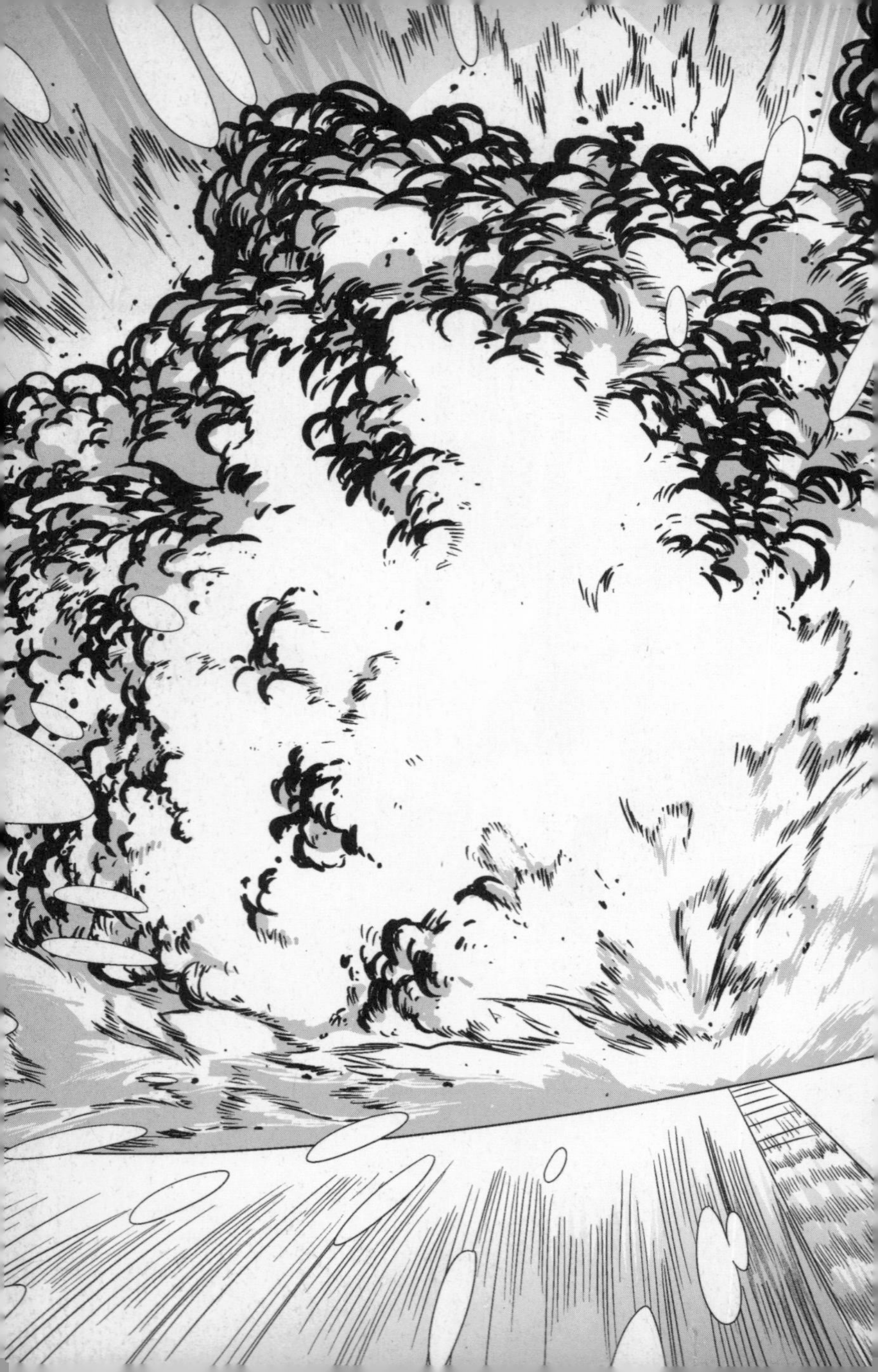

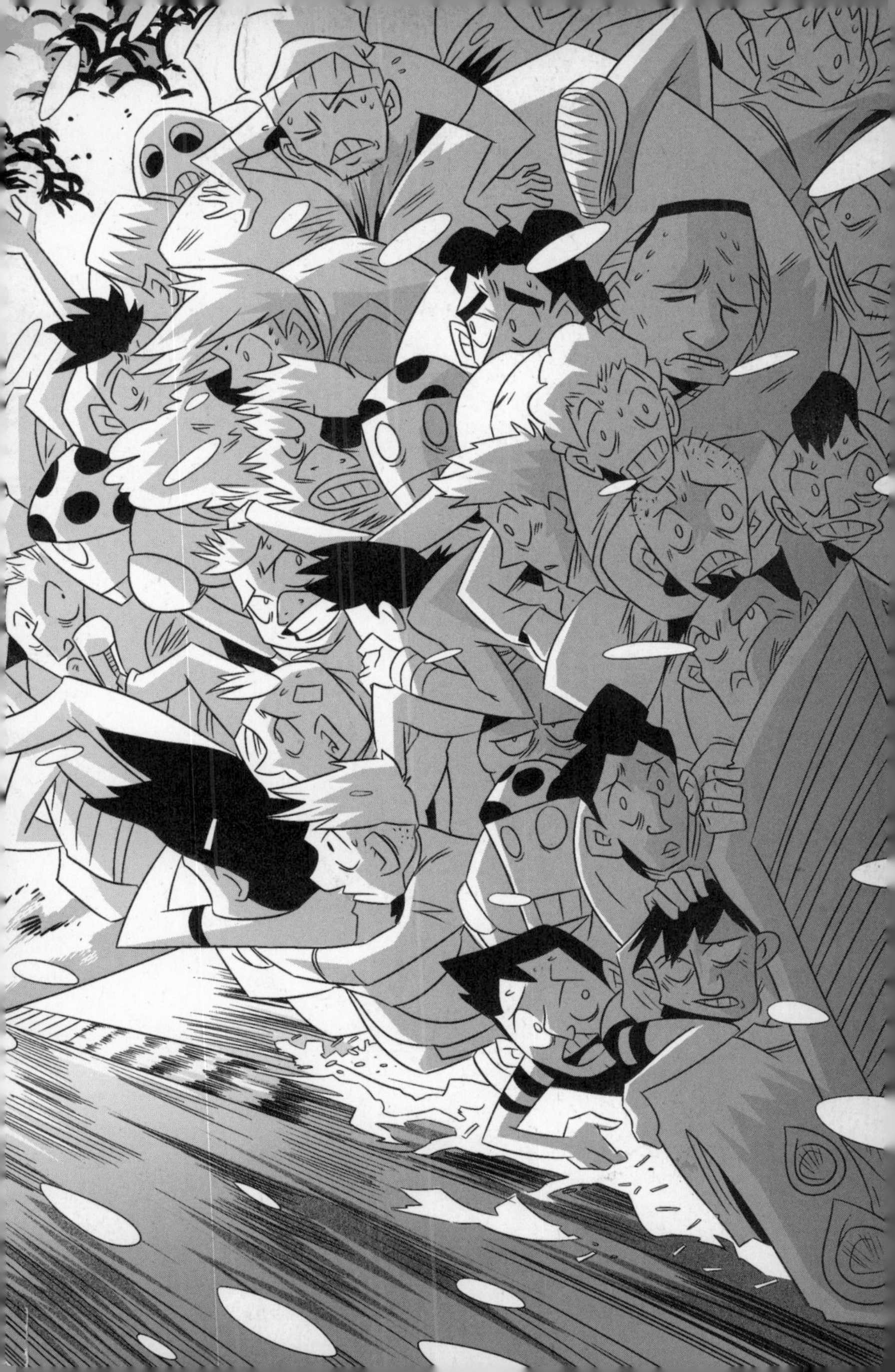

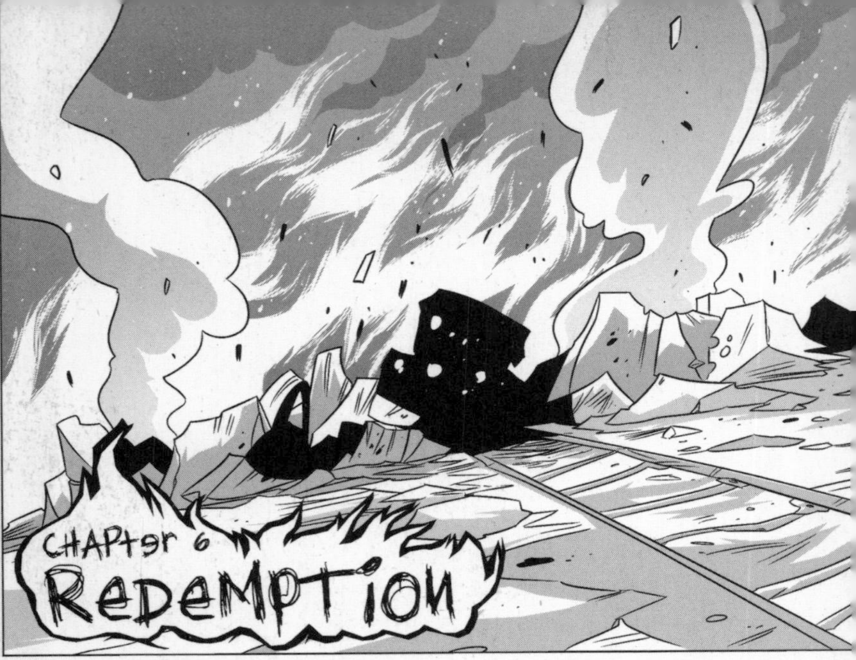
CHAPTER 6
REDEMPTION
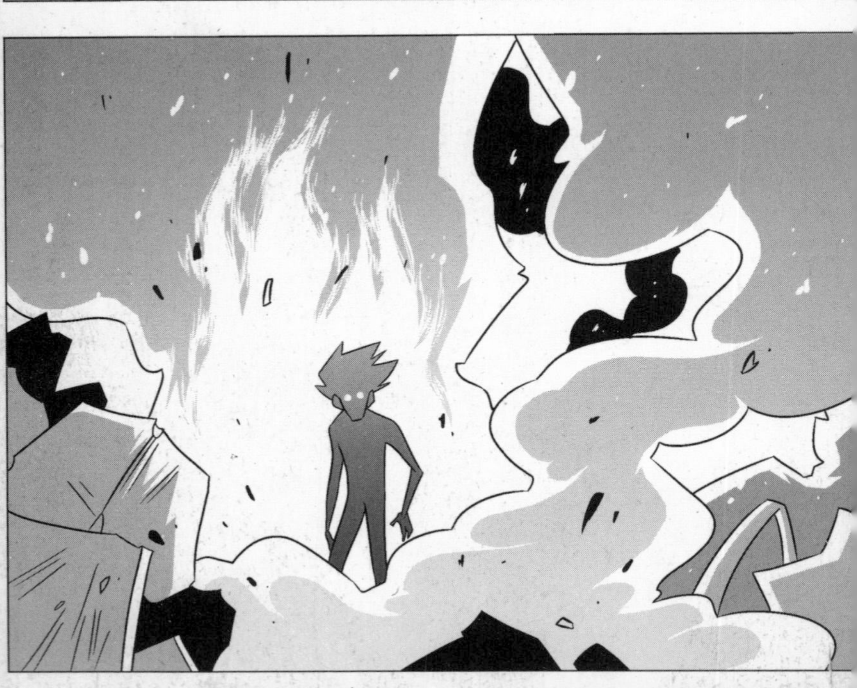

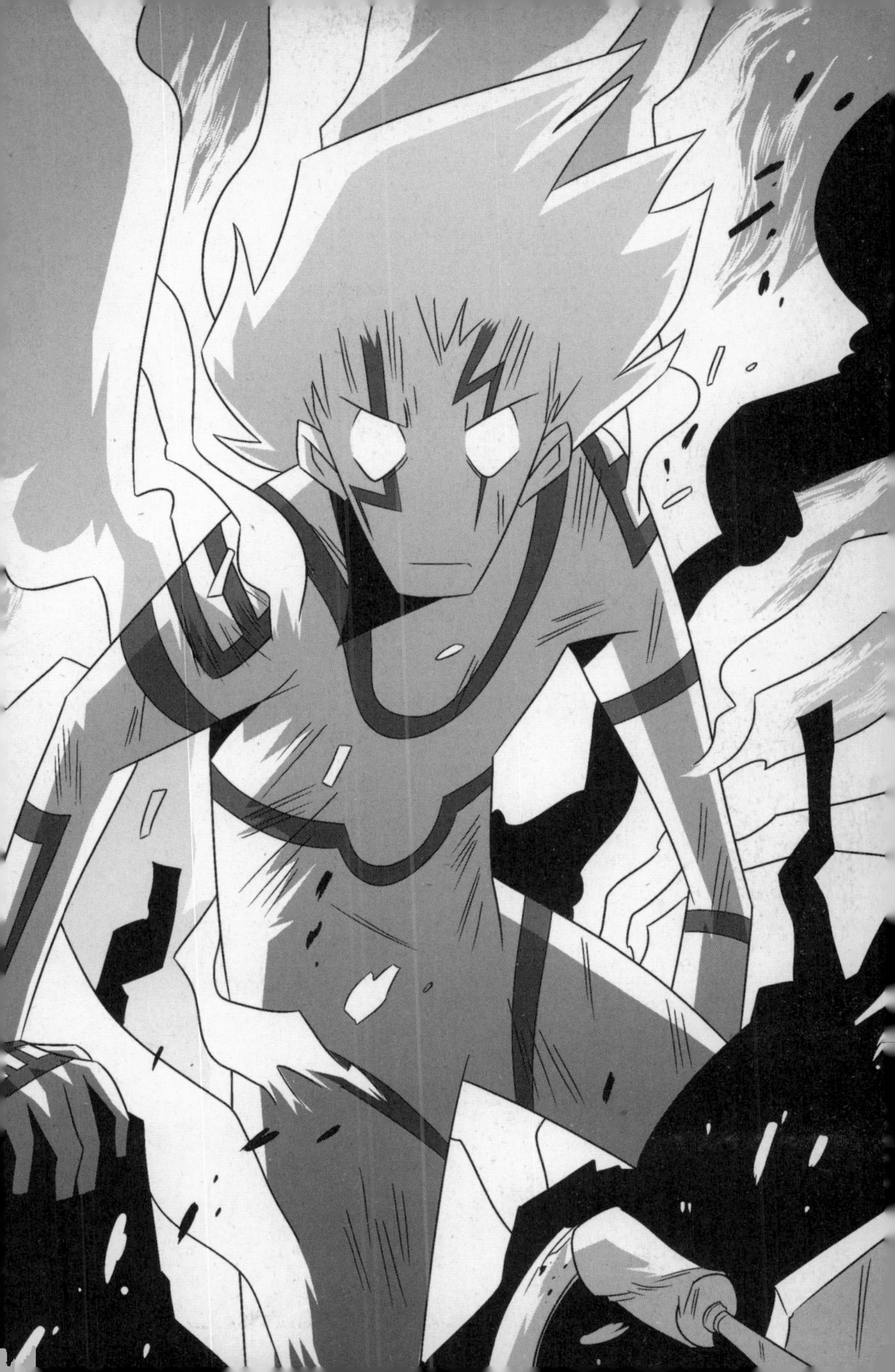

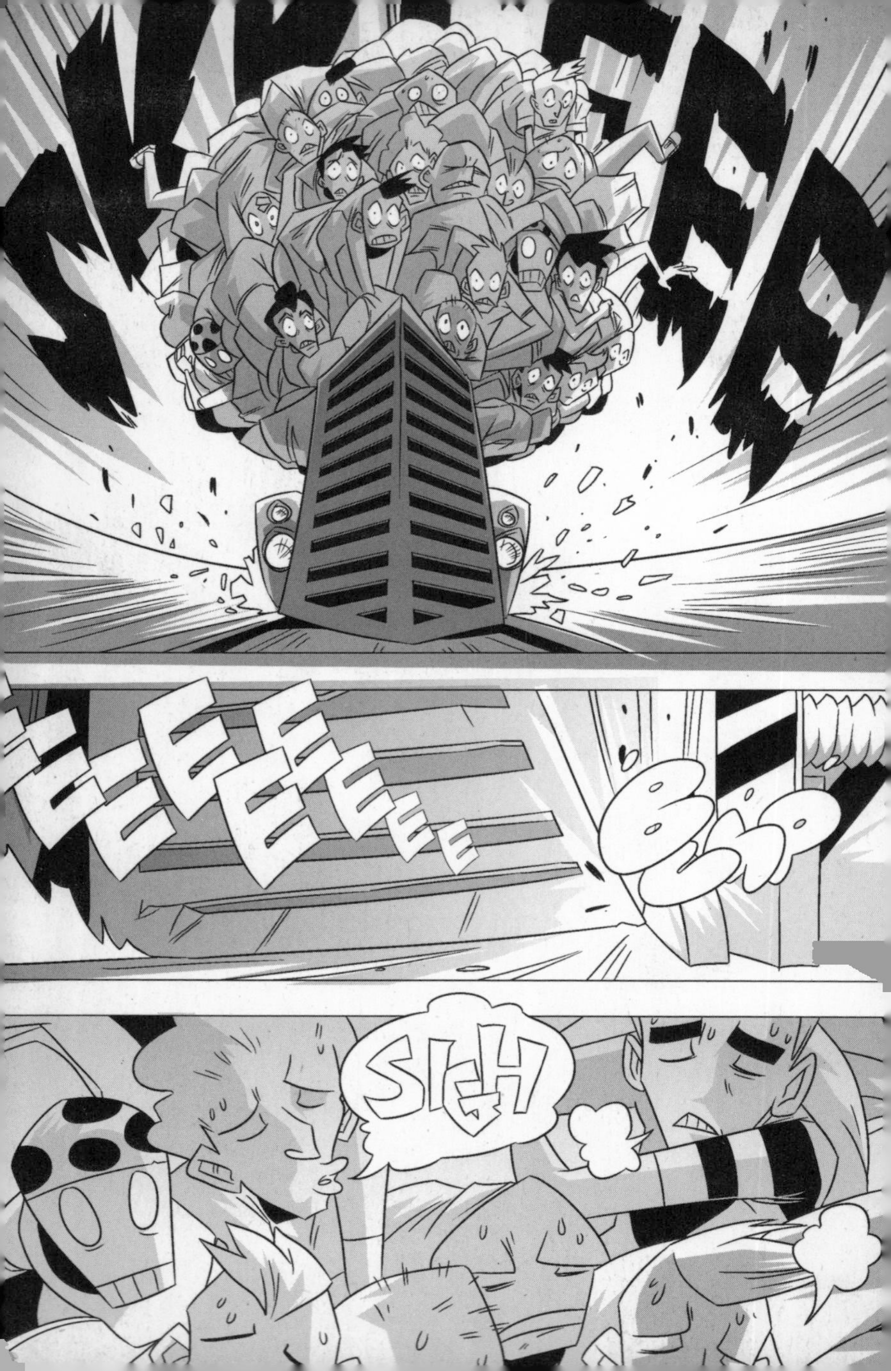
EEEEEEEEEEE
SIGH

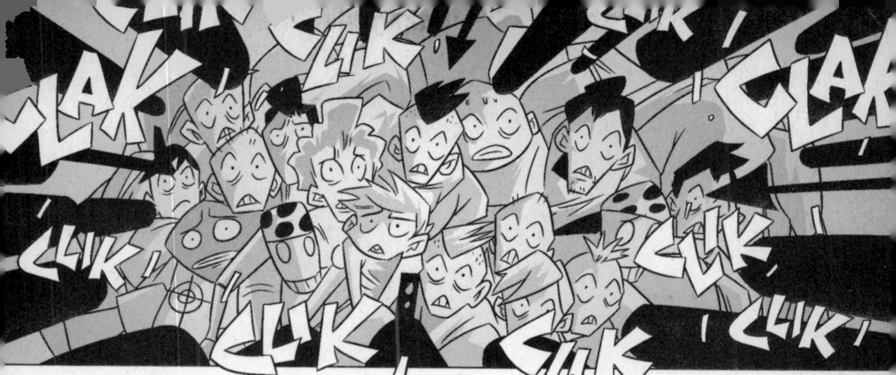
CLAK
CLIK
CLAK
CLIK
CLIK
CLIK
CLIK
CLIK

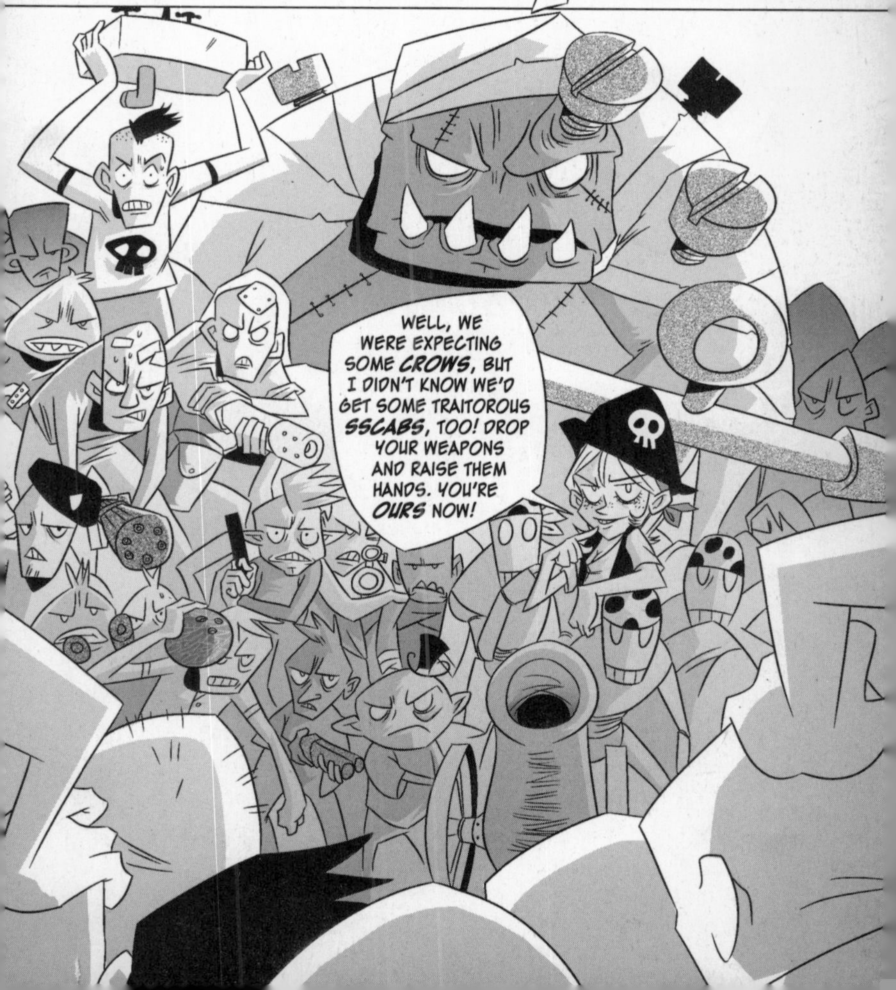
WELL, WE WERE EXPECTING SOME *CROWS*, BUT I DIDN'T KNOW WE'D GET SOME TRAITOROUS *SSCABS*, TOO! DROP YOUR WEAPONS AND RAISE THEM HANDS. YOU'RE *OURS* NOW!

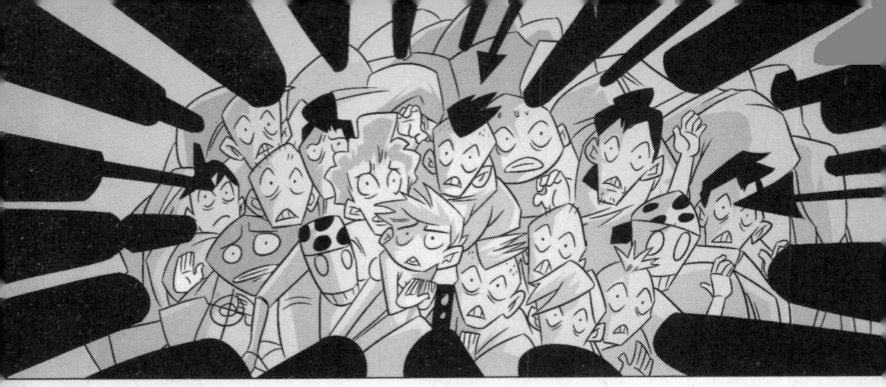

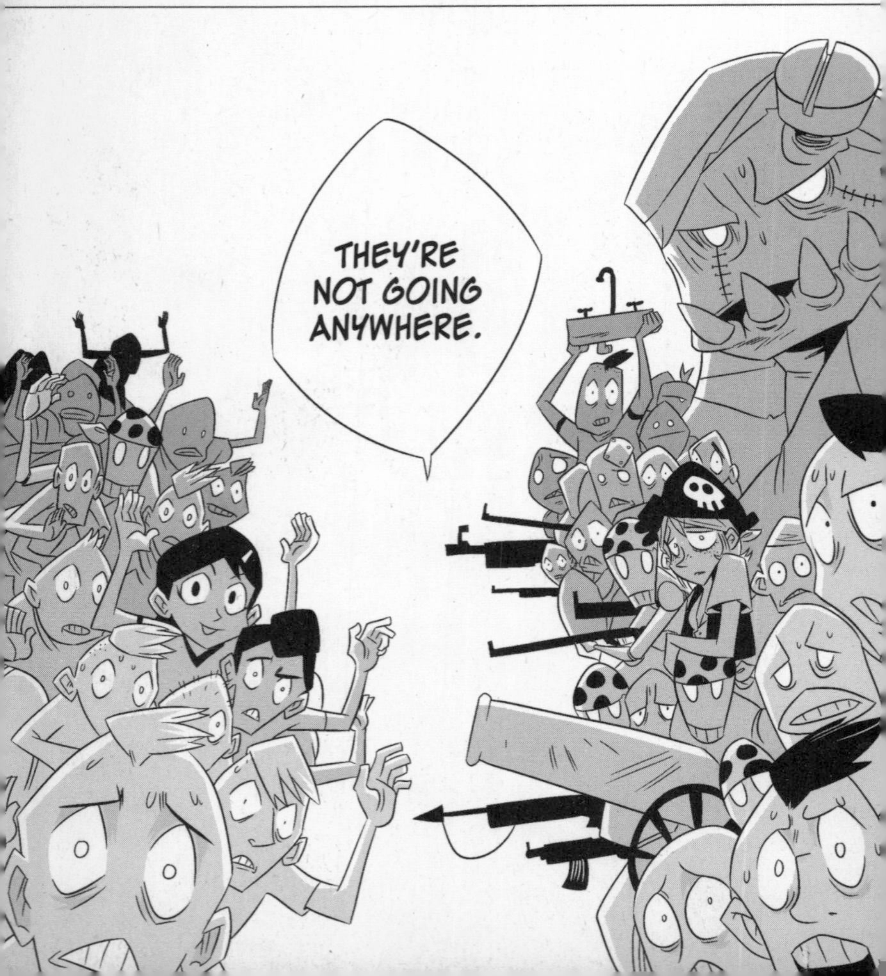
THEY'RE NOT GOING ANYWHERE.

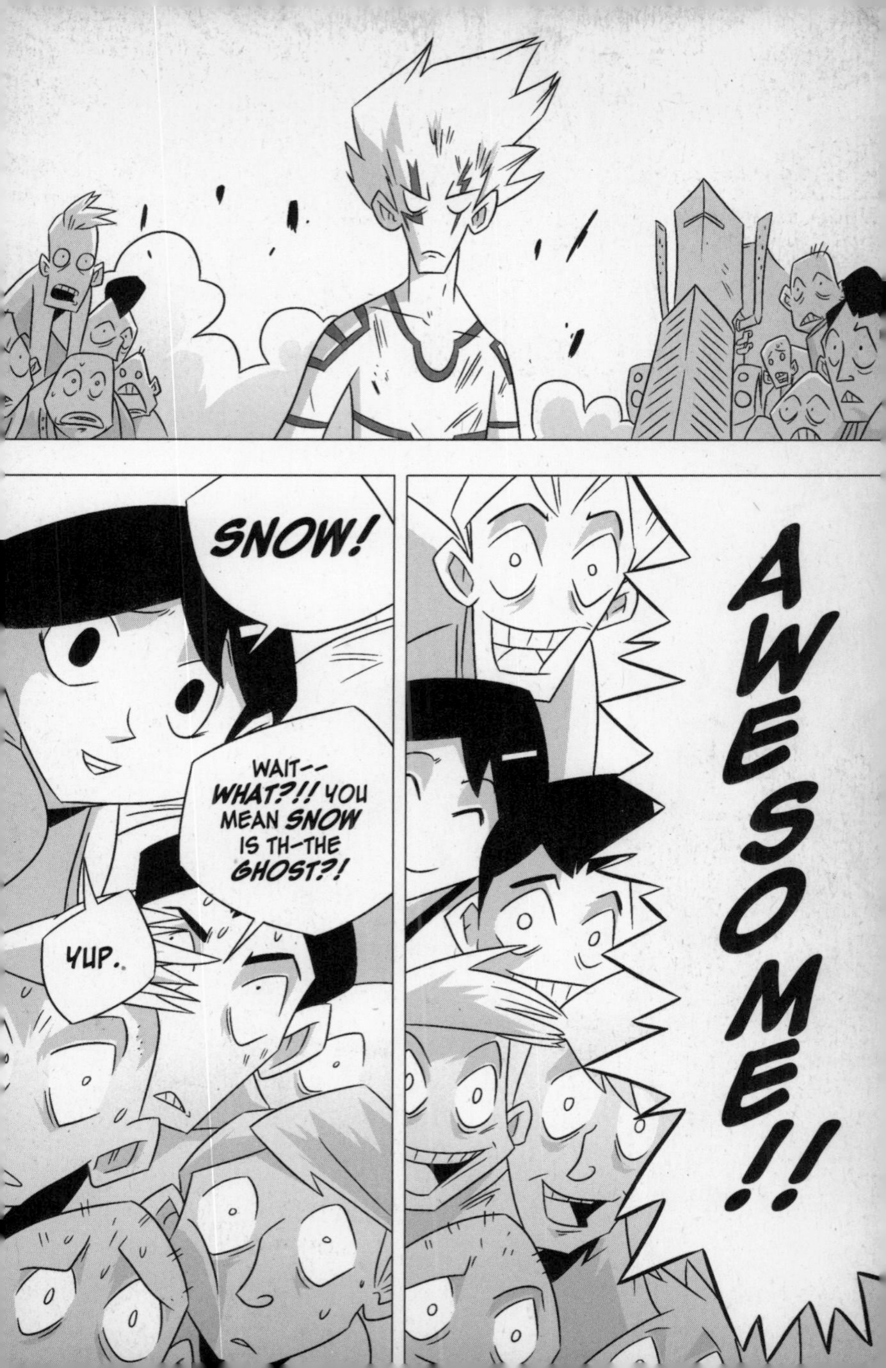
AWESOME!!
SNOW!
WAIT-- WHAT?!! YOU MEAN SNOW IS TH-THE GHOST?!
YUP..

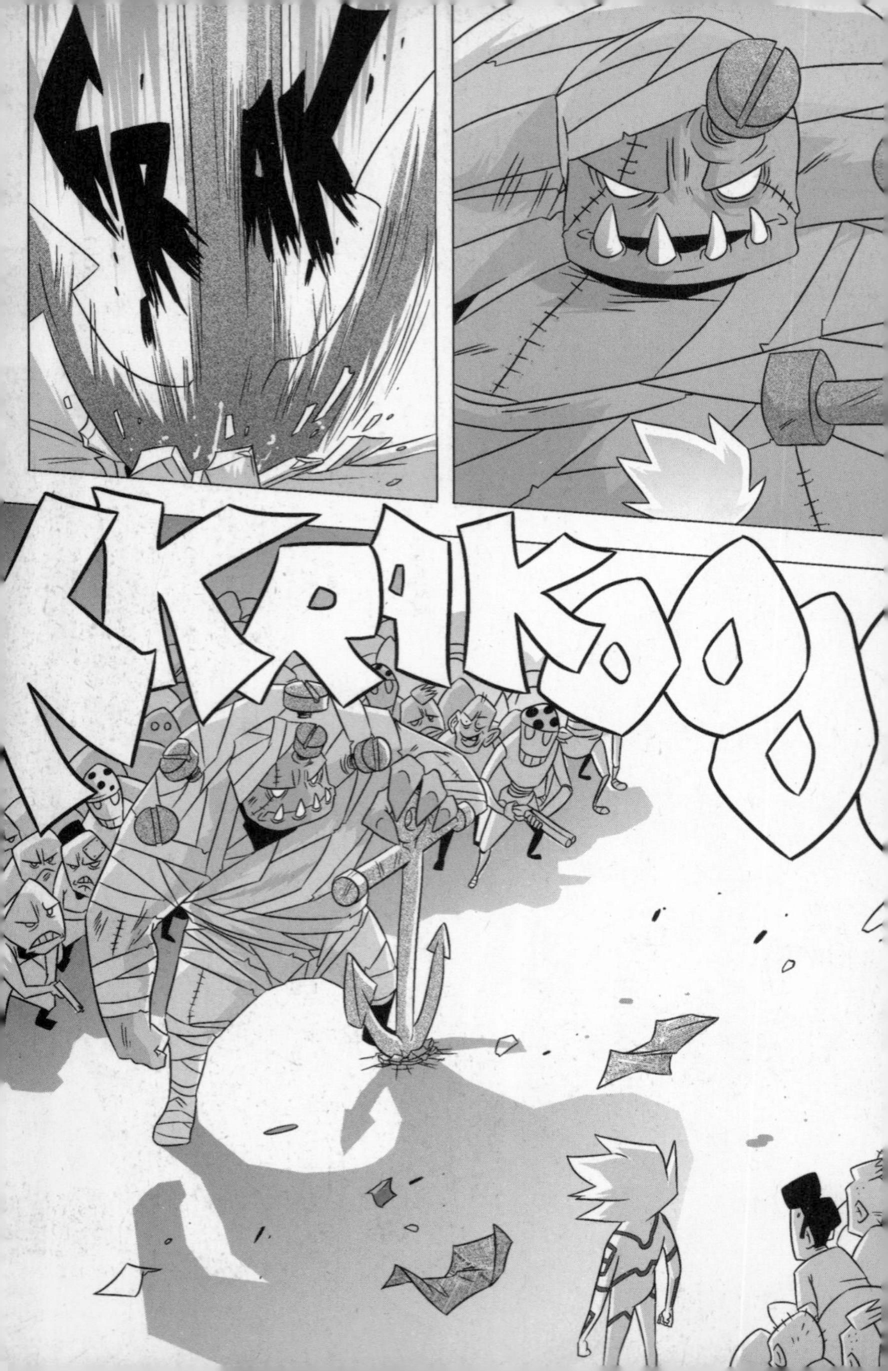
GRAK
KRAKOOO

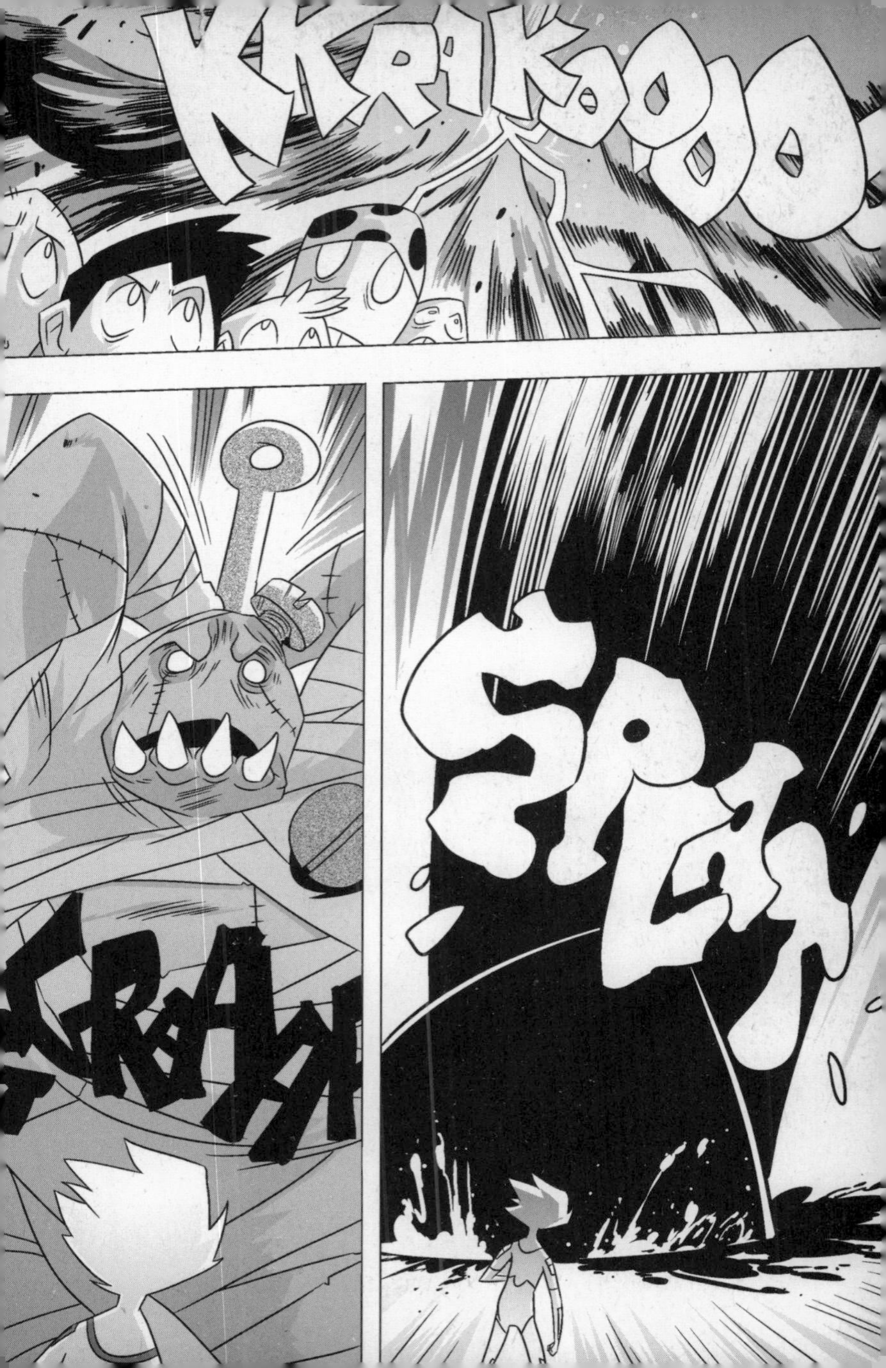
KKRAKOOOOO
SPLASH
KRAAM

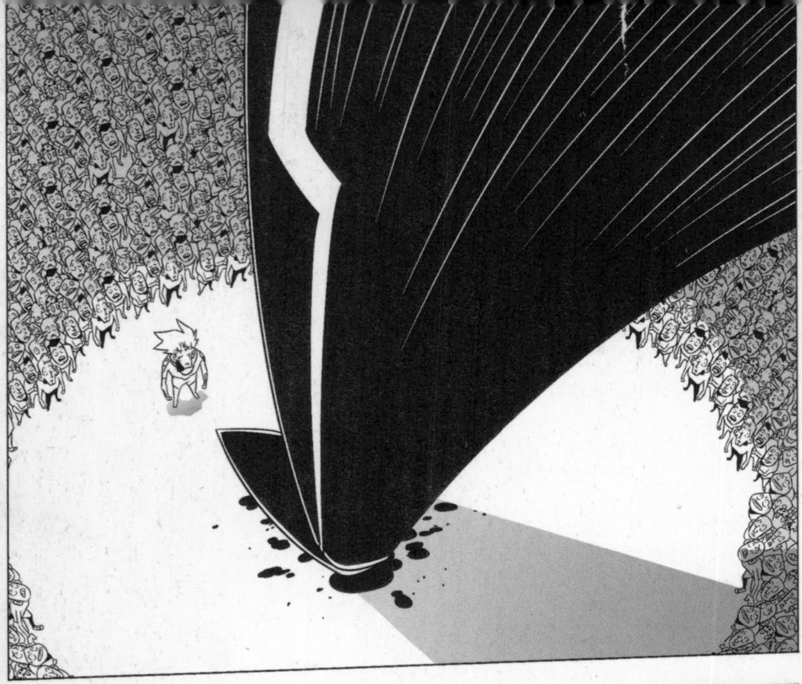

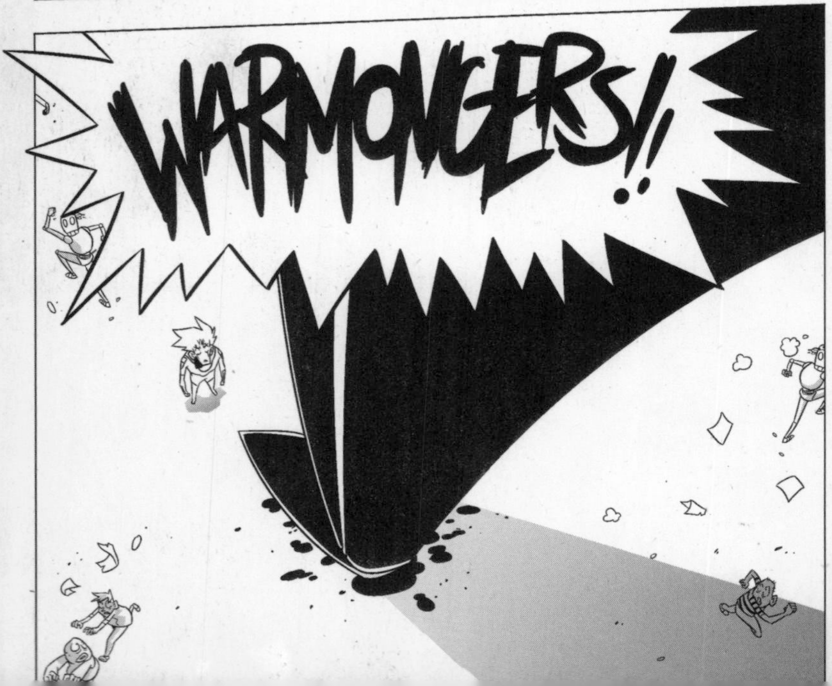
WARMONGERS!!

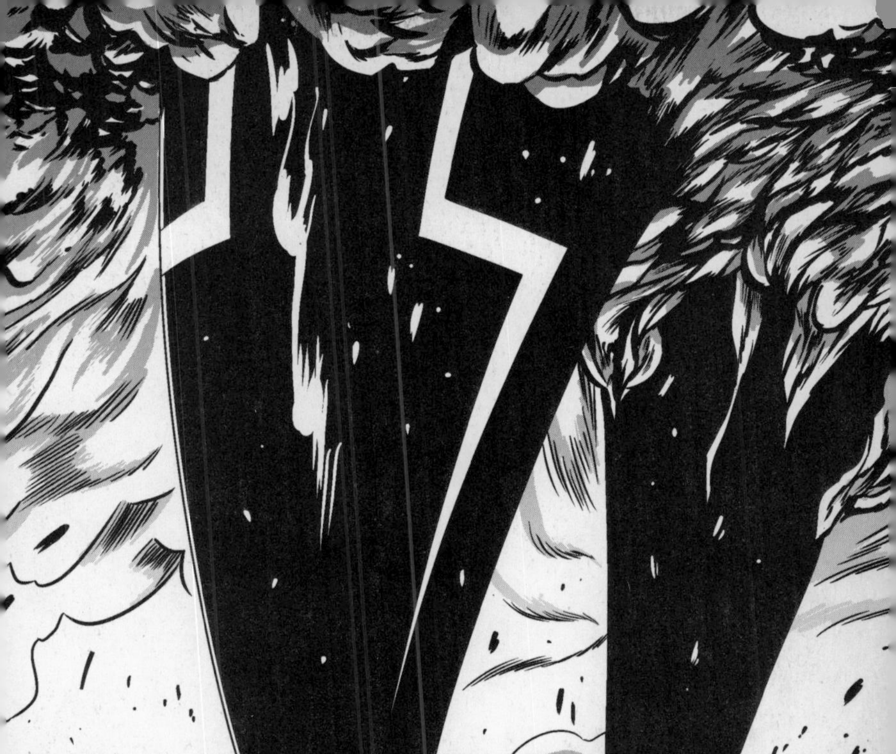

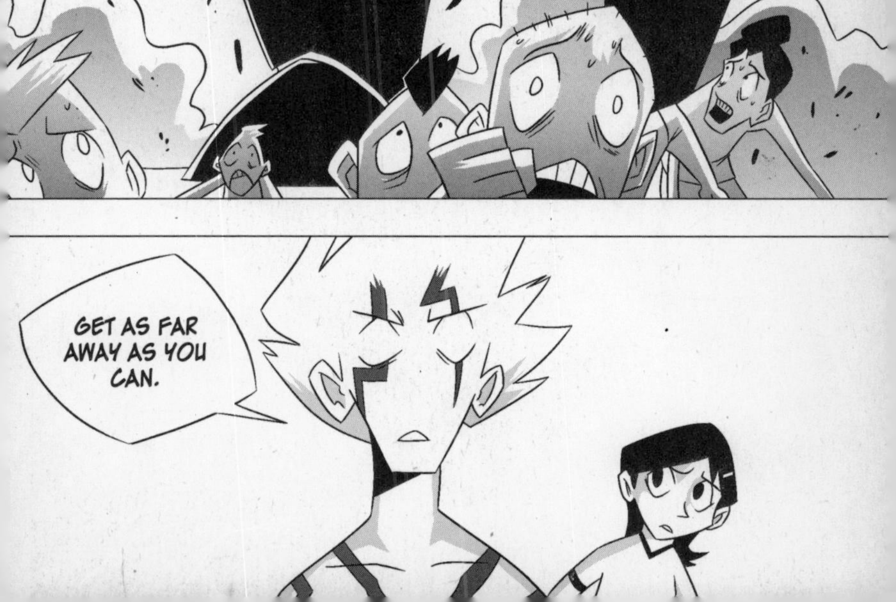
GET AS FAR AWAY AS YOU CAN.

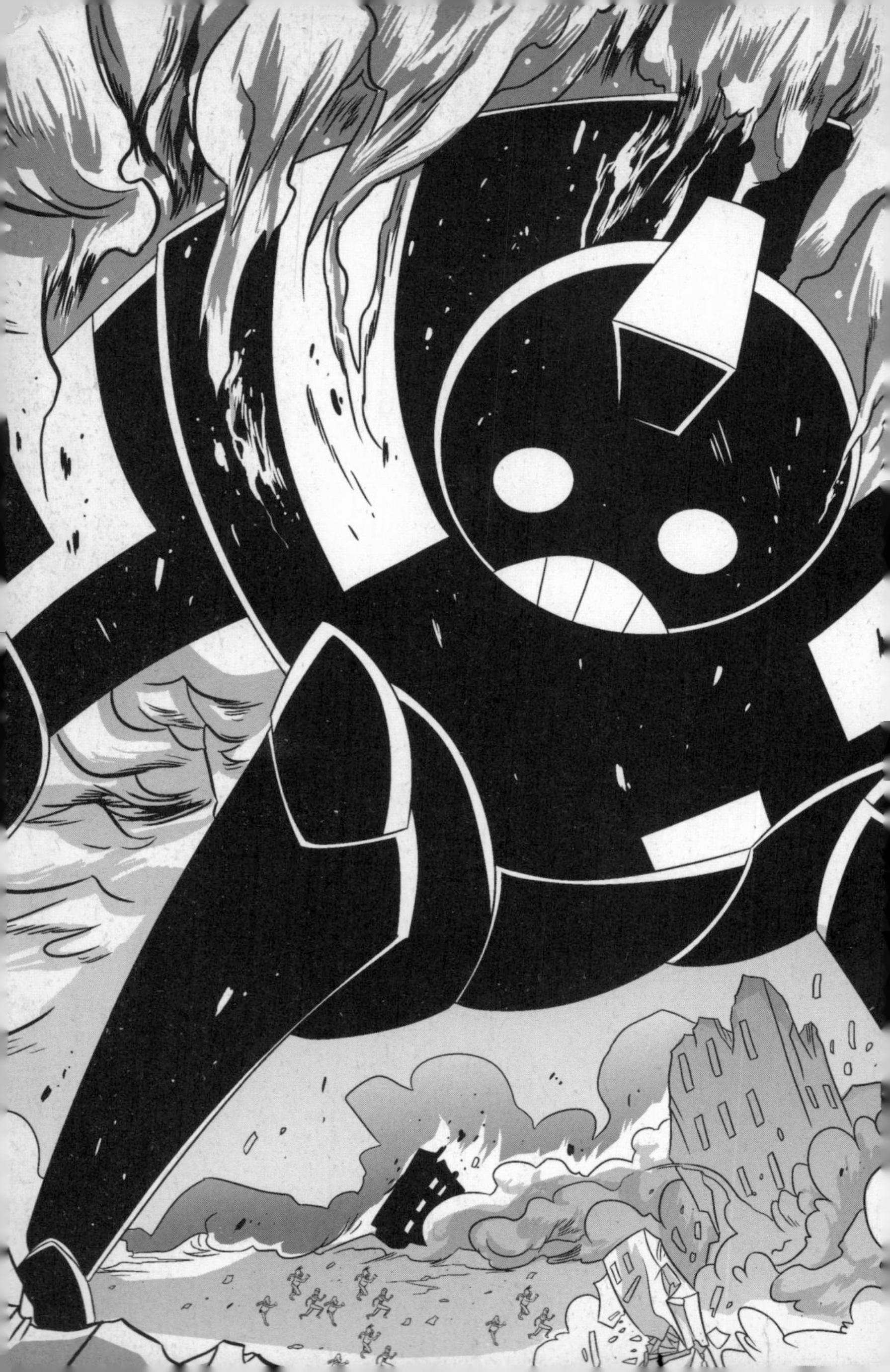

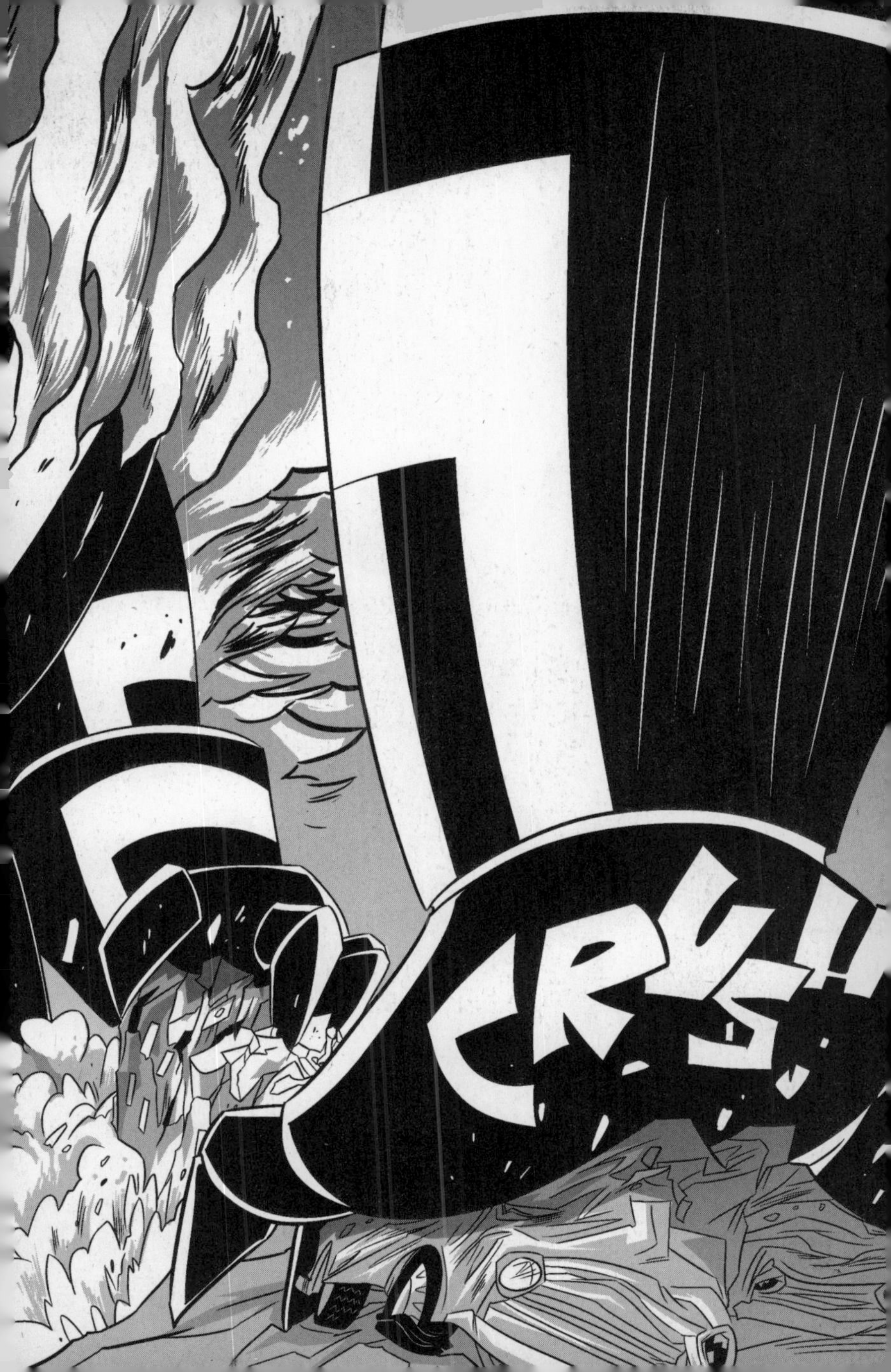
CRUSH

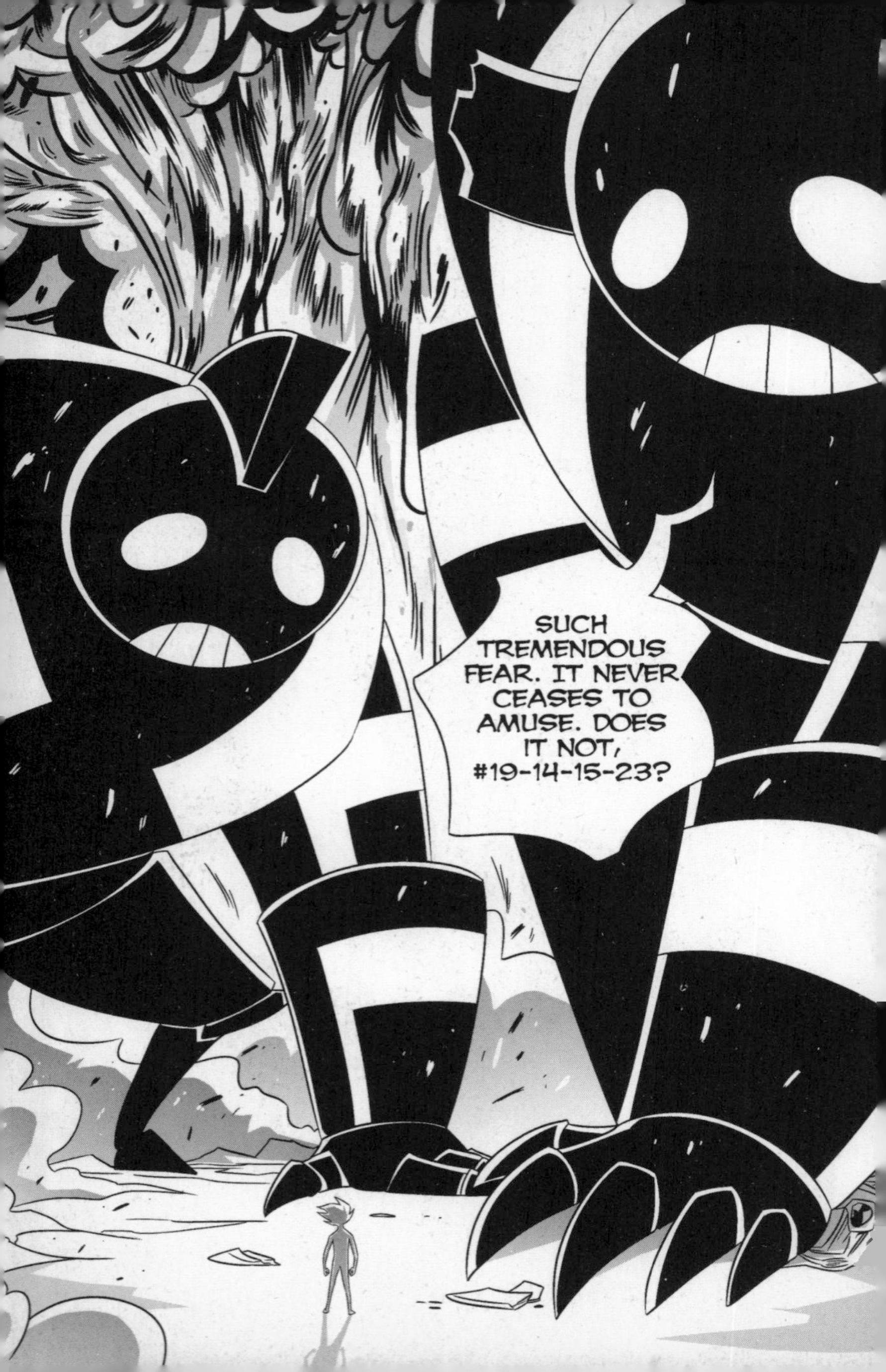
SUCH TREMENDOUS FEAR. IT NEVER CEASES TO AMUSE. DOES IT NOT, #19-14-15-23?

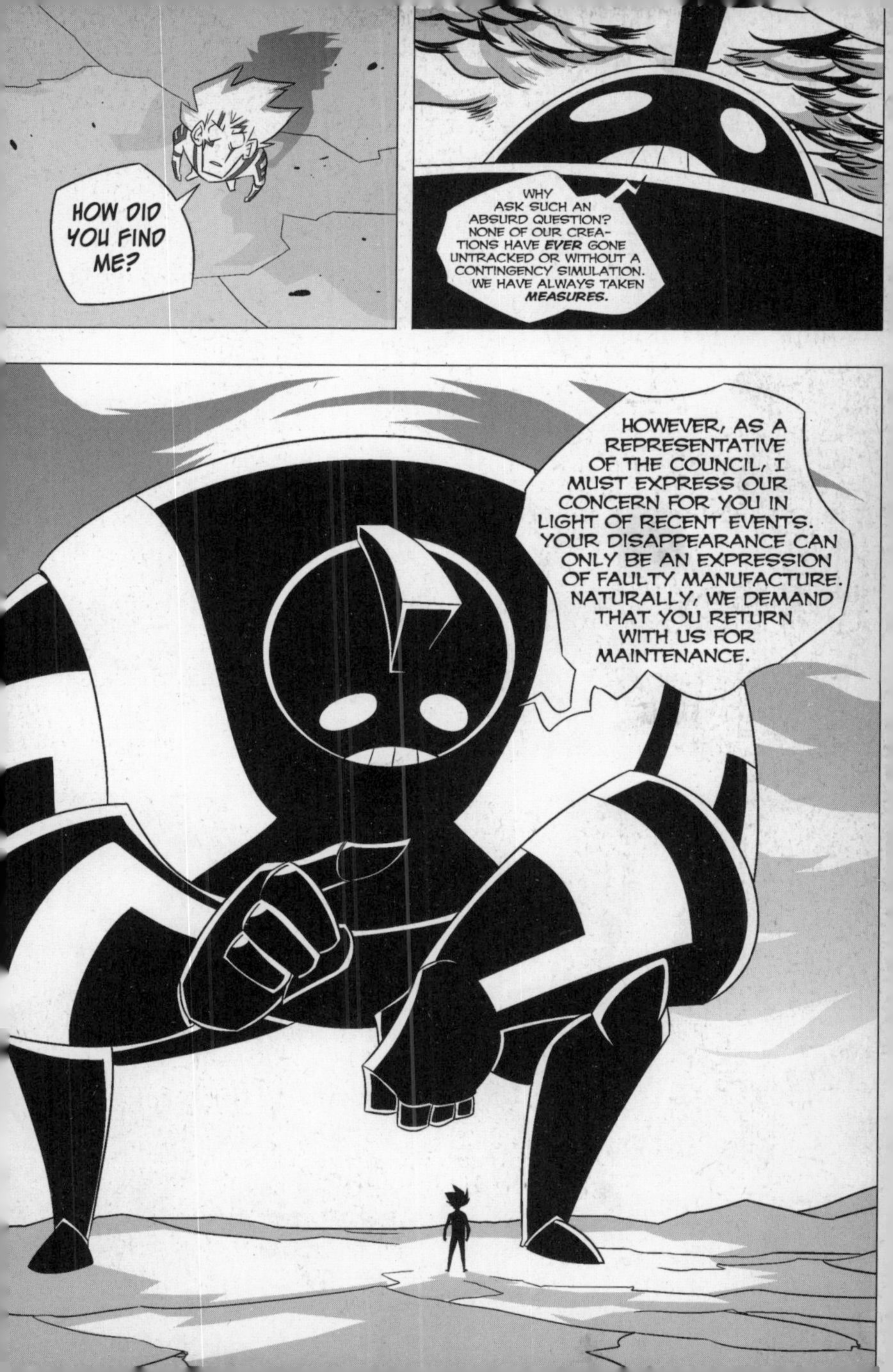
HOW DID YOU FIND ME?
WHY ASK SUCH AN ABSURD QUESTION? NONE OF OUR CREATIONS HAVE EVER GONE UNTRACKED OR WITHOUT A CONTINGENCY SIMULATION. WE HAVE ALWAYS TAKEN MEASURES.
HOWEVER, AS A REPRESENTATIVE OF THE COUNCIL, I MUST EXPRESS OUR CONCERN FOR YOU IN LIGHT OF RECENT EVENTS. YOUR DISAPPEARANCE CAN ONLY BE AN EXPRESSION OF FAULTY MANUFACTURE. NATURALLY, WE DEMAND THAT YOU RETURN WITH US FOR MAINTENANCE.

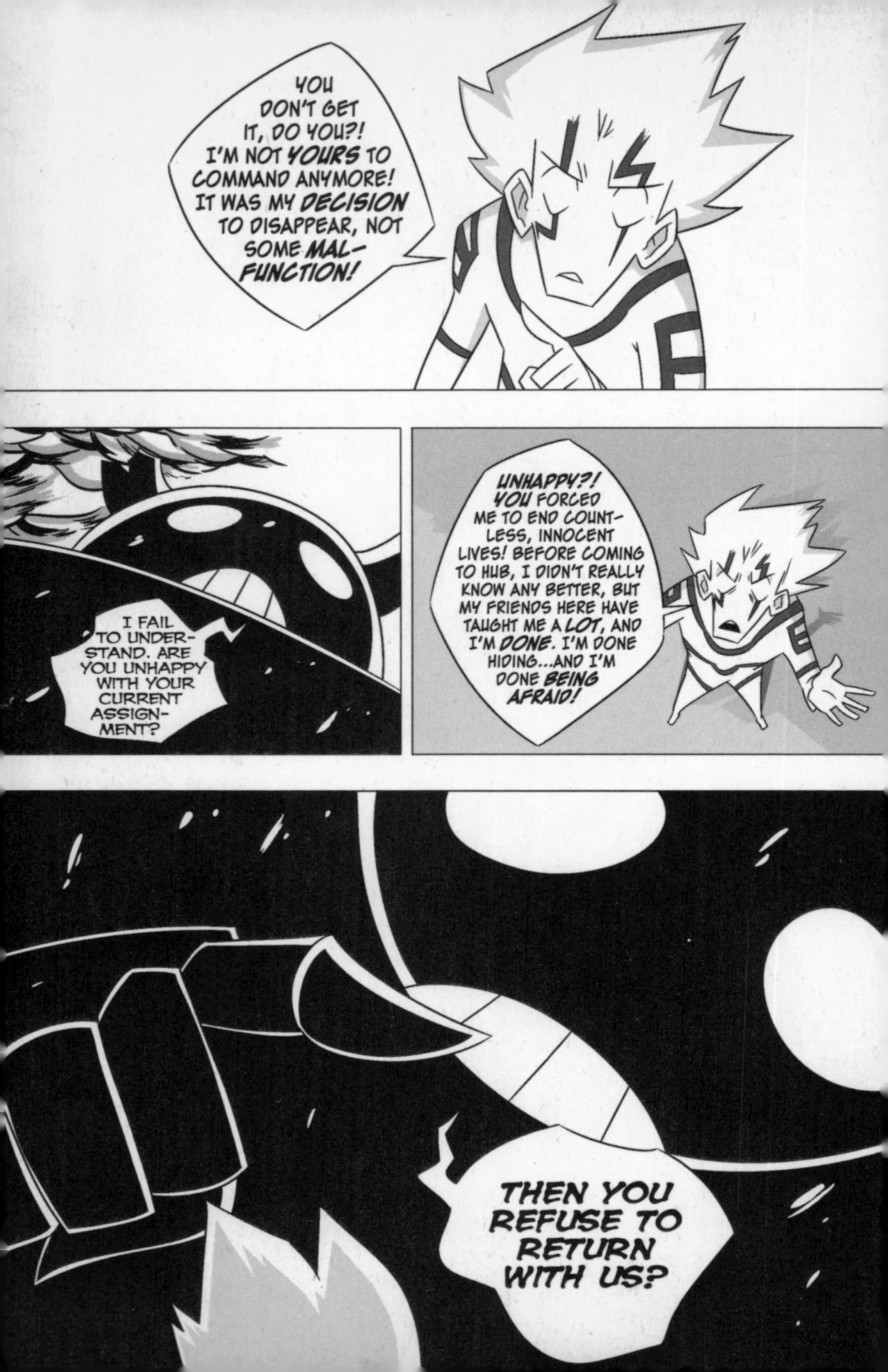
YOU DON'T GET IT, DO YOU?! I'M NOT YOURS TO COMMAND ANYMORE! IT WAS MY DECISION TO DISAPPEAR, NOT SOME MAL-FUNCTION!
I FAIL TO UNDER-STAND. ARE YOU UNHAPPY WITH YOUR CURRENT ASSIGN-MENT?
UNHAPPY?! YOU FORCED ME TO END COUNT-LESS, INNOCENT LIVES! BEFORE COMING TO HUB, I DIDN'T REALLY KNOW ANY BETTER, BUT MY FRIENDS HERE HAVE TAUGHT ME A LOT, AND I'M DONE. I'M DONE HIDING...AND I'M DONE BEING AFRAID!
THEN YOU REFUSE TO RETURN WITH US?

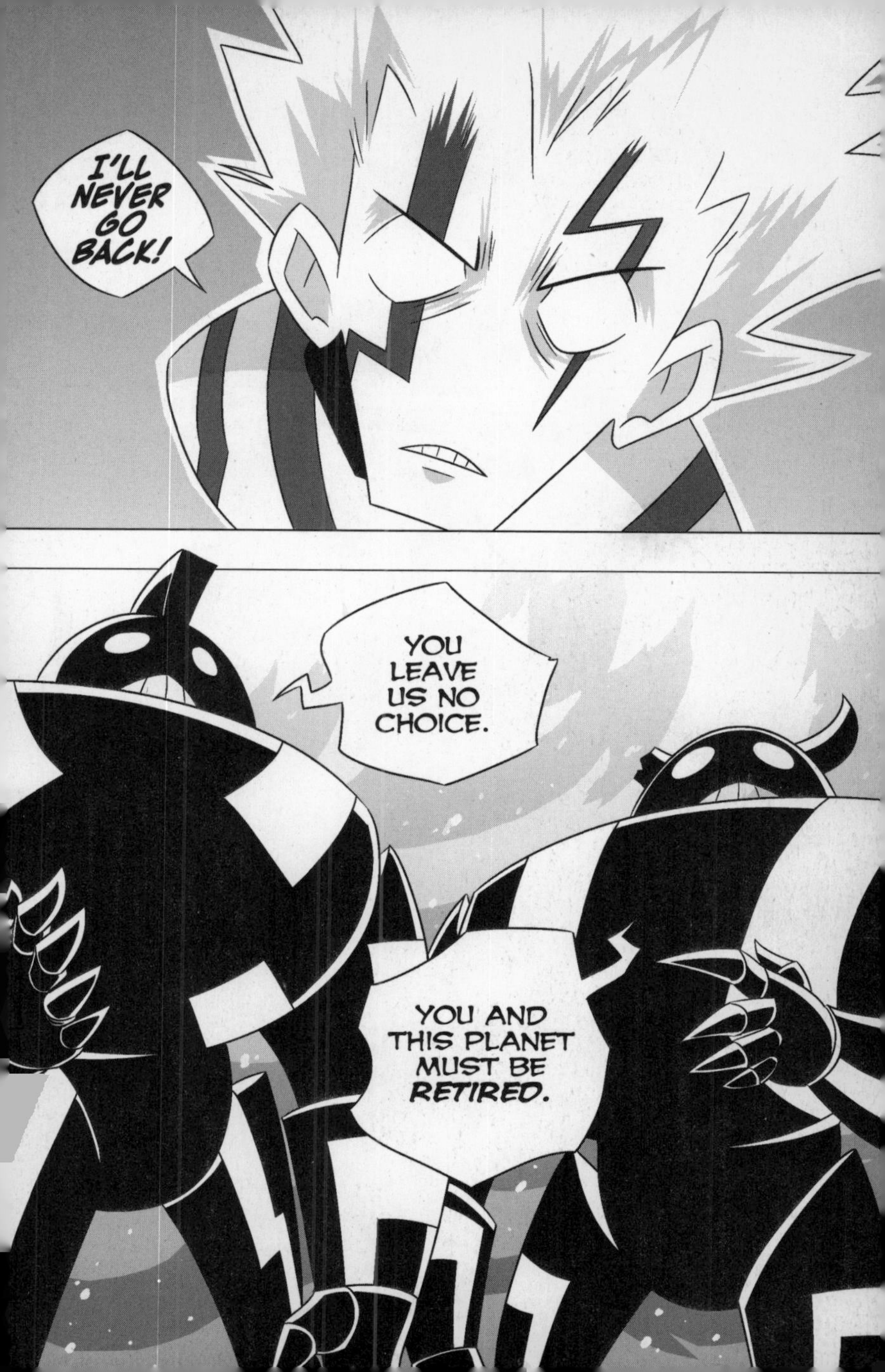
I'LL NEVER GO BACK!
YOU LEAVE US NO CHOICE.
YOU AND THIS PLANET MUST BE RETIRED.

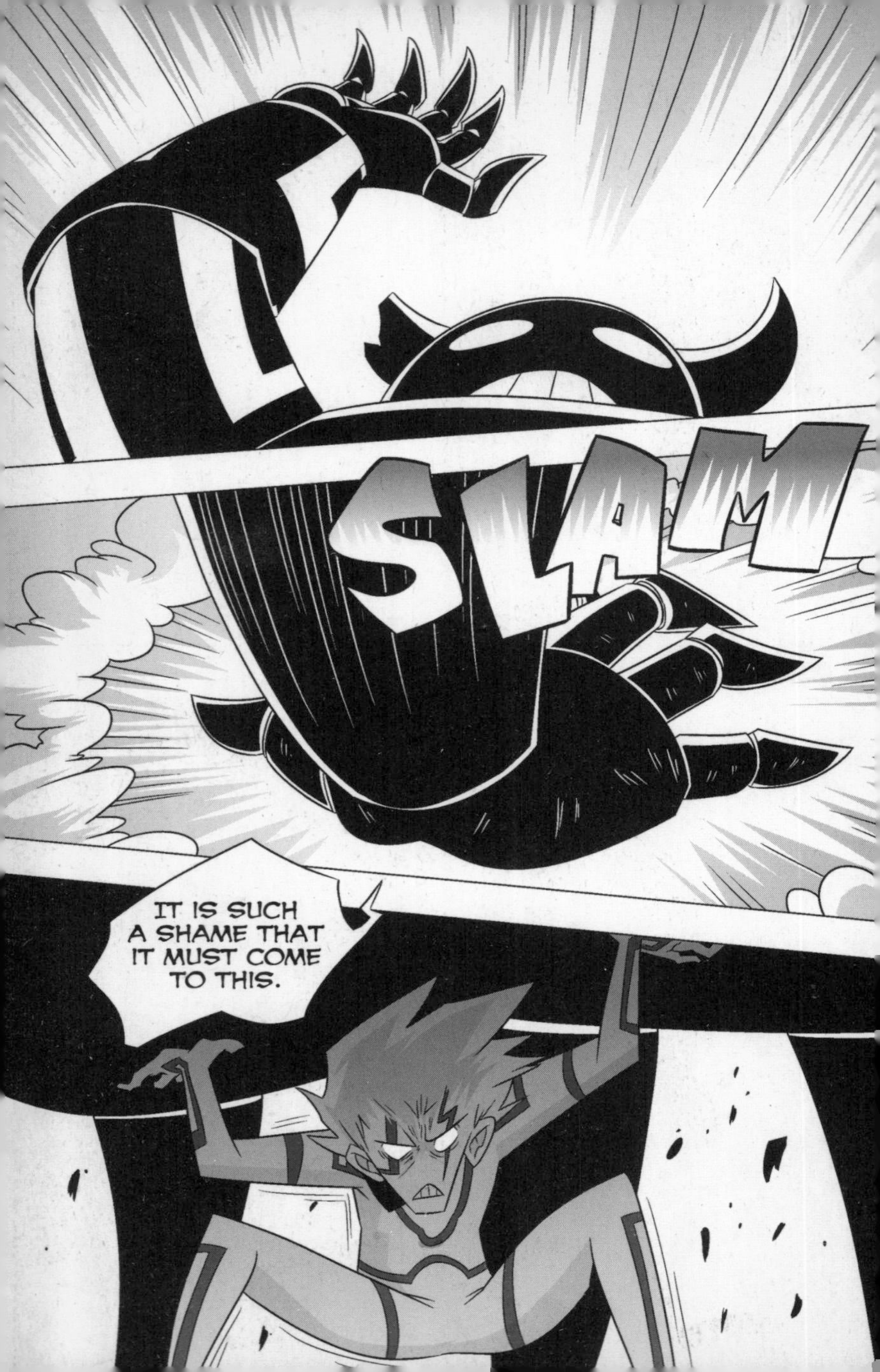
SLAM
IT IS SUCH A SHAME THAT IT MUST COME TO THIS.

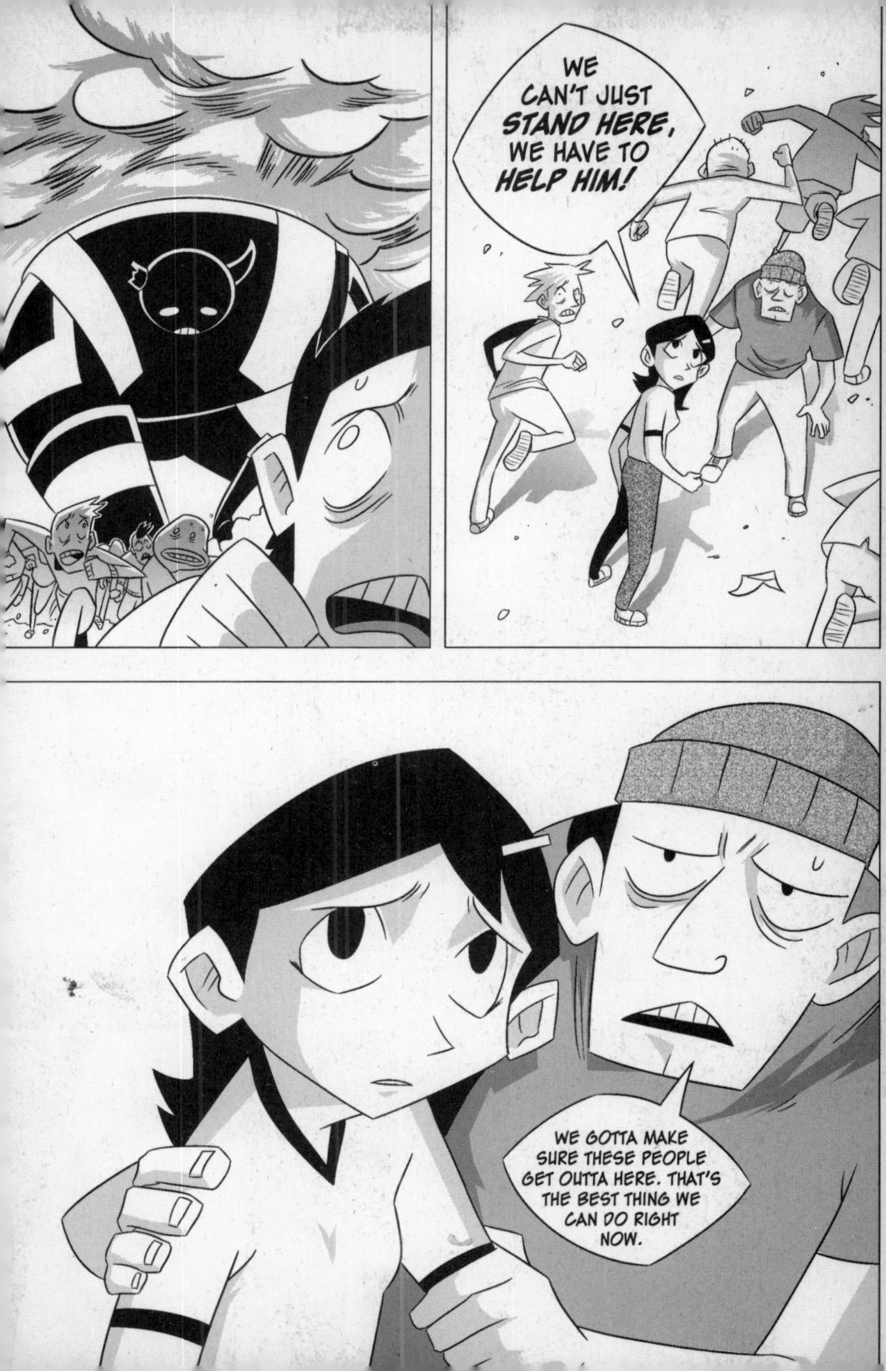
WE CAN'T JUST STAND HERE, WE HAVE TO HELP HIM!
WE GOTTA MAKE SURE THESE PEOPLE GET OUTTA HERE. THAT'S THE BEST THING WE CAN DO RIGHT NOW.

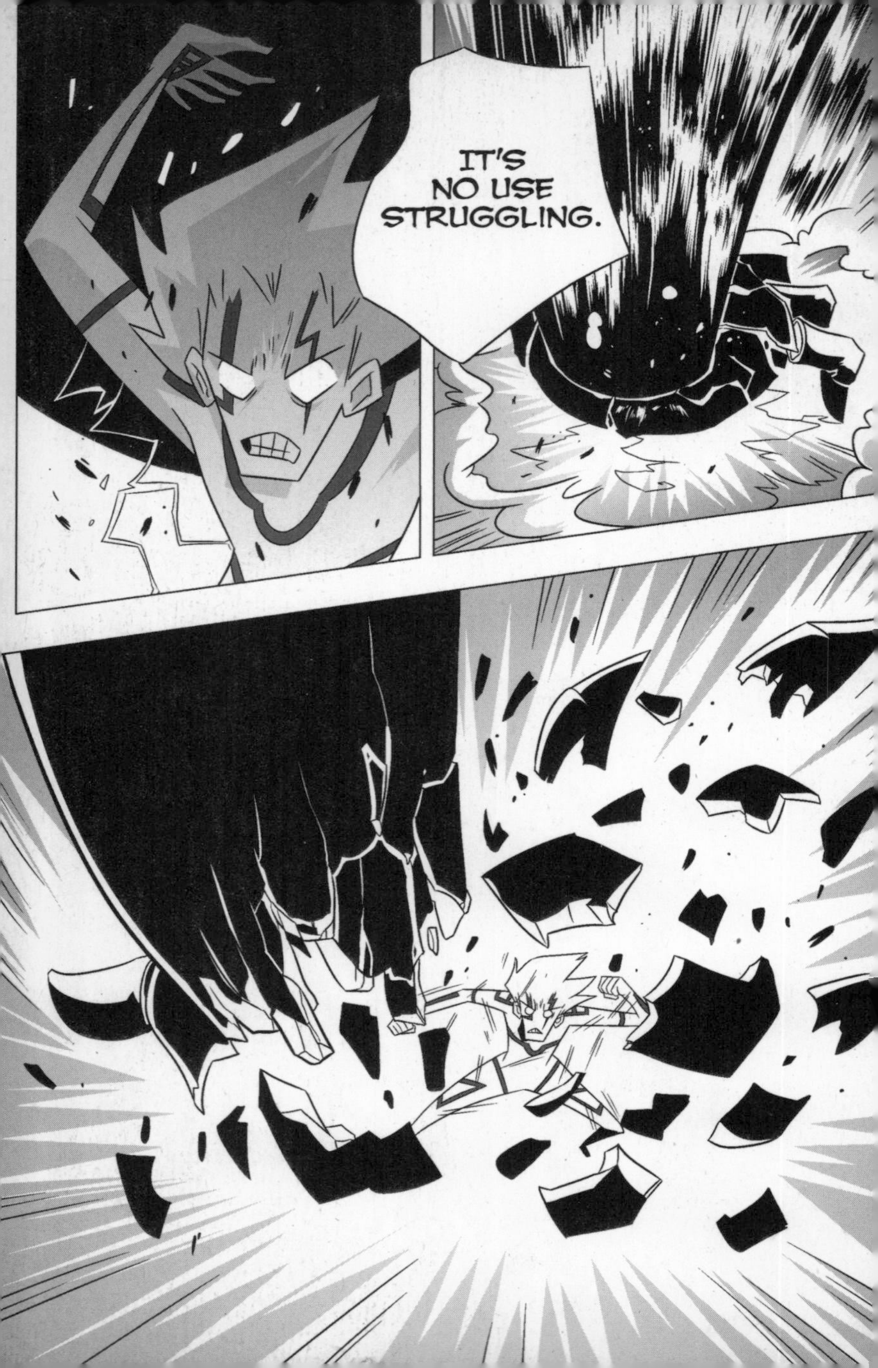
IT'S NO USE STRUGGLING.

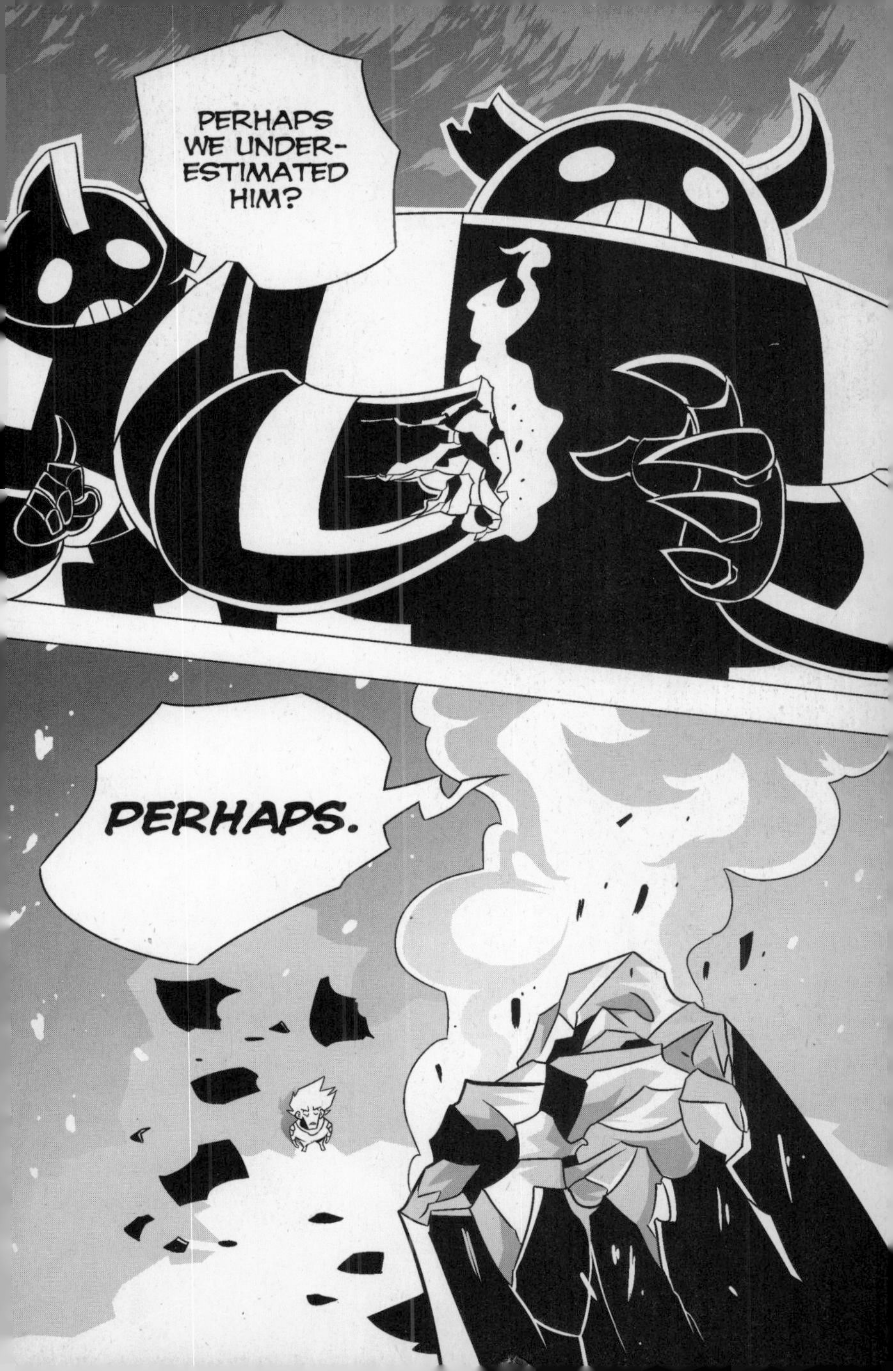
PERHAPS WE UNDER-ESTIMATED HIM?
PERHAPS.

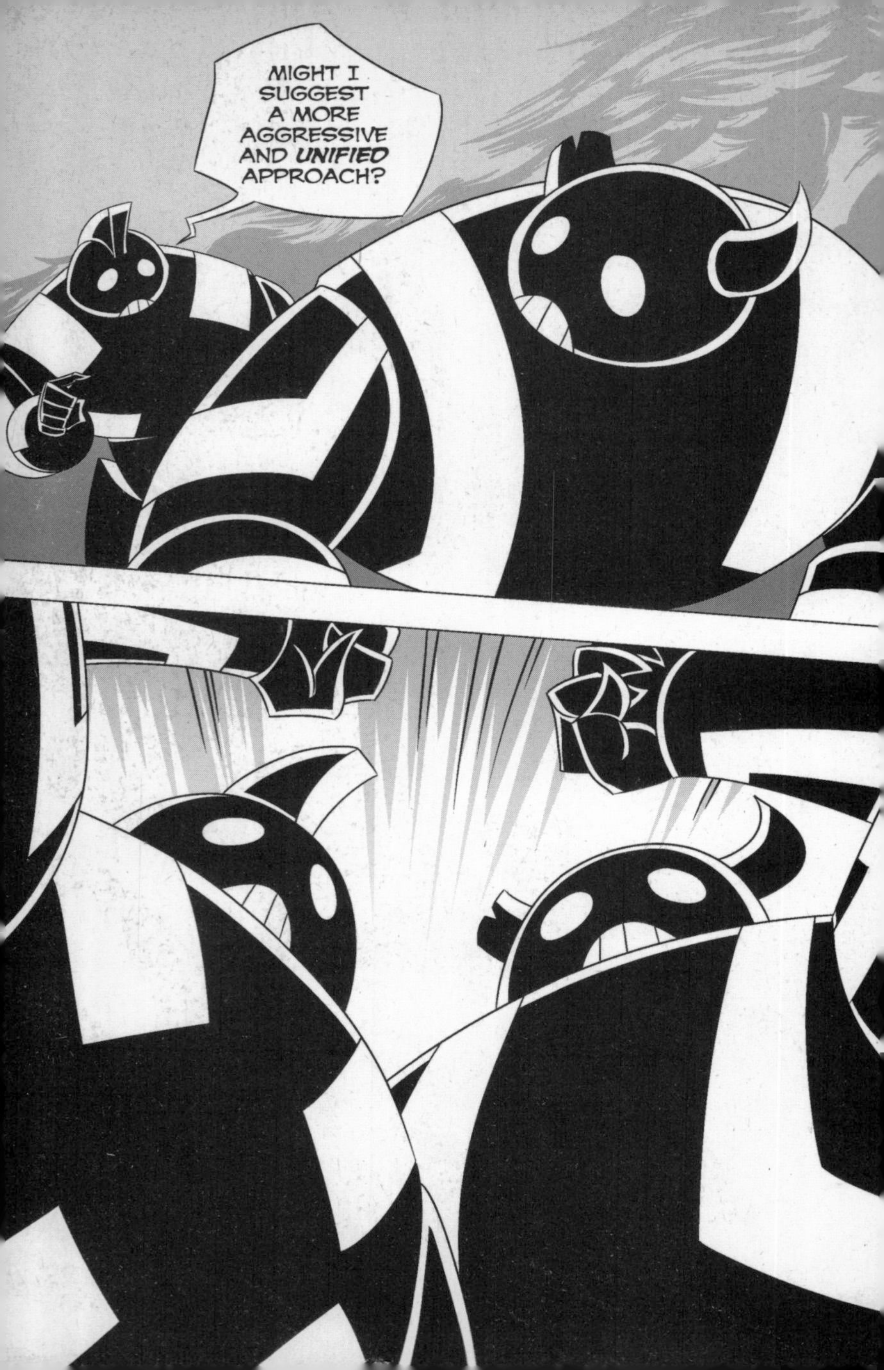
MIGHT I SUGGEST A MORE AGGRESSIVE AND *UNIFIED* APPROACH?

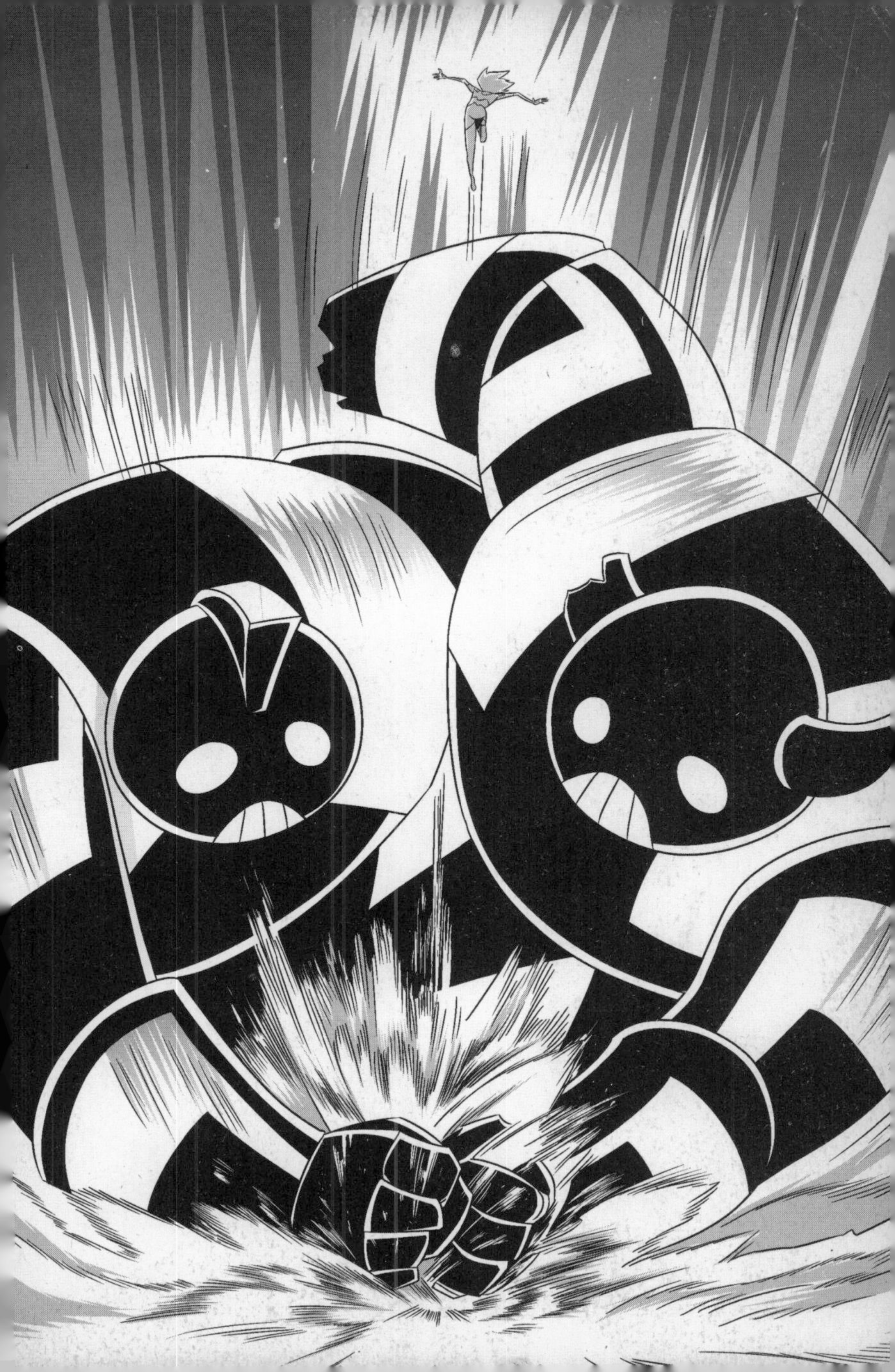

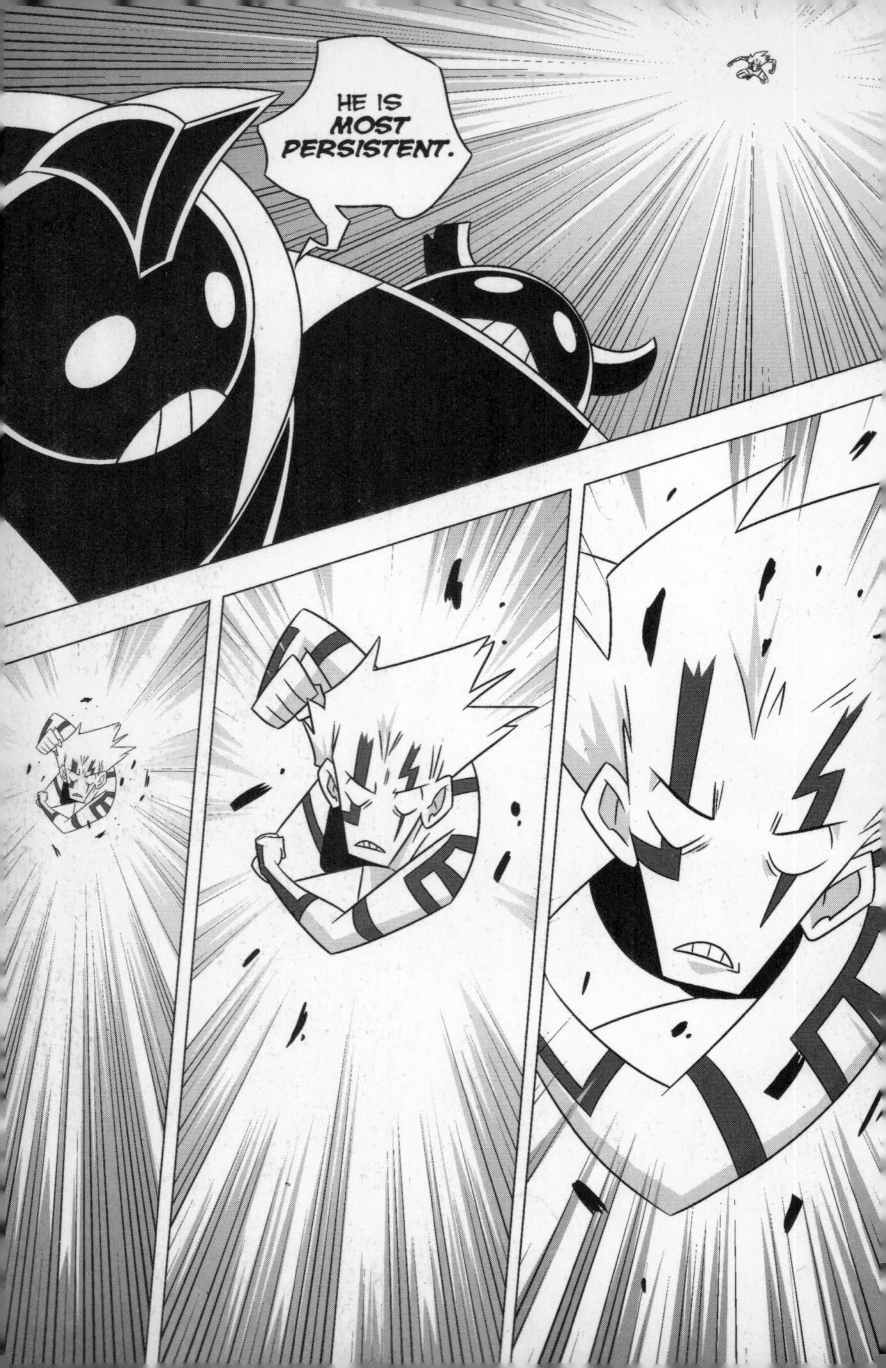
HE IS MOST PERSISTENT.

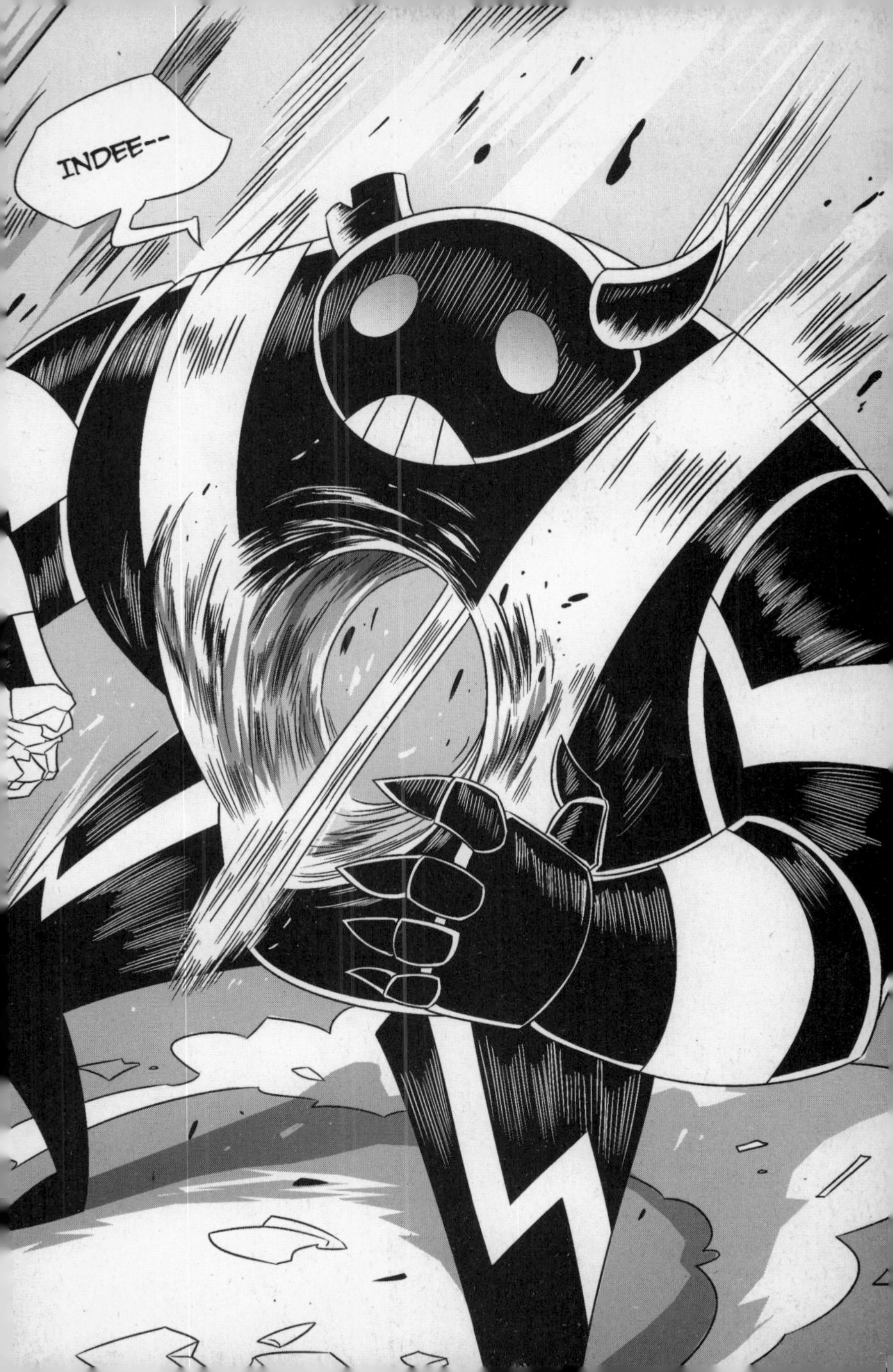
INDEE--

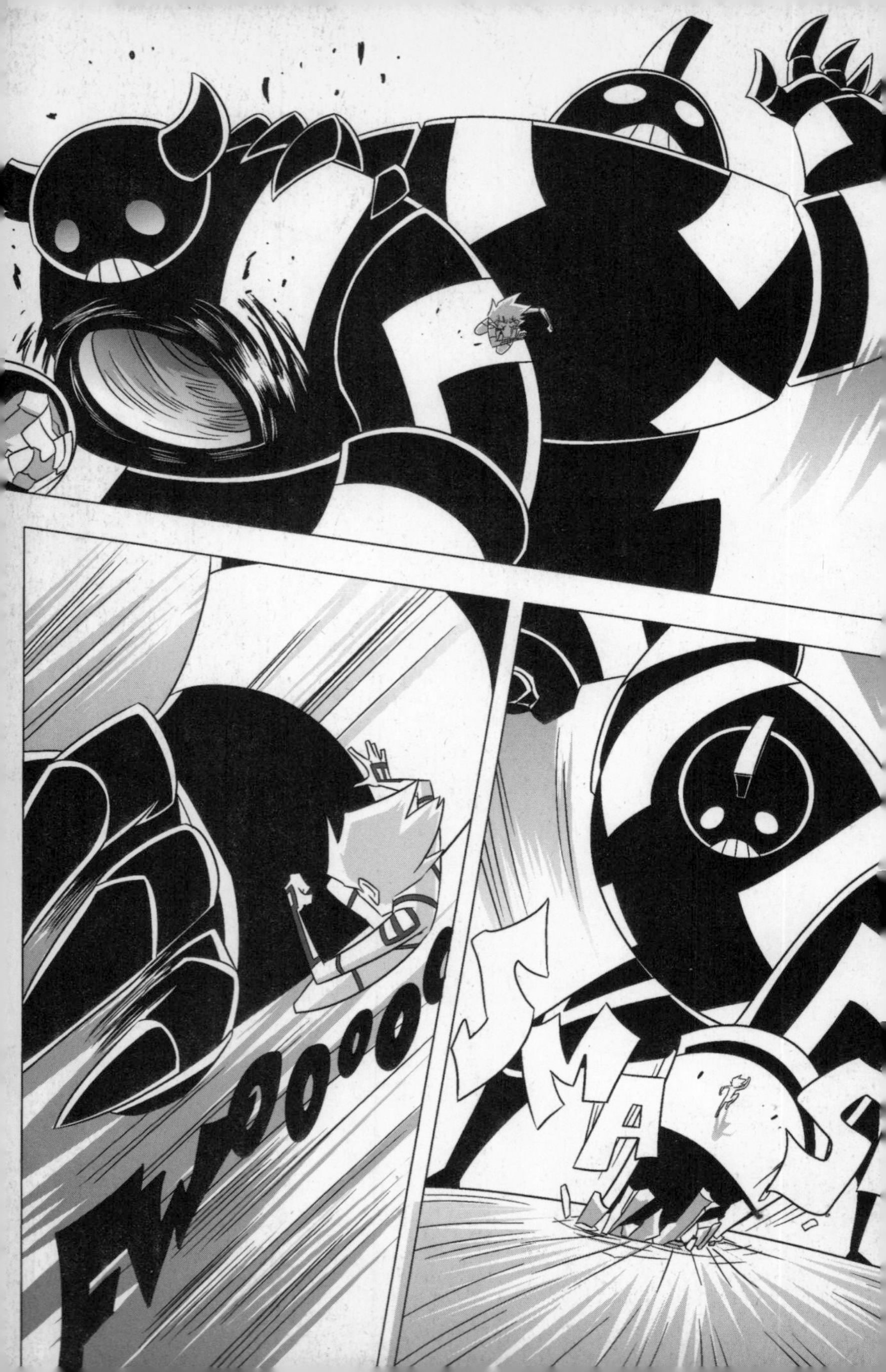
FWOOOOO

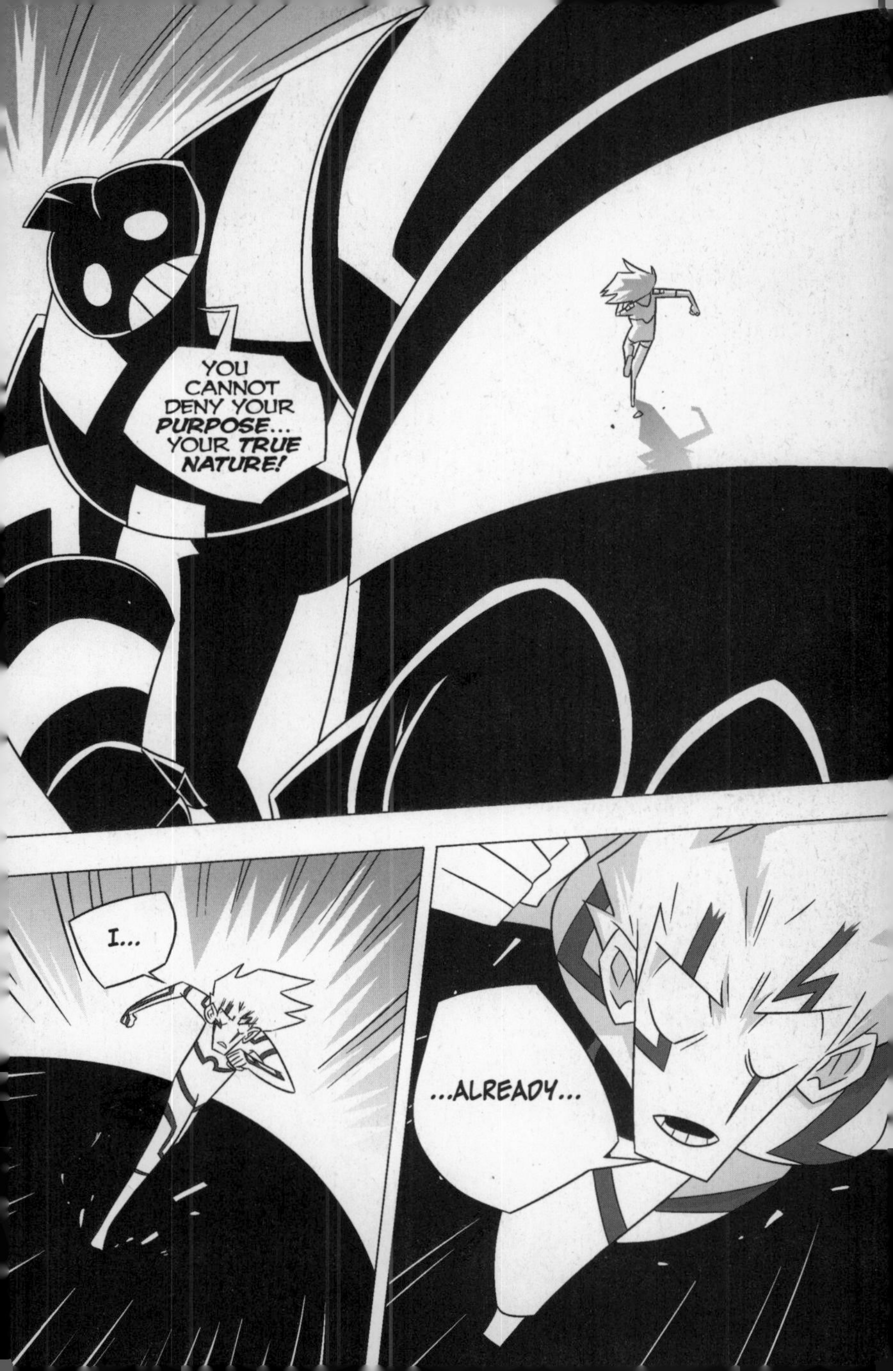
YOU CANNOT DENY YOUR PURPOSE... YOUR TRUE NATURE!
I...
...ALREADY...

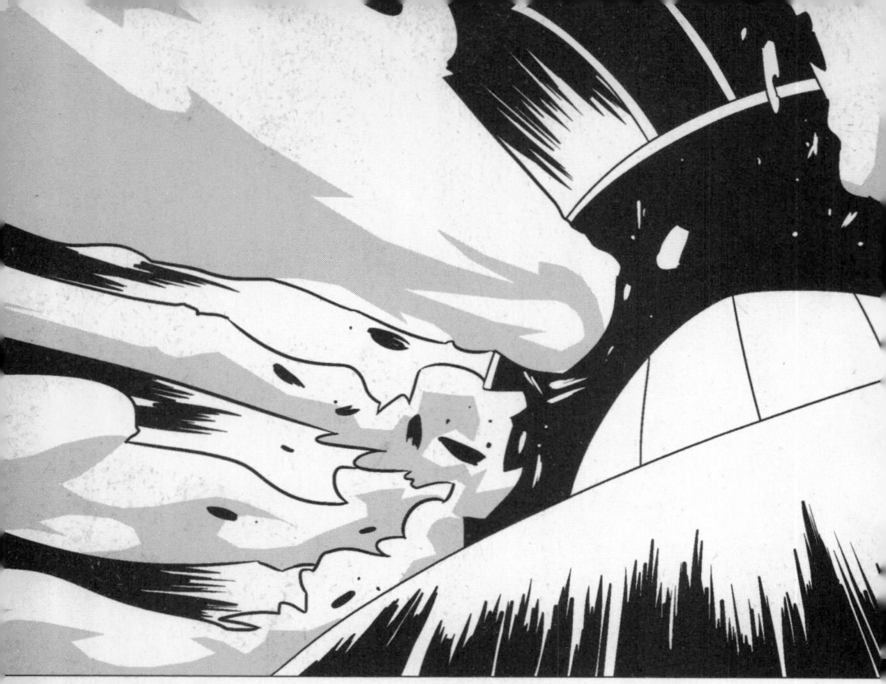

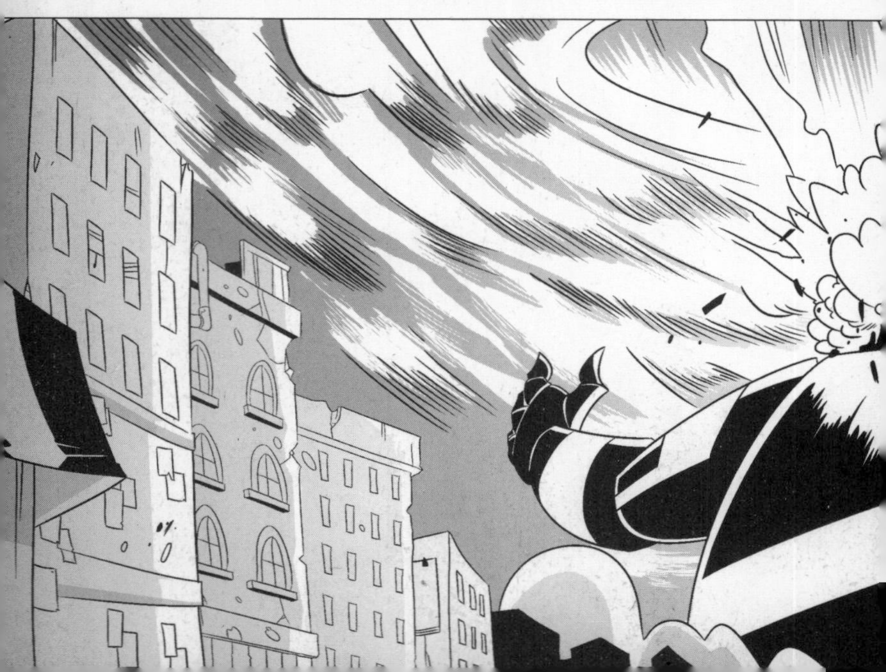

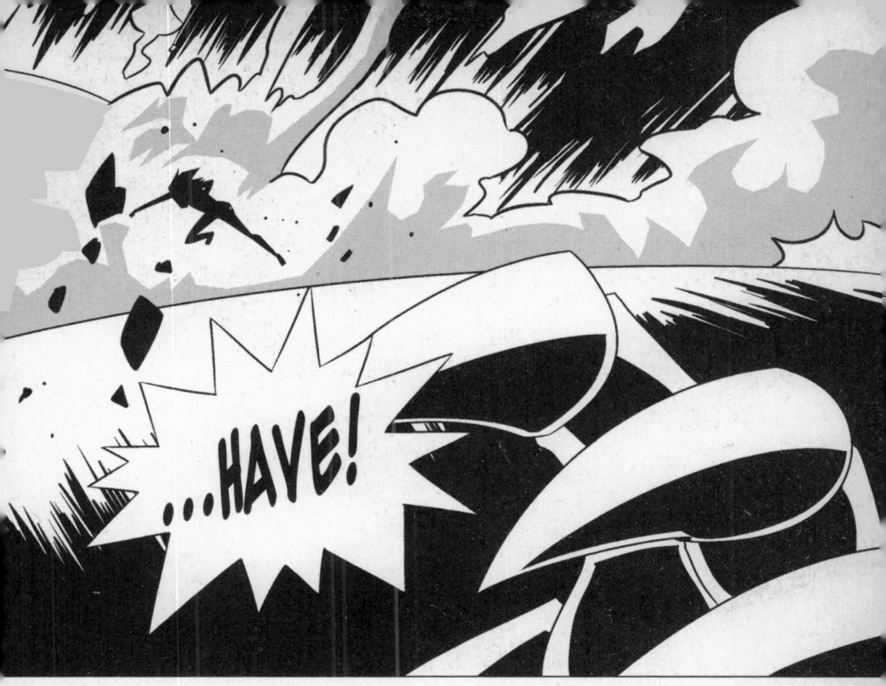
...HAVE!
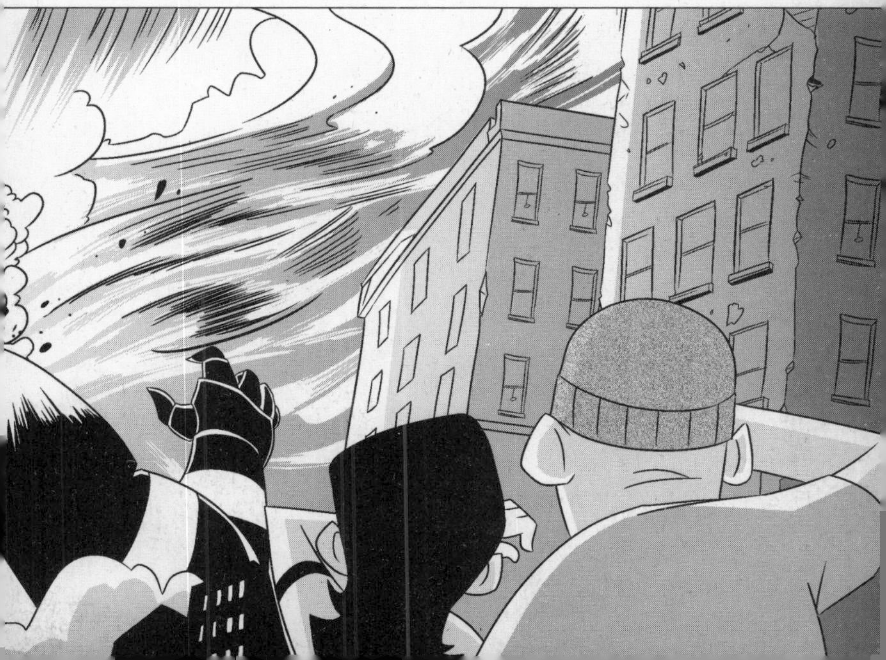

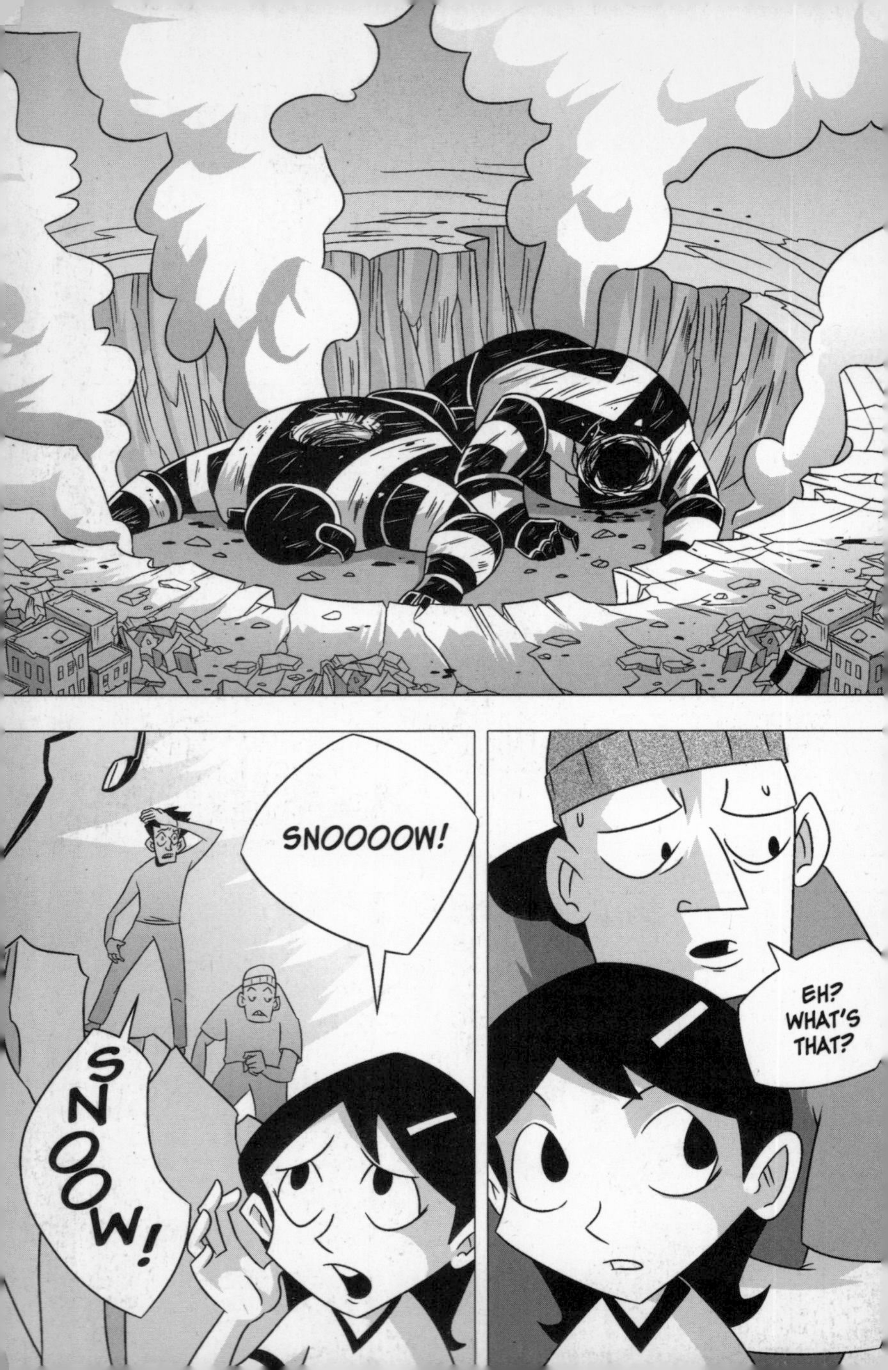
SNOOOOW!
SNOOW!
EH? WHAT'S THAT?

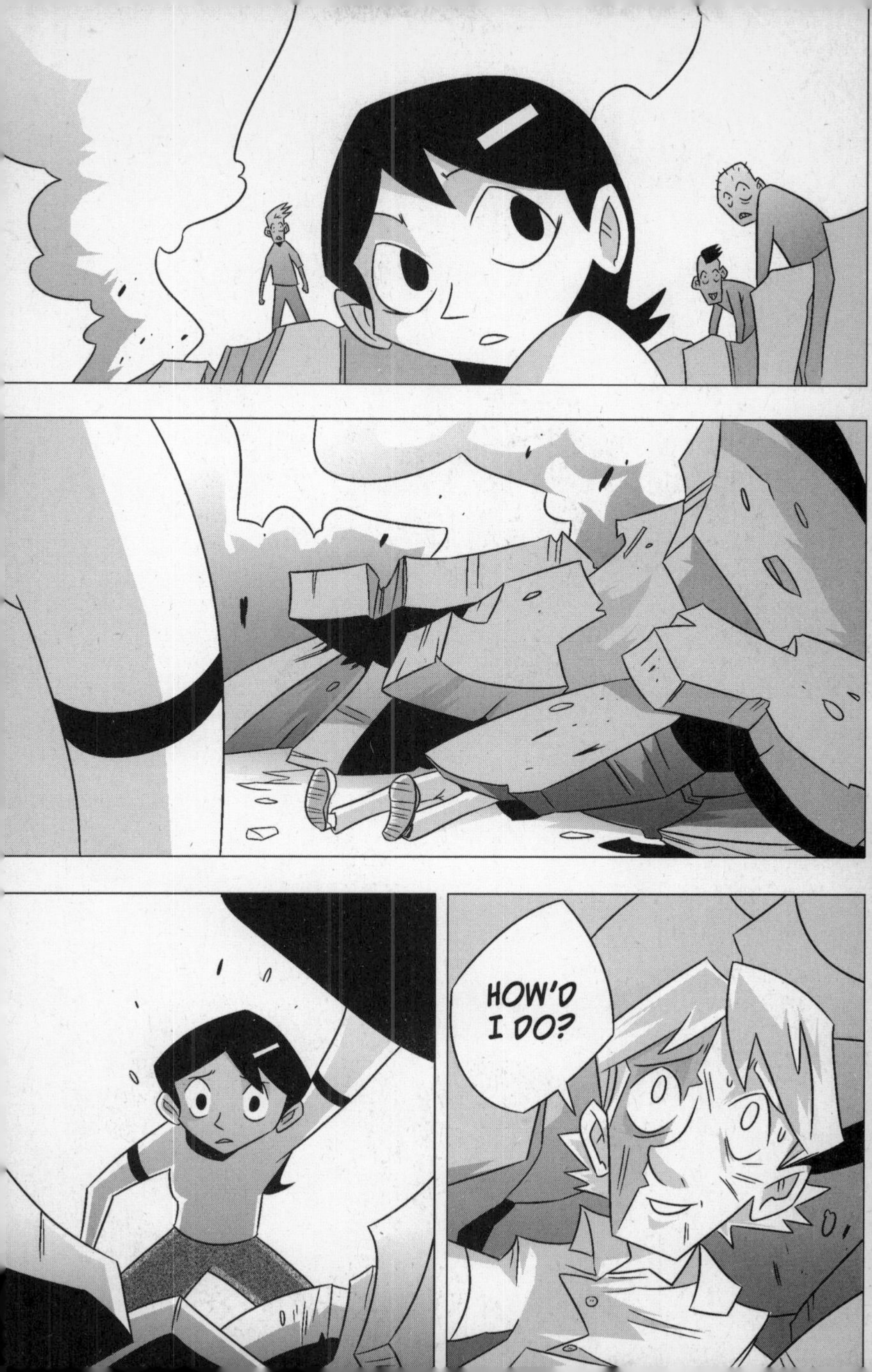
HOW'D
I DO?

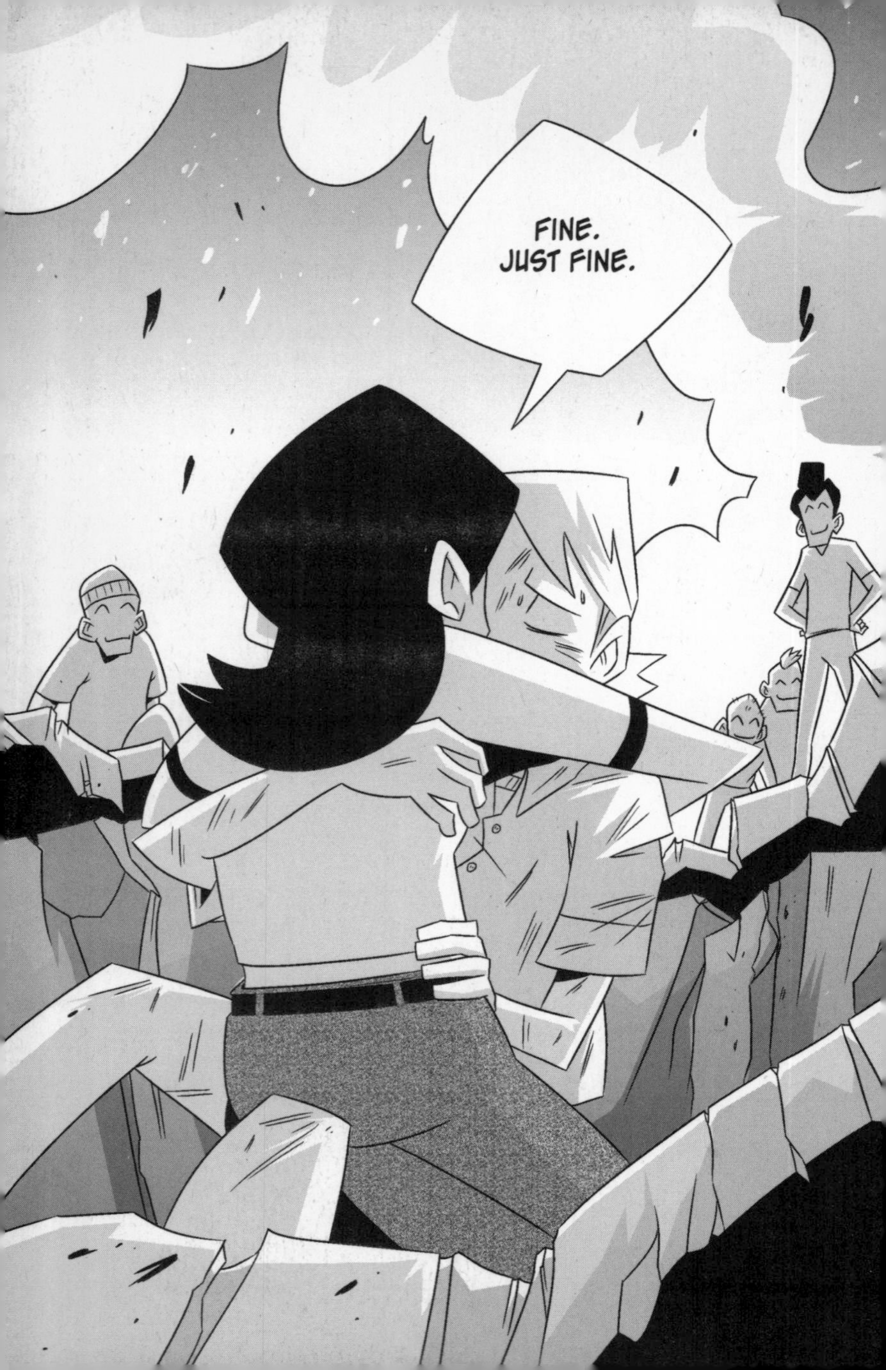
FINE.
JUST FINE.

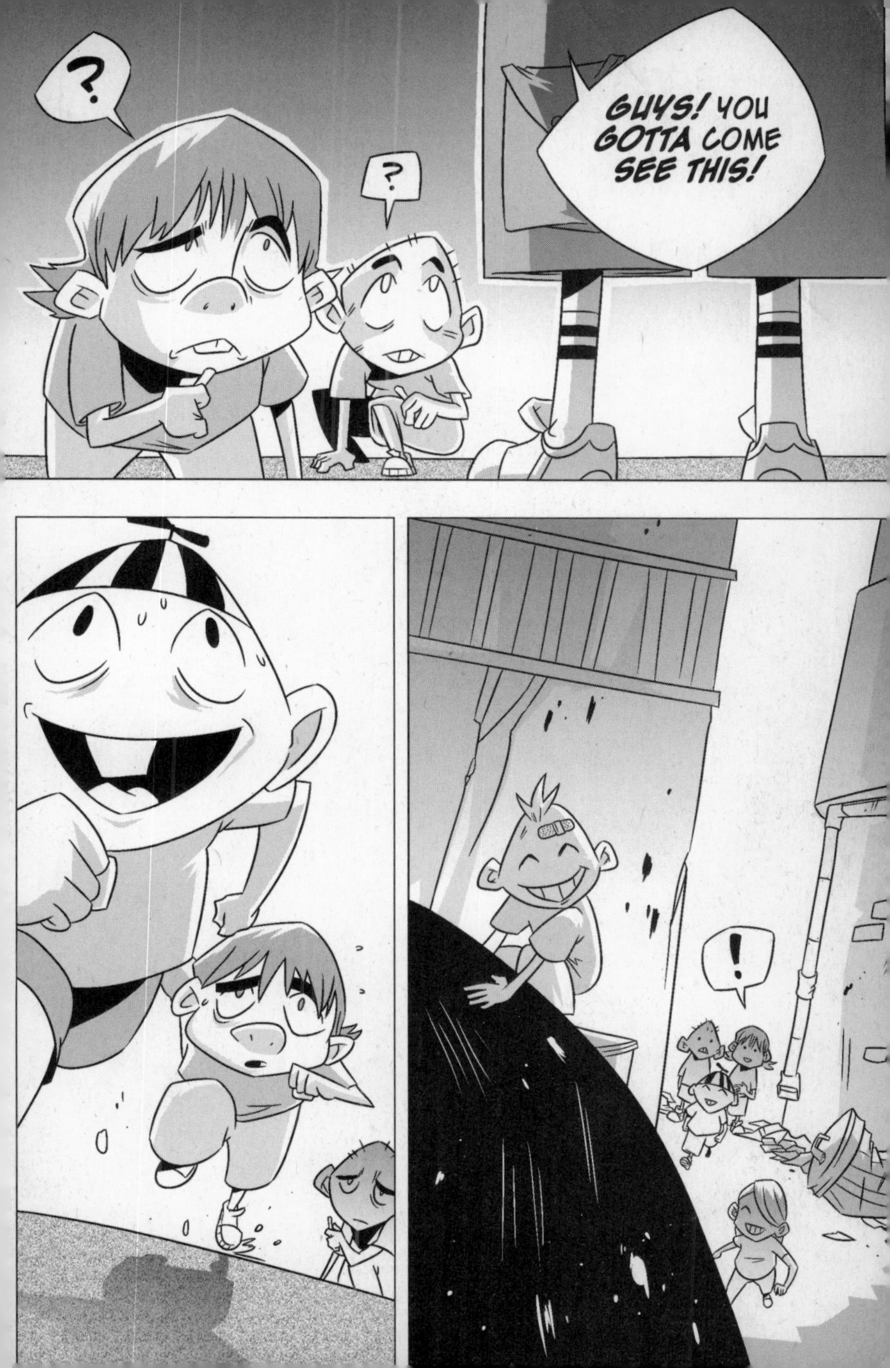
?
?
GUYS! YOU GOTTA COME SEE THIS!
!

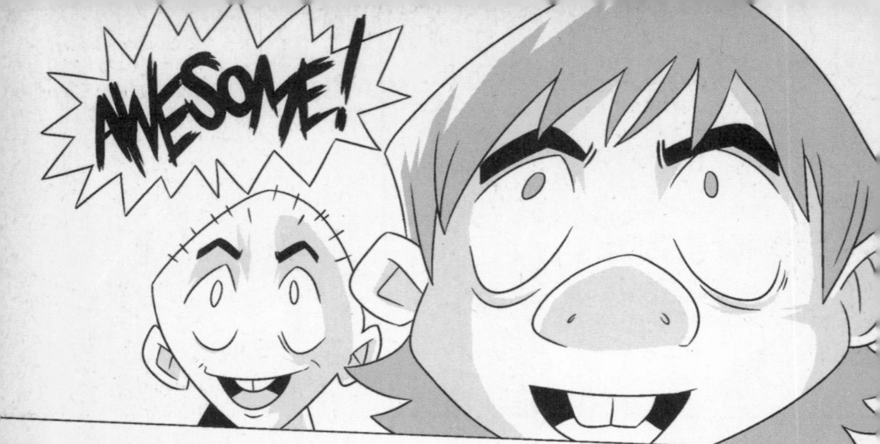
AWESOME!
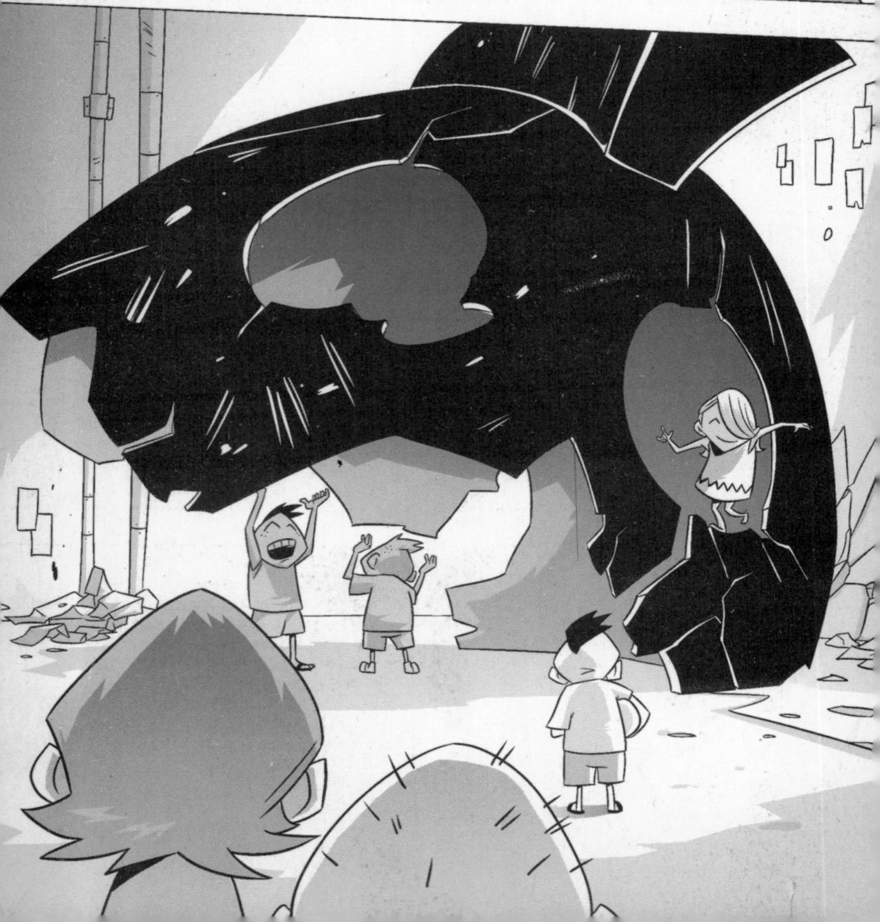

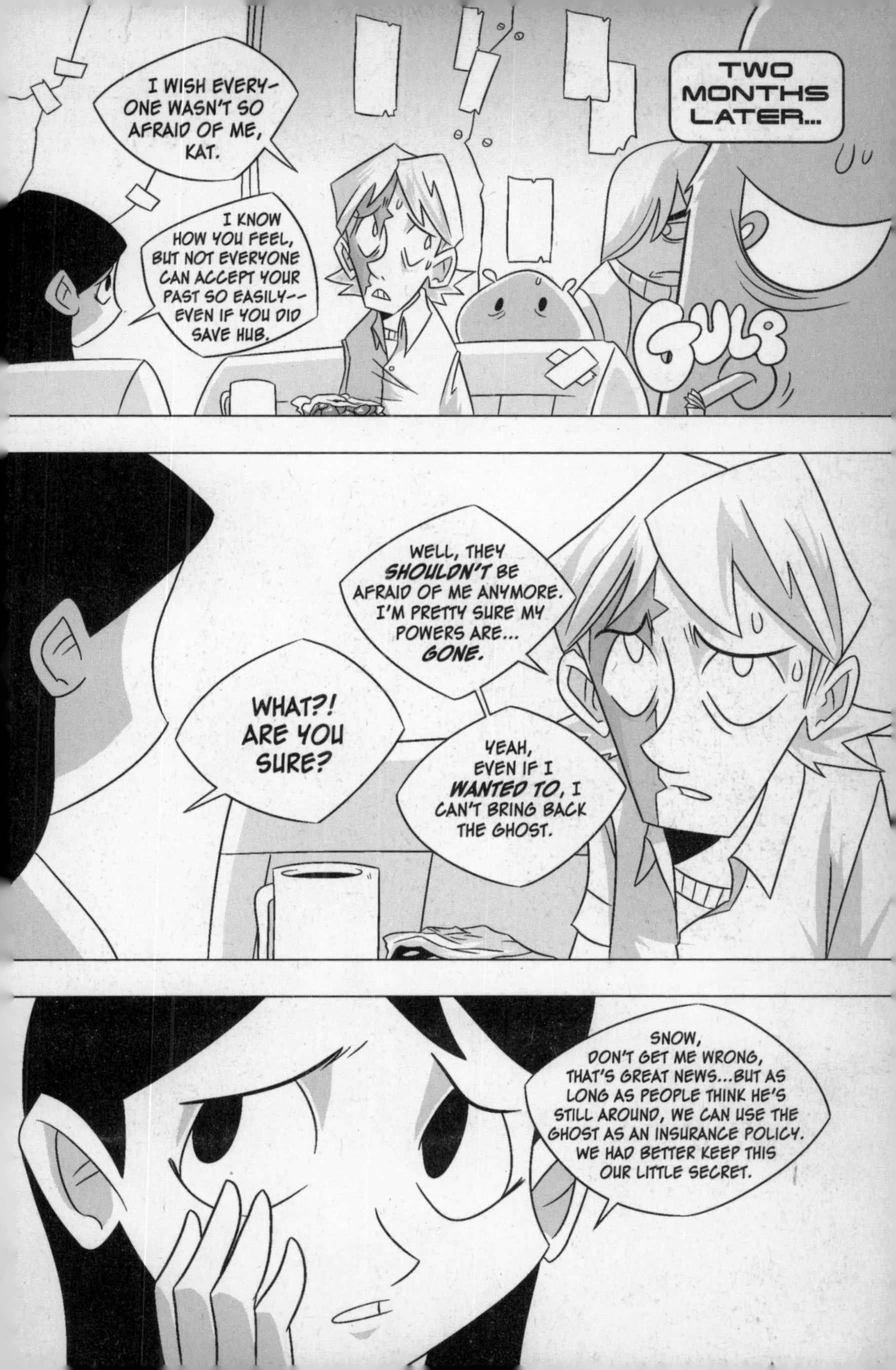
TWO MONTHS LATER...
I WISH EVERY-ONE WASN'T SO AFRAID OF ME, KAT.
I KNOW HOW YOU FEEL, BUT NOT EVERYONE CAN ACCEPT YOUR PAST SO EASILY-- EVEN IF YOU DID SAVE HUB.
GULP
WELL, THEY *SHOULDN'T* BE AFRAID OF ME ANYMORE. I'M PRETTY SURE MY POWERS ARE... *GONE.*
WHAT?! ARE YOU SURE?
YEAH, EVEN IF I *WANTED TO*, I CAN'T BRING BACK THE GHOST.
SNOW, DON'T GET ME WRONG, THAT'S GREAT NEWS...BUT AS LONG AS PEOPLE THINK HE'S STILL AROUND, WE CAN USE THE GHOST AS AN INSURANCE POLICY. WE HAD BETTER KEEP THIS OUR LITTLE SECRET.

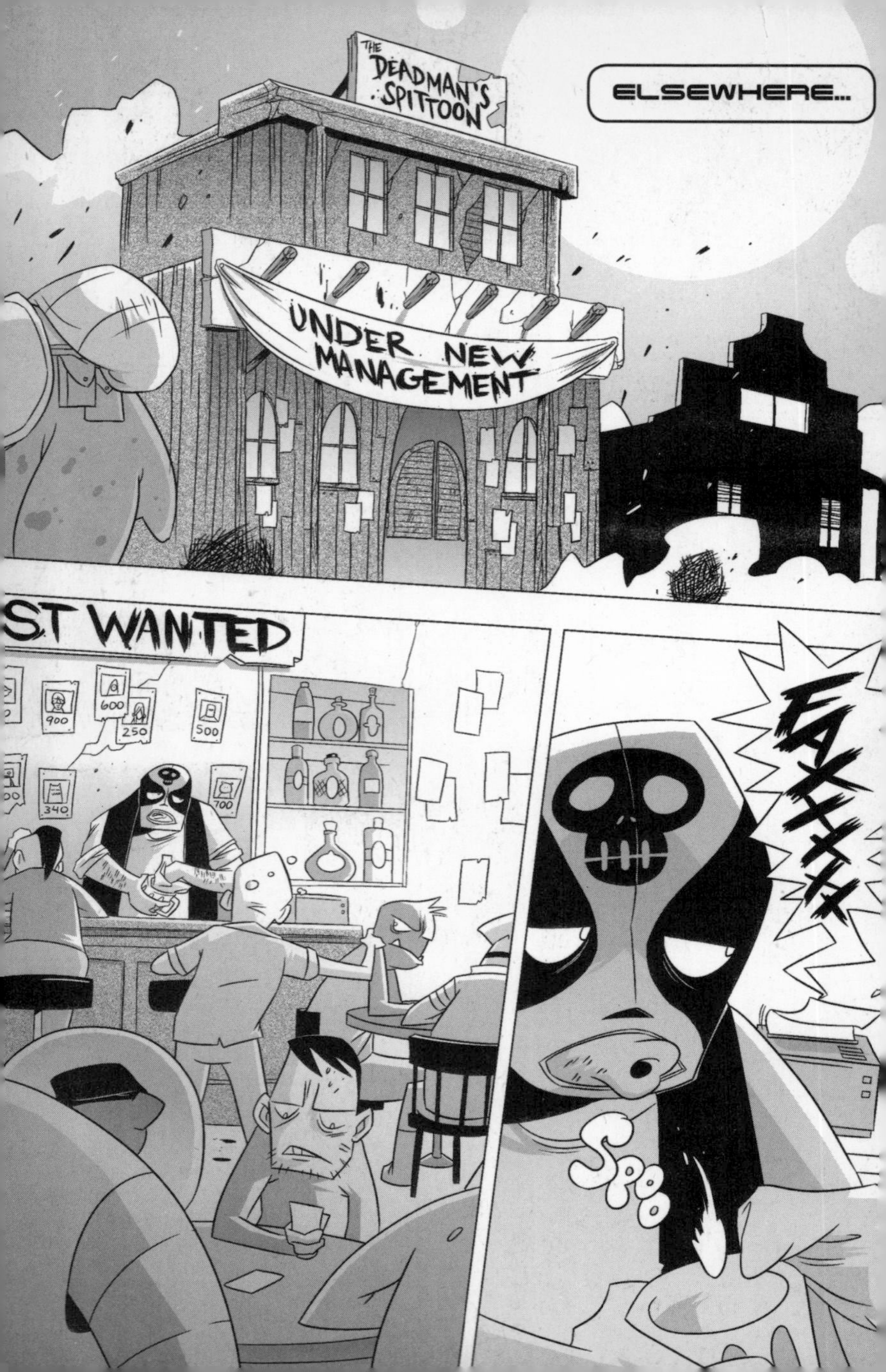
ELSEWHERE...
THE DEADMAN'S SPITTOON
UNDER NEW MANAGEMENT
ST WANTED
900
600
250
500
340
700
SPOO
FAXXXXX

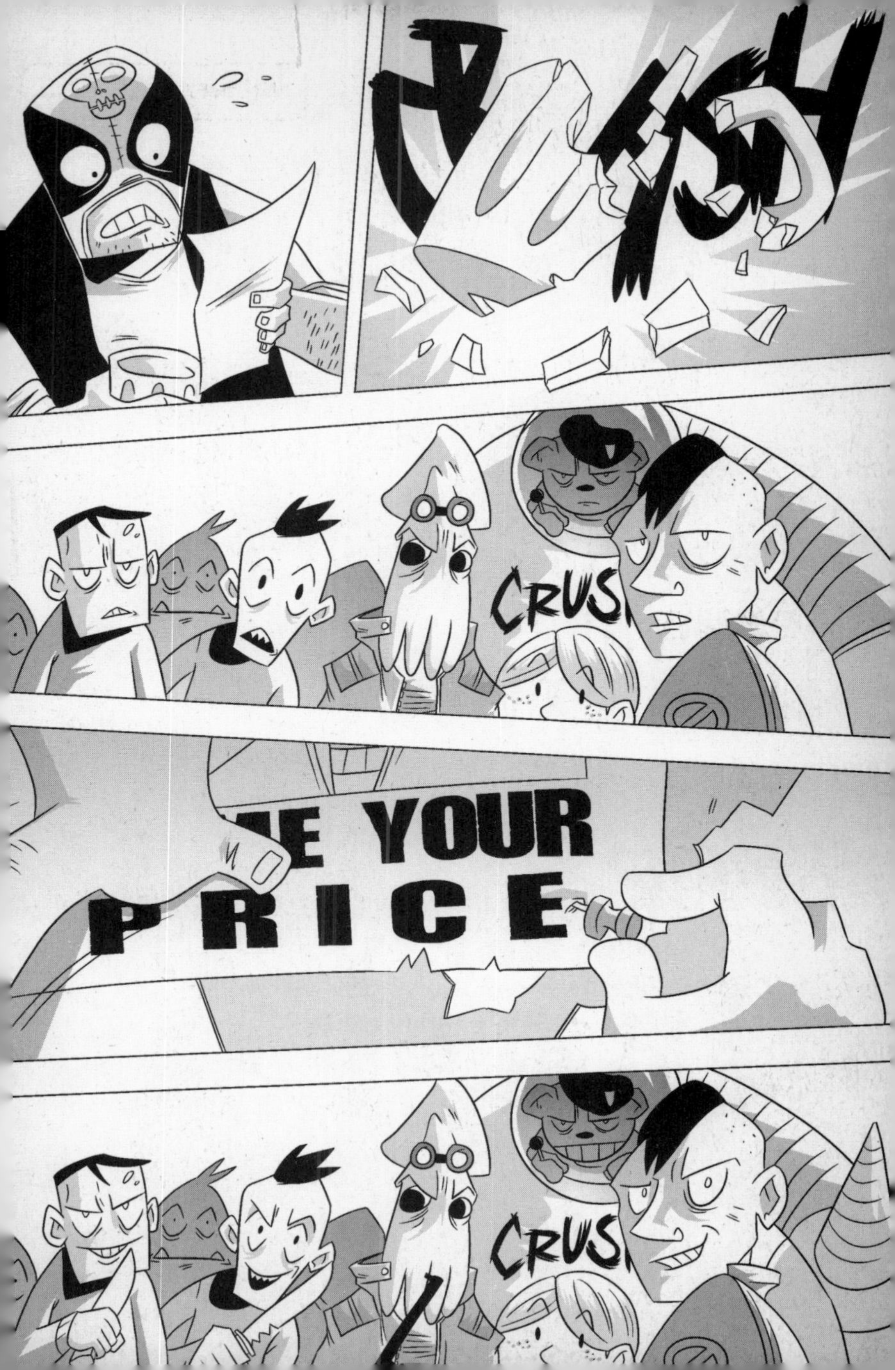
CRUS
E YOUR
PRICE
CRUS

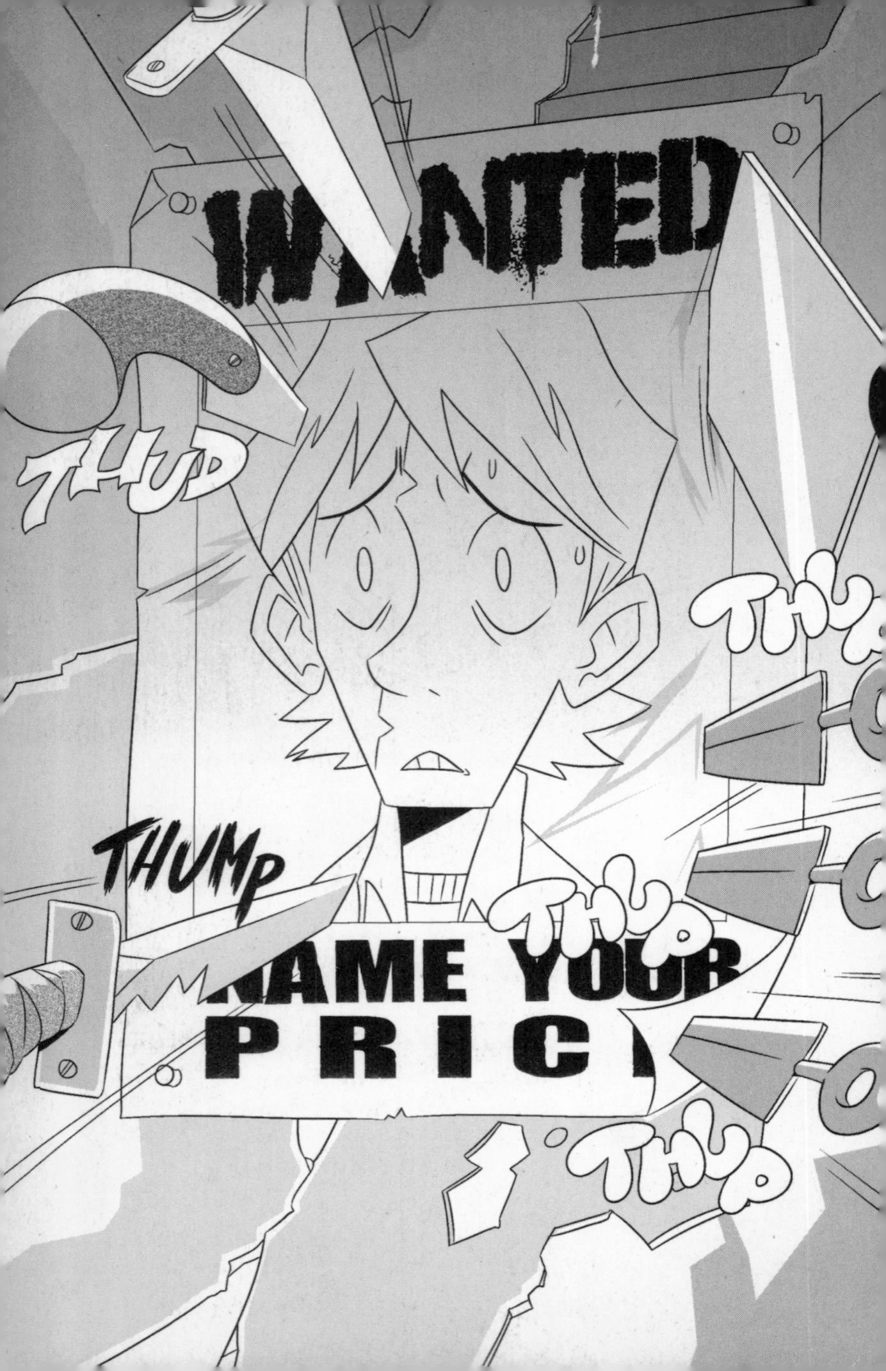

WANTED
THUD
THUD
THUMP
THUD
NAME YOUR
PRIC
THUD

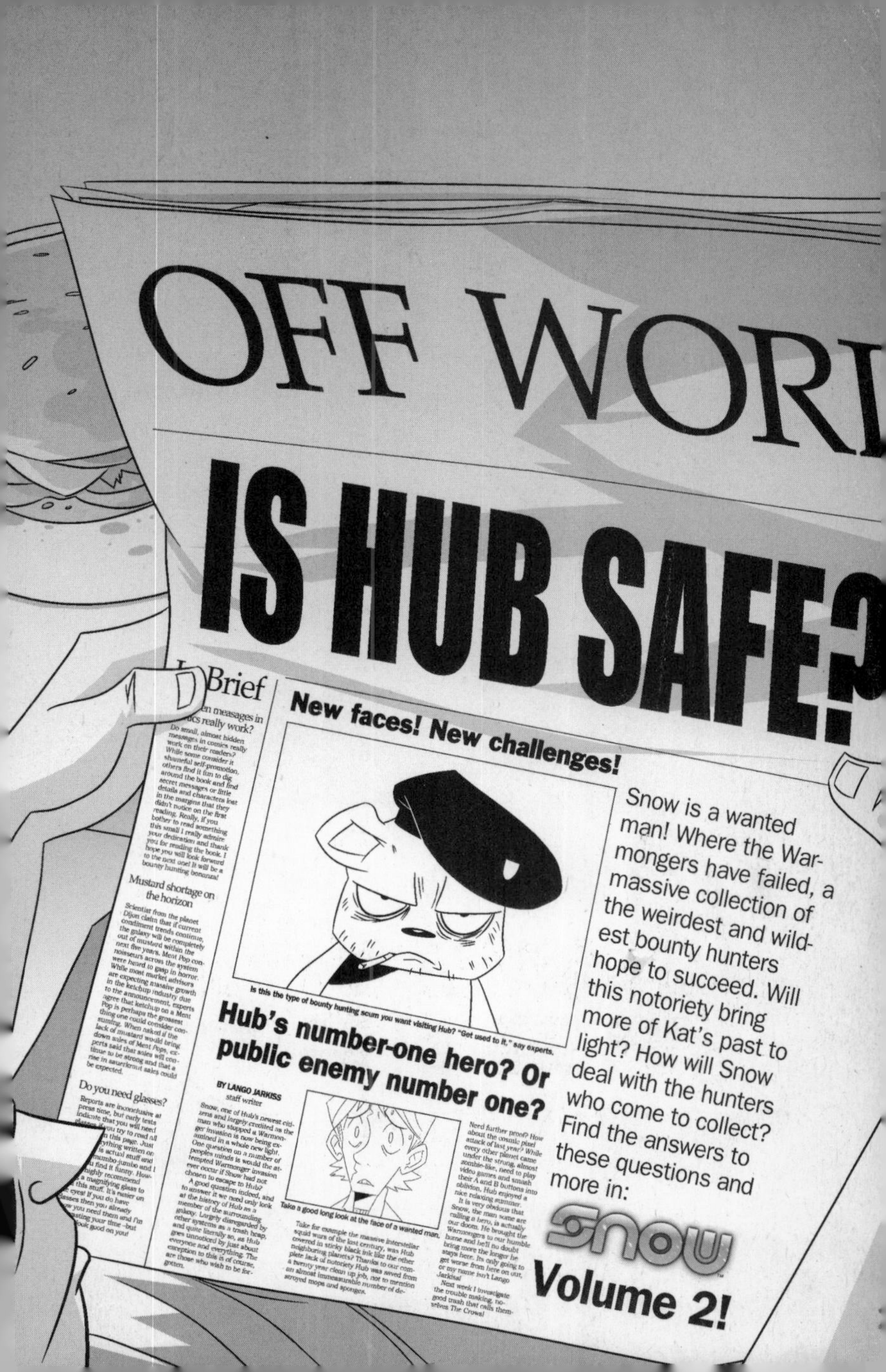
OFF WORL
IS HUB SAFE?
In Brief
en measages in
ics really work?
Do small, almost hidden messages in comics really work on their readers? While some consider it shameful self-promotion, others find it fun to dig around the book and find secret messages or little details and characters lost in the margins that they didn't notice on the first reading. Really, if you bother to read something this small I really admire your dedication and thank you for reading the book. I hope you will look forward to the next one! It will be a bounty hunting bonanza!
Mustard shortage on the horizon
Scientist from the planet Dijon claim that if current condiment trends continue, the galaxy will be completely out of mustard within the next five years. Meat Pop connoisseurs across the system were heard to gasp in horror. While most market advisors are expecting massive growth in the ketchup industry due to the announcement, experts agree that ketchup on a Meat Pop is perhaps the grossest thing one could consider consuming. When asked if the lack of mustard would bring down sales of Meat Pops, experts said that sales will continue to be strong and that a rise in sauerkraut sales could be expected.
Do you need glasses?
Reports are inconclusive at press time, but early tests indicate that you will need
New faces! New challenges!
Is this the type of bounty hunting scum you want visiting Hub? "Get used to it," say experts.
Hub's number-one hero? Or public enemy number one?
BY LANGO JARKISS
staff writer
Snow, one of Hub's newest citizens and largely credited as the man who stopped a Warmonger invasion is now being examined in a whole new light. One question on a number of peoples minds is would the attempted Warmonger invasion ever occur if Snow had not chosen to escape to Hub?
A good question indeed, and to answer it we need only look at the history of Hub as a member of the surrounding galaxy. Largely disregarded by other systems as a trash heap, and quite literally so, as Hub goes unnoticed by just about everyone and everything. The exception to this is of course, are those who wish to be forgotten.
Take a good long look at the face of a wanted man.
Take for example the massive interstellar squid wars of the last century, was Hub covered in sticky black ink like the other neighboring planets? Thanks to our complete lack of notoriety Hub was saved from a twenty year clean up job, not to mention an almost immeasurable number of destroyed mops and sponges.
Need further proof? How about the cosmic pixel attack of last year? While every other planet came under the strong, almost zombie-like, need to play video games and smash their A and B buttons into oblivion, Hub enjoyed a nice relaxing summer.
It is very obvious that Snow, the man some are calling a hero, is actually our doom. He brought the Warmongers to our humble home and he'll no doubt bring more the longer he stays here. Its only going to get worse from here on out, or my name isn't Lango Jarkiss!
Next week I investigate the trouble making, nogood trash that calls themselves The Crows!
Snow is a wanted man! Where the Warmongers have failed, a massive collection of the weirdest and wildest bounty hunters hope to succeed. Will this notoriety bring more of Kat's past to light? How will Snow deal with the hunters who come to collect? Find the answers to these questions and more in:
SNOW
Volume 2!